ALMOST FAMOUS

ALMOST FAMOUS

DAVID SMALL

AN AUTHORS GUILD BACKINPRINT.COM EDITION

AN AUTHORS GUILD BACKINPRINT.COM EDITION

Published by iUniverse.com, Inc.

For information address:
iUniverse.com, Inc.
620 North 48th Street, Suite 201
Lincoln, NE 68504-3467
www.iuniverse.com

Originally published by W. W. Norton

Grateful acknowledgment is made to Mrs. Chester Hudson Hatch for the use,
on pages 402–404, of portions of the journal of her great grandfather,
Captain Josiah Mitchell.

ISBN: 0-595-09373-6

Printed in the United States of America

FOR
ROBERT RUSSELL

"What is this earth and sea, of which I have seen so much? Where is it produced? And what am I, and all the other creatures, wild and tame, human and brutal, where are we? Sure we are all made by some secret Power, who formed the earth and sea, the air and sky. And who is that?"

—D A N I E L   D E F O E, *Robinson Crusoe*

ALMOST FAMOUS

O N E

M o t h e r ," the kid once said, "has revised and updated Descartes. She despairs, therefore she is."

Even now Sarah lay in the bedroom dreaming backwards at a rapid pace, traveling as fast as she could away from now, back to then. Probably by now she had worked her way through 1941 and was ready for 1940.

Ward Sullivan sat at the kitchen table with a cup of coffee in hand, calculating where his mother wanted to be. Sometime before 1924, he decided. Back in the good old days before Scott got horsewhipped off the place, and the old Captain lost the last of the money. That's it. That's the right place for her.

You make a wrong turn in time. You go against fate and tide, and something goes out of joint. You get lost. Your life slows down, almost stops. You wallow in a sargasso sea where time stagnates and you're hardly able to lift your hand or move your leaden feet. Everything that happens is slow and dreamlike. Everything past and done with is worth remembering and somehow full of life and color. Sarah was trapped in such a place. It was God's punishment. Some people get locked up in jails for their sins, she said. Others get locked up in time.

Fornication was the big word for it. Caught in the barn when she was thirteen with her cousin Scott, that's what locked her up in time. That was the beginning. That's when she began to experiment with insanity, being careful not to overdose on the dangerous power it afforded. Several times over the years she had locked the bathroom door, stepped into her bath, cut her wrists, and dyed the bath water a deep ugly red. On those occasions the old man shipped her off to Rosemont, her favorite sanitarium in Massachusetts, just as the old Captain had when she was his charge. But she really wasn't crazy. She just acted nuts to get out of now back to

9

then. It was a form of revenge, a way of beating up on people who made her unhappy: Althy, for her part in the family conspiracy to drive Scott away from home forever, and the old man for having had the audacity to marry her. 1923, make it. That would be about the perfect year. Not exactly too young, but too young to be suspected.

He could hear his grandmother and the kid in the bedroom, trying to coax Sarah into having a bowl of clam chowder. They both felt better if Sarah took occasional nourishment on her long journey. They liked to get her to perform certain reassuring stunts, like sitting up in bed and fumbling through a book, or lurching to the bathroom in a vertigo blur to manipulate the plumbing while someone stood guard at the door lest she do violence to herself.

Some days she tried to play Bushman to their Lincoln Park. But it sounded like today she just couldn't be bothered.

"Please, Sarah," he heard Althy say.

He shook out a smoke and hung it on his bee-stung lip. He rolled the pack of Camels back into the sleeve of his black T-shirt. He couldn't feel the cigarette, but he knew it was there. He didn't mind the fine white threads of scar tissue that cut up his eyebrows and made him look like a boxer. He'd grown used to the dull throb of his bum leg. But he never had gotten over the fact of having no feeling in his lip. He was always surprised to look in the mirror and discover a bit of food or a flare of cigarette paper stuck there. It struck him as a fresh little insult every time. He exhaled a cloud of blue smoke and ran his hand through his thick black hair.

Ward tried to think baseball since the new season was about to begin, but it was no good. He couldn't get clear of the talk going on in the bedroom. His leg was really starting to kick up. A little hot wire ran from the hip socket to the knee cap. Sometimes he just wanted to take a knife and dig into his leg and cut out that piano wire of pain before it drove him crazy. He rubbed his leg fiercely.

"Please?" said Althy from the bedroom.

Now don't let this get to you, he thought. Just study the mares. Sit here and finish your coffee. Then go see the old man.

From where he sat in the kitchen he looked right down the sloping lawn to the big pasture. To the left the low white stable, with its toy corral out front, clung to the mildly rolling ground. He and his father built the little building and the maze of white fences just a few years back, a fact which gave him some satisfaction. There were damn few things he could say that about since he'd come home from playing baseball more than twelve years ago.

The sky was dying, giving up its color by degrees. Some birds exploded out of the live oaks beyond the pasture. They looked extra dark in the faint sky as did the mountains over behind Merkleburg.

In the dusk two mares in the pasture inspected the claw-foot bathtub which served as a water trough. The others nibbled at the hay he'd forked over the fence. The grass was coming back, but it would be a while before he could give up on the hay.

The washboard roof of the stable, shiny as a foil gum wrapper in high daylight, had turned a dull nickel color in the dissolving light and the egg-white walls of the building were fading into the pale wide pasture. One of the mares, a bay, dipped her smoky nose into the tub water which mirrored the rose-colored sky.

"Come, come, dear. I made this good nice clam chowder just for you. Have just a cup for Mother."

"Give it a try," he heard the kid say. "Maybe a little chowder will remind you of Maine and perk up your spirits."

Yes, Ward thought. Invoke the state of Maine. That ought to get her off her ass.

When Ward was a little fellow his great-grandfather, known as the Captain, took him by the hand one day and walked with him to the top of the hill behind the old house at Dunnocks Head.

"See this," cried the little man. "See all this?" The soft white hair on his pink scalp danced on the air, light and soft-seeming as baby fluff or the puffballs of dandelions.

Indeed it was a pretty day up there by the cemetery. The iron fence was down in places and some of the tombstones were reeling, worn smooth as old coins. Down across the field beyond the abandoned shipyard where the half-built *Arzamas* moldered on the ways, the Kennebec wound through the pines and ledges down to the sea.

The Captain however was not referring to the scenery. He was referring to history. He was seeing it the way it used to be, the way it *really* was except for the accident of now, back when the shipyard was alive, before he sold the land to put bread on the table, before Uncle Tyler managed the bank into bankruptcy, and the hotels in Portland and Bangor lapsed into ghostly firetraps with a few aged "guests" who couldn't pay the rent and the Captain couldn't bring himself to evict, before the timberland was cut off and the granite quarry and the ice ponds were abandoned.

"All this," said the Captain, "belongs to you. It always has, and it always will."

Tempus fugit, as the Captain used to say.

But it didn't matter. It was still there if you went back far enough. Surely Sarah believed that. She was still struggling to live in the kingdom of the old Captain's imagination. That was why she had no time to get out of bed and go see the old man who, after all, was only dying. A traveler through time has more important things to consider.

She didn't want him to come home either. You could tell that when the subject came up, the way she looked weak and bleak at the same time even though she didn't say anything.

When and if you could get the kid to go see the old man, he'd have to go in the john and hang over the toilet bowl or sit there in the chair with his head between his bony knees, a fine cold sweat covering his face.

"I am not resigned to the laying of loving hearts into the hard ground," the kid quoted and had at least the decency to look embarrassed afterwards.

"Well, this is a real education," his father said as he sat up in his hospital bed. He weighed 220 pounds a year ago—solid muscle, padded out with a little healthy flab. Twelve months ago he didn't look forty, much less fifty-four. Now the hospital gown bagged on him and the plastic I.D. bracelet was loose on his wrist. He was still a damned fine-looking man, but by God he looked his age now. That was for sure.

"A real education," he'd say softly. He said that about everything, and depending on the circumstances it meant different things. But you couldn't tell how he meant it this time. It lacked the right tone. He said it absently, as though his mind really wasn't on the subject. It gave Ward a hollow feeling in the pit of his stomach. Had his father given up? He hadn't given up, had he? Ward couldn't stand it if the old man just went belly up on this thing.

"You have to have balanced meals, Sarah. How can you feel good if you don't let me take care of you."

No doubt his father would think the little play unfolding in the bedroom was a real education too. Finally Ward couldn't stand it. He had to go see for himself. The name of this play was: Will Sarah speak or not? Or will these other dinks just go on talking to the wall forever? He walked down the hall and stood in the open doorway.

Sarah was still as a snapshot under her pink satin quilt. Her mouth was open, suggesting unconsciousness. Wearing those sunglasses as she did day and night, it was impossible to tell whether she was awake or not. She looked unnaturally flattened in the bed, as if the heavy hand of gravity was pushing her right down into it and chances were good that she would be on the floor by midnight and in the cellar by six o'clock tomorrow morning.

"Dear?"

The others silently acknowledged his presence and he, along with them, waited for some sign of life.

The room was charged with the concentrated atmosphere of an operating theater, as if a medical team were working hard to save a life and the situation was touch and go. Maybe she was dead, finally, she lay so stock-still. There was no way of telling. Till she spoke. If she spoke. Then there was always a chance she'd float off again in mid-sentence.

The kid's face reflected sympathy and concern as he leaned into an imaginary wind. He seemed to have an overabundance of the bland variety of these emotions. Maybe it was a natural outgrowth of his artistic nature, so to speak. There was something smooth and unformed in his mild face as if he'd been taken out of the oven too soon. Indeed he'd spent some time as a baby on the oven door at the old house in Dunnocks Head.

He was born eleven weeks before full term, a horrible-looking red thing that gasped for breath, whined feebly and constantly.

"It don't look good," said old Doc Coffin, looking down, gripping his black bag tighter, as if he had a demon bottled up in there.

They all thought the kid was going to die. There was something especially horrifying in this for the old folks—the old Captain, Uncle Tyler and Aunt Dorcas, as well as for Althy and Granpa—because it reminded them of the time Sarah had lost her first baby by miscarriage late in the term, when she'd fallen downstairs after being fetched home from Boston that time she ran away with Scott. A terrible time in the life of the family, and now this pathetic not-quite-human creature seemed like the repetition of a

deadly curse or a collective nightmare they were doomed to dream
again and again.

But Althy, a natural-born nurse, swaddled the kid in a blue
blanket and stuck him in a dynamite box Uncle Tyler had found
over at the shipyard and put him on the stove door, the warmest
place in the February house. She stayed with him night and day,
sleeping in a rocking chair by the stove.

Ward, who was four at the time, prayed hard for his brother's
survival. He was shaken by the gloom that had descended on the
family, on all except Althy, whom he stayed close to. His mother,
as usual, was in bed and not available so he wasn't sure how she
felt, although he knew she generally subscribed to gloom, and in
fact was often sent away to Rosemont by his father to get rid of
it.

"Don't you go in there and bother your mother," he was told
when he was caught upstairs by someone.

He checked on his brother's progress two or three times a day.

"He ain't rising," he reported miserably to his grandmother after
a week of watchfulness because he full well expected that if the
baby were to show signs of improvement, he would begin to rise
like a loaf of bread which, in his experience, was the other thing
that Althy sometimes set on the oven door.

But the kid survived and prospered and, although skinny and
puny when little, he was now quite healthy if a little more nervous
than most, but that could be put down to what you might call his
artistic nature. He painted his girlfriend Avis in every awkward
position it seemed he could imagine, always without a speck of
clothing on; he painted trompe d'oeil toilets and flowerpots, pictures Ward puzzled over for the apparent waste of talent which
they represented, but, amazingly, these bizarre creations won
prizes all over the place. Now studying his brother's bespectacled
face the thousandth time for answers, the ruddy high color that
he'd never lost from baby days, Ward was still disturbed by something unformed, some subtle underdevelopment which he could
not put his finger on.

"This is lovely clam chowder," Althy was saying. "You said last
week how much you wanted some just like we make back home."

Althy, dressed in a short-sleeved housedress with a flowered
print, was peering intently at the figure under the rosy quilt. In her
hand she held a soup ladle and her apron was tied high on her

belly, just under her shapeless bosom. Her gold-rimmed trifocals flashed with sympathy as she coaxed the woman in the bed. From the way Althy acted you would think she was dealing with a six-year-old instead of someone fifty-five years old.

The figure on the bed spoke. The effect was electrifying, as if a picture on the wall had spoken, or as if a pilgrim at Lourdes had risen from prayer, thrown down his crutches, and walked away. What Sarah said was simple, and nobody in the room missed her meaning.

The voice, husky and thick from disuse, said, "There's a smell in here."

By God, she is still alive, thought Ward. She's just been on one of her trips through time and space, and now she's come back to say she's picked right out of the atmosphere the fatal scent of the old man's imminent death.

He preferred to take this light cynical line instead of facing the hopelessness which underlay Sarah's words. It would make him mad, if he thought about it, as if she were robbing the old man of his last hope for survival by making such remarks. From the first, she had said he was going to die. Now that it looked like it was turning out that way, Ward couldn't help but hold her partly responsible. Goddamn Sarah always expected life to go sour and with her repeatedly predicting it, it usually did.

"That's not true," said Althy. "I opened the windows and aired out the room. I've changed the sheets on Gordon's bed. It's just lovely in here."

"Yes, Mother. It's just fine in here," said the kid somewhat nervously because he was sensitive to what he believed were his mother's intuitive powers.

The old man was alone at the hospital and here they all stood around, trying to get Sarah to eat soup. He ought to get out of there, get his keys, get in his car and go see him. It was getting late, and the old man would be waiting for his visit. The minute he got in the car Ward knew his own nerves would start to smooth out.

"Have some clam chowder, dear," said Althy.

"Why are we talking about soup?" cried Sarah. Her voice seemed to flatten Ward's ears against his head. "Can't you smell it? You smell it too, don't you? Can't you smell death in this room?"

Her insistence shocked even Althy into silence.

"Don't talk crazy," he heard himself say. He had meant to leave the room without saying anything, to just get out of there. Sarah's sunglasses jerked in his direction. "Darling—"

"Keep your voice down," he said. "Don't go screaming about death. If you want to do something, put on your clothes and come along with me to see him tonight."

"You know she can't do that," Althy reproached him.

"No?" he said, looking from Sarah to Althy. "Why not?"

"You know why not. She's ill. She's been sick all these years. This is too much for her."

"I think it would be nice if she could find a way to visit the old man just once."

"You know she can't," said the kid.

"Why don't you let her speak for herself?"

They all studied Sarah, who pressed her hands up under her sunglasses and began to cry.

"You'd better leave, Ward," said the kid. "You're upsetting Mother."

"There's nothing wrong with her that a kick in the ass wouldn't cure." He hadn't meant to say that either. It was cruel and harsh and unfair—and it felt good.

Althy said, "That's enough. You leave this room now."

"Well, she's not screaming any more is she? She knows I won't put up with her theater."

"I'm an old woman," said Althy. "But keep it up and I'll still box your ears."

Now that he'd started he couldn't seem to stop.

"She never gave a shit about him. But you think she could drag herself out of bed and go see him now that he's dying."

He looked over at the bed where Sarah clutched the top of her pink quilt, returning his gaze fearfully.

"He's dying, Sarah," he said bitterly. "Just the way you said he would a year ago." All the insulation had burned off the wire in his leg now but the pain was clear and vibrant, singing, not burning.

"Come on," said the kid. "Cut it out. You're just making everything worse."

Althy said, "Never mind your brother. *I* told you to get out. Now you get out."

She was no bigger than a chimpanzee and more than eighty years old, but it was plain she meant to do battle if he didn't leave.

"My, you have a regular little army of defenders," he said to the hank of frizzy hair and sunglasses peering at him from above the pink quilt. "I got news for you, Sarah. Nobody can fix it for you this time."

"Come on. Out."

The kid laid his hand on Ward's chest. It cleared a little pathway for the pain in his leg and the anger building in him. He accepted the outrage gratefully and grabbed the kid right by the throat. He drove him against the closet door, his fist in the kid's Adam's apple. The kid was four inches taller and four years younger, but it didn't make any difference.

"Goddamn you," he told the kid. "Keep your hands off me."

Althy stung him like a hornet on the side of the head with the soup ladle.

"Get out!" she cried.

Ward brushed past the old woman and leaned down into Sarah's crying face.

"You lay there boneless as a squid while he dies. He put up with your shit for years and you can't even—"

"Mother!" cried the frightened voice.

"Get—out!" The old woman tattooed his back and shoulders with the soup ladle. He turned. His fist arrested the silver blur in mid-motion. The ladle, soundless and wingless, flew through the open door and clattered in the hallway.

"To hell with all of you," he said and walked out.

Back in the kitchen he heard Sarah begin to cry.

"Oh, Mother. Gordon's dying. What will I do? How will I get along without Gordon?"

"There, there," he heard Althy say. "It's all right, child. It's all right."

Althy still carried trays of ginger ale and coffee ice cream to the bedroom to provision Sarah for the long trip to Somewhere. That time-traveler no doubt still visited the Boston hotel room where she and Scott had lived for four months in 1929 and could tell you some new thing about the water stain on the ceiling over the bed, if you asked. The house still smelled of homemade molasses cookies sometimes, the mares were still in the pasture, the kid still

pushed his glasses back on his nose with the old characteristic
self-abusive stabbing motion and peered through the lenses at the
melon-ripe wonder of his girlfriend Avis where he seemed to
think he would find answers to the mysteries of the universe. The
old house still stood in the wind at Dunnocks Head. The baseball
season, and the sun were on their way back. But it was not all
right, and Althy damn well knew it. It had not been all right for
a number of years. He stood in the middle of the kitchen, rubbing
his sore leg.

The kid came into the room wearing a pained expression.

"What the hell got into you?"

"I just get sick of her bullshit sometimes. I don't want to talk
about it. Just let me cool off."

"Okay," said the kid. "All right. But we've got to talk. This can't
go on."

"You want to come along?"

"No, I can't. I told Avis I would take her shopping for her
mother's birthday."

"Suit yourself, kid."

"Ward?"

"What is it?"

"He's *my* father too. I feel as bad about it as you do."

"I know you do, kid."

"Hey."

"What?"

"Don't act like such a tough guy all the time, okay?"

Ward started down the steps. Maybe really what had set him
off was how treacherously life went along in its old furrow, how
everybody in the family could grow used to the idea of the old
man's fatal illness, take for granted its slow consuming course, and
go about their business. Therefore, his impatience with the pur-
veyors of clam chowder, time-travelers, and picture-painting paperheads.

His room was full of the relics of his former life, so to speak.
The silver bat over his bed and the gleaming trophies of miniature
ballplayers on the dresser mocked him gently. Against the far wall
under the window waited the student desk, the chair, and the
golden goose-necked lamp under whose burning eye, late at night
in the silent house, he played the baseball game or brought his

records up to date when he couldn't sleep. Just looking around the orderly room made him feel better. A place for everything and everything in its place, was his motto.

He got the car keys out of the top left-hand dresser drawer. He went back upstairs, made a quick pass through the living room and kitchen, and out to the garage without a further word to anyone. And he drove over to Harrisburg to see the old man at Cooper Memorial.

T W O

THE CADILLAC COUPE DEVILLE soundlessly powered
him through the night along the Harrisburg Pike. Ward Sullivan
peered over the tailored gloss of the long elegant hood, his battered
face bathed in the green glow of the dash lights. The tension in
his body seemed to ebb right into the black leather seat. Just
driving the big yellow car calmed him down.

The car was beautiful. He could never look at it or work on it
or drive it without remembering with satisfaction that the Boston
Red Sox had given it to him back in 1955 as the final installment
for signing with them three years earlier, the summer he got out
of high school. Even though it was twelve years old it was still
almost showroom perfect. It was no exaggeration for Ward to say
that he knew how to take care of things. If you knew how to take
care of things, they might last forever.

For example, every night when he came home from work he
wiped the car down with a rag. He never let road tar or dirt build
up. That was important. Then, too, twice a week he polished the
chrome. On the weekends he washed it and once a month he
polished it. Twice a year he gave it a wax job. If you looked at it
that way, it was no accident that the car was still beautiful. He
changed the oil himself. He had all the right stuff, the drain pan,
everything. He bought Quaker State cheap at the discount chain.
He stacked it in neat pyramids, like canned goods, under the
workbench in the garage. He had a spark plug wrench and meter
so he could handle that job. He even put in new points when she
needed them and he had the stuff to fix the timing just right. If
he found a nick in the paint, he didn't put off fixing it. That's how
rust got started. He fixed it right away, using the yellow touch-up
paint expertly, applying the perfectly matched paint on the care-

fully prepared spot with the deliberate intensity of a woman painting her fingernails.

If you loved something you had to be the doctor. You had to know everything there was to know about the thing. You really had to *want* to know. Unless you were really interested there were always a hundred things you would never learn because you weren't serious enough about It. But if you were really serious, you learned everything there was to know. And in fact you might even develop a sixth sense. After a while you might be able to pick the slightest trouble out of the air and go right to fixing it. Of course this was no substitute for regular work. You still had to have a regular schedule. You couldn't let the routine slide because if you did that's how you made problems. Ward felt good, as he rode along, knowing that the car would always stay beautiful so long as he kept after it.

Yes, this car brought back memories all right. Especially of that July day in 1952 when he had tried out for the Boston Red Sox at Fenway Park—back in the days before everything turned to shit. That day, all the brass watched him from behind the screen, sitting there in brown suits puffing on cigars behind home plate. Boudreau, that year's manager, was the only one in uniform. The rest of them looked like a bunch of hotel dicks. Except for the old man, who'd been invited to join them and who was dressed in his usual white shirt and grey pleated pants. In addition, he had on an expensive blue blazer with brass buttons that Sarah had bought him on one of her trips south. So far as Ward could remember— and he could remember everything—it was the only sports coat he had ever owned. At least the only one he had ever worn. His father might have looked jaunty if his face hadn't worn the expression of a man who has just fallen out of a balloon. What in hell were these men doing with his son? his expression seemed to ask. Why the funny shoes and the knickers? Well, the old man never was a ball fan. He never could figure out what his oldest boy saw in the game.

The truth was he never did get over the fact that his son, at age three, began to read road signs as they traveled along in the car back and forth between Portsmouth, New Hampshire, and Dunnocks Head, Maine, and later between Carlisle, Pennsylvania, and Dunnocks Head. Just like that. With no coaxing. All at once the

boy knew what the words meant. This little kid! His father
couldn't get over it. His little boy, reading big words! *Portsmouth,
Desert of Maine, Bath, City of Ships, You Are Now Leaving Vacationland,
Come Back Again, Merritt Parkway, Welcome to Pennsylvania.*

It was too much for the old man to handle. He was convinced
he had a little genius on his hands. Given the circumstances—the
implacable circumstances of his life as Sarah might say—it was
understandable how the old man could kid himself into thinking
like that.

For instance by the winter of 1938, he had one little boy who
spent his time in a dynamite box on the stove door. That would
be his newborn son, Gordon, Jr. Meanwhile his wife, Sarah, was
upstairs in bed, drifting semi-comatose in the front bedroom, the
one she favored because it looked out onto the Kennebec. She
spent her time watching the day slide by on the ceiling, the light
reflecting off the river in rippling patterns, the gold dapples swimming upstream against the slowly shifting light, the gold itself
dying as the theater on the ceiling went dark at the day's end.

Most of the time, the old man was back in Portsmouth running
the newspaper and feeling lonely, maybe even perplexed, at how
he got this newspaper to run, the crazy wife, and the two kids he
hardly ever saw. No doubt he wondered how he'd let his life
become so complicated. Twice a week Althy, or Granpa, would get
into the 1938 tan Dodge they had to keep down to Cousin Waterhouse's place because the Captain wouldn't allow the damn thing
on the premises, not even in the barn, and one or the other would
take Ward down to see his father and stay overnight at the little
white Cape Cod that was supposed to be home, but wasn't, because everybody's home was the Captain's house in Dunnocks
Head and always had been since 1700.

On those nights when little Ward Sullivan was a guest in what
was supposed to be his own house, his father would put him on
his lap after dinner and have him read stories out of the Portsmouth paper, which Sarah's cousin, Scott Prothero, had won in a
poker game in 1933.

Gordon Sullivan was a kid reporter on the paper in those days,
just down from Skowhegan after having worked for *The Kennebec
Journal* for a year. One spring morning he walked into the newsroom and this Scott Prothero was standing there in his three-piece
white suit and his carefully knotted green polka-dot tie, with that

vivid black hair which belonged to all Webster blood and that fine little moustache penciled on his handsome lip, looking a little like Zachary Scott, only bigger and less ratty, maybe more like another handsome loser, name of Lee Bowman. He was smiling at the old man, his gray eyes crinkling with good humor and friendliness.

The old man liked him right away. Of course, the old man was awful young and inexperienced. In those days he wouldn't have known a snake-in-the-grass if it had crawled up his pantleg while whistling "Dixie."

Scott told him, "I'm Scott Prothero, the new owner. What the hell do I do?"

Disarming bastard.

Well, the old man thought he was wonderful. The old man walked to work. And this fellow, this Scott what's-his-name, drove a white LaSalle around town. And he wasn't much older than the old man, about twenty-six then. It seemed he played cards for a living. Or maybe ran a little booze now and then. He owned part of some race horses in Florida and he'd been out in California and helped to produce a movie. Young Gordon Sullivan was overwhelmed. Jesus, what a fellow.

Then pretty soon there was this beautiful woman striding through the newsroom. She had dark, vivid hair, stark gray eyes, high cheekbones. She moved, impatient and graceless, on long legs through the dying clatter of the newsroom, a cold and lovely young woman who never looked at the dumbfounded pit dwellers who worked there, cutting through the noise and people, losing no time to get to that cubbyhole of walnut and frosted glass in the back where Scott Prothero sat and bit his pencil over his daily racing sheet.

Some said she was the prettiest woman in Maine. She'd even been called that in print by *The Brunswick Record.* But the old man said that was the wrong word to describe Sarah Rideout. She was not pretty, that was too mild a description. She was beautiful. Absolutely beautiful in the same undebatable sense that a Greek temple was beautiful. Yes. Because her perfect face was too haunted merely to be called pretty.

His father claimed he'd never seen a lovelier woman anywhere —and, of course, anywhere for him until then, added up to two towns—Portsmouth, New Hampshire, and Skowhegan, Maine. But it didn't matter. Because, country boy or not, Gordon Sullivan damn well knew there was not a more beautiful woman anywhere.

He watched her, not exactly understanding the hypnotic effect she had on him. He was fascinated just to see her move. It seemed like that was enough for him, that he would never ask for any more, except the privilege to see her walk across a room. Sarah Rideout was trim as a racing hull, cutting through peoples' stares like a good boat through choppy seas. Oblivious to the effect she had on others, it was said, though this would later prove inaccurate. Because Sarah saw everything, but was just coldly indifferent to it all, like a cat.

After Gordon Sullivan watched her passing through the newsroom for a while he discovered she was the new owner's cousin. Since Gordon was half in love with her already, he almost hollered aloud out of pure joy and relief when Scott told him that this beautiful creature happened to be a close relative. Well. The old man was still fresh out of Skowhegan and he could no more figure out what was going on than a cockatoo in the subway. And by the time he figured it out, it was too late. For, by that time, he loved her. He had discovered too late that she was crazy. But she was beautiful—that was for sure, even reported as such in the papers —and maybe the old man thought that was enough. Or, that with love, a special kind of cement rumored to have healing properties, he could repair the cracks in her head. One thing led to another and suddenly he was in the middle of it. And Scott was telling him that because Sarah was unstable, she needed special understanding.

"Maybe you could supply that," suggested Scott. "Do you think you could?"

Sure, the old man could supply special understanding—an endless steady plasmic river of it. By that time he was hooked and ready to take a bullet in the heart for that beautiful face.

About that point cousin Scott had to cut and run. Some people in Chicago, as he called them, were anxious to make his reacquaintance and he was obliged to put considerable distance between himself and the invitation.

"Those people want my antlers over the fireplace, Gordon. Take care of the paper till I get back. I'm making you a partner. I want you to take care of Sarah for me too. Will you do it?"

Of course the old man would do it. He wasn't twenty-one for

nothing. When you're that young you think you can do anything, even restore a crazy girl to sanity by doing everything for her and suffering anything for her. All this happened right after Christmas in 1933—not only Jesus' birthday but Scott's as well, an accident which had ruined the holiday at Dunnocks Head since 1924.

Since Scott had won the paper in a poker game in May, that meant he'd actually stayed in one place for half a year—longer than anywhere since he got run out of Dunnocks Head. So far as anybody knew, it turned out to be the longest he ever stayed in one place for the rest of his known life.

The night Scott packed his bag and told Sarah he had to leave town, she said she was all grown up this time. According to the story, she told him the Captain couldn't get him for kidnapping this time and could she go with him. When he said no, she went into the bathroom and took a bottle of sleeping pills. They say the last thing Scott did in Portsmouth that night was to wrap his cousin Sarah in her sealskin coat and drive her to the hospital in his white LaSalle. From there he used the pay phone to call Gordon Sullivan, his new partner, and told him to drop everything and get over to the hospital, for here was his chance to take care of this beautiful girl he was so crazy about. Then Scott climbed into his LaSalle and bailed out of town as fast as he could go, no doubt keeping an eye on the rearview mirror.

When Sarah woke up there was the old man sitting by her bed, wearing an expression like Lucky, the Captain's black Labrador, when it wanted to be petted.

Her first words were, "Goddamn the bastard, he's left me again."

And her second words were, "Get out of here, Gordon, and leave me alone." Said with no particular vehemence.

Fate is made of such moments as these. The big ones, it seems, always come in disguise. If Gordon Sullivan had listened to this thick mumble, taken it to heart as the best advice he would ever hear, perhaps his life would have been entirely different. But he didn't listen. He decided he was going to help. He was going to be everything she needed. Convinced, so the story went, that he had the necessary strength and good health to make her well, that somehow this healthy vitality he was so confident about would just naturally flow from him to her in the form of love and this crazy girl, who had already attempted suicide once or twice, would be magically restored to health. He was not the first man to make such a mistake.

Once the critical moment passed, things moved fast. The Captain came to see Sarah, took one look at his granddaughter and put her back in Rosemont. She had a psychiatrist there, young and handsome, whom she admired and who seemed to do her some good. Gordon drove to Massachusetts to see her every chance he could. Then on Sundays he would drive down to Dunnocks Head to make reports and counsel with the family. The family saw plainly this fellow wanted to marry Sarah as soon as he could.

The Captain, with his finger in a copy of Horace, listened to this young fool quietly, almost remotely, his gray eyes—*her* gray eyes too—steadily watching him, calculating the odds, as Gordon reported on her progress, but not listening to the report so much as listening beyond, for the answers to his unasked questions. Gordon Sullivan would recall this attitude of quiet watchfulness years later and tell his son Ward about it, making kind of a joke of it.

The old man said the family treated him with the same reserved courtesy they would have extended to a tattooed visitor from the Fiji Islands. Later, he said, he realized he would always be an outsider. He would be accorded guest status, just like Uncle Tyler and Granpa; Sarah, on the other hand, could go crazy or run away to China, but she would always remain part of the family, just as Scott would, although in his case an unmentionable part. Sarah was really the Websters' problem, not Gordon Sullivan's. But if he insisted on being helpful, they would use him, as they might the services of a specialist. He could contribute his health, his strength, his patience, and, later on, his money to offset her fits of violence, mostly self-directed, and her long bouts of depression. What he got in payment for this was not their business. It was strictly between him and Sarah. Or maybe between him and God. The Websters really owed him nothing since they hadn't asked for anything and whatever he did he had volunteered to do. They had merely seen his usefulness, that was all.

One night when Ward and the kid were sitting in the kitchen having a drink, Ward said something along this line.

"How do you know that?" asked Gordie.

"I know," said Ward. "The same way you do. Through osmosis. How else?"

Yessir. Althy says something when you are five years old, and she's giving you a bath. Maybe Sarah bursts out with some terrible intelligence from the past, and you hear it before you can escape from the room. One day the old man mumbles something while the two of you are currying a horse. And in this manner, without intending to, you realize one day you know a hell of a lot more than you ever wanted to.

Gordon told Dr. Walker, Sarah's psychiatrist at Rosemont, of his plan to marry his patient as soon as the doctor pronounced her fit to go home. Ward knew about that through osmosis too, and, on pain of death, could have reconstructed the dialogue.

"You know that she is a very sick woman?" asked the doctor.

"Yes, I know that," said the old man. There is an old photograph around the house, taken when he was a kid reporter with the *Kennebec Journal*. In this picture he has just turned to the photographer as if in answer to a call and there he is, in his hat and his suit, lean as a rake handle. His handsome face is alive with intelligence and energy. He looks like he could do anything. That's probably how he looked as he answered the doctor.

"I believe I can help Sarah find herself," he said.

"Sarah has tried to commit suicide on several occasions. Not just this once," said the doctor.

"I know that," said the old man. "I believe I can make her happy."

Now here he got some more grade-A information that could have made a difference.

"Sarah," said the doctor, "doesn't believe anything can make her happy. She says God is punishing her, punishing all Webster blood, for sins known and unknown. She says she would be happy if she could. She says that God has rolled a rock in front of the door of her soul and nothing can move it, only God."

"I still believe I can make her happy," said the old man quietly.

"Sarah," said Dr. Walker, "has a certain capacity for destructiveness, for violence. Mostly she directs it at herself. Someday that violence may turn outward."

"I believe—" began the old man.

"I know what you believe," interrupted the doctor.

He married her the day she got out of the sanitarium. They drove directly from there to a J.P.'s on the New Hampshire–Massachusetts border and then drove on to the house at Dunnocks

Head where they were welcomed with tea and grave discourse.
Afterwards, so the story goes, Uncle Tyler took the old man out
to the barn where he kept a bottle of Apple Jack hidden, as the
Captain didn't allow intoxicating beverages in the house, and they
both took a couple of pulls on that by way of celebration. It was
colder in the empty barn than it was outside, which was cold
enough. Their breath was vaporous, and they slapped themselves
between tugs.

The newly-marrieds honeymooned for the weekend in the front
bedroom, the one with the fine view of the Kennebec. Then Gordon, newly-appointed partner, managing editor as well as husband, got up early on Monday morning and drove down to Portsmouth to work. Sarah, feeling tired, stayed on at Dunnocks Head.

That was late February. In September of that same year Ward
was born—early, as though Sarah was anxious to get it over with
but he was no ugly gasping little red worm like his brother would
be, born after barely six months.

Tempus fugit, as the Captain used to say. Life is full of extraordinary passages when so much happens and time moves so quick it
takes you years to sort it out, if you ever do. Gordon Sullivan sat
in Portsmouth, New Hampshire, with his three-and-a-half-year-
old baby on his lap and another one on a stove door in Dunnocks
Head. This lap baby could read almost anything. No doubt the old
man must have wondered whether a whiz-reading baby and a
crazy but beautiful wife was just what he had in mind forty-nine
months ago when he first set eyes on Scott Prothero.

In the space of the first thirteen months he had found out that
he'd been done in by a beautiful face. He discovered that he, a man
of fair character, didn't really care what his wife did so long as he
could have her around from time to time to look at her. On the
plus side, he learned to manage a newspaper and found he had a
natural gift for making money. He woke up to the fact that cousin
Scott was his silent partner in lots of ways and would continue to
be whenever he could duck the mob or later, the war, and hotfoot
it back to Portsmouth. The worst news was that his wife was truly
crazy, and it was unlikely anything he did would ever make a
difference. He also seemed to accept the fact that Sarah would
never love him, but it didn't matter because, in any case, Gordon
Sullivan was going to stick with her.

That was a fair amount of discovery in such a short time. God

the postman had delivered him a letter and he signed for it, accepted the message with finality. Gordon Sullivan was going to be
one of those people who took care of everything, so to speak,
while other people drank and screwed and jumped off window
ledges. One of the nice rewards, it seemed, was this little reading
kid on his lap, twice a week.

"*Gee, that's wonderful son. Boy, you little thing, you just read right along,
don't you?*"

He just couldn't get enough of it. It just gave him fresh pleasure
every time Ward farted up a little story.

In high school Ward made straight A's even though he didn't
study much. What he really worked on was his baseball. He made
the varsity in his freshman year, and he led the team in virtually
every offensive category. Granpa was four years dead by that time,
but the lessons he and Jack Coombs had drilled into him in the
summers at Dunnocks Head ever since he was little, had taken. He
remembered everything the old battery mates had ever told him,
it seemed.

*What are you jerking the bat for? Just put it out there at the right time. You
hit it right, that ball will go far.*

His grandfather never saw him play high school or town team
ball for Dunnocks Head, but Mr. Coombs saw him play a couple
of times in Dunnocks Head and once even in Carlisle, coming all
the way from Kansas City especially to see him and that day he
did stick the bat out just right and he hit three home runs. Granpa
was still around for Little League, even coached him in Legion ball
in 1947. He saw him play, but he never saw him when he was
soaring, when it was clear that he was *good* and no doubt going to
be the major leaguer that his grandfather himself would have been
if he'd taken the contract the A's offered him at the same time they
signed Jack Coombs. But he had sickly parents to take care of, and
when they died he succumbed to Althea Webster, married her,
moved into the old house at Dunnocks Head, and the Captain put
him to work in the shipyard.

They were both just schoolboys, but already Jack Coombs and
Ward Rideout were baseball legends in southern Maine. That was
back in the late 1890s when people spent more time on the important stuff, like baseball. Every little town knew about these fellows
at Colby College who looked like they were going to be better than
Sockalexis or at least fulfill that drunken Indian's promise. In 1898

in his rookie year Louis Sockalexis of Old Town, Maine, hit .338 for the Cleveland Indians. That was before he discovered the pleasures of booze. One shining season. That was it. Then the bottle took over. For the next two years, he led the league in drunkenness before fading back to Old Town.

Mr. Coombs restored the nation's confidence in Maine as the birthplace of sober ballplayers. One year he won thirty games for the Philadelphia A's. He always said Ward Rideout was the best catcher he ever had, and said he was sure if he'd stuck to the game his old battery mate would have made the Hall of Fame. Mr. Coombs was quoted in *The Portland Press Herald* after Granpa died in 1948. Mr. Coombs was kind enough not to talk Hall of Fame when Granpa was alive. Because Granpa must have wondered sometimes if he hadn't sold out, settled for too little, although he never talked about it.

This good memory of Ward's was a curse which he shared in common with his mother. He seemed to remember everything. Everything. Without trying in the least. Why, he could not say. Only he could run movies in his mind containing the record of virtually every event in his life. If he wanted to know exactly what Wally Shaw looked like on a given afternoon as he mopped up a hopeless game for Louisville that golden summer twelve years ago, why, all he had to do was stop the film in his head at the right frame and trace defeat in every line and pore of that ugly face— right down to the drop of sweat hanging off his banana nose as the old relief pitcher fidgeted on the bench between innings.

And Blue. If he wanted to, he could recall her beautiful face perfectly. Even how she looked that day he met and fell in love with her at the ballpark. He could remember the slant of the sun, shadows, columns of light. Cleverdon, the fat little manager, stood pigeon-toed on the top step of the dugout that day, spitting tobacco juice over the railing, and the ground so hard and bone dry the juice just balled up with a coat of dust over it and sat there like mercury. He could even remember details like that. But he liked to think he was too smart to run these movies very often. Those memories had to do with the old days, dead and gone. And if a man wanted to live simply without much fuss he had to learn to get along with as few memories and as little imagination as possible.

The difference between, say, him and his mother was that she

didn't seem to be able to turn the memories off. She could not turn
to the projectionist and say: listen you, I've had enough of that
movie, put it away. Or say: run the happy movie about the time
Scott and I went fishing down to the cottage at Birch Point. Or say:
turn on the lights, I'm tired of movies. Ward could do that, but she
couldn't. That is why she is crazy and I'm not, he thought. Except
sometimes at night when Ward was asleep the projectionist put on
any damned film he wanted and then Ward had to thrash about
and grit his teeth till he struggled awake in a cold sweat and turned
off the movie himself.

Yes. He could remember everything if he wanted to. For example, as he drove along to the hospital that night, he heard Mr.
Coombs say something as clearly as if he were sitting right next
to him in the car at that moment. Something Mr. Coombs had said
to him twenty-five years ago. "Young fella," Mr. Coombs said,
"you're going to be a fine ballplayer just like your grandfather."

In the movie Mr. Coombs threw the ball to Granpa, bending
stiffly at the knees, his suit coat binding his arms, his black shoes
flattening the slippery weeds. The boy in the movie hit the ball
effortlessly and sharply all over the big empty open space of the
shipyard. He hit one onto the deck of the old half-built ship at the
other end of the yard, and Mr. Coombs declared it a homer.

In this particular version of the memory or the movie, the
weather was especially fine and the old Captain had come out of
the house to watch the two men and the boy. He too was in a black
suit like the other old men but with his coat off, displaying a
Sunday afternoon informality of white shirt and vest and sleeve
garters, a small dignified figure before the tall gaunt old house.

He was in his nineties then and he moved slowly but his gray
eyes were lively and followed everything. And when Ward hit one
onto the deck of the old ship, the Captain guffawed and cried out,
"Why you little gnat! You hit that one a country mile!"

The ball glowed a magical white against the black cloth of Mr.
Coombs' suit as he paused and peered in at Granpa for the sign.
"Come on, Colby Jack," said Granpa. "Show this rube your good
stuff."

Mr. Coombs cackled and started into his antique pitching motion. As he flipped the ball to the plate his coattails flew and the
ball, not fast but heavy, danced in, turning slowly like a midget
planet in its orbit.

A patrician figure, parchment skin, and elegant manners, a fine
old man in a black suit—that's the way Ward remembered Mr.
Coombs. The tip of the forefinger on his pitching hand was just
naked bone. Ward never asked him about it. He just assumed Mr.
Coombs had worn away the flesh throwing fastballs past Ty Cobb
and Nap Lajoie and the like.

Thanks to Mr. Coombs and Granpa as he stood out there in the
deserted shipyard with a bat in his hands, Ward had discovered
the wonderful mindless world of talent, where the head and all its
fancy ideas were subordinate to the mysterious intelligence of the
body.

There were times when his body did things without consulting
him at all. For instance sometimes he would have no idea how to
deal with a certain pitch and yet hit it hard—say, one of Mr.
Coombs' curveballs. Nevertheless the body went ahead and dealt
with it and left the mind wandering alone in the rear. And it felt
very good. There was more satisfaction in the mysterious properties of talent than in the plodding, struggling groundhog business
of the head, surely more pleasure in baseball than in the horrible
front page stories about Mussolini and Hitler and Chamberlain
that his father often obliged him to read aloud.

Which was how it came to pass that the old man found himself
in Fenway Park one July morning in 1952 sitting among a bunch
of fat men in brown suits. He was saddened to discover that these
men, who smoked cigars to the last man, were seriously considering laying out good money so his son could go on playing baseball
right into adulthood.

Out on the mound that day, one particular day in July of 1952,
Sid Hudson, a big lanky righthander from Tennessee, threw batting practice for Ward Sullivan. Sammy White was the catcher. At
first Ward couldn't even see the ball, he was so nervous. The ball
slid across the plate from Hudson's fluid motion in a continuous
slightly dipping arc, as if it ran on an invisible wire from the
pitcher to the catcher's mitt.

"Come on, kid," said White. "Show those fat guys what you can
do."

And he did. He began to drive baseballs all over Fenway, hitting
the walls, hitting them into the seats. The crack of the bat echoed
in the empty stadium as he hit balls to all fields for fifteen minutes.

The fat guys watched him shag flies in the outfield and throw to the infield. They timed him running to first. Someone suggested they all go up to "Mr. Yawkey's office" and Mr. Yawkey was apparently among them, but Ward had met so many people that day he couldn't keep the names straight. Upstairs in the big plush office, they talked to him while, as inconspicuously as possible, he examined the blown-up pictures of current and former Red Sox stars which comprised the main decoration on the walls. They were pleasant and seemed interested in the dumb answers he gave to their questions.

And at length they all left the room except for a little fellow with his hair parted in the middle who wore a polka-dot bow tie to go with the cigar he sucked on thoughtfully. He had hard eyes like little blue pebbles and as he stood opposite Ward and his father he gestured for them to have a seat in front of the desk. The man, who, as it turned out, was Tom Yawkey himself, sat down upon a creaky old cracked leather swivel chair, his eyes still on Ward who had never been appraised so coolly for so long before in his young life.

"Son," said the man, taking the cigar out of his mouth, "you look like a ballplayer."

"Yessir," said Ward and shifted uneasily in his chair.

"Yessir," sighed the man and blew some smoke at the ceiling. "You sure look like a ballplayer to me."

There was another moment's silence.

"You must be this boy's father," Mr. Yawkey said to the old man who looked somewhat startled.

"I am, yes," answered the old man.

"You must be proud to have a son who can run, throw, and hit like this young fellow. Son—"

"Yessir?"

"How would you like to play for the Boston Red Sox?"

"I think I would."

"Good. Good. Because we'd like to have you. Now, I know there's other teams interested in a boy of your talents. So I want to make you a fair but attractive offer. To tell the truth, I want to make it so fair and attractive you'll sign with us right now, here this morning, with no further fuss."

Mr. Yawkey leaned back in his chair, put his cigar back in his mouth and studied Ward's face carefully as if by minute inspection he might find the right price stamped there for an es-

pecially shrewd man to discover if he knew just where to look.
"Baseball is a wonderful game," he said. "A wonderful game.
But it has its irritations. For example, there's a rule says if a club
gives a young man more than $5,000 he has to sit on a major
league bench instead of going to the minors where he can be
properly prepared for his destiny, whatever that may be. It's a silly
rule. A despicable rule, really."

The conversation, it seemed to Ward, took a puzzling turn for
the worse just at that moment. For Mr. Yawkey turned his hard
bright eyes on the old man.

"What line of work did you say you're in, Mr. . . . ?"

"Sullivan," finished the old man helpfully. "I'm in the shoe
business."

"You sell shoes?"

"No, I make them, manufacture them."

"Oh, I see. Manufacture. You design your own models and such
like?"

"Well, as a matter of fact, sometimes I do."

Mr. Yawkey grinned pleasantly, as if he had scored gin in a card
game.

"I been thinking about going into the shoe business myself, Mr.
Sullivan. I bet you're surprised to learn that."

"Yes, I am."

"No doubt," chuckled Mr. Yawkey. "I could use a man of your
obvious abilities to assist me. I'll pay you, let's see—." Here Mr.
Yawkey rolled his cigar about in his mouth and studied Ward
again coolly and deliberately.

"What do you say to $30,000, Mr. Sullivan? Show me some
designs for some nice shoes. . . . What kind of shoes do you
manufacture?"

"Baby shoes."

"Good. Some designs for some nice, long-wearing baby shoes.
Nothing too detailed or complicated, of course. A few sketches
will do nicely. What do you say to that?"

"All right," said the old man. "Fine."

"Excellent. I'll have my lawyers draw up the necessary papers.
Now, young man, how would you like to have a nice Cadillac to
drive around in?"

"Yes, I guess that would be all right."

Mr. Yawkey laughed. "Well, you think about it. Maybe you

want the cash. Maybe you want a different car. By golly, this is nice. Here I thought I was just going to talk baseball this morning but now, just by pure chance, it looks like I might have found a partner for that new baby shoe business I've always wanted to go into."

In the pause which followed, Ward and the old man had time to register silently a stupefied admiration for the Red Sox owner, who suddenly stood up, smiling broadly as if standing up suddenly was a joke.

"Now I'm going to leave you gentlemen to think these propositions over, and when you're ready to talk, you just stick your head out the door. I'll wait for you in the hall. Take your time now. This is a big decision for everybody. And we don't want to make any mistakes, do we?"

He gave them a big grin again and suddenly disappeared out the door, closing it softly behind him.

"Good God," his father said.

"It's better than what the Dodgers said they'd do," said Ward.

"What do you care about the Dodgers anyway?" his father asked him. "Isn't this the baseball team you always wanted to play for?"

"Yes, it is."

"Then go ahead," his father said. "Go ahead and take it."

For indeed Ward Sullivan had always pulled for the Red Sox. He and Granpa died little deaths listening to that soap opera every summer over the crackly radio at Dunnocks Head. Back in the late forties, Boston had the best team in baseball. But, of course, they could never win a pennant. It was enough to kill you. Nevertheless, Ward and his grandfather and two million other fools still loved them to distraction no matter how many times the team, so splendid in mid-season, stumbled in September and finished second, as usual, behind the Yankees. It was a trick and a joke the Red Sox pulled on the population of New England every summer, and everybody fell for it year after year.

Mr. Yawkey came back in the room and Ward said okay, he would sign, and his father said he'd be delighted to draw him pictures of baby shoes. Mr. Yawkey chuckled and called the others back in the room, and the fat men laughed in relief and milled about as everybody congratulated each other and shook hands.

Sure, he could have held out for more from some other team.

But in a sense there was no *other* team. It was the Boston Red Sox or nothing. That's how dumb he was in '52.

While still in his borrowed uniform they took a picture of Ward with his arm around Billy Goodman, one of the Red Sox stars who happened to be at the park that morning. Mr. Goodman seemed like a quiet pleasant man, though slightly cross-eyed. It made you wonder how he hit a baseball so consistently.

Naturally the men invited Ward and his father to stay for the game that afternoon and, both somewhat dazed, they watched the Red Sox put it to the Tigers from Mr. Yawkey's field box. Hoot Evers hit a three-run homer that afternoon, which was very nice. The next day Ward was on his way to the Carolina League, where he did very nicely and made the men happy to send a representative periodically to Carlisle to hand the old man an envelope containing several thousand dollars in cash.

They were still happy three years later, when Augie Jatras of Blake Cadillac–Olds drove over to Carlisle and delivered the beautiful yellow Coupe DeVille. Augie looked admiringly at Ward as he stepped out of the car which shone like a mirror.

"Lucky," he said. "You dog. When you drive into camp with this, I bet the ladies go crazy."

"I'm not taking it to Florida," said Ward. "I'm going to put it up on blocks."

His father and Augie looked at him.

"I'm going to save it," he explained.

And that's what he did. Even after he got home, after everything was all finished, booked up, and sold out forever, he just let it sit on the blocks. When he went to work at the Distelfink Peanut Butter Company his father dropped him off in the mornings and picked him up in the afternoons. In good weather he rode Gordie's ten-speed and chained it to a pipe in the hallway where the time clock was. Finally, after he'd been home maybe three years, he took the car off the blocks and started using it. Sparingly. With great caution. Now, twelve years later, it was still beautiful. It was all he had left. Everything else was crap. True, he owned some land in Maine, but the car—that was the only real thing left over from his former life.

These days, he led a neat and orderly existence. Some might find his daily routine a little dull. But it suited him just fine. For instance, he kept his shoes shined and lined up in his closet in two rows like soldiers. A matter simple as that gave him considerable satisfaction. The copies of *Sports Illustrated* were neatly stacked on the shelf of the night table by his bed. He washed his own underwear in the downstairs bathroom sink, even ironed his own socks. Daily, he did a series of exercises including a hundred push-ups and a hundred sit-ups, hooking his feet under the bed. He did his work at the peanut butter factory and was never tardy. He took a great interest in a tabletop baseball game which was his principal hobby, apart from taking good care of his car. Everything was just the way he liked it.

Once or twice a week he saw Terry Delaplane, a girlfriend of sorts, you might say. He'd go down to her apartment and roll her around the bed and the floor and feel better for it. In a manner of speaking, he regarded her rather like a chiropodist. Yes, that was it. For he had his standing appointment with her, just as one might have a regular appointment with a foot doctor. All in all he had to say, if Sarah had not been quite so crazy and if the old man's health had been okay, things taken in balance were about as good as could be expected, under the circumstances.

Tonight he had barreled out of the house in good, if not record time, but not before he had snatched up the *Times* and *The Sporting News* from the coffee table and a bottle of vodka from the liquor cabinet. No doubt when he unsheathed the bottle from the rolled up *Times* his father would be surprised and then delighted. In the privacy of the old man's room, they would throw a little party and keep the hospital at bay.

They had all the right things to do this—the newspapers and the booze. They would swap stories, quote news items to each other, and drink a little sauce. Possibly he would tell his father a story or two. Maybe the one about the time Wally Shaw, the strange old relief pitcher, found romance in the Texas League and what the woman in question gave him to remember her by, for all time. That was a good story, one that kept coming back to him lately for some reason, which troubled him. Why would a man, who had taken a pledge to ration carefully his memories of the past, keep remembering the pathetic life story of a washed up relief pitcher he'd known and more or less despised twelve years ago in Louisville? It was a puzzle.

His father liked his stories even though he wasn't a baseball man.

"I've come to believe," he said, "There's no such thing as a ballplayer who can't tell a fascinating story about the game."

And he seemed to be right. When it comes to the game every man has his own story.

Well, they would have a good time. They would tell the stories and read the sports news. Eventually the old man would attempt to get serious about the front page. Generally the time would pass smoothly. The conversation would be harmless, if not good medicine.

We won't think about dying, Ward thought. We'll just talk a little baseball.

If they were careful, nothing bad would come up and they could both forget their troubles for a time. Ward would help his father fill the long slow hours of evening with bullshit and shut out the questions, and, what with the talk of baseball, the vodka poured neat in the hospital tumblers, and quotations from the. newspapers, he would do what he could to add to the old man's education.

T H R E E

Hᴇʏ, ʙᴏʏ!" cried his father as he entered the room.

"Hello, Dad."

Ward smiled with his surgically invented mouth, which, when cold, tended to turn chalk-white.

"What have you been up to, son?"

"I've been thinking a little baseball."

"Good God! That's right. It's baseball season again. How do the Red Sox look?"

"Leonard Koppet in the *Times* here says they look bad. He picks them for last. But I think they'll do all right."

The old man's piercing blue eyes, stark in the pale face, looked active and alert. They had shaved his father today which made him look younger somehow. His hair, matted in the back, stuck up like a rooster's tail feathers. The hospital gown, not white but not gray either, looked uncomfortable, too loose and shapeless— too borrowed—to feel good.

"How's your mother?"

A tough question right off the top. She's crazy, Dad. Crazy. He sat down still holding the rolled up newspaper with the bottle of vodka hidden in it. His father watched him carefully, waiting for the answer.

"She's okay."

"She's okay, you say?"

"Well, you know. She's about the same. She stays in bed pretty much. She doesn't get up all day. She might wander around for a couple of hours at night. But mostly she stays in bed."

"What does Dr. Terrill say?"

"He hasn't been up to see her."

"Well, call him. Get him up there before she gets too bad."

"Sure. Okay. I was going to anyway—"

You poor chump, Ward thought. You've spent thousands on
psychiatrists and hospitals, and Sarah still plays her game. No-
body, nothing can talk her out of it. She's fixing you for marrying
her in the first place. You can't even let it go and die peacefully.
"Get him up there. Don't let it just ride. You know how she
gets."
"Right. I'll take care of it." If that's what you want, thought
Ward, that's what you get. It's your money.
"Your poor mother," his father said.
"Now you sound like Althy."
What a sucker, Ward thought. She's tattooed and buffaloed you
for years and now you can't even let it go to die, can you.
"Well, your grandmother," said his father. "Althy's done everything she could. She never really knew what went wrong or how
to deal with Sarah. But she never stopped trying."
Ward had to admit he was right there. Althy had never stopped
working on her little doll baby. Every feeb needs a nurse, he
guessed, somebody to take care of him or her. So, if you took a
mean slant on things, it might be argued Althy had a guaranteed
reason for living so long as her daughter Sarah couldn't get out of
bed without feeling dizzy. But of course the world would look in
and say, *My how that woman's suffered. She's tried so hard!* And for a
certain breed of New England woman that opinion was reward
enough. Was that unkind? Was that cynical? He supposed it was.
All he knew for sure was that Althy took jealous care of the old
Captain, her father, till he outfoxed her and sailed away; then she
nursed her sister, Dorcas, after she had her stroke. Poor Aunt
Dorcas, who lay speechless and paralyzed for three years on her
bed, just the pleading eyes still alive, as they followed her animated sister around the room.
   And today as in the past, Althy cared for her daughter, now in
her fifties, who apparently had always been slightly demented and
not totally a product of that day when she was caught on the barn
floor with her cousin Scott. From piecemeal stories of her early
childhood, Ward suspected Sarah's natural rhythm of violence
punctuated by periods of depression was caused by what you
might call bad wiring, not anything Scott Prothero had done. Was
that unkind? Was that cynical? He supposed it was. At any rate
he was sure of one thing. Althy would outlive them all. And the
world would say, *My, my. How that woman tried and tried.*

His father looked out the window and thought for a moment. "You should have seen your mother when she was young. She was beautiful."

The old man said it with relish. Plainly it was the subject of a lifetime of study. Ward said nothing. The old man was dying. He was remembering how he sold out to a crazy woman, and he was trying to feel good about it. Now what the hell could you say about that?

"Look what else I brought you."

Ward pulled the bottle of vodka out of the rolled-up newspaper with a magician's flourish.

"You're a man full of good ideas," his father grinned. "How about some of that right now? I haven't had a drink in ten days. The sight of that bottle suddenly gives me a spasm."

"I'll get the glasses. How much do you want?"

"No more than five fingers to begin with."

Ward got two squat glasses out of the bathroom and poured them half full.

"I wish we had some ice," Ward fretted. "This is like drinking stump juice."

"We don't need ice. I'll think about the frosty caucuses."

"What?"

"Shakespeare, son. Shakespeare."

"Okay, Dad. Shakespeare."

After he got his father freshly propped against his pillows, Ward pulled a chair close to the bed so he could rest his aching leg on it. They settled in with their drinks. The old man put on his Ben Franklin reading glasses; he had already papered his belly with the business section of the *Times,* underlaid with *The Sporting News.* Now he took the front section and folded it into threes like a paper boy, only inside out, and he had himself a nice, fat, solid wedge of print. Given such conditions there was very little need to say anything, which suited Ward just fine. Better to read the papers and drink and sit together in the nice, easy silence. Ward, his leg propped on the spare chair and somewhat less painful, felt quite satisfied to sit like this, thinking as little as possible.

The old man said, "A friend of yours came in to visit me the other day."

"Who is that?"

"Terry, is who."

"Terry Delaplane?"

"Yes, she works in Pediatrics she says, and when she heard I was in here she came up to introduce herself and see if there was anything she could do for me. She's a pretty little thing. Friendly as anything too."

"No shit."

"I didn't know you had a girl, son. Why don't you tell me these things?"

"Is that what she said?"

"That's right. She said she was your girl."

"That's a laugh. She's just somebody I see sometimes."

"Just somebody you see?"

"That's right."

"Well, she seemed like a nice person."

Yes, Ward thought. Tell me about it. You're a good judge of women.

It made him mad that she would try to pass herself off as his girl. How did she get that idea, anyway? Just because you saw someone more or less regularly, the way you might, say, see a chiropodist if you had a bothersome corn, did that automatically give her the right to go around telling people she was your girl?

"Hi, you must be Mr. Sullivan. I'm Ward's girl."

He could see her now, the perky stride of her short legs, bound by her starched white uniform. Terry efficiently squeaking around the room on the crepe soles of her nurses' shoes, her cap floating like a paper boat on top of her lacquered, blonde bouffant, patting the old man's pillows, smoothing his sheets and blanket. The picture was enough to make you puke.

In this little movie, Terry planted her white shoes apart and, with a cute frown on her forehead, studied his father's chart. White stockings, like the paint on a mime's face, emphasized her sharp anklebones, reminding him of a pony's fetlocks. The bouffant gave her a lollipop head, which she wagged from side to side as part of her cheery act. She smiled, displaying prominent white teeth, somewhat in the manner of a chipmunk with its cheeks packed full of nuts. He could see her clear as day and he knew just how she would act.

Sometimes he wondered if her baby blue eyes—comic book

blue—were really blue or just the sky showing through the back of her head. Who the hell was *she,* to walk in on the old man and claim she was Ward's girl, a sugar water description for her foot doctoring?

"You're not much on friends, are you," his father said.

"No, I guess not."

"Reach me that bottle and pour me a few more fingers. Thanks, boy. This stuff's better than the medicine they give me. Well, she is nice. She's the cheeriest thing in the place. She says she'll visit me tomorrow, too, and I'm looking forward to it."

"Good. That's nice of her."

"Don't like her, huh?"

"She's all right. I just don't want any big involvement. I like to keep it simple."

"Yes, you do like to keep it simple. No friends, no girls, no nothing much. Ever since you came home from baseball, you've been like that."

"Dad, don't get on my back."

"I'm not on your back. I'm just worried about you. You got to pick up your life and move on."

"I'm doing all right."

"Yes. You're doing all right. Trouble is you're too much like your mother."

"Bullshit. I'm nothing like her. Nothing at all."

"She lies there in her bed all day, waiting for history to rewrite itself. But it won't. It's done with."

"I'm not like that. I got my feet on the ground."

"Good. I'm glad to hear it. Because I thought you were grieving, boy."

"What do you mean?"

"I thought you were still grieving over the game and that girl, Bluette, and all those times in Louisville."

"I still think about it sometimes. But I can shut it off when I have to."

"That's fine. Because it's over with. And all the thinking in the world won't bring it back. I'm not trying to be cruel, boy. You know that, don't you?"

"I know that."

"You come from a line of people who did things. The old Captain was a hero at sea even though some might call him a fool in business. Uncle Tyler gave away the bank but he was a fine, gentle creature. He grew a beautiful garden every year. How the Captain loved those fresh greens. And he and the Captain could quote pages back and forth to each other from *Paradise Lost* and *King Lear* and you name it. They still talk about your grandfather's ballplaying days with Jack Coombs. When the Websters got there all Maine was trees and rocks and Indians and snow and ice and salt water. So they dug up the rocks and sold them. They built ships from the trees. They cut the ice out of the rivers and ponds and shipped it to the Indies and even India. They started Bowdoin College. Don't you think there's anything you can add to the record?"

"I don't know."

"You don't know. Let me tell you something. Those people didn't stop to ask themselves if they were happy. They just worked. And the work gave them contentment. Are you unhappy?"

"I'm okay. I get along fine."

"If you're unhappy, find some work to do. I know you think you lost your chance when you lost your baseball talent."

"I tell you, I'd rather not talk about it."

"I suppose not. But I got a couple of things to say. You can't lie here for ten days and not think of things to say. Give me a little more of that stuff. You better have some yourself."

"I'll do that."

"One thing I have to say is that everybody is responsible for his own happiness. Or, better, his own contentment. Now *that* is a bitter lesson to learn. You don't know how bitter, I'll bet. You can't rely on other people."

"I know that, for sure."

"That's not the end of it, boy. Lots of people lay their disappointments or even their self-hatred at the feet of some unlucky devil. They're like children who expect their father to fix a broken toy. 'Fix it,' they say, meaning: 'fix me.' Hell, it's impossible. Ask me, I ought to know."

"I guess that's right."

"Yes, that's right. That's damn right. All you can expect from people is pleasure. Not salvation. You take pleasure in them the way you might take pleasure in identifying the markings of an exotic brand of waterfowl. You don't expect the bird to *make* you happy, do you? You don't say, 'Bird, make me happy, damn it. You owe me that.' You either are or are not happy or, better, content, watching the bird. If you enjoy it, you enjoy it for what it is. The bird can do nothing for you, except be itself."

"I have never expected much from the birds I've met."

"That's it. Make light of this. But I'm not finished yet. 'Are you happy?' I ask. But I'm not really interested in the answer. What I'm really interested in is seeing you find something to do. That's the real point. Besides, happiness is a recently invented idea. It may even be a decadent idea. Never has a great nation been so preoccupied with its happiness as this one. That's because people have nothing worthwhile to do. *Contentment* is a better word than *happiness*. It means you are in harmony with the rest of the world. Next to contentment, happiness is just a whore. Give me some more of that stuff."

As Ward canted the bottle to freshen the old man's drink, a nurse came into the room.

"Now just a minute!" she exclaimed in a Sunday school voice. "No alcoholic beverages are allowed in this hospital. Mr. Sullivan, I'm ashamed of you. I thought you were more responsible. You know you are on a very strict diet."

"A little snort will not hurt me, Miss Sims. If you lay in this bed for ten days straight you might feel differently about a drink."

"I'm sure I would not," replied Miss Sims. "There are few things worse for you than alcohol. I'll take that bottle, young man. I'm afraid I must report this to Dr. Terrill."

"Miss Sims, you have little imagination," said the old man.

"Young man, give me that bottle." Miss Sims wore glasses which gave off light like old-fashioned flash powder. No doubt she had just recorded a picture of Ward's soul on her retina. And not a very pretty picture at that.

"The hell you say. If you want a drink I'll pour you one. But you don't get the bottle."

"That's my son, Miss Sims. He's not going to give you anything unless I say so."

"Give me that bottle," insisted Miss Sims.

"Go to hell, Miss Sims."

"You can't act that way here. We have rules to follow. We have other patients to consider. This is no barroom. If I have to, I'll call the police. I won't stand for disorder."

"I'll tell you, Miss Sims," said the old man. "You tell Rogers Hollister about this. I've put a little money into this place from time to time. Now I want to throw my weight around. Besides, I'm dying. You know it, the boy knows it, and I know it. So why don't you get out and leave us to our business."

"I cannot condone—"

"I'm not asking for you to do anything. Just get out. I'm going to die in my own way, Miss Sims. And you aren't going to have any say in the matter."

"I will call the police if necessary."

"You do that. It'll keep you busy."

Miss Sims' starched white back retreated angrily.

It was quiet then. The room transfixed with a certain glitter, the night a glossy negative within the single window.

"What's wrong, boy?"

"Maybe we should have given her the bottle. You think she'll call the cops?"

"You're not worried about that. You're wondering how long I've known that I'm dying."

"Terrill's been talking to you. Who the hell told him to open his mouth—"

"Yes, he's been talking to me. A damn good thing too. Does he have to have your permission to tell me the truth? A couple of weeks ago he had me still thinking that this blurred vision and dizziness thing was just a side effect of the medicine. But finally I told him, I said, give it to me straight. Am I dying?' What could he say? He came clean."

"That damn quack."

"What are you upset for? He owes me the truth. How long would it take you to get around to telling me?"

"I think he ought to let the rest of us know what's going on."

"Well, I'll tell you what he said so you're up to date. He said it looks damned bad. It looks like I'm going to die."

"He can't be sure of anything. Sometimes the thing turns around, people get better."

"That's right. That's right. Sometimes it happens that way."

"Just don't you give up hope. You've been feeling pretty good except for this last episode haven't you?"

"Yes, I've been doing all right. And of course I won't give up. But you got to know what you're up against. It makes me kind of mad to think you didn't see that right away. I don't know how long Terrill would have kept me in the dark if I hadn't come right out and asked him I gave him a little hell about it. A man has a right to know and make his own decisions. How much do you know about the old Captain's death?"

"All I know is when he was very old he went out sailing one day and never came back."

"Yes, that's right. That's just the way he wanted it too. Althy doesn't talk much about that one, does she? But I was pretty close to the Captain at the end—I think he finally took me on as a grandson instead of a house guest. I was in the room when Doc Coffin told him the truth."

"What truth was that?"

"They were about the same age. Doc Coffin was somewhere in his nineties and your great-grandfather was ninety-six. He had some circulatory problems and took to his bed. Doc Coffin told him that funny odor he smelled was gangrene. He told him his leg would have to come off, otherwise he'd die. You know what the Captain did when Luther Coffin told him that?"

"No, what?"

"He laughed. He lay there and laughed at the doctor. He said, 'I'm sure you're right about that, Luther.' The question, he said, is not if, but how and when. He said he wanted to think about this subject. He said it was a subject worthy of an old man. Doctor Coffin told him he better think fast and when the doctor came back the next morning, the Captain said, 'I think I'd rather go for a sail.' I was in the room. I remember Coffin said, 'Does that mean you decline the invitation?'

" 'Yes,' said the Captain. 'I decline.'

"The doctor told him he was sealing his own warrant.

" 'Exactly,' said the Captain. 'Every man should enjoy a similar privilege.'

"And he thanked him for not making a professional scene about it. That's what he said. He said, 'Thank you, Luther, for not making a professional scene about this.'

"Doctor Coffin reached in his bag and put a bunch of pain pills on the nightstand and got up and left.

"That afternoon the Captain got dressed. He put on one of those stiff cardboard white shirts he favored and one of his six black suits. I helped him down the path to the place where the catboat was tied up.

" 'I just want to go out on the Kennebec again, Gordon,' he said. He said, 'Let me exercise the privilege of the dying. Help me do this last thing.'

"Which I did. And I watched him haul up that gaffrigged sail and the wind billow out the white sail and the little boat glide down the glassy gray river. I watched him till he went out of sight. And he never came back. I suppose I knew he wouldn't."

The old man looked at Ward a minute, saying nothing, and then he said, "I want you to promise me something, boy."

"What is it?"

"Never mind what is it. *Promise* me."

"Okay. I promise."

"Promise me you won't let anybody take my life away from me. When I say something, I want you to do it. If I'm flat on my back and I ask you to take me canoe paddling, you do it. Or anything else. Will you do it?"

"You know damn well I will."

"Good. It's my life and I want to be in charge of it. The doctors and the lawyers, they will be happy to take it over if I let them. But you do what I tell you, even if it doesn't make sense."

"I will."

"Good. I figured I could count on you. You know, I've been thinking about things. You can't lie here for ten days and not think about things. It's a real education, just to lie here day after day. You've been through it, you know what I mean. When you get into a tight spot like this, a great clarity comes into your mind, doesn't it? I lie here and I think about things—about your mother and me, our life together and her feeling that everything touched of Webster is for some reason unaccountably cursed. And I think of Scott, lost in the war and lost to his family before that and just plain lost. And I think of the Captain, all he tried to do, his heroism in the long boat and the forty-three days at sea and how he tried to hold all that was Webster and Maine together and how it all came unraveled in his fingers. I think he felt cursed too, finally. Maybe not. He was such a gentleman about life, it's hard to know for sure how he felt about it. And I think about you and your brother. I wonder if I've done everything I ought to have done and what there is left that I can do."

"Why don't we read the papers for a while instead of talking like this."

"Because I feel like *talking* like this."

"You haven't even reviewed for me the grave significance of this evening's headline."

"That's because I've got other things on my mind. I've written a will, sitting here these ten days. Here it is," he reached in the drawer of the steel nightstand with the baked-on white paint and handed Ward a few pieces of folded blue stationery. "Put that in your pocket. I didn't have any paper, but your friend—your casual acquaintance—she brought me some paper, when she learned I had some things I wanted to write down."

"That's nice of her."

"What you have in your pocket now on that blue ladies' paper is my last will and testament."

"Dad, what—"

"Just listen. I thought about this in the sitz baths and in the middle of those G.I. series. I wrote it out in my mind before I ever saw that blue paper. And I tell you what I want you to do. I want you to take this down to Sharfman's office. Have him and you witness it and put it in his safe. He can call me if he wants to verify it."

"Jesus. I thought you had a will."

"Yes, you would think so, wouldn't you? But I never did. The thing is, I never thought about dying."

"Dad—"

"No. Let me finish. Damn it, every time I try to tell you something you try to stop me. Until a year ago I felt wonderful. Hell, I never thought about being in my fifties at all. It wasn't as if I felt that I was going to go on forever. It was that I'd never given it any thought at all. I don't believe I'd been sick a day in maybe thirty years. Do you ever remember me sick?"

"No, I don't."

"Well, now I am. I'm going to die, boy."

"No. No, you're not. Is Terrill telling you that shit? You're going to fight, aren't you? Didn't you tell me you were going to fight this stuff?"

"All right. Yes. I'm going to fight this stuff. But I don't like this slow shit. I'd like an answer fast. This stuff gets on your nerves. So you listen to me. Don't give me any pep talk. I've been thinking about things and writing them down on that blue paper. I want you to know what's in that will."

"I don't want to know. I don't need to know."

"I don't care whether you want to or not. You look on that paper. You'll see I've made your brother trustee of the estate. That means he controls the works—the shoe factory, the newspaper, the stocks, bonds, and so forth. Now it all goes to your mother, but he manages it in her behalf. What do you think?"

"I think you're crazy."

"I thought you'd think that. If you read further you'll see I've left you $20,000. Not much, is it? But it's enough to get you out of that peanut butter factory. And out of the house. You don't belong here in Pennsylvania—none of us do, for that matter. But you especially. So you take that money and go somewhere else and make a fresh start. Go back to Maine, maybe. But you ought to go somewhere because hanging around here is killing you. I know you think you lost your chance when the ballplaying came to an end. But that was a long time ago. It's time to forget and move on."

"I don't think about it much. I already told you that."

"Yes, I know. But I see something different on your face. Don't let the bad luck work on your mind. You have to make something of your life. Do nothing, and it will sink you in the end."

"Nothing's going to sink me."

"Good. Good. I'm glad to hear you talk so silly. It means you still have a chance after all. You take this money I give you and run. You underrate your brother too."

"I do?"

"Yes. You think he's just an artist, a child. But *I* think he'll lap this up. He is really the businessman. Are you the businessman— my trustee? Hell, no. You are the ballplayer, my three-year-old reading baby. You are the damn *artist,* not Gordie, although he's the fellow who lives the life. You are the artist, but you don't have any apparent talent, except that lost one which involved hitting a ball. So I don't want to saddle you with this estate. You already

feel weighted down because you don't know what you're in business for. This damned estate would sink you. But it won't bother
Gordie."

"It's your goddamned money. I don't care what you do with it."

"Yes, you do. You think I've sold you short. But I haven't. I've
given you a break. But I know this: regardless of what you feel
you'll do what I say. So you take this down to Sharfman as I said,
and you swear to it and he swear to it and then have him put it
in his safe."

The old man was wiped out. The lines etched deep into his pasty
face and now his eyes went flat. His arms, sticking out of the
clumsy hospital gown, looked more naked than they should.

"Dr. Terrill says you can come home soon."

"Yes, he does. I'll be glad to be clear of this place. I'm tired of
all the probing and pinching. Look, get Terrill to take a look at
your mother. Don't let it go."

"I won't."

"We've kept her home for five years. I'd like to keep it that
way."

"Okay."

"She hasn't said anything about Carol, has she?"

"No. Carol's name has not come into it."

"Good."

Indeed Sarah had given no sign that that thirty-eight-year-old
mythical baby she carried in her womb, the one that everybody
else thought she lost on the stairs in 1929, was stirring these days.
She talked to this child and the child talked to her. Sometimes the
child forced Sarah's mouth open and talked for herself in a kind
of Baby Snooks' voice. When all this happened, it was time to call
the booby hatch.

Now it looked to Ward like he had two crazy people to deal
with. The old man babbled on in a tired monotone. The disease
had not only laid waste the flesh on his bones but it had enfeebled
his wit and left him gently mad. Under the bed lamp his skinny
yellow face with its taut shiny skin was tranquil as an idiot's. To
make Gordie executor of the estate was crazy. Everything would
go down the sink. Everything the old man spent his life for: the
baby shoe factory, the newspaper, the horses, the house and fifty

acres, the stocks and bonds of his blood and breath. Why doesn't
he see that? But of course he was crazy. It was too late for him to
see it. Terrill said the dizzy spells, the blurred sight, meant the stuff
was in his brain. He asked me to help him, Ward thought. So now
I will help because he needs it. When I get a chance to think it
through, I will know what he would want to do if he could do it
for himself.

One thing sure was that will on the ladies' blue writing paper
was never going to reach Sharfman's office. He was damn sure his
father wouldn't want that if he was healthy, no matter what this
disease-riddled shadow babbled from the bed. Ward felt a powerful urge to get away from this man he no longer knew or trusted.
It was a little like talking to Sarah's Baby Snooks character. He got
up and that damned fist of pain he got regularly grabbed him
under the breast bone so he had to hold on to the metal nightstand.
He sucked for air and then he said, "You want me to leave the
bottle?"

"Give me one more. Then you take it. Here, stick it in this paper
bag so you look like a real drunk as you walk out."

Downstairs he found the kid sitting on a little plastic settee that
had as many angles as he did.

For a split second when the kid looked up—his glasses that
flashed like Nurse Sims', the smile on his thin face, the long blonde
curly hair slightly reddish in tint, the khakis, the tattersall shirt—
the whole program of innocence was more than Ward could stand.
This dink was the old man's choice to handle hundreds of thousands, this dreamy flamingo who cried at concerts and who had
to be restrained from kissing pictures in museums. This clown
with a mind like white paper which had never been smeared with
death's snot-scented blood—this was the man to run things? Bull
shit.

"What are you doing here, kid? I thought you were going to take
your old lady shopping."

"How is he tonight?"

"He's bad. He's not making any sense. He's just kind of babbling up there. Don't go up there, it'll make you sick. How long
you been here, anyway?"

"I just got here. Besides, I couldn't go up and see him anyway.
I can't handle it, man. He looks so bad. The damn smell in here

gets me, too. Why do they always keep these places so hot? You say he's pretty bad?"

"Yes, he's pretty bad."

"What'd you talk about?"

"Nothing much. I brought him the papers. We had a couple of drinks."

"A couple of drinks? Is that what you have in the paper bag?"

"Yes. I got a bottle of vodka in here."

"Why don't you come over to the house for a few minutes and share your bottle. I know Avis would appreciate the company. She gets bored as hell if nobody stops by in the evenings."

"I ought to get back."

"Come on. It's on your way. Just for one drink."

"Okay."

They separated outside the door as Gordie had parked on the street and Ward in the parking lot. Ward practically staggered to the car. His chest hurt like hell and his leg was kicking up again. The long, low, elegant car shone like a ghostly topaz under the carbon arc lights in the parking lot. It was pure relief to put the crown-headed key in the car door and fall back onto the black leather seats. He sat there in a fine cold sweat, the blood beating in his head like coffee in a percolator. His hands squeezed and slacked on the steering wheel in rhythm to his pulse beat. God-damn. *Goddamn.*

The old man had cut him out. What was this shit? It was bad enough to lose everything that counted because of a bunch of dirty tricks. Now he was even going to be cheated out of the booby prize. Ward didn't want anything for himself, just a quiet life with a regular routine of exercise and television. He would continue to wash his underwear and socks in the sink, a habit from baseball days. He didn't want anything fancy. He would take care of the car and play the baseball game. Nothing much would change. If the old man had to die, Ward would take care of things—keep Sarah in ice cream, see that the horses were fed and watered and wormed, and that everything stayed the way the old man would have wanted it.

But he was damned if he would be cheated out of this as he had been of everything else. If he let this ladies' paper be the fuse, everything would blow, sending horses, factories, stocks and bonds, newspapers, even what was left of Dunnocks Head, sky-high. The old man's life would hemorrhage away in nickels and dollars unless Ward put a compress on it to stop the terrible invisible bleeding. At least he could see that the stocks and bonds remained intact. The coral under his skull glowed with electric schemes, none of which made any sense. He had to get off by himself to figure this out.

The thickly padded car was so soundproof it created an island of dead air which calmed him down. After a while he turned the key. The Cadillac responded with a muted but powerful growl.

He put on the lights, illuminating the tightly wound buds on the trees, green as brussel sprouts. Maybe some music would smooth him out. He turned the knob and pressed the Wonderbar, the radio dial searching for the closest, clearest reception.

Mahalia Jackson was belting out a spiritual:

> He's got the 'hole worl' in his han's.
> He's got the 'hole wide worl' in his han's.
> He's got you and me, brothah in his han's.
> He's got you and me, sistah, in his han's.
> He's got the liddle biddy babies in his han's.
> He's got the liddle biddy babies in his han's.
> He's got the 'hole wide worl'—

Ward snapped off the radio.

Slowly he drove the few blocks to Gordie's house on the alley off Fourth Street, taking extra time. Be cool, he thought. Get a grip on yourself.

He hated to leave the beautiful yellow car just sitting at the curb in this neighborhood, but what could he do? He could have one drink and leave fast, that's what he could do. He took the bottle out of the paper bag. After locking the car and checking up and down the dark street for possible car thieves and vandals, he walked up the white stone steps and rapped on the door of the narrow brick row house Gordie had bought and fixed up for peanuts.

Put on your clown face, he thought. Be a funny fellow.

Avis answered the door, the broad continent of her forehead disheveled with black woolly hair, her pug nose ugly with boredom. Since it was mild for an April night, she was in her summer gear of faded cut-off jeans with some patches and provocative holes and an old oxford cloth white shirt which she wore outside her cut-offs. Beneath this shirt her breasts moved freely as she shaded her eyes to see him against the street light.

"Hey, Ward! What do you say, Gimp? Come in."

He stood on his good leg, grinning back at her.

"Gee, there for a minute I didn't recognize you with your clothes on."

"Very funny. I stand around bare-ass in the name of art. What do you do—shell peanuts for a living? Come in, you jerk."

She led him into the living room. He sat down on the beige couch over which hung a four by six air brush painting of Avis' ass.

"Frankly, you look better with them on."

"Right. Thanks. Another compliment." She laughed shortly. "I stand around bored to death, catching pneumonia so your brother can play at being an artist, and a washed-up ballplayer who shells peanuts for a living makes with the yuk-yuks."

The place was a mess. Plants, books, and magazines everywhere. An ironing board and an easel stood with equal authority at one end of the room.

Gordie shambled in from the kitchen.

"Here he is! Hello, hello! Give me that bottle. I fear I am dying, Waldo. Bring on the dessert. Let's have a drink, what do you say? I'll get some glasses."

"Here you go, kid," Ward handed Gordie the bottle.

"Your lips are blue, girl. He have you working again today?"

"Of course he did! Your brother is so damn slow it's pathetic. Degas was fast as a whiz. Isn't that what they say? He was full of ten-second studies. Your brother thinks I ought to be able to hold a pose on one foot for an hour. He is so slow it's pathetic. Genius is quick, that's my idea. Degas was fast, lightning fast. That's a sign of genius. Your brother labors at the thing. He doesn't paint pictures, he pumps out cesspools, hangs wallpaper, cleans furnaces —all that slow dull shit. What makes you think you're a painter, anyway?" There was a kind of sullen anger in the question. Gordie grinned at her happy as a dog that's just been tossed a stick.

"Hell," he said. "I'm a painter. Look at these paintings! Would you like to see my clippings? I'll be happy—"

"No! No!"

"I'll be happy to present you with a complete, wonderful set of my artistic triumphs from Pittsburgh to Philadelphia, Maine, even New York occasionally. You suffer for a good cause, lady. You have to remember: not all artists are quick, not all famous by thirty and dead by thirty-five. How do you want your vodka, Bro?"

"Put it on the rocks, kid. You have any olives?"

"Do we have any olives?"

"In the fridge."

"Pop a few olives in there, kid."

"Okay. What do you want, Avis?"

"Oh boy. A party. Give me a beer, Sweetie."

Gordie disappeared into the kitchen.

Avis looked him up and down as he slumped on the couch, his bad leg propped on the coffee table between the stack of *The New York Review of Books* and the cactus plant in the gray pottery crock. She sat down next to him.

"Where'd Gordie run into you?"

"Over at the hospital."

"He actually went to see his father?"

"No. I found him in the lobby on my way out."

"You mean he was just sitting there? He didn't even go up to see him?"

"No. Hospitals always make him sick."

She sprang to her feet and began to walk around the room.

He watched her walk up and down. She was pigeon-chested and swaybacked. Her breasts, which fell away from the high ground of her breastbone, were heavy and soft-looking and big-nippled. As she walked he watched the piston action of her ass, which was high and narrow. Her hips thrust forward at a sharp angle causing her belly to stick out in a mellow curve. Altogether she had a Negro build, reminding him of those bare-breasted women who used to darken the dusty old copies of the *National Geographic* he pored over in the study in Dunnocks Head when he was a kid. In fact, in build she was the female counterpart of the fellow who played shortstop for Louisville in '55, Lamont Baltimore. Old Lamont was pigeon-breasted, and pigeon-toed too, all legs and arms just like Avis.

"I don't understand your brother," she said. "I ask him to think about his father—his father must feel terrible that Gordie hardly ever comes to see him. What does he say?"

"Nothing. He never talks about it."

"He doesn't? You sure? I'd sure as hell talk about it."

"No. You don't understand. The old man is never bitter. He expects people to fall down on the job. He's had thirty-four years of Sarah. He doesn't expect anything. Everything to him is a real education. He is the birdwatcher, and we're the birds. In that way he is almost a saint. The kid gets sick in hospitals. It doesn't make him mad that the kid stays away. Those are just facts to him."

"Well, he is a saint. It's a damn shame—"

"Yes, it is."

"What do you suppose will happen to your mother?"

"I don't know."

"I guess she'll have to go into a home."

"Why is that?"

"Well, who's going to take care of her? Gordie sure as hell won't, I think you know. He's got his art to think of. That's his excuse for any act of selfishness. And you—I guess you've got your own peanuts to shell, haven't you?"

"I'm sure we'll work out something."

She sat down on the couch again. He could see the faint dark circles of her nipples against the white shirt.

"Do you think your father will leave all his money to your mother?"

"That's his business."

"Okay, I'm sorry. I apologize. I'm getting into things that are none of my concern. But somebody's going to have to manage things—"

"He'll know what to do, don't you think? Besides worrying about the old man's money, what have you been up to?"

"Aren't you unpleasant. Well, not much. The usual. If you knew how *bored* I was all the time."

"That's too bad."

"Yes it is. I'd like some fun sometimes. You still see Terry?"

"I see her once in a while."

"You do? I'm surprised. No, I'm not either, come to think of it. You'd go for the blonde lightweight type."

"I thought she was a friend of yours."

"She is, but she's still a lightweight. God, am I *bored.* Gordie never wants to do anything except paint. I'm just a piece of furniture to him. I said, if you're so great what are you doing in Harrisburg, Pennsylvania? Why don't we move to New York where I could at least have a little *fun* once in a while."

"Where the hell did the kid get to?"

"I don't know, he's probably washing out the glasses. If he's not painting, he's reading, or walking along the river. Do you have any idea how boring that is for me?"

"It sounds like you're bored."

"Very funny. Terry says you're a good lay."

"Terry says that?"

"Well, no. I would just figure. You're the family athlete. Aren't you athletic?"

Gordie burst into the room, carrying a tray of glasses, a bowl of ice, the bottle of vodka, a can of beer, a glass dish full of peanuts.

"Okay! Here we are. Drinks for everyone. Jesus, Avis, what a shambles the kitchen is. What do you do all day?"

"Nothing. I don't do anything. And I'm getting sick of it."

"Hey, don't get excited. I'm sorry. What'd you do to her to get her going?"

"Don't put me in the middle, kid."

"That's right, this peanut vendor didn't do a thing. I just told him what a bore it is to stand around bare-ass all day. I told him you were a bore. I told him I'd like to have some fun. Then I asked him if he'd like to take me to bed."

"Don't get so upset. Everything's cool, lady. Take it easy."

"Piss on you—*kid.* Everything's cool, huh." As he stood there with his mouth open she took the can of beer off the tray. "Thanks for the beer," she said. "I think I'll watch the news."

And she walked out, that Hottentot ass of hers boxing with her shirttail.

"What the hell got into her?"

"Don't ask me, kid. That's your problem."

"God. I don't understand it. I do everything I can for her."

"It doesn't matter. They get mad no matter what you do. You might as well do what you want."

"That's tough talk, pal. Just what I'd expect from a jock. But sometimes you have to think of the other person. If she's unhappy it's because I've failed her in some way."

"There's a fine crock."

"No, it's true."

"That's right, I can't tell you anything. I mean you're a college kid. You read about it in a book somewhere. But if you were open to a little down home advice, I'd say don't be such a candy-ass."

"A candy-ass?"

"Yes, that's right. A candy-ass. You're always worrying about how you failed her. She doesn't think like that. A friend of mine, an old guy down in Louisville—he was a relief pitcher, and he'd had a few rough dealings with women—he once told me that when a woman looks at you she's looking in her mirror. She wants to see herself in your face, played back and looking good. Now what do you give Avis?"

"What?"

"What you give her is nothing. She looks at you, and your eyes are all glazed over. You're thinking about *Paradise Lost* or something."

"*Paradise Lost!* Hey, pretty fancy ballplayer."

"That's all right. I pick all that stuff up by osmosis. She just told me you treat her like furniture."

"I treat her like a human being and an equal. All this stuff about mirrors, that's the most chauvinistic description of women I ever heard. Where'd you get these ideas?"

"Forget it, kid. You know what you're doing."

"I'm honest with her. I treat her with respect."

"That's good, kid. Hand me a drink."

"Okay. Fine. Enough of this frivolous stuff. Let's get down to some serious drinking."

Ward took a gulp of his drink. It was cold and clear going down and burned pleasantly in his throat afterwards.

"Here's to us," Gordie said. "Here's to art and baseball—one and the same thing."

"Good. Here's to us."

"You know? You're my brother. I love you. What gets into you? Like tonight I thought you were ready to hit Mother."

"I guess I was."

"Well, what gets into you? Nobody can act like that. You can't treat people that way. I know Mother gets on your nerves. She gets on everybody's nerves. But she's sick. You have to take that into consideration."

"I don't have to take anything into consideration. I don't have to think about any of it."

"When Dad dies we'll have to take care of her. We'll have to do something about her. We have to think about it."

"Fine. We'll think of something."

"Has Dad said anything?"

"About what?"

"Well—about his plans. What he wants us to do. About everything."

"Hey, listen. He isn't dead yet. He might just surprise everyone. Don't count him out yet."

"I'm not counting him out."

"Good. I've got to go, kid."

"Stay a little longer. Have another drink. Let's talk some more. Remember when we were kids in Dunnocks Head—that old ship on the ways? I sometimes dream of that old ship in the moonlight and the Captain and the old house itself. You were the hero in those days."

"I wasn't a hero. I was just a kid."

"You were a hero."

"The Captain was the only hero I ever knew."

"Yes, he was a real hero. Where you going?"

"I told you, I have to get home. Besides you better tend to Avis."

"Stick around. Have another drink. Let's talk a little bit."

"See you, kid." He set the glass down on the coffee table and started for the door.

The kid ran after him, laughing.

"Hey, when you say you're going you mean it."

"That's right, I mean it," Ward grinned crookedly from the doorway.

Standing there skinny as a stork, his glasses flashing as he smiled back, the kid looked like a real dink.

When Ward got home he went right down to his room. He was tired as hell and he sure didn't want to run into Sarah or Althy. He folded the paper bag with the old man's will in it neatly and stuck it in the nightstand till he could think what to do next.

In the downstairs sitting room, the telephone rang. Then pretty soon he heard Althy shuffling outside, clawing at his door. "Ward!" she cawed in that horrible old lady voice.

"What now?"

"That girl's on the phone. She says she has to talk to you."

"Tell her to go to hell."

"You tell your own girls to go to hell. I'm not doing it for you."

"Tell her I'm tired. I'll call her in the morning."

"Why don't you tell her yourself."

"You just tell her. Help me out, Althy."

"Humph. Help *you* out."

Then she went away and he crashed back onto the bed and fell asleep like a man falling through a trap door. He didn't even have time to hang up his khakis.

Blue shuddered and shook out her glossy blue-black hair. She rode above him in a slow rockinghorse motion, her shoulders hunched against the pleasure. Her eyes were closed, her head thrown back, showing the pretty curve of her throat. Below the tanned shoulders her full breasts were cream-white triangles, beautiful as sculpture. She rode slowly, smiling, the whites of her eyes showing in new moons behind her almost closed eyelids. She seemed to be listening in rapture to a pleasing voice that only she could hear. *No,* he thought even as he sank. *I won't remember this. I don't want to remember this.*

He struggled against the troubling image, and it dissolved. In its place stood Shaw, with his arms bent like chicken wings and his question-mark posture, squinting against the sun which added ten thousand new lines to his already hundred-year-old beaten and pathetic face. *Yes,* thought Ward. *I'll remember Shaw.*

So he dreamed. Not original dreams like other people had, but selected short subjects from the memories of his former life. So far as he was able, he picked the material for these dreams. He could not always do this but it seemed like a good plan to try. A man's a damn fool just to let go and do the first thing that comes into his head and that goes for his dreams too. That was his idea, anyway. He'd

learned that the hard way, a long time ago, and the lesson had even
reached into his nightmares.

FOUR

As a nineteen-year-old kid with what he claimed was a blazing fastball, Shaw got called up to the Detroit Tigers for a look-see in 1936. He wasn't up there for more than a cup of coffee. He pitched a total of two and a third innings, collected a major league lifetime ERA of 34.74, and sank back into the obscurity of the bush leagues where he was still drifting around twenty years later when Ward ran into him on the Louisville club.

On the road they roomed together, mainly because nobody else could stand to be around such a pathetic hangdog figure and because Ward didn't really give a damn who was in the room with him, since he wasn't thinking about anything in those days except seeing that baseball and whaling hell out of it. He took no more note of Shaw than he would of a cockroach.

In the summer of 1955, Ward and the strange old relief pitcher roomed together and traveled the hot humid circuit of cheap hotel rooms in southern country towns. Sometimes at night when they were in the room doing the mild domestic things that ballplayers do on the road—Ward maybe writing Blue a postcard, since she always liked him to send a postcard a day when he was on the road, and Shaw maybe darning a patch on the oldest damn pair of socks Ward had ever seen—Shaw would attempt to tell Ward what he had discovered about life, God, and women. This damn fool, this big-nosed, bald-headed relief pitcher with the deep-carved cheekbones and Mongolian slits for eyes thought he had some lessons worth passing on. But, hell, he was just a loser and had been all his life. He walked around under a little pet black cloud all the time. It made the other fellows nervous just to have him around. But he didn't bother Ward any. "Let the old fart rant," he thought. Possibly Shaw might turn out to be funny or at least ridiculous, useful as an object of contempt similar to his little four-eyed brother at home who read all the books and painted all the pictures and generally lived up to the old man's expectations.

He didn't listen to Shaw, at least not at first. He just watched him expectantly, waiting for him to look foolish so he could report it to Wayne McLain, the witty big leftfielder, or the other fellows in the locker room, and together they could weave the latest ridiculous description into the comic yet cautionary tale that had dogged Shaw all through his baseball career.

In 1955 nothing was worth listening to anyway. Ward already had the answers. Back in Louisville he had this twenty-eight-year-old beautiful woman who was crazy about him, who made love to him three or four times a night all over her nice apartment where she insisted he hang his glove when he was in town. It was June, and he was hitting .410 in Triple-A ball.

He was the hottest prospect in the Red Sox chain since Ted Williams, and he wouldn't even be twenty-one till September. They took a long look at him in the spring. Williams told the press he was a natural hitter, the best young hitter he'd seen. He even put his arm around Ward and grinned at the cameras with him. They told him to go out and learn to play first base.

"You'll be back," they told him. "You'll be back to stay."

He knew that spring he was already the second-best hitter on the Red Sox. They wanted him to go out and learn first base. It made him damn mad, but he'd do it. He'd show them.

There wasn't anything more he needed to know. He and Shaw had nothing in common. Shaw had blown his chance. Maybe he had had a little talent once, but it took a damn sight more than talent. You had to know you were born for the game—that nothing, no one could stop you.

Ward knew he was one of the elect. He'd been brought up among them. Granpa and Mr. Coombs had duly prepared and catechized him over the long golden summers of his childhood. He was like a freight train on the tracks, and there was no stopping him.

But after a while, rooming with Shaw on the road got to him, made him a little jittery and edgy at times. The damn guy was creepy.

He'd sit on the bed thinking about something. His face would begin to glow, become a mask of undefinable danger. Ward, without looking up from the sports page, could feel old Shaw building up like a thundercloud.

"Did I ever tell you about the time down in the Texas League when I thought they's going to vote me on the all-star team?" Shaw would begin, and Ward would know how it was going to turn out, with some travesty of expectation transformed into miserable failure.

Ward would slap the sports pages to the floor and shout, "Shut up, you son of a bitch! Just shut up!"

Old Shaw would meekly resume his darning or his reading and that would be the end of it for a while.

Shaw's whole story was nothing but misery and gloom. He had come home after school one day when he was eight and found his mother, who was nothing but skin and bone anyway, sitting at the kitchen table with a colander of snap beans in her lap, and she was just plain outright dead sitting there in her chair, still holding the beans in her now cold and tideless lap. She was just sitting there, casually dead, having died from boredom apparently in the process of snapping beans, and be damned if they didn't have those beans along with some ham hocks for dinner that same night.

His drunken father, who mowed lawns and set up pins in the local bowling alley for a living—he was the only forty-three-year-old pinboy they had in that town, maybe the only one in Arkansas —undertook haphazardly to keep the family together, which consisted of a thirteen-year-old girl who had to lock herself in her room at night when her father came home drunk, lest he do something unnatural, and four brothers, including an idiot whom it fell to Shaw to take care of.

One day Shaw's father was scything out back of an old overgrown farm house when the earth gave way, plummeting him into the cesspool where he drowned without further notice. Wally Shaw had to quit school at twelve and go to work in a bakery. That's what he did at night. During the day he took care of his idiot brother. His brother was one of those rubbery rigid defectives with clammy little white claws for hands. He had fuzzy short red hair that didn't seem to grow. Shaw wheeled him everywhere in a baby stroller, dressed in just an old plaid shirt and diapers. The kid was fourteen but not much bigger than a three-year-old. He

wheeled him out to the town ballyard when he played ball. The
kid just sat there and flapped around a little bit, making faint
noises in his spit. He had a dead-white complexion, so Shaw
always parked him in the shade of a nearby tree so he wouldn't
crisp up in the sunlight. The kid's name was Johnny but the kids
called him "the Dribbler." Shaw fed and tied the Dribbler in his
crib at night before going to work at the bakery.

So there he was, one of a brood of four melancholy orphans plus
one citizen of the world, spending his nighttime on the job at the
bakery instead of experiencing the deep untroubled slumber of
more fortunate children. He spent his days in spoon feeding the
Dribbler, wheeling him around town in his stroller, shackled to
him by the sudden recognition of kinship in the eyes of passersby
who mentally calculated the point spread in their I.Q.s. When
Shaw was sixteen, the Dribbler caught pneumonia and died. At
least that's what Shaw thought he died of. They never did call a
doctor. His sister said they couldn't afford one, so they just kept
him covered up and tied in his crib. The kid grew raspier and more
bubbly, till he was blowing bubbles out of his nostrils with each
labored breath. Two blue bruises began to spread in a malevolent
tide under the black rubber buttons of his eyes. Shaw watched the
spread of these blue patches with dread. The black rubber eyes
grew more blank, and the expression on the wax-white face was
one of astonishment, if it could be said to approximate anything
human. The only sound in the room was the child's hoarse phleg-
matic breathing, the only sight, the rapid pulsation of its abdomen
as it struggled for breath.

Then one morning he was dead. Shaw shook the little rubbery
body, swore over it, and cried, hugging it like a doll to his chest,
and swaying on the floor in real grief. He thought he hated the
Dribbler. Now clutching the cold, lifeless body, he discovered he
loved the poor bastard.

The sun poured through the naked window in a solid yellow
shaft, and Shaw sat on the floor hugging his parcel, surprised by
love and grief, fixed in amber for what seemed forever. Something
stirred in the battered and empty house. They were poor, dirt poor.
And maybe a three-legged chair in the kitchen had started for the
door, to escape, and fallen over. Anyway, after a time he rose up
and wrapped this eighteen-year-old child, still no bigger than a

three-year-old, in the dirty, sour-smelling patchwork quilt which their dead mother had made especially for the Dribbler and finding outside the house in the dirt yard a packing box and the right tool among the dreary trash his father had dragged home one time or another—the old rusting disemboweled automobiles, worthless wringer washers, and doorless refrigerators—he carried the kid, tool, and box through the wild overgrown orchard of barren apple trees into the rocky upland pasture, where it was clean and quiet, where you couldn't see the old Hudsons and Chevrolets, the backless chairs, the rust-eaten wash tubs, or the bleak house itself. And there he buried him, using the packing box as a coffin. Then he threw that rusty spade as far as he could, and set out for the railroad track, not taking a damn thing with him. He caught the four o'clock freight. He never did go back there again.

End of childhood. Beginning of twenty-three years of wandering the bush leagues. Except for that brief moment in 1936, when the Tigers brought him up. Naturally he blew it. In his one and only start, he gave up nine runs and thirteen hits in two and a third innings. Since then he'd been drifting around the minors with a black rain cloud stationed permanently over his head.

Shaw had nothing to be cheerful about: his mother dead in the kitchen over the snap beans, his father turning up as just another turd floating in the cesspool, the work at the bakery, the life and death of the Dribbler. Then to get to the majors where it took just two and a third innings for his pea-size talent to fail him, giving him maybe thirty minutes on the mountaintop in the fresh air.

At first Ward couldn't figure out why Shaw was so down on women. It seemed to make him real gloomy when Blue came into Ward's life.

One night, as they sat in a rented room on the road in one of those duplicate hot nights of that long ago summer, Shaw told him of his brief love affair with a West Texas sheriff's wife. Shaw sat there on the painted iron bed, rhythmically squeezing that little black rubber ball he carried to strengthen his pitching hand, staring off into the night as if hypnotized, and told the story in a halting, nasal monotone. The eyes looked at Ward sometimes but did not see him. He was somewhere else, lost in the misery of his own history. The big-knuckled, veiny hand worked the little ball hypnotically as Shaw unfolded his story.

This little morality tale was supposed to explain why he didn't like women but it didn't do the job. The real cause might have been genetic, because there are, after all, just some natural-born loners around, people who pack light and travel fast. Shaw was one of these, and so was Ward likely.

It was in 1937, the year the Yankees won 102 games and finished 13 ahead of Detroit. Detroit had only one pitcher with an ERA under 4.00. They could have used a good pitcher. They had the hitting sure enough. Hank Greenburg hit .337 with 40 home runs and an incredible 183 runs batted in. Charlie Gehringer won the batting title with .371. The damned *team* batted .292.

Meanwhile Shaw, twenty years old, was eating dust down in the Texas League. He was mighty discouraged. But he was nurturing his pea-sized talent and getting along, hoping Detroit might give him another break but afraid that Mickey Cocherane, the manager, had seen all he needed to in those two and a third innings in 1936.

That's when he fell into the arms of Noona Perault, a forty-year-old frizzy-haired redhead, the sheriff's wife in Amarillo. That was his first three mistakes, right there: getting mixed up with a married woman, a gun-toting sheriff's woman no less, and doing it right in the team's hometown.

It wasn't like he seduced her. She caught up with him in a bar one Saturday night, the same night that her sheriff-husband left town to take a prisoner down to Corpus Christi, a trip calculated to keep him out of Potter County for a week. She and the sheriff were childless and the sheriff not much interested in the means of producing offspring. His job was too taxing, she said. She was a hungry, empty woman and she latched on to the twenty-year-old Shaw desperately. She had a big banana nose, knobby shoulders, long slab-like arms and hands almost as big as Shaw's, but she was passionate and her homeliness had probably only heightened the intensity of her emotions. Ugliness can be a great aid to clarity of feeling since ugly people have plenty of time to think things out.

"She was half-crazy with loneliness," allowed Shaw. "Like most ugly women she wasn't quite right in the head when it come to men. And me, well, I was a real sick puppy. I guess she knew right away I was in no condition to care what a woman looked like. Before you could say Jack Robinson I was in big trouble."

Shaw said ol' Noona sneaked him into the sheriff's white clapboard house and held him a virtual love prisoner under the hot iron rusty roof of that miserable place. She followed him to all the games—the Amarillo team was conducting a long homestand that week—so she could keep a ravenous eye on him.

The fellows on the team noticed this and began to rib him. They all offered to chip in and send for his mother if that was what he really needed, not knowing Shaw's mother had been dead forever, that Shaw himself suspected sometimes that he'd never had a mother at all and had just hatched out under a rock somehow.

Shaw's salvation and release from virtual imprisonment came when the sheriff was due to return to town, so she had to let him go reluctantly, but Noona would sneak out of the house and call him on the hall phone at the boardinghouse where the team stayed and implore him to meet her out in the mesquite somewhere.

Shaw was in a panic, afraid of the sheriff, and besides he'd taken all the ribbing he could stand from his teammates. He may have even been unkind when he told her to blow it out her ears.

They were on the road right after that, and Shaw was breathing easier. It was a great relief to get shut of that passionate big-nosed woman. By the time they got back to Amarillo, he thought he was in the clear. But the night he took his turn on the mound, she was there, right down front on the first base side, fixing him with a glittering wild-eyed stare. It made him nervous as anything. The trouble was he had to take his warm-ups practically right next to where she was sitting. He couldn't keep the ball anywhere near the strike zone, she made him so jittery with that glittery, crazy stare.

No sooner had the umpire cried "Play ball!" than old Noona had jumped out onto the field to play her particular version of the game. As she crossed the first base line the entire park was stunned into silence. Shaw, on the mound, with ball in hand, turned into the vortex of that threatening silence, to see what was going on. And saw Noona advancing on him with her husband's six-gun in hand.

"No, no, Noona!" he cried in a high squeaky voice. Shaw was one of those people, even on the point of being murdered, who was doomed to look ridiculous. "No, no, Noona!" would soon become a legendary cry of the Texas League shower rooms. It would persist long after its origin was forgotten.

Shaw turned his back on Noona and collapsed to his knees. His legs simply gave out from fear. He clutched his head with glove and meat hand, sagging in that abject posture, and there he waited publicly on the pitcher's mound for Noona to plug him, for a piece of skull bone to fly away, for rivers of blood to spout from his young back. Shaw told Ward that turning his back on her like that had been the final mistake.

"A woman in love uses you for her mirror," explained Shaw one evening while darning a sock in one of the rented rooms. "She looks in your face to see herself there—hopefully reflected back beautiful. Turn your back on her and it's like she don't exist. Where the hell is she, she asks herself, if she can't see your face. They go crazy, even get violent. Only I didn't know that then."

No, he didn't. He turned his back on her and fell down on the mound. Slumping there passively, making disgusting little whimpering noises before teammates and crowd alike—it was an open invitation to violence. It was also a gesture of rejection. All she could see was a back. Not only couldn't she see herself in that back, she couldn't even take it for a person. A back was just a thing, not a person, just something to blaze away at. Using her husband's gun coolly, if inexpertly—Shaw wanted him to note how she'd picked out her husband's own gun as the weapon for vengeance—Noona plugged him three times before the first baseman and the umpire tackled her and threw her out of the game, as it were.

Doubtless she would have emptied all six chambers into him otherwise. Shaw pointed out that if you read the stories in the papers you would see that men in anger might shoot someone, but usually not more than once, while women always seemed to keep shooting till they ran out of bullets or time.

She shot away the top of his right kidney, hit him in the fleshy part of his waist and shattered the collarbone on his pitching side.

"It never mended right," he said. "My motion was always stiff after that. I still had a chance to get back upstairs before that."

But even more than the physical damage was the emotional effect.

"When somebody shoots holes in you," Shaw said, "it just knocks the vinegar and piss right out of you. I never did feel the same again. Never could really stand up to things. It took the fight out of me."

While he was playing for Louisville, Ward happened to run into a fellow by the name of Gee Walker who hit .353 and played left field for Detroit the year that Shaw pitched his two and a third innings. Gee remembered Shaw. Maybe not a famous name, but Gee Walker was some fine ballplayer and hitter. Mr. Coombs had mentioned him sometimes on the porch at Dunnocks Head in the summers years ago, and Mr. Coombs was an authority on talent, having discovered, among others, Dick Groat, the great shortstop for Pittsburgh and St. Louis. So Gee Walker was certified by proxy as a judge of talent too, and when Ward pressed him, Walker politely confessed that Wally Shaw was, in his memory, a no-talent who had been promoted only because Detroit was desperate for pitching that year. "He had no velocity on his fastball as I remember," Gee said. "But more than that, he didn't seem to have a grip on himself. He looked like a loser right from the start."

Shaw thought he was talented and full of fight before that woman shot him full of holes but the evidence suggested that he'd been beaten long ago and just never admitted it till the sheriff's wife took a gun to him.

Second chances rarely come to anyone. Either you're up for the thing when it happens or you're not. If you're not, one of the ways you go on living is to delude yourself periodically into believing that life is now offering you a second chance *on the same terms* as the old-time deal you managed to blow. This way you get second, even third, and fourth chances, without disturbing anyone. And you go on living.

No doubt Shaw thought he was working on a second chance down in the Texas League till Noona Perault came along and blasted him off the pitcher's mound. As a result of that episode, which knocked all the vinegar and piss out of him by his own admission, he missed an entire season of baseball. He was laid up into winter with his injuries. One of the wounds turned septic, and he almost died.

But eventually he got well enough to travel and, having no place to go, he decided to stay down south where it was warm with the idea that the good weather would help him heal faster. Naturally the Tigers gave him his unconditional release.

He went down to Fort Worth and got a job in a tractor factory.

The next summer he was playing ball in a fast industrial league and the next winter he went down into Mexico and played winter ball in Juarez. The next spring the Red Sox invited him to camp and at the end of it signed him to a contract for Class A ball.

It seemed like he'd worked himself back into the picture. Not exactly in the picture, but to the edge of it. He was laboring in the vineyards once more and that at least made him feel alive again, not free-floating and invisible, the way he'd felt ever since Noona had thrown him out of the ballgame. And he kept on laboring, without distinction, seeing signs of progress where no one else could, eating alone in the notion that loneliness purified his dedication, thinking about pitching, analyzing the hitters, taking extra running, his sheer pathetic earnestness depressing the hell out of the manager and the coaches. They saw all that serious plodding ineptitude as completely futile, and it probably frightened them as well as the players, because they had to wonder whether they too were victims of the same self-delusion. Am I kidding myself? Am I really made for this game? Am I going anywhere? Or is this something I just fell into because it was fun and at first it was easy to do. Did I take the line of least trouble, and now am I caught up in a joke? Shaw was an unsettling man to have around.

He pitched all through the war. The war didn't touch him. Noona had at least exempted him from that ordeal. He was free to concentrate on the game, while the young and unmaimed suited up for catastrophe. The war at its height was a field day for the halt, the maimed, and the ancient. Pete Gray, a one-armed outfielder, made it to the St. Louis Browns. Rip Sewell, thirty-five years old, won twenty-one games for the Pittsburgh Pirates.

Periodically hope welled in Shaw like a case of heartburn, but nothing came of it. He found himself flinging away, without distinction, registering 8-8 seasons in Double-A ball.

About 1946 he developed a trick pitch he called a Vaseline ball, which acted like a knuckler. It took a little daub of grease on the seams to activate this pitch, and what he did just before game time was pack his big nostrils with Vaseline. Whenever he was in big trouble, he'd go to his nose and throw the old Vaseline ball. In this way he won six straight ball games which made everybody sit up and take notice, including the umpires.

One day in the middle of the third inning an umpire named

Katcovich called time out with a three-two count on the batter and
started out toward the mound. Shaw wiped the ball on his pants.

"What are you doing out here, Shaw?" asked Katcovich suspiciously.

"Nothing," said Wally. "Why?"

"How come you all of a sudden developed some talent?
Where'd you get that breaking pitch you been throwing today?"

"You like it?" Shaw said ingenuously. "I worked on it last
winter down in Mexico."

"How come you pick your nose so much? Didn't your mother
teach you any manners?"

"I dont' pick my nose much," said Shaw.

Katcovich was a short umpire and at this point a funny expression came over his blunt-featured dull face.

"What's that *stuff* on your nose?" asked Katcovich.

"Snot," said Shaw, hanging his head and moodily asking himself why Katcovich had to be so short, for when he talked to most
pitchers he had no choice but to look right up their noses. "I got
a summer cold."

"Your summer cold is over, pal," said the umpire. "It's lasted for
six weeks and as of now it's gone for good. If you ever develop
it again, I'll bounce your ass out of this league."

Katcovich made him take out his handkerchief and honk two or
three times, blowing the whole secret mess of his recent success
into his already snot-stiffened handkerchief. Katcovich told him
that he was disgusting and returned to home plate.

That day Shaw reverted to form and was shelled from the
mound in an 18–6 loss. As a result, Shaw became famous for
something besides ineptitude in that league just as he had in the
Texas League many years before. He was known as the man with
the perpetual summer cold, whole opposing teams were known to
sneeze in unison when he took the mound and the first batter
invariably asked the ump to check Shaw's first delivery for snot.

He was suddenly famous again for the wrong, painful reasons,
this time as the inventor of the snotball, a pitch known to dip, clip,
and splatter across the plate. His catcher was advised to cut eye
holes in a linen handkerchief and glue it to his catcher's mask for
protection. It was awful as usual.

But as he grew older and no better, the ridicule fell away from him. He was too grim and pathetic, too hopeless and old, to be the butt of jokes and so he became what everybody was afraid of becoming—old and washed-up with no place to go. And everybody gave him a wide berth.

But nobody is ever through with fooling himself. And even in 1955 when he was thirty-nine years old Shaw could still be tricked into thinking that God, time, and the Red Sox had relented, and he was going to get a second chance.

It had to do with the annual game with the Red Sox. Every year—this year in late July—the parent club came down and played an exhibition game with Louisville, their Triple-A farm club.

The fans and the Louisville ballplayers loved these games. The fans, because they got to see the real thing, and the ballplayers, because it was a chance to show the big fellows what fine talent they had down on the farm. The Red Sox ballplayers always looked bored stiff during batting and fielding practice, but when the game started, they played for blood. The game was baseball's version of the Oedipus complex, according to Elwood Flowers. He was the second-string catcher, wore glasses, and was the team intellectual. Because he was the recognized, certified team intellectual and well-liked to boot, he could get away with saying fancy things. Ward thought that Elwood's description was pretty good but he kept out of things like that. He was a hitter, and ornery. It would surprise and alarm his teammates if they knew he understood a term like Oedipus complex. In this life, Ward knew, people are easily confused.

That year, Louisville was right in the thick of the race for the pennant of the International League. It was a good club, especially with Ward leading the attack. Rudy Cleverdon, the manager, no doubt was hoping the Red Sox would forget about Ward and leave him right there in Louisville to help old Rudy win his pennant. Even though it was only July, Rudy was developing the lean and hungry look of a man starved for recognition. He'd kicked around the minor leagues for twenty years or so, played parts of three seasons with the Philadelphia A's, and carried a lifetime batting average of .239.

About two weeks before the Red Sox exhibition he called a club meeting in the locker room right after Indianapolis had shut them out 3–0. Everybody was sitting around naked with just towels draped around their middles.

"Okay, listen up, you niggahs! Massa Cleverdon got somethin' he wan' to tell you cotton choppers!" shouted Lamont Baltimore, the shortstop.

Wayne McLain, the witty leftfielder who was sucking up a beer tried to burp at this point, couldn't, and farted instead. Everyone laughed.

"There's your entrance music, Rudy," said Elwood Flowers.

"Okay, all right, you clowns. Shut up for a minute," said Rudy.

He pulled himself up to his full five feet three inches and looked them over for a minute till they settled down, looking back at him as if he were the camera for the team picture. He paused to spit a little tobacco juice into a paper cup about half full of cold coffee, a deplorable habit which made Ward want to hit him sometimes. It was further aggravated by the fact that he used to set these abominations down all over the locker room, the team bus, and in hotel lobbies and restaurants, sometimes even in the dugout when he had ground all around him to spit on. He drank coffee constantly and the stuff seemed to have dyed his skin permanently, so it looked almost as brown and dead as a grocery bag. He was dingtoed and stood and walked as if he had sore feet. His mouth was always wet, and he spit at you a little bit when he talked, so Ward always stood off from him out of the spray. His big belly rolled out over his belt. Wayne McLain once told Ward he bet Rudy's belt size was almost as big as his lifetime batting average.

"I know you fellows are real disappointed about losing this game to Petit, but there's always tomorrow," began Rudy.

"Oh yeah. Right man. Okay," burbled the ballplayers. Wayne McLain tried to fart again but couldn't. Wayne always had a smile on his face. He had red hair and a saddle nose, and it made you just want to smile when you looked at him. He was a big fellow, about six feet four with a barrel chest matted with orange hair. He had arms big as hams and a little waist and skinny legs. He was always good-natured. The only thing that made him mad was if you called him Colonel Leghorn.

"In this game," said Rudy, "you play them one day at a time."

"Oh, mother," said Elwood.

"What's that?" said Cleverdon.

"Nothing," said Elwood. "I just forgot my mother's birthday, that's all."

"Well, keep it to yourself," said Cleverdon.

He didn't like Elwood Flowers too much. He felt that Elwood would have been a much better ballplayer if he hadn't gone to college. College, he had been known to mutter, had messed up Elwood's mind and ruined his eyes.

"Now some of you boys," said Rudy, "have pretty good talent, and it's plain you're going places. All you have to do is keep your mind on the game and work hard. Even the best of you aren't going to get anywhere without the right attitude." And he looked right at Ward.

"So work hard and concentrate on the game. I want you to have a good time and all, but I expect you to act like professionals, which is what all of you are. We have a tough schedule coming up. But I think we can win it all, if everybody plays the way they can. In a way it's too bad we have the exhibition game with the big club when we do because we got a bunch of doubleheaders coming up just after that, including several key games with Montreal. Anyway, I have decided on the starting pitcher for the game with Boston. We're going to give a hard-working man a chance. That will be Wally Shaw."

This news was greeted with stunned silence. Wally, who was sitting on a stool in front of his locker, in just his blue baggy boxer shorts and one sock, looked as surprised as anybody. It was his first start all year.

"Wally has earned this honor by his hard work and good attitude. Wally, I want you to do some extra throwing in the next few weeks, since it's been a while since you had a start." And then Cleverdon went on to other business about throws that missed cut-off men, screwed-up signs, and other ball club matters. Wally sat there, hearing nothing, with a strange look on his face.

A few days later Ward and Shaw were staked out behind a big rubber plant in a hotel lobby, idly watching the women pass by on the other side of the big dirty plate glass window.

They talked about the weather and compared notes on the passing ladies. Gradually Shaw worked the conversation around to the pitching staff of the Boston Red Sox.

"They ain't got nothin'," Shaw was saying. "Who they got?

Once you get past Frank Sullivan and Kinder, who they got?"

"No-names," agreed Ward.

Then Shaw said the thing that was on his mind. The incredible thing that made Ward realize that even Shaw, despite all the evidence piled up over twenty years, still thought he had a chance.

"So I figure if I pitch real good in the exhibition game, maybe they'll bring me up. They need all the pitching they can get."

"Wally, you're thirty-nine."

"Ellis Kinder is forty-one," he said stubbornly, "and he's pitching for them"

Ward almost told him the naked truth, that the only reason Cleverdon gave this halfwit the start was because the game didn't count and Cleverdon was saving his good pitching for the regular season, since Louisville was right in the thick of the race that year. Cleverdon wasn't doing Shaw any favor. He was just throwing him away, using him as cannon fodder. Instead Ward decided to have a little fun with the old fart and teach him a valuable lesson too. When a man is no good at something—especially a man you take for a fool anyway—he ought to know it and stop doing it because it's an insult to the people who do it well. And if a fellow is too stupid to realize his own ineptitude, he ought to be told. Or at least shown in some humiliating fashion. That way, maybe he'd step aside and let those who can, do a thing without any comical characters hanging around to detract from the seriousness.

"You got a point there," said Ward, pretending to take him serious. "Maybe if you showed them something, they'd bring you up. Lord knows they need pitching."

"That's my point exactly," said Shaw. It was hard to take a man seriously who stood around with his mouth half-open all the time. Ward clapped him on the shoulder.

"Tell you what I'll do," he said. "I'll let you in on some of my training secrets, help you get ready. Cleverdon will have me over on first base. They'll want to see me there 'cause they got the good outfield and they're fixing to bring up Sigafoos and me to play the corners. During the game you and I can talk. You still throw the snot ball?"

"Where did you hear about that?" asked Shaw darkly.

"Word gets around," said Ward.

"I never throwed it in this league."

"Come on."

"Only but maybe once a game."

"Well, I'll have the stuff on me, and if you need help just ask. See, that way you stay clean."

"I couldn't do that in this kind of a game."

"The hell you couldn't," said Ward. "How do you get ready for a start anyway? I know you don't get the call often, but what do you do?"

"Well," said Shaw, "I usually eat a bowl of cream of wheat and go to bed about 8:30. I like about twelve hours sleep before a start."

It was all Ward could do to keep from laughing outright. "That's interesting," he said. "Too bad it isn't oyster season. Oysters make great training food. You like oysters?"

"I'd rather eat spit," said Shaw.

"Too bad," said Ward. "I eat them all winter at home. That's how come I come to spring training so strong. I even like shucking the devils. They teach you to hang in there. You get after them with an oyster knife, and it's like they're never going to open. You just pry at them, and it seems like no way are you ever going to open them, and then suddenly they just give up all at once like a girl."

"I wouldn't be for that," said Shaw.

"You ever do any extra running?"

"No. I try to save my legs," Shaw explained.

"I'll stop by for you tomorrow. You got to beat the body a little. If it doesn't hurt a little, it won't listen when you ask it to do something."

"I don't know—" said Shaw.

"I'll stop by," Ward said, chuckling to himself.

And he did, banging on Shaw's door till the old pitcher stumbled through the dark and opened it, and under Ward's bullying and steady cursing he pulled on sneakers and a pair of ancient gray sweatpants with the knees out, strapped what looked like a piece of black inner tube around his middle to make him perspire extra, and struggled into a sweatshirt.

They went padding quietly along the night sidewalks in the faint dove-gray light. Ward was running easily and feeling good, on the verge of laughter about old Shaw, maybe just because mirth was the natural overspill of that inexhaustible energy he had then, with Shaw in his ancient running costume not so much running as staggering stiffly twenty yards behind.

They went along the gravel paths of a nearby park where it was still cold in the blue shadows under the towering trees. When they came to a small hill, Ward heard the old fart stumble, the gravel fly as he pitched headlong. He lay there face down, his arms flung out like a man who has just been shot in the back.

"What the hell you doing, Shaw?"

"Catching my breath."

Chuckling, Ward helped him to his feet. Yes, a loser like this, who didn't know when to quit, really deserved a lesson. Right then and there Ward decided to bang on his door every morning and get him out to run till he made his start against the Red Sox.

"He thinks he's got a chance to go up if he looks good," said Ward.

"He don't," said Wayne McLain.

"Yes. He thinks it's an important game, that Cleverdon's bestowed some kind of honor on him."

"Shit, you say," said Wayne McLain.

"I'll have him so worn out by game time I bet he doesn't last more than a third of an inning."

"I wouldn't take that bet," said McLain. "He never goes more than a third anyway."

The night before the game, Ward collared Shaw and dragged him off for Mexican food.

"No warm milk tonight, Shaw. This Mexican food will make you *mean*. Maybe all that baby food you ate over the years made you soft. How your legs feel?"

"They're feeling good," Shaw said. "Surprisingly good."

Which surely surprised Ward. Just that morning Shaw's legs had gone rubbery only a mile and a half out and they had had to quit and walk back to the boardinghouse.

They had another bowl of eye-watering, sweat-popping chili and washed it down with another bottle of Carta Blanca After which Shaw beat a hasty retreat for the toilet.

Ward sat there smiling to himself, thinking Shaw wouldn't be able to run for it when he was standing out there on the mound. He wondered just how drunk he ought to get the old fool. He didn't have any official bet with Wayne McLain, but it might be a good joke if Shaw was still drunk at game time. For his own part, he knew he could drink Shaw under the table three times. He wasn't worried about himself. He had the body that would take it.

Ward ordered two more beers and as Shaw approached the table and saw the bottles, a look of despair and resignation fluttered across his face.

"How you feeling?" he asked as Shaw sat, or more like fell back into his seat.

"I wish I had some ice cream," said Shaw ruefully. "I feel head-achy. My gut hurts from all that burny food."

"Never mind all that old guy talk. You'll be fine. Drink your beer. We're getting ready for tomorrow. We're going to change your life."

"It's almost nine o'clock. I should be back at the room, going to bed," muttered Shaw.

"You aren't going anywhere. You've been going to bed every night at eight-thirty for twenty-four years, and where did it get you? Tonight you do what I say."

Shaw looked around the room miserably for some form of res-cue—a cop, a teammate—and having confirmed what he already knew, that no help was at hand, he fixed his gaze on his beer glass.

"Here, drink up," said Ward, sloshing Shaw's glass full with a four-inch frothy head.

"I won't be able to pitch tomorrow if I keep this up," said Shaw.

"You could never pitch sober," said Ward. "Maybe you can pitch drunk."

"What about you?" asked Shaw.

"Me?" Ward showed him a mouthful of white even teeth. "I can hit sober, drunk, or cockeyed."

They went to another place, dark and smoky. This place was crowded and noisy, with a jukebox and many unattached women. They had several more beers. About this time Ward looked up to see Shaw, drunk by now, ogling a young dark-haired skinny child who sat languidly at the bar. Her skirt was hiked up, offering for review a good deal of adolescent leg. She had a small body and seemed to be all arms and legs like a spider monkey.

"What you looking at?"

"Huh? Nothing. I'm just sitting here wondering when we can go home. I'm so tired I'm almost cross-eyed."

"Be patient. You haven't changed enough yet to go home. You're not ready for tomorrow. Wait here till I get back."

"Where you going?"

"How long's it been since you had a woman?"

"What?" Surprise and fear spread over Shaw's face at the abrupt question. His big-knuckled hands gripped the edge of the table, his narrow almost mongoloid eyes widened and bulged and ran from side to side in panic. "Now listen, don't do anything funny. I don't need nothing like that. I'm all right like I am."

"Remember, old man," said Ward as he got up. "I can run ten times faster than you. You'll never make it to the door before I catch you. You just sit here, and I'll be back in a few shakes."

Her face was round, a perfectly blank white oval populated by small black eyes and a small sullen mouth, purple with moist, dark lipstick. This girl had redesigned her tiny eyes with black paint to demonstrate, he supposed, the kind she would have given herself if she'd been God. In this corrected version, they were big and almond-shaped. In addition she had loaded her eyelashes with mascara and painted her lids electric blue. Short dark hair framed this brooding child's face. She seemed under a bell jar of silence in the midst of noise. She was looking down at the tall, frosted cylinder of her drink, which looked more like a frappe than anything alcoholic, and he could see the beautiful curve of her almost turquoise eyelids as they lay on the ovals of her eyes. There was in that expression something virginal, sculptural. If his little brother had been there he'd have probably wet his pants at such a sight. She was twisting her straw into knots as he came up to her and said, "Howdy, miss. How about a drink on me?"

"Sho now. That's mighty nice of you. I didn't think anybody was ever going to talk to me in this place. Phil, give me another Tom Collins. And put some sugar in it."

She looked about ten years old under the paint and she was all straight lines except for the hard-looking baseball-size breasts under her tight, glossy multicolored blouse.

"Well now," she smiled, as she fiddled suggestively with the straw in the fresh drink.

"How old are you anyway?"

"How old do you want me to be," she asked, showing him a row of tiny gray teeth.

"It doesn't matter," he said. "My friend over there thinks you're beautiful."

"Where is he?"

"He's over there at the table."

"That old guy?"

"Yes, that fellow. How about a date for my friend?"

"He kind of old and ugly, ain't he?"

"What do you care? You're not going to marry him, are you?"

"No, but with the old ones sometimes it takes a lot of work."

"That's all right. Never mind about that."

So they went to the table, Ward carrying fresh bottles of beer and a bag of popcorn and she with two fresh tall drinks. Falling halfway down her arm was the strap of a shoulderbag about as big as a mail pouch or an average knapsack, and probably just as serviceable. As they approached, Shaw's eyes widened in panic again. She smiled seductively as she sat down, sticking out her small round ass, pausing in mid-motion as if she were going to putt, and then tucking in and sitting down neatly. The whole act was compact, suggestive, and promising. "Howdy, pop," she said and put her hand into Shaw's lap. Shaw nearly fainted. He looked at Ward. His eyes, sadder than a hound dog's, pleaded *no.* Ward looked back coldly and poured another four-inch head on his beer. Her name was Sharmaine and she kept claiming to be eighteen. She was from a little town no bigger than a flyspeck, she told them, called Waterproof, Louisiana. She was trying to get to Nashville where she had a friend who would get her a recording audition.

And that was about all he remembered for a while; the rest was a blur of music, beer, and babble. Then there was the painful blurred odyssey through a bad section of Louisville, staggering together down the silent streets till they came to her apartment. Then a dim recollection of a room with large-flowered wallpaper and pictures of country music stars torn from magazines taped to the wall. Ward sank heavily into a bloodhound brown overstuffed chair, his consciousness settling slowly like a torpedoed ship into the alcoholic and peopled darkness below the bright burning faggot of consciousness, half-remembered snatches of dialogue, bats and balls frozen mid-way in orbit, laughter and cackling hypnotic cribbage counts, the vague faces of old men, blued by the icy light pouring through the parlor window—the seaworld dance and music native to his mother's existence. Then he woke up in the girl's bed, still dressed down to his shoes, and she in his arms, warm and cozy-feeling in just her black shorts and lacy harness. On the other side of her lay Shaw, as white as a corpse, the only naked one in the bed, his face wearing that slightly flattened look that corpses have, as if gravity were pushing on it with both invisible hands. Ward was young and strong then. He was strong now. But in those days he burned with a strength that was as bright and merciless as some perfected anger. He always awoke fully awake, sometimes cursing, his head clear the instant he opened his eyes. In that wide-awake supercharged state he would sometimes hop on Blue before she woke and be halfway through with his errand before she even knew what hit her. Then he'd go out and run, run, run, till that clarity—that surge of energy like great anger—calmed down, and his spirit began to flow within its banks again. It was no different this morning. He woke up clear-headed and dead sober, with that tight ball of fury in his chest that by now he knew was just excess energy. He started the day with a string of curses. He got up and punched the wall. He did fifty jumping jacks. His two companions slept on boozily. He threw open the window, discovering she had quarters over a liquor store, and took deep gulps of fresh air. "All right," he roared. "I let you sleep extra. Now get off your dead ass!"

The girl got up readily, even feeling good enough to giggle about it. In the early dawn light she looked younger than ever. She helped Ward drag Shaw from the bed to the floor, each grabbing him by a hairy ankle.

"No, no," the old man whimpered like a puppy.

"I'm dead," Shaw moaned from the floor, with the blanket wrapped around him. "You and the girl have kilt me."

"Shit," said Ward. "As soon as we get in our run, you'll feel fine."

"Oh no," whimpered Shaw and tried to climb back into bed but the girl held him back firmly. "Come on, Dad," she said. "Unless you want to play some more at the usual rates." Together they dressed him. She made some perk coffee and toast. In the little kitchenette she bent her incredibly round and childlike face to

Ward's ear and asked, "You really think he'll be able to pitch?"
"Hell, no," said Ward. "He couldn't have pitched dead sober
either. That old fart's a loser. He's been a loser all his life."

"You don't sound much like a friend," she said.

"Oh, no?" he said. "What's a friend sound like? That fellow in
there has had a good drunk and the pleasure of your company on
me. That's more than most would do for him."

"You could have celebrated tonight. Seems to me you deliberately set out to tire him out. I don't call that friendly. He was
telling me while you were asleep in the chair that this was the
biggest game of his life," she said, picking her teeth with a wooden
match and standing there on one foot, dressed now in the
housecoat with flowers on it which for size matched the ones in
the wallpaper.

"This is no big game," said Ward. "It's just an exhibition. The
manager gave him the start because it doesn't count. *He* thinks it's
important. But it's nothing."

"If he thinks it's important," she said, "it is. To him. If you were
a friend, you'd see that."

"Shit," he said. "I haven't got all day to jaw with you."

The two of them helped Shaw dress and poured a couple of cups
of coffee in him. He looked awful. Just before they went out the
door, Sharmaine touched him on the arm.

"Don't let nobody tell you you ain't any good. You let them do
that once, they'll never stop. People are bastards, even if they can't
help it. They like to see you fall on your face. Don't let them do
it to you, hear? Go out there and win that ballgame. Then you
come back here tonight and we'll celebrate for sure."

"Thank you, Sharmaine," Shaw said. "You're right about people. Once you let them call you no good, they never let up. I'll try
to win that game."

Ward was astonished and embarrassed by the exchange. He
didn't know what to say. Sharmaine was there looking at him as
if to say *well?* and Shaw had already turned and was hobbling
down the dim scarified stairs. Silently he turned and trailed after
him.

They ran in the park that morning, but this time Ward's intention was not to wear the old man out but to sober him up. They
ran slowly through the mild bright air, their feet on the gravel the

only sound in the park except for the birds and the squirrels. Ward felt bad about how he'd set up Shaw. The man of course needed to be taught a lesson but somehow Ward didn't feel so good about being the teacher anymore. Maybe because Shaw had gone along with it innocently, partly because Ward had bullied him into it but partly too because he believed this young kid was really trying to help him get ready for his big moment. The old guy felt flattered no doubt that such a sure-fire major leaguer would take an interest. Looked at that way, he could see Sharmaine's point: it was nothing a *friend* would do? Hell, it was nothing *anybody* with any sense would do. When you find a loser, even if he doesn't know he's a loser, the best thing you can do is leave him alone. Even if he is an insult to the game. How did I get so mean? he wondered. He didn't know the answer. Maybe it was because he wanted to play ball so bad it made him almost inhuman, figuring anything that didn't have to do with hitting a baseball didn't count. Then there was the chance, the outside chance, that somebody who had it all going for him could by some trick end up all washed up like Shaw. A thought like that made your mouth go dry, and it too could make you mean and ugly.

They sat on a bench at the end of their run near the park exit. Shaw was looking better. His color had come back and his head looked three-dimensional again.

"How are you feeling?"

"Better," said Shaw. "I'm not drunk anymore, and my head doesn't hurt so bad."

"Wally," Ward had said then.

"What?"

"I really hope you win today. Remember, I'll have the stuff if you need it. Just call me over. I'll touch you on the elbow or somewhere, and then you'll have it."

"I don't think—" Shaw began.

"Well, if you need it," said Ward. "Maybe if you show them something, they'll bring you up." This time he said it kindly and not to make a joke. What was going on here? Well, nothing he could put his finger on exactly. Maybe he had learned that even old ballplayers were entitled to the dignity of their dreams, no matter how foolish they looked to the young.

Near game time Cleverdon found Shaw asleep in the metal toilet stall of the locker room, his baseball pants down around his ankles, his head resting on the toilet paper dispenser.

"Wake up, you damned drunk," he cried. He looked around blackly for Ward but he was already out on the field, going through infield practice.

The first pitch Shaw threw in the direction of a Red Sox batter missed the back stop completely. Ward trotted over to him from first base.

"Don't be nervous," he said. "Just relax and pitch your game."

"I ain't nervous. That pitch just slipped. I'll be all right."

"Go get 'em," said Ward and trotted back to his position. He was hoping like hell the old guy wouldn't look too bad. Everybody deserved some kind of mediocre performance that in later years he could make into a great exploit and carry like a suitcase into old age with him. There wasn't a middle-aged man alive in America who hadn't worked on that. This old relic's moment, if it came, would just arrive a little later than usual.

Shaw's next pitch was a soft melon which floated right across the heart of the plate and startled the batter so much he hit it on the ground wide of first base. Ward went after the ball and Shaw pounced off the mound like an old cougar to race the batter to first base. Ward flipped the ball to Shaw who tripped over the bag and pitched forward into the dirt, landing with a sickening thud; Shaw writhed in the dirt, clutching his shoulder.

Cleverdon pigeon-toed quickly down the base line, wagging his belly like a mailbag and then stood there absently spitting tobacco juice to one side while Shaw thrashed around.

"Are you all right?" asked Ward. "How's your arm?" But he was watching Cleverdon's little duck's eyes calculating which dead-head he could afford to throw in next if this one couldn't stand up. Get up, Shaw, Ward thought. Show this bastard you're not through yet.

"I am all right," answered Shaw, tight-lipped and grim.

"Then get off your ass and pitch," said Cleverdon and walked back to the dugout.

Pitch he did. He struck out the next two batters with what looked to be pretty hard stuff. He beckoned Ward over to the mound.

"Somethin' happened," he said. A toothy smile creased his ugly face. He looked like a hound that had snagged his lip on a tooth.

"What happened?"

"Something snapped when I took that fall. My arm's looser than it has been for years. You see those fastballs?"

"I see them," Ward said. "They're beautiful."

"I'm going to strike out this son of a bitch too."

"Good. Go to it," said Ward.

"See Kinder over there on the bench. See him leaning forward? He trying to figure out how an old guy like me can throw so hard."

"You better get to work."

"You got her number?"

"I got it."

"Right after the game."

"All right."

And he struck out the next batter, blowing him away on three straight swinging strikes, high, look-like, ninety-mile-an-hour fastballs.

When Shaw ducked into the dugout, Cleverdon was standing with his hand on his hips, glowering at him fiercely. "Where'd Sullivan take you last night, old man?" he said. "I want to take the rest of the pitching staff there tonight."

"Never mind, never mind," Shaw cackled asthmatically. "It's my secret place."

And Cleverdon whispered to Ward, "Where'd he get that fast-ball? He ain't got a fastball like that. He never had anything like that."

"That's all right," said Ward. "He thinks he's got one today."

In the bottom of the first, Ward picked on the Red Sox pitcher's first pitch and laid it against the boards for two bases. Sigafoos singled him home.

On the mound Shaw stood in a sunstruck golden haze of dust, looking tough and old and shrewd, cackling between pitches, looking suddenly like a winner. He had an easy second inning. And an easy third and fourth. Although by that time he was beginning to finesse them more often than throw smoke, and he'd called Ward over to the mound a few times for a little Vaseline and dipped a few pitches that had batters swinging wildly even though the ball finished in the dirt.

On the bench between innings, his face bright with sweat, his breath sour with excitement, Shaw said, "I'm pitching like the old days before Noona plugged me. I got my old fastball back."

In the fifth with one out and still throwing a no-hitter, Shaw
had the Red Sox manager standing on the top step of the dugout
absorbedly squinting out at him.

He called Ward over. "See that fellow look at me now. Now this
next one gets smoke. I give this first fellow my slow stuff. Now
I go to my Sharmaine pitch."

"You have a pitch that giggles in bed?"

"No, this is my newfound fastball, thanks to you and Sharmaine. By God, I can bring it today!"

He pitched the next batter razor sharp. He hit the inside corner
under the fists, an impossible pitch to handle. He wasted a three-
quarters-speed on the next, high and outside. He came back inside
high with the fastball and the batter swung and missed. He threw
a balloon ball change-up on the outside and low that the batter
took for a third, called, strike.

Shaw called Ward over again.

"I can do it!" he said. "If I pitch a no-hitter against them how
they going to deny me the chance?"

What an afternoon for the old guy, thought Ward, moving deep
behind the bag. Who knows—with that fastball, maybe he *is* the
next Ellis Kinder, at least for an hour or so.

In the sixth with two strikes on the batter and still throwing his
no-hitter, Shaw served up another balloon pitch which the batter
timed perfectly and hit like a bullet right at Shaw. The old guy
froze. The ball cannonaded off his skull, high into the air like a ball
off a fungo bat. It plopped into Ward's glove. Shaw sprawled in
the shape of a swastika on the pitcher's mound. *Good God,* Ward
thought. *He's dead, just like Ray Chapman.* Cleverdon and the others
surrounded him. Cleverdon held a cold wet towel to the egg which
was appearing on Shaw's forehead like a demonstration of high-
speed photography.

He was dead all right. He lay still as a picture. Poor son of a bitch
looked peaceful as a turnip laying there with the whole team
clumped around him, taking him seriously for once. It was fitting
that the old man should have a moment of glory just before being
killed by a baseball. It was the only happy ending possible to an
otherwise miserable career. Ward had already accepted Shaw's
death as fitting when the old relief pitcher's eyelids fluttered and

his breath rattled in his chest like a string of boxcars slamming into motion again.

"Can you pitch?" asked Cleverdon. "You done enough. You can quit now if you want."

"Yes," said the old relief pitcher.

"You're not quitting," said Ward. "Get on your feet, Shaw. Goddamn. I never heard of a pitcher walking away from a no-hitter. Stand up!"

"I can't," moaned Shaw.

"What's got into you, Sullivan?" asked Cleverdon. "Look at the egg on his head. Klaus knocked him goddamn silly. He might even have a fractured skull."

Ward could not figure the sense of dread he felt when he saw the flutter of the old guy's lids and a trace of color creeping back into the dead gray face. *Oh no.* That was what ran through his head involuntarily. Not, *thank God, he's alive.* But, *oh no.* Maybe because he felt Shaw had been denied a satisfactory way out of an impossible situation. Ward gaped in outrage and anger as Cleverdon and the others helped the old fart to his feet. Now time would move on. It would no longer be arrested on this pinnacle.

But *oh no* was all he thought then. Suddenly he was so mad at Shaw it made him dizzy and he didn't know why, which only made him madder. Years later he would think he had the answer: *because the old crook duped me.* Because he actually had Ward believing for three or four innings that a fellow could escape his fate. By coming back to life, Shaw had only mistakes to make. Either he would continue to pitch and they would beat his brains in or, unable to continue, he would commit the sacrilege of leaving the game in the middle of a no-hitter, proving again that even when he was doing something special, he was still, and always, a loser.

All there was back then was the hot vertigo, the realization that the others were asking after him solicitously as Shaw staggered around the mound and then the doleful shake of his head, inducing the pitiful jiggle of the bloodhound creases of skin beneath a jaw pitted with whiskers as dark, ugly, and definite as blackheads. No, the sad face confessed. He could not go on.

"What?" yelled Ward, grabbing Shaw by the front of his shirt. "What? You're quitting in the middle of a no-hitter? You can't do that!"

"Let him go," said Cleverdon. "What's wrong with you? Didn't
you see him get shot by that baseball? He might even have a skull
fracture."

"He hasn't got any goddamned fractured skull. He's just a quit-
ter. Why the hell did you throw that goddamned dink ball anyway?" He shouted, straining over the top of Cleverdon's cap trying to get at Shaw as he stood there dazed and woebegone. Now
the others held him back, because it was clear he wanted to get at
Shaw and maybe widen the crack in that fractured skull that he
didn't have.

"What's wrong with you? Have you gone crazy?" Cleverdon
grunted as he and the others grappled with Ward.

"You old bastard!" Ward howled. "Nobody quits when he's
throwing a no-hitter! You're worthless! I always knew you were
worthless!" Ward looked around at the astonished clutch of ballplayers. "Nobody quits!" he growled as Shaw, assisted by a spare
outfielder and the bat boy, skulked off the field.

Naturally they lost the game 6–5. But that didn't matter. What
mattered, he saw now, was that Shaw had quit, given way in face
of the facts. He had admitted he was a loser, which made the world
more dangerous for other people who were trying to go on with
their lives. You did your job. You fought the bad breaks. Then you
looked up and there was Shaw, with defeat written all over his
face like a newspaper headline. It was enough to drive you crazy.
No wonder everybody hated him.

So that's how it was with Shaw. Ward never forgot him. He
never forgot anything. It was all there on the movie memories in
his head. Shaw stood there in his memory with the posture of a
question mark, his pitching arm two to three inches longer than
the left one from flinging baseballs for countless years to no purpose. His glove, so ancient it was gray instead of brown, dangled
from his knobby wrist like an old paperthin hornets' nest. There
he was, with his hangdog face, looking almost at you but a little
to one side as if there was some invisible, horrible, but interesting
presence hovering just over your left shoulder. Nothing could
wipe the misery out of those sad Mongolian eyes, or make his
perpetual sour stomach come right, or sweeten his stinky breath,
or give him a respectable fastball.

That was the dark, disturbing side of those days and even that was good, and it only looked especially dark and troubling years later. The good side was whaling hell out of that baseball, coming on with the irresistible rush of a locomotive. And of course it was Bluette Fingers too. He would never forget Blue either.

F I V E

WARD walked right up to her, this big good-looking girl with skin translucent as honey and long black hair, and he kissed her hard on the mouth.

"Thanks, sweetheart," he said, taking the check and the trophy from her. "Why don't we take this money and have ourselves a hell of a weekend?"

"I don't know you from shit," she said looking at him steadily. "And next time you do that I'll kick you into a tree."

Ward blinked. In 1955 no woman, certainly no *southern* woman, talked like that.

"What's your name?" he said.

"Bluette. Bluette Fingers."

"Well, Bluette Fingers. Miss Bluegrass Queen. My name is Ward Sullivan. I guess you never heard of me."

"No, I guess I never did."

"Hell," he grinned. "I'm almost famous. I'm hitting .410 and traveling fast. Couple of months I'll be playing in Boston next to Ted Williams."

"Fascinating. Who's Ted Williams?"

"It doesn't matter, only that I'll be doing it." He grinned, "You're tough, aren't you?"

She just looked at him. He could tell something good was happening inside both of them, some mutual acknowledgment. When they talked they knew just what the other one meant, as if they had invented the language. People who belong together are never strangers, not even on first meeting. Blue had already taught him that, within the first five minutes of their time together.

All this happened at the ballpark one night in early May of 1955. *This year's Miss Bluegrass Queen,* said the announcer over the loudspeaker, *Miss Bluegrass Queen will give out the check and the trophy to the lucky winner of tonight's pre-game home run hitting contest. Won't you welcome,* he asked, *Miss Bluegrass Queen?*

Won't you welcome Miss Bluegrass Queen?

Yes, indeed.

The gates opened in center field. They drove her out in a glossy white Cadillac convertible, ohe sitting up on the trunk lid dressed in her swimsuit, wearing the silly sunburst crown and the red robe with the phony ermine trim. But somehow the effect was electrifying. The crowd hushed. Here was a *real* queen, dazzling and resplendent. The scattering of women in the crowd saw themselves perfected in her, and the men found that their dreams had come true. For a minute she had an entirely healing effect on the crowd. Then the people began to buzz again, the magic moment crumbled as they took solace in their hot dogs and beer.

"I can't even *look* at her," said Big Jim Honeystill, the first baseman. Big Jim was thirty-five and had a Triple-A average of over .330. Yet he'd never been able to make the jump to the big time despite several trials. He looked major league all the way, but for some hidden reason it just didn't work out for him.

"I can't even *look* at her," he confessed in a heartbroken voice and turned his face to the water cooler.

"Hell, she's beautiful. She's easy on the eyes."

Yet he needed an answer. Her beauty pierced him like a spear. He was standing there feeling half-sick. What the hell was going on?

"What's the matter, Big Jim?" Ward said. "Since when did you turn away from a beautiful woman?"

"I tell you, son," said Big Jim, looking sad. "I've had enough sad times in my life. I don't want to stare at some beautiful creature I'll never even get to meet."

That was it. That loveliness tore you to pieces. She nearly killed with her beauty, and yet she didn't even know you existed.

That's when he learned that beautiful women could be a source of misery, reminding you of all you weren't and of all the things you'd never have. He felt sorry for Big Jim. He didn't like the clutch of pain he felt on first looking at this beauty queen, but by damn he was going to do something about it. She wasn't going to leave him feeling all hollow and moony like Big Jim.

He decided right then and there that he was going to win that
hitting contest. Bluette Fingers, the beauty queen who made you
hurt all over, was going to present that trophy and check to him,
nobody else. He would see her up close, study her with the same
intensity his little brother might waste on a painting. And goddamn, he would *do* something to make her remember him. She
would have to look at him—really *see* him. She would feel the
electric surge of his lust and admiration, and she would have to
acknowledge that he was serious or dangerous or *something* and in
so doing give him back his soul.

Bluette stepped out of the car. He saw for the first time that long
black hair fall in glossy waves to her shoulders and the flawless
movie-star smile and her eyes blue as cornflowers. His knees grew
weak as she stepped down at home plate and some flunky relieved
her of her royal robe and scepter. She was dressed in a white Miss
America tank suit. A broad blue satin ribbon with "Miss Bluegrass
Queen" scrolled on it ran in subtle diagonal undulation from her
sweet breast across the margin of her stomach and caressed her left
hip. The effect of that suit, which showed off her long legs and
high-riding lovely bosom, was so physically dazzling the pulses in
his neck, his armpits, and his thighs all began to throb like crickets.
The electric tension in the crowd had broken. No longer was she
the fulfillment of their dreams. She was just a spectacle now, and
they clapped wildly and hooted and stamped their feet and did all
kinds of farmerlike parodies to cover up the hungry emptiness
which this lovely woman had filled for a spellbinding minute.

That is the most beautiful girl in the world, he thought. He felt
so weak he thought he might have to sit down.

The fellows were lined up on the top step of the dugout. They
were all knocked speechless. Till Wayne McLain shouted, "Hey,
Queenie! You want to try out the grass in my backyard?"

Ward told him to cut it out.

"What?" said Wayne McLain.

"I said cut it out, you baboon. Don't dirty this up with your
smart remarks."

Wayne looked at him, and his smile faded.

"Dang if you ain't serious," he said.

Shaw was the pitcher for the home run hitting contest which
made it harder because Shaw's fastball looked like a regular
pitcher's change of pace and you had to supply all the power

yourself. Honeystill, McLain, and Sullivan were the Louisville entries and Toronto had three pretty good hitters in it too.

Both Honeystill and McLain had more native-born power than Ward. They were big fellows and Ward was just 6 feet, 160 pounds. But Wayne McLain saw everything as funny; and, deep down, Big Jim, as pretty a first baseman and hitter as you ever wanted to see, was soft and moony. And when they all went out there for that contest, Ward knew he was the only one who had the iron to win it. And he did, just the way he knew he would. It seemed like Shaw tried to get tricky with him a few times, but he whaled hell out of everything he threw up there anyway.

He went up to get the check and the trophy from Blue. He didn't know where to look, she was so beautiful all over and it seemed impolite to look at her anywhere. But the worst part was he couldn't keep from looking at her breasts, and it was a struggle not to walk up to her and put his head right down in there between those warm and glowing shapes.

But he toughed it out. He walked up to her and kissed her right on the mouth when she attempted to give him a little congratulatory buss, kissed her right on the mouth and held her in a long clinch. The crowd loved it.

It was then as he walked her to the VIP box which was right next to the dugout, that she offered to kick him into a tree and he told her he was almost famous. But the big thing was that they *looked* at each other. They fed on each other, they drank each other in. They both became slightly manic. She was verbally punching him around pretty good. He decided he'd better get to work in a hurry.

That's when he said, "I tell you what. Why don't I try to repair my manners. You're a beautiful woman. There's something in the way you talk. It's like I've heard your voice before. It's almost like I know what you're going to say before you say it, now that I'm over the shock of your first offer."

"You ought to try football," she said. "You reverse your field so well."

"I'd really like to take you to dinner, to get to know you. Really —no funny stuff."

"I never go out with ballplayers."

"Isn't that kind of unfair? Some of us are all right fellows."

"Thanks, but I'm not your type, traveler." And now her voice did flatten out, and the light went out of her face.

He opened the door of the box for her.

"Why not?" he wanted to know.

"Well, to tell the truth, I don't date much. Under this tank suit beats the heart of a librarian. I like to stay at home and read. I don't like to arm wrestle and I'm not much of a sport. Sounds dull, doesn't it?" He hated the sound of that dull hopeless voice.

"No, not necessarily," he said desperately. "All my people are readers."

"Your people?"

"I mean my family. They're all readers. I've got a little brother at home who I bet can read circles around you."

She smiled. "Remind me never to enter a reading contest against him."

"I get the idea you think I'm just another dumb athlete."

"No, really, I don't think that."

"Mr. Sullivan!" Cleverdon called sarcastically from the dugout. "Would you like to play ball today? Or are you out here just for the sunshine?"

"Keep your shirt on, Rudy," he said to the manager and turned back to the girl. "How about dinner?" he said. "Come on. Take a chance."

"All right," she said. "I never do this, but this time I will."

That night Ward's mind was not fully on the game. He tried to hit a long ball for this woman called Bluette Fingers. He never got his pitch, although he had a pair of nice singles.

Shaw watched him with interest as he hurriedly showered and started to dress after the game so as not to keep Bluette waiting too long out in front of the ballpark in her red Studebaker.

"Where you going in such a hurry?" asked the old relief pitcher.

"Where am I . . .? What are you, Shaw, my mother?" he said, suddenly feeling mad about it. Up till then he'd felt good about Blue, still feeling the galvanizing effect of the kiss, still thinking about the scent of her, of *her*, not any perfume, and that smooth translucent skin and her lovely voice. But the ominous tone of the old relief pitcher's voice, the insidious suggestion of peril, pitched him into an angry inner admission of some unspoken danger.

"I'm going to see that girl. That one they call the Bluegrass Queen," he said.

Shaw looked away in disgust as if his worst fears had been confirmed. "Women," he muttered.

"Why, that woman's beautiful!" Ward said. "Anybody would wish me luck."

But the old relief pitcher stubbornly refused to answer, to acknowledge any promise of pleasure or happiness from women.

Then he mumbled something Ward couldn't quite catch.

"What? What is wrong now?" said Ward.

Shaw was fumbling with his shoes and socks, his bald head bent down. He was sitting there on the narrow bench in the hot, cramped ill-lighted locker room. He looked more like a derelict than a ballplayer in his old blue gabardine suit that looked like he'd just pressed it with a tractor. The other fellows wore sports coats and slacks and shirts open at the throat. They *looked* like ballplayers. But this old fart looked like he'd been pulled out of line at a Salvation Army soup kitchen. The others glowed with youth and healthy exuberance. Shaw was sallow and hangdog; the sad slots of his baggy eyes were furtive. Always first on the bus and last off. He was quiet as a ghost in the locker room, on the ballfield, and in the hotel lobbies. He was a silent spectator in the bars where the boys on the team whooped it up. Out of the sides of his eyes he watched the women who flocked around the fellows, and said nothing. Everybody felt uncomfortable with him around. He always sat to one side, away from the jokes and the fun, and he always seemed to see something in the bottom of his drink. He was a real pain in the ass.

"Be careful of your talent," Shaw said, hardly above a whisper.

A chill passed through Ward as if cold fluid had been injected into his spine.

"I thought we were talking about a woman!"

"All the same," muttered the old relief pitcher.

Ward stared at the top of his old bald head as Shaw tied his ugly black shoe.

"Ah, shit," Ward said and walked out into the evening to meet Bluette.

She was just a woman, one in a long parade of women that were fated to come into his life, give him pleasure, and exit without leaving a trace. One in a parade, he repeated to himself uneasily, without much conviction. Because he knew with a sinking sensation that he was never going to forget this one, that he wasn't going to be able to ignore her or discard her or use her or leave her without it half killing him. She was into him. He felt the pain of knowing that she already counted more than any of the other women he'd met and casually abandoned through his brief and glorious sojourn in the minors.

Won't you welcome, please, Miss Bluegrass Queen? urged the melancholy voice again in his head. He would be damned if he would! She might be here, a fact like gravity, sitting across from him and making him dizzy smiling at him, filling up all space with that smile and that beautiful face, but somehow he would keep a grip on things.

He was going to be rich and famous and acknowledged as the best ballplayer of his time. Someday he would probably be in the Hall of Fame, the way Jack Coombs would have been if he hadn't ruined his arm with his dogged feats of endurance, or like his grandfather if he had not felt compelled to take a "steady" job. He would make it. He was made for it, a perfect mixture of genetics and timing. The women—women like Bluette Fingers—would seek him out as they do famous athletes or anybody notorious, and he would accept them as he would the rain, a natural phenomenon, benevolent but not figuring in the real business at hand. Because nature, God, destiny—something—had made him for ballplaying, and that was what he would do, better than any man of his era.

He listened uneasily as she became exuberant in the restaurant, and began to babble the facts of her life. As if they'd wasted a lot of time by not knowing each other and now had to run to catch up. *Slow down,* he wanted to tell her. *You're moving so fast I can't jump off.*

Her father was an ex-Navy man and now chief of police in Memphis, Tennessee. His hobby was coon hunting. It was her daddy who had insisted she enter all the beauty contests when she was a kid. She did it to please him. It was easy enough at first to enter those things and win them one after another.

"My daddy is a simple man," she said. "He thinks all a girl needs to be is pretty. I can remember him saying to me if he found me reading a book, he'd say, 'What are you bothering your pretty head over that for, Honey?' God, my poor daddy! How I loved him and how bad he was for me."

Now that she'd given up a glamorous New York life she didn't see much of her parents anymore. They all felt uncomfortable. Her daddy, as she called him, was especially bewildered and hurt when she had quit New York for Louisville. He couldn't understand why she'd just thrown everything away and taken a job as a stewardess on Southern Airways.

She'd lived with a man named Spurgeon in New York. He was vice-president of the advertising agency that was trying to make a certain brand of Canadian whiskey famous, and she was the lovely lady featured in the advertisements in the magazines. Spurgeon was forty-five. He was going bald. He had a sailboat. He drank too much. He liked her to drink with him. Pretty soon she was taking uppers to get over her hangover in the mornings. Because the booze made her wakeful, she was taking sleeping pills at night.

"One morning I woke up," she said. "We were both on the bed. Spurgeon had managed to get one shoe off before passing out so he was the temporary champion. I still had my dress on—shoes, stockings, the whole thing. There was a trail of puke leading from the bathroom to the bed. I had no idea which one of us did it. No memory at all of the night before. I looked over at Spurgeon. He was asleep with his mouth open. I said, 'This is enough of this.' I got on the telephone to my friend Kathleen who's now my roommate. I said, 'Kathleen, I need some help quick.' She said, 'You come on down here.' She said, 'I'll help you, sweetie.' So I did. It's the best thing I ever did for myself. It was hard to leave Spurgeon. He was really good to me, always a gentleman, drunk or sober, and he really needed me. It really hurt to let him down. It really hurt, traveler. But down here I live my own life, not one invented for me by my daddy or Spurgeon. Except every once in a while I slip back, I guess, and turn out to be a Miss Bluegrass Queen all over again," she smiled. "But I'm making progress."

"Why are you telling me all this?"

"Because I want you to know me. I want to be honest with you. I like you, that's why it's important. I'm sorry to come on so strong. I don't want to scare you to death." She searched his face quickly to see what kind of damage all this serious talk had done to them.

"That's all right, I like to hear you talk," he lied because she *was* coming on too strong, and he'd just as lief relax and take her purely as a beautiful woman right now without any complicated stuff thrown in.

"It's okay. I'm used to it," he said, trying to help out. "Every pitcher in this league's trying to scare me to death."

"Really? Why is that?" She was grateful to change the subject herself.

"I see you don't understand baseball," he said. "I'm hitting .410. That's a lot. A pitcher hates a batter who eats up his best pitches like so much candy. They can't get me out throwing fastballs and curves, so they're trying to see if I scare."

"If you scare? How do they do that?"

"They throw at my head," he looked at her coolly. "They throw that hard ball as fast as they can and they try to nail me right between the eyes. That ball clocks around eighty miles an hour, faster with the good ones. It doesn't give me much time to duck."

"That's terrible," she cried. "You could get killed. Aren't there rules against that? What do you do about it?"

"I spend a lot of time kissing the ground around home plate," he grinned again. "Sometimes when the fellow gets too murderous, I go after him."

"What do you mean 'go after him'?"

"Well, I try to get out there to the mound before his teammates and the umpires get to me. If I get there in time I try to bloody his teeth or maybe rip off an ear."

"Mercy," she said. "I thought this was a slow-moving dreamy sort of game. What does the pitcher do?"

"He usually runs if he can," he said. "See, I have a reputation for being slightly crazy. They know I'm not out there for a dance like some fellows. Pitchers are generally big, but they don't want to get hurt. So they don't like it when somebody comes out there throwing real punches. They're hoping for big league careers, so they may be big but they're mostly chickens."

"You sound tough, traveler," she looked a little scared. He wanted to touch her, to calm her down. He had such a need to touch her. But he didn't know how to. He glanced at her breasts again, and his mouth went dry.

"Nobody's going to stop me from doing my job," he croaked. "If you let them, these fellows will drive you clean out of the

league. Pitchers and batters áre mortal enemies. It's nothing personal. It's just the way it is."

"You're not afraid of anything, are you?" she asked softly. Her
blue eyes sparkled like jewels.

"Are you making fun of me again?"

"No, really I'm not," she said. "I'm just fascinated by this.
You're not afraid, are you?"

"No. Why should I be?" and he was truly puzzled, even irritated
by the question. It sounded like something Shaw would ask. "Listen," he said, "I don't want to brag or anything, but I've got more
talent than that whole team put together. It's a gift. I'm just making the most of it. I work hard at it. Someday I'm going to be the
best ballplayer in the big leagues."

"Why?"

"Why? Because that's what I want. That's what I'm meant to
do."

"Is that how you really feel? Like it's your fate?"

"Yes, I do. I'll be playing for the Red Sox before this season's
over. And I'll tell you something else. Once I get up there, they'll
have to hold me down and cut the uniform off me to get me ever
to take it off again." He gave her a big grin. He wondered if he
should take her by the hand.

"My, you are young," she said.

"Now I suppose you want to make something of me being too
young. Hell, I'm twenty years old."

"No, no, it's just that you sound so sure of yourself."

"Is it bad to know what you're doing? Does that make me wet
behind the ears?"

"Most people—if they ever have your kind of confidence—lose
it as they go along. Life—what—throws a fastball at your head and
things change."

He couldn't tell whether she was making fun of him or not.

"You say I'm tough," he said. "I say you got to be tough. That's
the difference between winners and losers. The losers don't have
the grit. They fold up when the pressure's on. Most of those
fellows on the team are losers. You can see it. Most of them have
the reflexes, but they don't have the spunk."

He was thinking of Jim Honeystill and Elwood Flowers now,
both good ballplayers going nowhere.

"I used to feel as sure of myself as you do," she said. "But I don't anymore."

"That's too bad. You've got all the reason in the world to feel sure of yourself."

"Let me tell you something about winners and losers, traveler," she said, and her voice was not honeyed and mildly southern now but more like when she had offered to kick him into a tree. "You're going to find out that the losers are the people you want to watch. Losing makes for character, and therefore your interesting people. Generally they have more heart and feeling for others. They know that life is bigger than anyone's puny ego. The winners are specialists. They stumble on something they can do well, and they do it over and over again obsessively. They keep away from the dark and the terror that way. The winners live in a dream world. They tend to be indifferent to others. They describe themselves as tough."

"So that's the way you see me. Just a cocky kid with a bat in hand." He wondered if she'd just strung him along so she could blast him. He had to admit he'd been sounding off.

"No, there's more to you than that," she said softly. "I wouldn't be here if I didn't think there was. See, the thing about you is: you're too loud and noisy about it. You're a little uneasy about the whole thing."

"Is that right? Funny, I don't feel uneasy, doctor."

"I'm sorry. I'll quit now," she smiled. "I don't blame you if you're a little sore."

"You say I'm an uneasy winner. Now what are you?"

"I can tell you what I'd like to be," she said.

"What's that?"

"I'd like to be a hero."

"The fire department could use someone like you."

"You say the world is divided into the winners and the losers," she said. "There's another group. The heroes. They are the people who know that hitting a baseball or being Miss Bluegrass Queen is really just a joke. They know that life is one heartbreak after another but it doesn't stop them. They don't pick out anything easy to do. They try to find something worthwhile and then they do it, knowing full well in the end that everybody dies. They've seen life for what it is, and they still go on."

"They sound like a bunch of losers to me," he said. The whole conversation was making him uneasy.

"No, they're not," she said. "They see the bad, but they see the good too. They're tough as hell."

"Well, that's too much for me," he said.

"I doubt if it is," she said. "You look like you've seen some of the dark side of the moon."

"Maybe I have," he said. But she was not going to drag some stories about Sarah out of him just because she sounded sympathetic. Back then he hardly ever thought of Sarah or the mild ascetic faces of the old men who peopled his childhood in Dunnocks Head—Mr. Coombs, Granpa, Uncle Tyler, and the Captain. *Fifteen-two, fifteen-foah,* went the cribbage count in his head and now it seemed to be marking off great chunks of time, even light years. He wrote his father a postcard once a week which usually started: "Dear Dad—I'm hitting like hell. . . ." He sent newspaper clippings to Althy because she was putting together a scrapbook of his doings, as she called it. Once in a while, he dropped the kid a postcard too. But Sarah? He never thought about her much. Sarah was irrelevant to his present life. Once, in ancient times, she had given birth to him—a primitive act, remote and dull like the doings of the ancient Babylonians. There, in that old unaccountable fact, their connection ended.

"Someday maybe you'll be a hero," Blue offered, pulling him back to Louisville.

"For now I just like to keep it simple," he said. "I know just what I want to do. That's enough for now."

"Yes, that's surely enough," she laughed. "It puts you one up on me."

She shook her lovely mane of black hair and smiled at him, taking him by the hand, a gentle, kindly act. And all of his uneasiness evaporated.

Later she asked to stop at a little neighborhood bar called The Green Door. She took a sip of her beer and said, "Will you do me a favor?"

"What's that?"

"Will you make love to me?"

"Good God. You just come out with it, don't you?" he was flabbergasted.

"I don't know how else to say it," she said helplessly. "I would just like for you to hold me and make love to me."

"There is nothing I would like better," he said.

"I wish I could take you home but Kathleen's there, and she has an early morning flight. I'm afraid we'd disturb her. How about your place?"

"I don't have a place. Just a room over on Jefferson and the landlady never sleeps. How about the car? You are never without a roof if you have a car."

"No, I don't go for that," she shook her head. "That's a little too whorey. Think of something else."

"I've got an idea," he said.

Indeed he did. He gave her directions, and she drove them over to the rooming house. There he took her upstairs to Shaw's room and flicked on the lights.

"Uhuh," Shaw mumbled. His face was creased by the sheets, his eyes swollen. He looked a hundred instead of thirty-nine.

"Get dressed," Ward said.

"Where we going?" asked Shaw.

"I need the room, Wally," said Ward. "I wouldn't do this to you, but I've got to have the room."

"That woman," Shaw muttered, suddenly inspired. "You got that woman from the ballpark in tow. Is that it?"

"Just get the hell out, Wally, before I go crazy."

Shaw sat there, his face criss-crossed with wrinkles from the sheets, blinking ferociously at Ward, the stare not a function of outrage but of fatigue and blurred vision. With a sigh Shaw started to pull on his pants.

"Damn women," he said. "They'll ruin you if they get a chance."

Blue was standing in the hallway. When Shaw opened the door to leave, there she was. Ward saw her with a fresh stab of surprise. Shaw didn't even look at her or say anything as he shuffled by.

"Who's that?" she said coming into the room.

"Nobody," said Ward.

He started taking her clothes off. She was long-legged and high-waisted. She wore gossamer-like goodies that made his scalp tingle —little tiny panties that glowed like flower petals and a brassiere as intricate and delicate as a spiderweb. Naked, she looked like an

Amazon. Her lower abdomen was a lovely creamy wedge rising gracefully from the dark exclamation of her sex in a gentle curve, and then curved back, creating a lovely plane just above her navel. It was breathtaking sculpture, one of the natural wonders of the world like the Painted Desert. Her shoulders were lovely, smooth, and white; her hands were finely shaped. Even her feet were unusually handsome. Women always had ugly feet no matter how pretty they were, but not Blue. Taking her in, he realized that he was going on the evidence that dazzled her father and the beauty contest judges, not the metaphysical stuff she counted as important. Right now, he thought, this is all that's needed.

They made love all over the room—on the chairs, the bed, and the floor. And there was nothing like it. He kissed her, and the sensation was wonderful. He drank in her kisses. Somewhere he'd read some romantic claptrap, some poet's description of drinking at the lips of his beloved. Now he knew exactly what the third-rate poet had meant, only the sensation was wonderful, not third-rate.

"What do you think of this, traveler?" she smiled that dazzling white smile of hers.

She had her arms tight around his neck, their bodies clasped together, and everywhere he felt sweet and delicious. Her crow-black hair was heavy and damp.

"I like this," he said. "Good gravy, this is fine."

"Not too bad for a town this size, if I do say so myself," her lip was beaded with sweat. "Hold me, traveler," she said. "I'm a serious lady."

"I'm holding you. I won't let go either," he whispered hoarsely.

"Hold me. Hold me. Please hold me," she was crying. The tears ran into the rich hair at her temples and into the pink shells of her ears.

"I'm holding you," he said desperately, holding her tightly. "See? I'm holding you really good."

"I'm getting scared this is so good," she cried. "I don't want it to be over."

"See? I'm holding you tight."

"Do you feel as good as I do?" she opened her eyes and searched his.

"I feel better," he said.

"How about we do this again tomorrow?" she said.

"Yes, yes," he croaked.

"Traveler, I think I love you already," and she began to cry again.

After that they were together as much as possible. Her friend Kathleen moved out, and he moved, in. Blue had an attractive little apartment over a TV shop. The owner, a thin, dry, dyspeptic fellow the color of leaf tobacco, had built it for himself and then decided to move to the country. The living room was pine paneled and equipped with a fireplace, no less, and built-in bookcases which displayed Blue's books of poetry and popular psychology.

A Wedgewood blue couch edged in white faced the fireplace. Before it was a low coffee table, and even though they had a little dining room, they did most of their eating and drinking right there. Behind the couch was a narrow library table of the same height. Copies of *Life, The New Yorker,* and *The Sporting News* appeared and disappeared from this table. There was a porcelain lamp here, a large graceful figure of an Asian man releasing a bird from a cage. The lamp gave off a good reading light. A low woodgrained AM/FM radio sat opposite it. She would sometimes switch on the radio, keeping the music sweet and low. Most of their waking hours together in the apartment centered around this arrangement of furniture, every object of which he could remember down to the last detail.

A little sundeck on the back overlooked a park. Here on her days off Blue sometimes sunned herself on a bamboo mat in a brief white bathing suit, her hair spread like a fan on the deck above her head. The perspiration would stand like big beads of mercury on her oiled and gold-glistening stomach and her thighs would darken to bronze. He sometimes watched her in dry-throated wonder out the window.

No doubt this sunbathing touched off the anonymous phone calls she got from the Breather. You couldn't call them obscene, because the fellow never said anything, he just breathed heavily, overcome by his dark need, dumbfounded beyond words. Blue thought the calls were funny but Ward was full of choking fury over them. Secretly, he blamed her. If she didn't lie out there in spectacular near-nakedness she wouldn't get such calls. He suspected she was even gratified. After all, the Breather was just one more unofficial contest judge and like all the other judges, her

"daddy" and Ward included, his strangulated breathing gave assurance that she was physically beautiful and therefore held in
high, or low, esteem—take your choice.

Ward was no better. He took her on the same standards as every
other man; because she was so damned gorgeous he could hardly
take his eyes off her. He loved her for all the classic wrong reasons.
He liked to see other men's heads snap around when they walked
by arm in arm. Wayne McLain, the rightfielder, said to him one
night when she showed up at the ballpark, suntanned and in a
white cotton sleeveless dress, "My God, is she beautiful." He said
it soberly, and Wayne was known never to utter a serious word.
She seemed to have the power to make frivolous men solemn for
minutes at a time and, he would discover, unhinge serious men for
a lifetime.

Ward wanted to undress her every time he saw her, unhook the
subtle closures of her flower-petal pastel goodies and lose himself
in the lovely delicious dance of their lovemaking. He was proud
of her too because she'd been a big league model in New York and
now was his girl.

She had a few extra bucks left over from her salad days and
bought him unexpected beautiful gifts. One time she bought him
a $200 navy blue suit and a white turtleneck because she wanted
to put on the dog and go out to dinner. He suggested one of Ollie's
Trolleys, a local hamburger chain, but she took him downtown in
her red Studebaker to Maurice's, a fancy New Orleans-type
French restaurant. When the bill came for her escargots and veal
Oscar—he stuck with roast beef, thank you—she picked that up
too. She was dressed in a frothy light blue dress with spaghetti
straps. He spent dinner getting drunk on her—the smooth mounds
above the margin of the alluring bodice, the glossy black hair on
the tawny shoulders—instead of on the wine.

On the way home she pulled the car off the side of the road
under the night-dappled shadows of some sighing elms on the
edge of the parklike university campus.

"Come on, traveler. Make love to me here and now," she urged.

Was there really a sad note in her voice or was that something
he'd added to the memories of those days, all so clear and unfor-
gettable in his head?

He did make love to her right then and there, did so excitedly,
the heady scent of her naturally aromatic skin spiced now with

just a hint of flowery perfume. He hauled her out of the cramped car, pushed aside the fragile beautiful clothes, and had her on the fender. She set loose a moist tongue in his ear as noisily and enthusiastically as a spaniel, whispered encouraging erotic nonsense, got her cool hands under his clothes and tweaked his nipples. He pumped away in desperation and despair, his member tangled uncomfortably in his underpants.

This lack of control, this total immersion in this passionate woman scared him to death. He had work to do, damn it. He needed his rest. He had to concentrate on hitting that baseball. He suspected all this lovemaking might lower his energy, affect his eyesight. If Blue had been less heedless he would have felt more comfortable. She wanted to be with him whenever she could. She was inventive. She planned charming picnics out in the countryside. She dragged him to a concert, an all-Sibelius program, saw that that was a mistake and cheerfully left early with him. She read to him from her books of poetry. She washed and ironed his clothes for him, she trimmed his hair as expertly as any barber, and she took showers with him and scrubbed his back. She somehow got for him a copy of Jack Coombs' book on baseball, which had been out of print for several years. It had some good old-time pictures in it. She bought an outrageously expensive, impractical piece of leather luggage with his initials on it in gold for him to use on road trips. She bought him a soft leather shaving kit. She packed his bag efficiently and neatly when he hit the road. She stuck love notes in his neatly packed underwear, that said things like, "I'll be Blue for you while you're gone." No doubt she wanted the same uncalculated passion in return. The whole thing seemed out of control, dangerous. Was this love? Yes, it was. It certainly made a body uncomfortable.

It wasn't always easy, being good to him. One night he came through the door to find a strange new aroma in the air.

"Looky here," she said. "Look what we're having for dinner tonight."

With a flourish, she lifted the lid of a pot.

"What is it?" he asked suspiciously.

"Chicken Cerubi," she kissed him on the neck. "Mm-mm! You're going to love it."

"I told you," he explained patiently, "I don't eat anything fancy. I like to keep it simple. Steak and fries is the answer for me."

"You can't eat the same thing all the time."

"Hearts of lettuce on the side," he said.

"You can get that anyplace. But you can't get chicken Cerubi everywhere."

"Sometimes I like a little applesauce," he said. "Nothing fancy. And I don't eat any desserts. You ought to know all this by now."

"Well, hell!" she exploded. "I work myself silly making you a nice dinner and what do you say? 'Steak and fries, steak and fries.' "

"Now, Blue. Don't get upset."

"You damn kid." She put her hands on her hips. "You won't listen to anything. You won't try anything new."

"Wait a minute," he said, noting that her ears were beet red, a sure sign she was mad. "Wait a minute. Don't go off the deep end. I'll try it. But you have to understand something. I'm in training. I'm one of those winners you talked about. I do the same thing over and over again. I have a regular routine. It's not just my body I'm preparing. It's my mind too. I don't want my routine changed. Call me superstitious if you want. But I know what works for me."

Her ears were fading back to their normal color.

"Okay. Okay," she said. "I can understand that. I accept it. But you'll try the Cerubi tonight?"

"I will. Yes, m'am. I told you that."

"Good. In turn for that magnificent concession on your part, I'll cook you a steak tomorrow night."

"Good. Good," he said.

"What a pain in the ass," she said. "How about a kiss, you lug."

She caught on pretty quick. A regular routine was what he wanted. So they had one. He came in through the door and sat down on the blue couch with the sports page. She got the chilled shaker of vodka martinis out of the refrigerator and brought them in on a cutting board together with the chilled martini glasses, the olives stuffed with almonds, a plate of guyere cheese and stoned wheat crackers. After the drink, the newspaper, and the idle conversation, it was time for dinner invented from a narrow range of steak and fries, sometimes steak and eggs and fries and mushrooms, a leg of lamb, fried chicken, always a salad. Before bed most nights he took a glass of milk with a raw beaten egg in it. They made love and went to sleep. He would rise every morning at 5:30, put on his sweatsuit and sneakers and go out for a run. When he got back, she'd have the coffee and eggs ready. This was the routine he liked and seemed to need when he was at home. And routinely once a week, he would go out with the fellows and have a few beers or go over to Elwood's and play poker. When he would announce his intentions, she would say, "I guess I'll call Kathleen." And the first time she said this, he said, "I thought you'd stay home. Kind of keep the home fires burning."

She looked at him coldly and said quietly, "Go to hell. No twenty-year-old kid is going to tell me what to do."

"You don't talk very nice sometimes," he said ruefully.

"You get better than you deserve," she said.

One morning at quarter of six he came out of the bathroom to find her smiling in the hall, dressed in a pair of baggy white shorts with green trim and an old gold-colored basketball shirt, sneakers and knee pads. She had her hair back in a ponytail.

"Where are you going in that outfit?" he asked her.

"I thought you might like some company on your run this morning," she said.

"Well, I tell you—that's a nice offer."

"But you have your routine," she finished.

"Right."

"And you're preparing your mind as well as your body," she said.

"Yes," he agreed.

"And if I go along, I'll screw it up," she said.

"I'm sorry, Blue. I know I'm not fit company."

"That's all right," she said. "Hell, you ballplayers are more temperamental than a whole company of ballet dancers. Guess I'll go back to bed."

"Would you like to play tennis this afternoon?" he said.

"Yes, I would," she said. "It's a deal."

"You're pretty good, aren't you?"

"Yes, I am." She was proud of her game.

"Well, I've played about six times," he said. "What do you want to bet I beat you."

"I don't want to take your money, traveler. Have a nice run." She turned away.

"Blue?"

She faced him again. "What?"

"Thanks."

"That's okay, traveler. We older women are understanding."

She came back to kiss him on the neck.

"Just out of curiosity," he said. "Tell me what the knee pads are for."

"In case I stumbled and fell," she said. "Then I wouldn't cut my knees."

"I see," he said. Women don't know anything about what a man does, he thought. And a man doesn't know anything about women and what they do. It's like two secret tribes living together uneasily in the same neighborhood. No wonder war breaks out from time to time.

That afternoon she beat him on the public courts 6–4, 6–4, 5–7, taking a little sweet revenge on him for requiring so much understanding and forbearance.

Idle conversation could trigger off a series of events nobody could account for or explain later. One night as they finished their drinks on the couch, he told her he was going to have to get a new glove now that it was clear he was going to get to Boston by playing first base.

"I'm using an old one of Big Jim's," he said. "But I guess I'll have to get one of my own pretty soon. No hurry," he added because he didn't want her worrying about Boston.

He came home the next night and there on the library table on top of his newspaper was a package wrapped in green foil paper with a yellow bow.

"What is this?" he said.

"What's it say on the card?" she said.

"It says, 'For the next great ballplayer—love from your secret admirer.' "

"Well for heaven's sake," she said. "It must be for you. Go ahead and open it."

Which he did.

"What do you think," she said. "Do you like it? I went in the sportings goods store and looked around at the gloves till I found the one with the highest price tag and that's the one I bought. Because nothing's too good for you. Do you like it?"

"Blue, it's the nicest damn catcher's mitt I ever saw. Elwood Flowers would cry if he saw it."

"What's Elwood got to do with it?" she wanted to know.

"A catcher's mitt is a catcher's mitt," he said.

"Yes?" She still didn't get it.

"You can't play first base with it," he explained.

"Oh. You can't?"

"I tell you, though. If I ever convert to catching, this will be just the mitt for me."

"I wanted to surprise you," she said.

"You did," he said.

"I guess you better come along when I take it back and pick out your own glove."

"I suppose so. It's very nice of you to do this, even though it's not quite the thing I can use."

"Well," she said fiddling with the bow. "I guess you will have this from time to time, as you travel west."

"I believe," he said, "you could use some basic education in the game."

"I expect you're right."

"Okay, stay right there."

He went to the hall closet and fetched the ball he kept in the pocket of his glove to keep it in good shape. He came back into the room and held it up between two fingers, delicately, as if it were an egg.

"Now this is a baseball," he said.

"All right," she said. "I've got that part. What else?"

For the most part things went along all right.

She taught him a whole bunch of new ways to make love. They tried bondage, lubricants, lingerie, and imaginative new positions, some of which required acrobatic skill. She was always surprising him. He suggested that if they kept going like this maybe they ought to join the circus.

"I don't want you to get tired of me ever," she squeezed his hand. The deep-eyed gaze was electrically fervent and sincere. "I love you. I want to keep you interested."

It rattled him, never knowing what she was going to do next. As for keeping him interested, he was in a permanent state of excitement that was harrowing and fatiguing. When she was away on one of her trips for Southern, he sometimes collapsed on her queen-sized brass bed in blessed relief. But before the night was over he would be missing her, feeling a hurtful emptiness in the chest, wondering where she was if she had not called him, which she always did if she could get to a telephone. Her encyclopedic

knowledge of sexual pleasure disturbed him. A girl wasn't supposed to know all these tricks. He wondered jealously if Spurgeon
had been the master teacher and she the prize pupil. He took to
making disparaging remarks about that poor old fish Sturgeon, as
he liked to call him.

One night he was lying there in a lathered daze on her big bed
after a bout of lovemaking.

"No wonder Sturgeon's hair began to fall out," he said.

She was hurt, bewildered, by this remark. She wore many rings
on her long beautiful fingers—an amethyst, a big diamond, a good
turquoise, antique spoon rings that had been her grandmother's.
She clutched his hand so hard the rings made his bones smart.

"Are you jealous? Don't be jealous of Spurgeon. I didn't even
know you then. I love you, traveler. Nobody else. I love you more
than my own life."

Now why didn't that settle him down? It just made him feel
more uncomfortable. Just what did he want from her anyway? All
that passion and no experience? All that love and no expectations?
It was puzzling. Love was the consolation prize, the thing people
settled for when they didn't know what to make of their lives. But
he knew where he was going. He was a ballplayer. This woman
wanted equal time. She acted like it was normal, natural, to drag
around a whole lot of emotional baggage. She would have been
amazed to learn he worried that maybe love would make him half
a step slower, or dim his eye, or flaw his concentration. So it was
a good time, but it was damn worrisome too.

One afternoon after a tough day on the field, he bought Blue a
newspaper cone full of daisies at the florist. He entered the apartment and passed through the still kitchen, eager to get to the couch
and his newspaper. A drink would do him nicely too.

"Blue!" he shouted.

A man sat on the couch reading *his* newspaper. He had a dark
moustache, pale blue eyes, a blonde balding head dominated by
a huge bony forehead latticed with blue veins at the left temple.
He was thin—the word was *emaciated.* Ward took him to be about
fifty. He got up quickly with a friendly air when Ward came in.
He brushed himself off, his hand moving quickly and lightly over
his double-breasted navy blue blazer and the thighs of his white
duck trousers. He fixed the little knot of his blue-and white rep
tie, a fussy little Ivy League sort of tie.

"Hello there." He extended a small well-manicured hand. "You must be Ward."

"Who the hell are you?"

"I'm Spurgeon McCall, Bluette's friend from New York."

"What are you doing here? Where's Blue?"

Spurgeon let his hand fall to his side. He flexed his fingers. He was still smiling under his moustache. "Calm down," he said. "There's nothing to be upset about. She just went out for a few minutes to shop for dinner. It'll give us a chance to get to know each other a little."

Ward slumped into a cane-back chair by the fireplace, still dumbfounded. He wondered how long Sturgeon and Blue had been carrying on this reacquaintance.

"Why don't you go put those flowers in a vase? You look a little silly sitting there holding them in your fist," said Spurgeon.

Ward looked at the flowers, foreign, bright little creatures, which he laid on the floor by the chair.

"How long you been in town?" he asked Spurgeon.

Spurgeon read his mind.

"I just got in," he said. "I called Bluette from the airport. She didn't know I was coming. It's as big a surprise to her as it is to you."

He beamed at Ward as if it were a good joke and smiling would help him get the point. He looked a little like the old tintypes of General Custer, only with less hair.

"So you're Bluette's young man," said Spurgeon.

"So you're the old fart she used to go with," said Ward.

That put his lights out.

"You're pretty abrasive, aren't you? Let's not make this ugly."

"I don't like that 'young man' stuff like I'm still in short pants," said Ward. "You're sitting here when I come in the door. You're the past as far as I'm concerned, a part of Blue's life I don't want around. And you don't want me to make this ugly? I tell you, Sturgeon, you haven't seen anything yet."

"Please," Spurgeon shook his head, his eyes shut, denying the reality of this behavior. "There's no reason to make threats."

"I'm not making threats," said Ward. "I don't make threats."

Spurgeon's pale blue eyes, round as a pigeon's, carefully examined Ward and saw that he didn't.

"Suppose you state your business," said Ward.

Again Spurgeon smiled, only there was a crack in it this time. He was a little nervous. "When I knew Bluette in New York I was a mess. I'm alcoholic. I can say that now, admit it to myself. I've been on the wagon for over a year. I've got myself under control again."

"Well, that's nice," said Ward. "You came all the way to Louisville to say that?"

"No," Spurgeon said. "I came here to ask Bluette to marry me." He said this quietly with surprising dignity. He looked at Ward. "I've always loved Bluette. I've loved her for years. It's only now that I have myself under control that I feel I can ask her to marry me."

"That's a nice speech, Sturgeon. Now why don't you fold up the newspaper and get the hell out of here. You might as well have stayed right in Connecticut."

"That's up to Bluette to decide, isn't it?" said Spurgeon.

This little skinny fellow seemed ready to hang on to the couch like a barnacle. Ward figured he might have to throw both man and couch down the stairs to get rid of him.

"No," he said. "It's not up to Blue, goddamn you. This is my life you're fooling with too. You sober up and find out you missed a good thing. Then you come down here, thinking you'll walk right in and grab a happy ending for yourself. To hell with other people's lives. Now you get out of here while you can still walk."

"Bluette invited me to dinner. I'm Bluette's guest," he said. His hands fluttered nervously against his jacket.

"I'll apologize for you," said Ward. "I'll tell her you developed a sudden case of indigestion."

"Look," said Spurgeon. "I don't want to cause you problems. But I love the girl. May I ask you something? How old are you?"

"What's that got to do with it?"

"Well, you're about twenty, I'd say. You look like a healthy young man. Bluette says you're a very talented baseball player. Someday you're going to be famous. Is that right?"

"That's right. Now get out," said Ward.

"You're twenty. You've got everything before you. I'm fifty— I've got maybe ten more good years. Fifteen, if I'm lucky. I'd like to spend them with Bluette. I'd make her happy. I'd do everything for her."

"So will I," said Ward.

"Look at it this way. In twelve years you'll be thirty-two. You're an athlete. You probably won't look much different than you do now. Bluette will be forty. She might look a lot older. It might be a little like having your mother tag along."

"You better reach for the door, Sturgeon," said Ward. "You're pushing me awful hard."

Spurgeon's eyes were suddenly full of tears. "Listen, son. I love the woman. You don't love her. No offense, but you're too young to know what you have. You want to make a career for yourself. Blue will just get in your way."

"Why don't you get on your feet," said Ward quietly. "Then if you say something especially funny, I can give you a ride across the room."

"Goddamn it, boy," said Spurgeon. "The woman's my last chance. What do you really care? You've got everything in front of you. At least give me a chance to talk to Bluette alone, let her make up her own mind."

The kitchen door slammed. Ward heard Blue deposit the paper bag of groceries on the kitchen table with a crumply thump. There was a pause. Then she strode into the room, smiling brightly. In this contest she was trying to win the prize for Best Personality.

"Hello, everyone," she said. "I guess you fellows have met by now."

"We've already met and parted company," said Ward. "Sturgeon here was just on his way out."

"You are?" she said. "What on earth for? We're going to have chicken Cerubi." She put a hand up quickly as if directing traffic. "You," she said to Ward. "You're having steak and fries. Come on, Spurgeon. Stay for dinner. We haven't had a chance to catch up on old times. There's a dozen people I want to ask you about."

"I guess it's inappropriate for me to stay, Bluette. Thank you anyway. Considering my reason for coming in the first place it's not realistic for us all to sit down and have dinner together."

"That's right. It's not realistic," said Ward. "You don't even *look* realistic."

"Shut up, Ward," said Blue. "Tell me. Why *did* you come here, Spurgeon?"

"It's simple. You must have guessed the minute you heard my voice on the telephone."

She smiled at him and said gently, "You came here because you love me."

"Yes," he said.

"You came here to ask me to marry you," she recited as if by rote.

"That's right, Bluette. I don't drink anymore. I got myself straightened out. I can offer you a good life now."

She put her hands on Spurgeon's who unconsciously had clasped his together against his breast.

"I will never forget this, Spurgeon. I will never forget that two years after New York, you came all the way to Louisville to say this."

"I take it," he said, "that your answer is no.

"I love him. I can't help it," she said. Neither one of them gave any sign that Ward was still in the room.

"He's just a kid," said Spurgeon.

"I know," she said. "It makes me feel pretty foolish sometimes."

"You know I'll treat you better than he will," he said.

"It doesn't matter, does it? When you're hooked, you're hooked." She leaned forward to kiss his pale hopeless cheek.

Spurgeon turned around and looked at Ward. He faced Bluette again and took both her hands. "A man would be mad not to marry you if he had the chance. If you ever change your mind, call me."

"It's a nice offer," she said. "But life moves on. Find a woman who loves you back, Spurgeon. There are plenty that will. You'll have a good time then."

Then old Sturgeon was gone, out the door.

"Well," she said sadly. "He's gone now. No chicken Cerubi tonight. He's gone forever." She looked at Ward. "I don't have any regrets. But to tell you the truth, it makes me feel older, now that all that is just history."

Later on that night she clutched him as he lay asleep next to her and startled him from oblivion.

"Don't leave me, traveler," she whispered. "Don't leave me now. You're all I've got left. Don't panic though. I'll get tough again. I'll be able to make it on my own after a while. But just don't leave me now." She began to cry.

He rolled over to take her in his arms. She punched him in the face.

"Hey," he said.

"You're just a kid," she cried. "Just a damn kid. I know you're going to leave me some day and break my heart."

"No, no," he crooned and held her till her shaking subsided, and they fell asleep.

S I X

ALL THE LOVEMAKING seemed to improve his eyesight, just the opposite of what he was afraid might happen. He saw the ball better than ever. Standing out in right field on a hot night with a circle of gnats above his cap in some dimly-lighted godforsaken ballyard with a bunch of yokels in the stands, he'd think of Blue, waiting for him back in Louisville. His skin would tighten all over and his heart would start to pound. Then he'd hear the crack of the bat and lope back toward the fence, easily, knowing he'd get there and reach up into the roar of the voices and come down with that little ball securely in his glove.

Hitting good, too. About that time he hit a third baseman in the chest with a batted ball and knocked him cold. The ball caromed out into left center. He made it into second base standing up. He went four-for-four that day, every hit a frozen rope.

An old lady came up to him as he headed for the bus after the game. She was dressed in shiny black, with an underglow of green. She reminded him of a crow.

"Are you Ward Sullivan?"

"All my life," he said, grinning.

"Would you sign my book?" She offered an old-fashioned autograph book, thick as a family Bible, with a gold clasp and tooled leather cover.

As he signed his name she said, "I've got all the big names in there—Babe Ruth, Ty Cobb, Hack Wilson—all the great ones. I've seen them play in all the parks—St. Louis, Chicago, New York. Followed some of them from the minors on up. You're the best-looking young hitter I've seen since Rogers Hornsby. You're going to be a great one." She shook her head and squinted at him, "Yes, a great one."

"Yes, m'am. I hope so. And thank you."

Shortly afterward, coming off a road trip for a long homestand, he suddenly stopped hitting. Never in his life had he been in anything like a slump. But now he went three, four, then five games without a hit or even a good cut at the ball.

"It's women," said Shaw. "They—"

"Don't tell me what they are," said Ward. Because he'd been listening uneasily to Shaw's babbling on the road, his stories about how a woman had shot up his talent for good and how bad luck and women all seemed bound up together.

He could still see the ball, the turning of the ball, knew where it would be, felt certain of the point of interception. But astonishingly, he would swing and miss it. Or pop it up. Or hit it weakly on the ground. It produced fresh amazement each time. Not only was it unprecedented, it was unnatural. He had always known where the ball was going a split second before he hit it—left field, right, or center—and he knew whether it was a base hit or not. Some instinct told him that. Now that instinct had vanished, and he had no knowledge of himself whatsoever. When he swung at a ball now he never knew what would happen, where before it had always been a certainty.

His teammates said nothing to him when he came back to the bench. Jesus Anduzar, the Cuban shortstop, crossed himself sometimes when Ward struck out at the plate. Jim Honeystill looked the other way and spit casually into the butt can. Elwood Flowers thumbed his glasses back up his nose. Wayne McLain scratched his armpit. They were a mite too casual. They knew they were witnessing something crazy. Ward sensed they were even gleeful, though they were losing games and falling back in the race for the pennant. Maybe they were relieved to see Sullivan hit weak grounders to first base, lift soft fly balls to medium left. It meant he was human after all. Now that he was scaled down to size, they didn't feel like a bunch of midgets anymore.

Only Shaw broke the taboo. One night, after a particularly bad game, Ward was dressing slowly. The relief pitcher, who was sitting down from him on the bench dressed in just his old-guy-type boxer shorts and a pair of white cotton socks, spoke up.

"That gal of yours—she's not keeping you up late, is she?"

"No she's not, Wally. Who the hell asked you anyway?"

"Okay, okay. Don't get testy. I'm just saying you're not sticking the ball anymore. You're just—"

"What are you hitting?"

"Say what?"

"I said: what are you hitting?"

"You know I ain't been to bat but twice all season."

"That's right," said Ward. "So don't tell me about hitting, you bald-headed bastard."

"Well, a pitcher sees things, son. He don't necessarily have to be a hitter to see 'em."

"Just never mind. I don't want to hear it."

"Okay, okay. Don't get sore about it."

"And one more thing. I don't want you to ever mention Blue again. I don't want you to ask how is she or nothing. Understand? Don't you even mention her again."

Shaw looked at him silently out of the sides of his eyes. The boisterous locker room had gradually quieted till the last of this was taken by the others in complete silence.

"You got it, Shaw?"

Shaw nodded almost imperceptibly. His sallow ascetic face was gloomy. His long skinny arms ended in a clumsy tangle of big fingers between his slack thighs. He bent his bald head to study the locker room floor, and his chin disappeared into the slack folds of his gun-blue skin.

Ward was madder than hell. He kicked his locker door shut. Shaw wasn't putting the whammy on *him*. Shaw attracted trouble and failure like a magnet collected iron filings. Son of a bitch was a loser. Who needed a fellow like that advising you about hitting or putting the whammy on your woman?

Ward tried to figure out what he was doing wrong, why his body had turned traitor. He was following the ball. He kept his bat back, his head down, his wrists and hips were right. He wasn't overstriding. Rudy Cleverdon said nothing to him about it, pretended with the others that nothing unusual was going on. Ward was tempted to go to him and ask him if he saw anything. But what the hell could Cleverdon tell him, Cleverdon who played parts of three seasons in the bigs and had a lifetime .239 batting average? Forget it.

Even though he wouldn't turn twenty-one till that fall he began to think about his body. Maybe he'd been abusing it too much. He studied it in the mirror. It was marble-hard all over, the muscles sculpted in bas-relief, the shoulders broad and sinewy, the stomach hard and scalloped, lean through the loins. Not like some of those clowns on the team who at twenty-one or twenty-two already had bellies that sagged slightly or carried an extra fifteen pounds of beef under the mistaken notion that extra flab gave them strength and stamina. Out the window of the team bus, he studied distant signs and could still read them when other people could hardly make out their outlines. An optometrist once told him that he had unusual eyesight.

"For most of mankind," the optometrist said, "a speeding baseball looks the size of a golf ball. For you probably the size of a grapefruit."

And so far as Ward could tell, it was still the same. The billboards and road signs clicked in as early as ever. He followed the ball as well as ever. He just didn't hit it. He just did not hit it.

He put in more running in the mornings, starting out before dawn. He sneaked out of the room—they were back on the road again—and ran through the silent streets of the medium-size southern cities they were passing through on this road trip. He wondered if it could be the long, jouncing bus trips. Maybe that caused some mysterious painless cramping of his body. His body wasn't meant to be at rest, to be still ever. It was made for motion, action, perpetual use. Always at home he ate standing up. He walked whenever he could. The brand-new 1955 yellow Cadillac which he'd received in February as the last installment on his bonus from Mr. Yawkey, owner of the Red Sox, remained on blocks in the garage. He rode Gordie's bike into town, rode it even in winter if the roads were clear, pumping up the hills as smoothly as any combustion engine. Silence in the streets, the calming sound of his measured footfalls and even breathing, all of it did him some good, but it did not help his game. He still could not hit.

He changed his diet. Maybe it was those vodka martinis and the olives stuffed with almonds. He cut back to one beer a day. He customarily had bacon, eggs, and coffee in the morning. He switched to wheat germ, fruit, and milk. He cut out steaks, fries, and salad. He started eating chicken, red snapper when he could get it, and oysters on the half shell. And he began eating desserts —ice cream, torts, cheesecake. Nothing dramatic happened. He still felt uncomfortable at the plate. When he got a hit it still felt accidental, not predestined.

Finally he had to decide it was Blue, just as Shaw had said. It couldn't be anything else. What else could it be? This woman had somehow unhinged his beautiful game. It was inescapable. Shaw was right. Women and baseball didn't mix. (Or was it that men and women didn't mix, that they were always certain to be in subtle opposition to the basic needs of the other? Was it the law of cosmic disharmony that Shaw had put his finger on?)

He went back to the three-room apartment they shared and started packing his bag. She took it silently for a few moments. Then she said, "What are you doing?" She was playing some records and in the background he could hear Teresa Brewer excitedly asking someone to put another nickel in the old nickelodeon.

"I'm getting out. I have to. Sorry, Blue. I can't get any rest here. I'm barely hitting .300. I've got to go somewhere and pull myself together."

"Look," she said. "Don't leave me now. Make it later if you have to. But not now. I can't take it. Okay? Is that a deal?"

When he said nothing, she said, "When will you be back?"

"I don't know. Soon. As soon as I start hitting again."

"It's not my fault," she said. "Why do you have to go? That won't make any difference. Why do you have to blame me?"

"No, it's not your fault. I just have to get away, Blue. It's not anybody's fault. I just have to get off by myself."

"No. Don't leave me. You can't. Ward, you can't do this to me. We love each other. Don't throw it away. I need you. You need me. Don't, baby, don't. It's like you're trying to kill me. Don't do it. Don't hurt me like this. I need you. I can help you. You don't have to run away."

"If I don't go, and I don't hit any better, I'm liable to kill you."

"Then kill me. You might as well kill me as leave like this."

He moved past her, but she grabbed at his neck and caught him off balance and they crashed to the floor, wrenching his throwing arm slightly. She was a strong girl, using all her strength to hold him down now.

"No," she sobbed. "You're not leaving me now. Not after all this."

She had her arms tightly around his neck. His face was crushed into the darkness of her robe. Slowly, with much effort, he disengaged her arms.

"No. No," she whispered fiercely. But he struggled to his feet and pinned her arms behind her, gave her a shove across the room, grabbed his bag and got out the door.

He was just a kid after all, like she and Spurgeon said. Kids believe in the magical properties of habit. As he went down the stairs, he felt nothing but relief. He didn't give one thought to the woman upstairs. He would go back to steak and fries and sleeping alone, confident that he would begin to hit again.

Downstairs he remembered his new fifty dollar ball glove was still on the closet shelf in the bedroom. That was part of the magic too. He had to go back for that.

He quietly opened the door to the apartment. She was nowhere in view. It was quiet, still as a sleeping house on Saturday morning. He started for the bedroom, spied the closed bathroom door, and was possessed by a terrifying certainty.

"Blue!" he shouted through the door. No answer. The door was locked. Blue never locked doors, never thought to, looked at him as if he were talking a foreign language when he asked if a door was locked.

"Blue!" he shouted, this time not expecting an answer but just making fearful outcry, certain some terrible and fateful act was in progress behind that door. He threw his shoulder into the door. The door jam splintered.

He was shouting something at the top of his lungs. The sound of his bellowing echoed in the little closet of tile as she clumsily fell or slipped off the edge of the tub, the bathrobe cord noosed around her neck jerking tight, and there she dangled spastically, trying to keep from clawing at her throat.

He bellowed, kept bellowing to keep from his brain the unbelievable scene of Blue hanging by the neck above the bathtub.

"No!" he shouted. Her thighs smashed into his belly as he grabbed for her. The two of them formed a tableau for an instant. Then the rod began to wrench loose.

"No," he grunted. His arms gripped her buttocks. His skull was planted between her breasts. She clawed at her throat. Slowly as in a slow-motion film, they began to cave in under their mutual weight to the accompaniment of wrenching metal and a shower of plaster. Halfway through this agonizing descent the rod gave way completely, and they slammed to the tile floor.

Ward's body thudded against her. Somehow she ended up under him, trapped helplessly under his weight, squeezed between

his flesh and bone and the cold tiles which ground against her
pelvis and shoulder blades. But her hands were free. Her breath
whistled and wheezed like the sound of the metal whistle in a
rubber pig's belly. She jerked loose the cord around her throat. Her
face was ashen; her eyes bulged as she sucked in air noisily. She
was at once as ugly and beautiful as he'd ever seen her.

"Are you all right?" he asked anxiously. She couldn't answer.
She sucked greedily for air.

He lay in the cradle of her body in the classic position for
intercourse. The buckled shower rod yoked his back. They remained in that position for some time, their heavy breathing the
only sound.

The cold tiles of the floor assumed a human warmth. As if the
position itself invoked passion, a strong sexual desire possessed
him. He pushed aside her robe and pulled down her pants and rode
her gently on the tiles. He cradled her close, his heart mingled with
both pain and joy at finding her still alive. Never did he feel so
tender towards her. Then he staggered into the bedroom leaving
her spread out on the floor with a smile on her face. After a short
time she joined him. He put his arms around her and she huddled
close to the curve of his body. His member rested against her
buttocks. He marveled at the warmth that only two bodies together can make, that cannot be duplicated by any artificial means
whatsoever. Those who had electric blankets on their beds and fur
coats on their backs never really knew what it was to be warm.
And so they slept without a further word, but it was clearly
understood by both that he would not try to leave again, that he
had to give up using that kind of magic and think of something
else.

Strangely enough, the next day he began to hit again. He went
on a fabulous binge. He collected twelve hits in a row, a new
league record—the hits were spread over four games and intersp-
ersed with three walks. Twice he was hit by pitches (he led the
league in that department, too). He never said a word to the others,
treating this new incredible display of his prowess as casually as
had his teammates his equally incredible slump. His average began
to climb. He hit line drives all over the park, off the shinbones of
pitchers, so many shots right through the box that he added to his
reputation among pitchers as a killer, a career maimer.

Blue's crazy attempt at suicide drew them closer together, just

as an illness might, where you hold the head of your beloved as
she pukes and retches and you swab the shit off her buttocks and
smooth the dirty hair from her fevered brow. The scene in the
bathroom moved them closer, maybe both unwillingly, to that
country of humiliating knowledge where each knows the limits of
the other's body and spirit. And each one stands revealed, com-
pounded of simple beauty and complicated ugliness.

Once they talked about it. But only once. It was a secret between them, an embarrassing secret injury.

"I'm sorry," she said. "I'll never try that again. I just went to
pieces. Never again. It was a damn fool stunt."

"Yes, it was," he agreed. "You looked damned ugly in the middle of it, too."

"Be serious, traveler. I'll never do it again. Just stay with me for
a while. I'll be all right. I'll get strong again."

She looked at him, a keen piercing look full of pain. He thought
she was going to cry. But when she spoke her voice was steady.
"You have your baseball," she said. "That makes it okay for you.
If I knew what I was going to do after thirty, maybe I wouldn't
need you so much." She gave him a pat on the arm. "Don't worry.
I'll be all right."

Maybe they weren't so different in their opinion on the basic
subject. Love was a canker for the strong and a mustard plaster for
the weak. Or did she feel weak because he was traveling fast, and
she figured someday, before she was ready, he would find a way
to get rid of her? Maybe she was waiting to get through the fever,
for the mortifying passion to burn itself out, so she could go on
to more rewarding people who were interested in things other than
baseball and steaks and fries.

But he never thought about it then. Why would he think at all?
Why indulge that most disturbing of all the faculties? He had his
baseball, he had his uneasy and sometimes unpredictable love life.
And he was going to be famous. He made a point of not thinking.
It was a very rewarding way to live. All his assurance flowed from
his powerful and magic-making body. For the most part it was
wonderful.

Blue would not have been surprised to know that he really
missed her when she was away working for Southern. He didn't
much like the idea of her serving those fellows coffee, tea, and
milk while they made a grab for her as she moved down the aisle.

She was so beautiful it was hard for him to let her out of his sight, much less sleep alone in their bed which seemed so empty when she was out of town. On the other hand he didn't miss her at all when he was on the road and *she* was home alone. He had to force himself to keep up the one-postcard-a-day routine: *Dear Blue: How are you? I'm fine. I'm still hitting. Love, Traveler.*

She would not be surprised either to learn that he thought love was a burden. People were baggage if you had someplace to go. Lonely? You were never lonely if you believed in your destiny, believed you were made to do one thing really good. It charged your life with meaning and excitement. Only the weak and uninspired were lonely.

The last Saturday in August following an afternoon double-header, featuring between games a baton twirling contest for high school girls, Ward sat before his locker drinking a Budweiser and thinking with some satisfaction about his afternoon's work. In the first game: double to right, two runs batted in, run scored; single to center; double to left, RBI. In the second game he had three more doubles, three RBIs, a walk, a stolen base, and a run scored. Making five doubles on the afternoon, six RBIs and two runs scored. He was leading the league in almost every department. His average after today was something over.380.

"Sullivan."

It was Rudy Cleverdon, his big belly pressed drum-tight against his uniform and dangled dangerously over the edge of his leather belt. He straddled the doorway to his office, his fists on his hips. Ward had stepped off the bag early in the seventh inning of the first game, and the batter had been called safe. It cost the team a run and the game. Is that what this pea-shooter wanted to tell him?

"What is it, Rudy?"

"Come in my office," said the manager. "I want to talk to you."

The old fellow closed the door. He had his cleats off and was hobbling around in his stocking feet. He ran his blunt tobacco-colored hand from eyebrows to the back of his creased neck, encompassing a bald dome and a gray fringe of hair, a head largely denuded by forty-five years of ball caps. His brown face had more lines in it than a spiderweb. He looked at Ward. The baggy brown eyes took him in. He's got a stupid face, Ward thought. The face of a .239 lifetime hitter.

"Well, kid," Cleverdon said. "It's happened. You're right on schedule. They're calling you up to the bigs. You're supposed to join the ball club in St. Louis tomorrow."

Ward grinned. "It's a great day," he said.

"Yes, it is." Cleverdon spat in his paper coffee cup. "If you play it right you'll be up there to stay. Maybe fifteen, twenty years. You got the talent. No question. But I want to tell you something, kid. I don't know why I bother. You never listened to anything I told you yet. But I'm going to tell you anyway. You got a million-dollar body and a ten-cent head. You ain't stupid. You just don't listen."

Ward just looked at the old lined face. Cleverdon's wet mouth hung open slightly at the end of his sentence as he peered at Ward to see if any of this was sinking in.

"I seen Ted Williams come up. He wasn't no farther along than you at this stage. Maybe a little. He was a better outfielder than they give him credit for. And he ran the bases well even then. Always used his head.

"He was bullheaded too. Just like you. He knew what he wanted, knew just how he wanted to go about it. But he used to soak up information like a sponge. He'd listen to you talk about pitchers all day, what they threw on three and two, who was working on a slip pitch, and so forth. But you. You *never* listen. Now you play beautiful ball. But you run into fences and overrun bases and try shoestring catches and slide head-first into home plate. You throw bats, brawl with your teammates, and jaw at the umpires. You make your own teammates uneasy. See, Williams was proud and he had this temper like you. But he wasn't— dangerous. You understand what I mean?"

"No."

Cleverdon sighed. "I didn't think you would. Well, anyway, good luck. And one other piece of advice. Williams liked women too. But ballplaying always came first. Don't get off on the wrong foot. Show 'em you came to play ball, not to impress the ladies."

When Ward told Bluette the good news she was sitting on the couch, arms folded, legs crossed, in his white terrycloth bathrobe. It was nearly six o'clock in the evening and she had just gotten out of bed, after arriving home late the night before on a flight from El Paso.

"Well, it's happened," he said. "It's finally happened. Those people in Boston have come to their senses. They're bringing me

up. I'm supposed to join the team in St. Louis tomorrow. They
should have kept me in the spring, damn them. But I forgive them
everything. I'm going to get up there and make them *sad* they
didn't have me all year." He pounded his fist into his open hand.
"I always knew I was going to make it! I knew it! I've waited so
damn long it seems. And I'm only twenty. But I've waited sixteen
years already."

He'd been looking at her all this time but not seeing her. He kept
on babbling, but now he started watching her. Behind her blank
blue irises, he saw the panic setting in. He kept on babbling. He
figured if he babbled fast enough he could outrace her panic, circle
it, and drive it off.

She lighted an Old Gold and began to blow smoke all over the
room. She crossed her legs and wiggled her foot and flicked ashes
all over his robe. She kept her eyes on him, said nothing, and let
him babble.

"Well, what the hell is wrong?" he finally blustered. "Here I am
on the verge of it and you sit there like stone. You haven't said
a word."

"I don't know what to say," she said finally. "What am I supposed to say?"

"I'd like to know what you think. I'd like to have you say
something like congratulations or kiss my ass or something."

"Okay. Congratulations. I'm happy because this is your big
moment. This is what you want. But I'm scared too. Because
maybe this means the end of us."

"What do you mean?"

"I mean, I guess you're going to do this on your own, aren't
you?"

"Yes," he said. "This is something I have to do on my own."

"Well, go do it then," she said.

He still had his ball cap on. He ripped it off his head and threw
it across the room.

"Look," he said. "It's just for a month or so. It's my big break.
I can get up there and get off to a good start. Then I'll be back here
when the season ends."

"No, you won't. You won't come back here." It scared him the
way she looked at him when she said this. As if she were giving
the weather report.

"I'll be back in a month or so. It's no big deal," he said. "Don't

act like that. It's my big chance. It's what I *was made for,* don't you
understand? I'm not leaving you. I'll be back."

Now probably he could have married her, or they could have
worked out some other deal. But he really meant it when he said
this was something he had to do on his own. He was young and
he was an American man. He had been brought up to think that
if you had anything important to do you did it alone or with a few
select male friends. He was just a kid. No matter how much he
loved her he couldn't see how she figured in this. It would just be
for a month or so, he figured. He was naturally a little nervous, and
he needed some time to himself. He couldn't worry about women
and apartments, cats and dogs. He wanted to think about nothing
but baseball. Think about that ball clocking anywhere between
eighty and one hundred miles per hour, and put that baby against
that Green Monster in left field. Blue could see the handwriting
on the wall. She was older and more experienced. She probably
knew him better than he knew himself.

He was getting mad. She's making a big deal out of this, he
thought. She's trying to force me to choose between her and baseball. By God, he thought, if she pushes me I know what my choice
will be. He was trying to work himself into a state of self-right-
eous anger.

But he wasn't fast enough. In the meantime she was coming
unseamed. She'd done a pretty good job of taking it calmly, albeit
a little grimly, but she just wasn't in shape to handle it. She still
needed him too much. She jumped off the couch and grabbed him
by the neck suddenly and jerked him off his feet. Damn good thing
he'd taken his cleats off in the kitchen. Otherwise she would have
snapped him off right at the ankles. She began to cry. "Don't leave
me," she said. "I love you. You said you'd never leave and now
you are. Don't. Don't. It hurts so much."

They were on the floor. The front of his uniform shirt was wet
and smudged with her eyeliner. He thought of the time she tried
to hang herself in the shower. He was afraid she might try something dumb like that again. She promised she'd never do anything
like that again. But he couldn't be sure. Poor Blue. She was really
a mess, and this was supposed to be a happy day. Her body
shuddered against his as she cried.

I'm trapped, he thought. What can I do? A flicker of hatred for
her passed through him. Why couldn't she just stay here in Louis-

ville while he went to Boston and put it together? Why did she have to make such a mess of it? But still, he couldn't take her crying like that. It hurt to hear her cry, such a heartbroken and lonely sound.

"Okay," he smoothed her rich hair back from her temple. "Stop now. You're coming with me. We'll figure out something."

"Oh God, I'll be good, Ward. You won't be sorry. I love you so much. We'll have such a good time. You don't have to marry me or anything. It'll be good. I'll call work tomorrow and give them notice. Kathleen can clean up this place. She'll be happy to do it. I can be with you in two weeks."

"Don't you have to give them more notice than that?"

"Two weeks," she said. Her face was shiny with tears. She was so beautiful. He couldn't say or do anything but hold her close.

"I'll leave you alone," she whispered huskily, her words hot against his throat. "I won't be any trouble. As soon as I get a little stronger and I'm able to handle it, we'll talk about whether I stay or not."

"That's all right," he smoothed back her hair. "I've made up my mind. You're coming with me."

It was un-American but he was going to try to grow up. He felt good about this decision for about five minutes. In his chest his heart hung heavy as a dead pheasant in a hunter's game bag.

In honor of Ward going up to the big club, Jesus Anduzar was going to uncork his famous bottle of Mexican firewater which had a dead worm floating in the bottom of it. The little send-off party that night was supposed to be just for the team. But he decided to take Blue and to hell with them if they didn't like it, which certainly Shaw and Cleverdon and some of the others wouldn't. He wondered if his reputation for being a bad ass would follow him around the way it had Hack Wilson. A dozen writers and ex-ballplayers were still pissed off enough to keep him out of the Hall of Fame.

They'd fooled around so long he didn't even have time to change out of his uniform. He just pulled on an old pair of sneakers, and Blue had to comb her hair in the car. It was raining anyway, and she always liked to have him drive when the roadway was wet. They were a little late getting there.

"Hey! Hey!"

The fellows made a big fuss when they walked into the private dining room of the restaurant. They had a nice bar set up on a table, chips and pretzels, and red plastic chairs all around the edge of the room.

"Who's the ballplayer?" somebody wanted to know.

"He always wears his uniform," said Wayne McLain. "Don't you know that? That way if a ballgame breaks out of a sudden, he's ready."

Some of the fellows guffawed over that.

"Never mind the ballplayer," said Lamont Baltimore. "Who's the *movie star?*"

Lamont was enthusiastic about Blue. "Hey! All right, man! Scored again! Safe at home! A real .400 hitter! All right!" Lamont gave it his full piano keyboard grin.

He was getting some laughs so he kept it up. "The man won the home run hitting contest," he said to Big Jim. "He won the money, the trophy, *and* the girl. Now he gets to go to the bigs. He didn't leave you *nothin,* man."

That got Lamont another laugh as Honeystill just stood there, big as a bear, bashful, and tongue-tied.

Elwood Flowers put an arm around Ward's shoulders. "Now Jesus will let that worm out of the bottle. He wouldn't open the bottle till you got here."

"Is there really a worm in that bottle?" asked Blue.

They crowded around to see her reaction. Jesus, small and dark, altogether wrong for shortstop since he was almost a midget, held up the bottle and smiled. "*Si.* There ees a worm. But he won' hurt you. He's dead," he explained gently.

"Oh, my God!" gasped Blue. "There really is a *worm* in there."

Jesus looked like his feelings were hurt.

"Uncork that girl and give me a touch of the worm," said Wayne McLain.

Jesus did so eagerly, as if anxious to restore the honor of the worm. He filled half a dozen glasses with the clear, powerful-looking liquid. The worm remained at rest in the bottom of the bottle.

"I swear," said Wayne McLain wiping his lips quickly with the back of his hairy hand, "that stuff's poison. No wonder the worm is dead."

They went through Jesus' bottle in good time, despite all the jokes about it. At the end Jesus poured the worm into his own glass and picked him out and, holding him with some elegance between two dark fingers, ate him like a canape.

"Oh God, Jesus!" cried Blue. "How could you?"

"Ees good," explained Jesus politely. "Crispy like a potato cheap."

As the party really got going, Ward spotted Shaw sitting in a corner by himself.

He went over to him. "Come on, you old fart. Why don't you join the fun?"

"I can see everything from here, right fine, thanks."

"Well, suit yourself, Wally."

"You taking that girl along with you?"

"Yes, I'm taking her. What of it?"

"Well, she's mighty pretty. I wish you luck."

"You want to ride back into town with us later?"

"Obliged, but no thanks. I like to walk. Gives me time to think."

"Hell, it's raining out, Wally. You can't walk back to town tonight."

"I walk in all kinds of weather, son. I got my rainhat, my raincoat. I like to walk. It's peaceful, just walking along thinking your thoughts. No offense."

Well, he was a funny old duck. What could you expect from an old no-talent who'd played nothing but baseball all his life? The party really got going. At some point Wally managed to sneak out. Nobody missed him. He wasn't the kind you missed.

Ward tried to relax and have a good time. But it was hard. He was plenty tense about it all—going up to the bigs, the deal with Blue. How the hell was he going to manage everything? He drank plenty.

"You ought to slow down," Blue said at one point, patting his hand.

You ought to knock it off, he thought and continued to drink more than his share. By the time the party broke up, he was pretty morose.

It was still raining when they started back to the apartment in the Studebaker. And as they rode along silently he suddenly worked it out.

Blue was going to sleep soundly tonight, no question. She was asleep now. He would throw a few things in a bag and sneak out. He'd be on his way to St. Louis before she'd even wake up. He'd leave her a note, tell her it was best this way. He'd explain he needed to get his feet on the ground. Don't worry, he would say, I'll be back for you after the season, maybe even take you along if I play Caribbean ball next winter. He was sure she'd understand after she thought it over. This plan cheered him up considerably.

Suddenly as they approached an overpass, a shadowy rain-drenched figure—was it a man in a raincoat and hat?—staggered onto the road, just discernable in the rain-blurred beam of the headlights. He jerked the wheel of the car to avoid the lurching shadow. The Studebaker began to slide. He tried the brakes but it made no difference. He saw they were going to hit the concrete bridge. The next sensation was one of flying, but his head felt hot and there was a large object turning in the air beside him.

When he regained consciousness, the rain was pummelling his face. The copious thick blood in his mouth tasted like snot. He looked around blindly but couldn't find Blue.

"Blue! Hey, baby! Help me! I'm hurt," he cried out. But there was no answer. He knew he was busted up pretty good. Then he passed out again.

He woke up under the lights in the emergency room at the hospital as they were cutting the uniform off him. His face hurt like hell and they were doing something awful to his legs. He wondered if his balls were gone. He felt damp down there. He wanted to scream, but they had something in his mouth. Then he passed out again.

When he came to after the operation, he asked how Blue was. They wouldn't tell him anything. But he knew. They didn't have to tell him.

The nurse said, "Your family will be here tomorrow to see you."

He didn't say anything.

And she said, "Is there anything I can do for you?"

"Yes," he said. He talked slowly and painfully. His mouth and lips were full of stitches, his jaw was wired, most of his teeth had been knocked out and it all hurt like hell. "My wallet. Picture of a girl. Tear it up. Throw it away. Get me a bottle of vodka. Then stay the hell out."

But she didn't do any of those things for him. When he was able several weeks later, he fumbled the picture out of his wallet himself. He took one last look at the flawless face, the incredibly beautiful eyes and the high cheekbones, the movie star smile. And he tore the picture into small pieces. But he couldn't quite bring himself to throw those pieces away. Instead he put them in an envelope in the drawer of the bedside table.

Some of the ballplayers came in to see him. Elwood Flowers came two or three times—but most of the others only came once. He understood that. Now that he was all gooned up, he was one of the game's untouchables. Besides Ward didn't feel much like having any company. Elwood told him Wally Shaw quit the team the day after the accident and headed for who knows where.

"He's probably playing ball down in Mexico," said Elwood.

Was Shaw the slouching figure on the road that night? Did Ward really see anything at all or was it just the booze and a trick of the rain? He was mildly surprised to discover that he didn't care if he knew for sure or not.

One day for five dollars he persuaded a practical nurse to bring him a bottle of vodka. He drank that bottle quietly, lying in bed late one night, trying not to think about any of it. His leg and hip itched under the cast and his whole body still ached as if he'd been beaten up. His eyesight was still blurred, but he could make out the shapes of things pretty good. He drank that bottle. He thought of Blue. He couldn't help it. He thought of the way the dark hair brushed back from her temple and the way her eyes seemed to see into him. He thought of how beautiful she was and how other men had envied him. He thought of his .386 batting average and the baseball season now ended, forever past and done with. He drank all that bottle.

Well, he thought, now you don't have to choose between Blue and baseball. There's nothing to choose from anymore.

S E V E N

The days passed in a haze. It was pleasant really. A sensation of slow movement accompanied by windblown fragments of music. Ward often woke with a smile on his face, coming back from a wonderful dream country he could almost remember. The smile opened the hot pain in his lips where surgeons had sewn together the shreds of his former mouth.

"Looks like a dog bit you right in the mouth, friend."

This one sentence came clear through the rushing haze of unsound, the slow delicious burning of lights, the deathlike sleep, the fugitive memory of distant music.

Then another: " 'Cept the lacerations are clean. But don't you worry. You'll have a fine new mouth when we're through with you."

The confident, smiling face of the intern floated like a balloon against the ceiling. The intern was taking Ward's pulse and talking at the same time. The pressure of the man's cool fingers against his steady pulse felt good. His sight blurred on the edges, but he could see this unblemished idiot talking confidently of a new mouth.

A new mouth.

Ward tried to speak but found that he couldn't. He was in a new place of understanding beyond the power and meaning of words. He looked at the intern's smiling face, stupid with youth and inexperience, and felt a profound contempt for him. A tube protuded from Ward's nose and another was taped into his mouth not unlike that saliva sucker at the dentist's. He was sheathed in a body cast from his chest down to his left ankle. He could tell by the delicate touch of the sheet that his right leg was free. A pain, subtle and deep, gnawed just under his heart. Gnawed and stopped; then gnawed again. The picture of the intern clouded over as the pain in the left side of his face took over. His cheek-

bone had been crushed. They'd gone in through his mouth to fix
it up. His jaw was busted in three or four places, too. But he didn't
know all this at the time. The pain in his face, as paralyzing as any
toothache, blotted out the image of the young unblemished doctor. At the same time his contempt dissolved, and as it did he got
to a place beyond the pain.

"Don't leave me," she cried. "Don't leave me here."

It was Blue.

Her voice was clear but frightened. She was bathed in a golden
light. He was centered somewhere outside of it. It was like she was
locked in a room. He could hear and see her, but he couldn't speak.
She knew he was out there, but he couldn't get through the wall.
There was nothing he could do to help her. It made him feel bad,
really bad.

"What am I going to *do?*" she cried. She put her hands to her
face. Her long dark hair slipped forward. The picture of her was
familiar and beautiful at the same time. He did not like to leave
her there where she was unhappy, but there was nothing he could
do.

He opened his eyes.

There was his father looking down at him. The handsome open
face, the texture of the skin, the muscle tone—nothing in the face
showed him to be in his forties. He looked so damned young, so
unmutilated by life. Gazing rapturously into the face of his father,
Ward felt safe, as though now that his father was here he was
beyond any real danger.

"Hello, boy," the old man gripped Ward by the forearm. Ward
tried to smile but his burning lips stopped him. The ceiling formed
an eggshell background in contrast to his father's smiling dark
head. His face shone brightly in the Kentucky humidity, glowing
highlights on the fine forehead and along the right edge of the
perfectly straight nose. Everything was terribly bright and clear,
suffused with a crystaline menace. His father's head was surrounded by a circle of cool light, faint blue in tone. The ceiling
feathered off into dove-gray shadows at the edges. Everything had
the special clarity usually reserved for a baseball spinning toward
him. Never had he seen people and ordinary objects with such
intensity. This is what it's like to be almost dead, he thought. This
clarity lasted about an hour one day and then his eyesight relapsed
into a bright swarming sea of granules, like a snowy TV picture.

"Hello, Dad," he croaked. He could have cried, he was so happy to see the old man again.

"Hey, Ward. Hey."

Gordie's four-eyed face popped into the picture. Tiny ears like rosebuds stuck out from the sides of the narrow block of his blonde-skinned head. The kid's eyes were full of tears. It was like being at your own funeral.

"Your mother's not well." His father's strong fingers continued to knead Ward's forearm. Understand, the fingers said. Understand. "She wanted to come. But I was afraid the trip would be too much for her. She sends her love."

Sure. Poor old Sarah couldn't make it. No question it was too much for her. Some days she couldn't find her way to the bathroom without help. Lots of times she'd lean on Althy, and they would stagger like a comedy team towards the plumbing.

One time he watched her fumble numbly for fifteen minutes trying to open a letter as she sat at the kitchen table. Her fingers crawled blindly over the envelope looking for a seam. At last she put the envelope on the table, snapping it down with her thumb like a card played emphatically. She pulled her bathrobe tight around her melting throat and averted her face.

"Some days," she said meekly. "My fingers just won't work." The dumb face with its lowered lids and its gone-to-seed loveliness filled him with an icy rage. It was all he could do to keep his hand from snapping out and wiping the meekness off the chalky face.

It was no surprise she couldn't throw a few things in a suitcase and get to the airport. The airport, not to mention Louisville, was a long way from bed. He was just as happy it had worked out this way. The sight of her weak hothouse face always made him mad, and he was too busted up to deal with it.

"How you feeling?" asked Gordie.

"Not so bad, hotshot. How about you?" Ward painfully spit each word through the wired jaws.

"Not so good," Gordie said. "I think I'm going to be—"

A face like Sarah's lived just below the surface of Gordie's mobile features. It was this face that flickered to the surface as he stumbled into the bathroom.

"Your brother can't take hospitals," said the old man. "He

wanted to come see you so badly. Even though he knew he'd probably faint or puke."

Ward started to laugh and so did the old man. Ward laughed very carefully, going heh-heh but it still hurt. It felt like a scalpel was lodged in his chest just under the skin, and every time he laughed it created a sharp piercing pain.

"The girl in the car," the old man asked. "Was she—a close friend?"

How could he tell the old man through the wired jaws and the pain? No, she wasn't a friend. We loved each other. We were at war. She screwed up everything. I needed her and hated her at the same time. She kept me up late at night when I should have been getting my rest. If not for her I would have spent my nights dreaming about the ball zipping in and how the eye and the mind, fully concentrated, made that glowing white ball look as slow as a toy balloon and big as a grapefruit. I would have been hitting to all fields in my dreams. But she got in my way. She breathed in my face and hogged the bed. She wanted to make love at three o'clock in the morning and again at seven o'clock. I'd drag myself to the ballpark, weak as a cat. She'd come to a ballgame sometimes, and as I stood at the plate she'd scream as if she'd been shot every time the pitcher released the ball. I'd want to go over there and punch her right in the mouth to shut her up. She thought she was just showing me what a big fan of mine she was.

In the mornings when I was looking at the sports page to see how Larry Doby and Al Rosen were hitting them, she'd fall across my lap with her face full of toast to give me a kiss and tell me with a smile full of bread how she loved me. The smell of her hair and her skin would make me giddy. She'd give me that movie-star smile as she got up to tend to the eggs. My heart would hurt, wanting her so bad. I'd look down and the sports section would be all crumpled to hell in my lap. That was Blue, loving me, screwing things up, busting me down, making me admit that I loved her too. She probably cost me six or seven hits on the season, with her loyal banshee act.

Goddamn her to hell anyway. He had never wanted her to count for so much. Now that beautiful girl was dead. In his mind he kept seeing the slow magic smile awaken the flawless face. God. She was beautiful. How could she be dead when he loved and hated her so much? Through the wired pain he could not explain this to the old man anymore than he could explain it to himself. So he just nodded. That's right. She was a friend.

"I'm really sorry," his father said.

Good old Dad, feeling miserable about the loss of someone he never knew. What would Shaw say if he were here? "That gal of yours—too bad," he might offer solemnly. The old relief pitcher's sallow face would collapse on his chest in gun-blue folds as he lost himself in his gloomy thoughts. But what Shaw would mean was that what happened was no more than what could be expected.

You turn around and there stands a crazy person with a gun just aching to shoot away your kidney.

You get a call from the big club. It starts to rain, the road slicks up, and you run your talent into a cement wall and kill your girl to boot.

Too bad, Shaw would say.

"How you feel?" asked the old man. "Good enough to read your mail? We got a bunch of cards and letters here. Here's one from the Red Sox. You want me to open it?"

Ward shook his head yes.

The old man's jaw fell open about halfway through the letter. Ward knew all along what it was going to be. The old man probably thought it was a personal get-well message from Tom Yawkey himself. It was a message all right. Ward recognized the pink form as his father unfolded it and began to read it innocently. It was his unconditional release. Goodbye, baby. We don't need no busted-up outfielders with body casts and wired jaws. The shocked expression on his father's face was almost comical. Ward felt the searing pain of a smile twitching on his lips.

"It's okay," he said. "I know what it is."

His father blinked back the tears. "Goddamn bastards," he choked out. "I picked out the one I thought would cheer you up the most. I picked a good one, didn't I?"

"What the hell," said Ward, his lips twitching. But he was thinking: I'll make them pay for that. They think I'm through. But I'm not.

"Listen, boy," his father said. "I'm going to get you home as soon as possible. As soon as they say you're able, I'll hire an ambulance and get you home."

The old man just let the rest of the mail sit. Once burned, twice a fool, is the way he figured it. When Ward was well enough, he tackled it himself.

Elwood Flowers came to see him again after the playoffs, before going back to Oklahoma for the winter.

"You're looking better this week," he said. "I never did see such a swollen cut-up face. Now you look almost normal. Wayne said you look like a Jap who was put through the meat grinder."

Ward carefully went heh-heh-heh.

"Can you see any better?" asked Elwood.

"Better," Ward said. "Better now."

"I talked to one of your docs last week. He says he figures your eyesight will be just fine again one day. Jesus asked me to bring you this," Elwood held up a bottle with a worm in it. "He couldn't come himself."

Elwood put the bottle in the drawer of the nightstand. "That's so the nurses don't complain," he said. "Big Jim says he's quitting. Says he's going to buy into a bowling alley down in Denison. He says when you get old this game gets too sad. Shit, I'll bet he'll be back in the spring. Don't you?"

"Yes," Ward whispered.

"I mean what's that big sapsucker going to do if he doesn't play ball?"

"Well," he said getting up. Elwood rubbed the back of his head. "I know you can't talk much through those wires and you're supposed to get all the rest you can. So I'll be on my way. I just thought I'd stop and see you before I head to Oklahoma. My Dad isn't feeling too good this year, so I promised I'd help him punch cows this winter. No winter ball for me."

"Thanks, Elwood," spit out Ward. "Thanks for stopping."

"Have a drink for me out of that bottle," said Elwood.

Ward nodded.

"Thanks, Elwood."

"Hell, boy. You get out of that turtle shell. You'll be back on a ballfield in no time. You know that. Nothing's going to keep you down, is it? Hell, no."

Elwood gripped Ward's hand and grinned at him and then he was gone.

It was five weeks before he was well enough to travel. In the meantime he floated. When he had too much pain they gave him medication. Then the movies started to roll. In the darkened theater of his mind he watched himself star in these dreamy productions. There he was—good gravy!—dressed in Yankee pinstripes, in the on-deck circle. The crowd was roaring. He recognized the place. It was Fenway Park. Tom Yawkey sat in his field box with his hair parted in the middle, the heavy face, the squinty blue eyes, looking like a cretin. George Susce, the Red Sox pitcher, struck out Andy Carey, the Yankee third baseman. The crowd roared its approval. The Yankee runner at first stood on the bag with his hands on his hips. The scoreboard showed two out and the Red Sox leading by one run.

Susce started off Ward with a fastball inside that wouldn't put a dent in a pat of butter. The next pitch, the whole thing, the windup, everything, was in slow motion. The ball spun out of Susce's fingers turning over slowly. The ball broke about knee high but away. He saw it good all the way and got all of it. The ball, brilliant white in the lights, arched high in the air above the field and disappeared over the Green Monster. Ward grinned at Mr. Yawkey as he sat glumly in his box like a defendant who'd just heard the judge say, "Guilty." Ward started down to first base. The fans up from New York were going nuts. Norm Zauchin faked indifference as Ward touched the bag at first. He heard a familiar loony scream: *Wheeee!* The sound a happy kid might make on a roller coaster. He looked up and there was Blue, in a box behind first, jumping up and down, her long dark hair in tumult. " 'Ray, hero," he heard her cry. He was glad she was here to see him put it to the Red Sox.

Suddenly as he rounded second he was in the dark, in a dark tunnel. In the distance, he could see the green of the diamond. He ran toward the light but the tunnel went on forever. His hip began to hurt. His breath came in short, searing gasps. He needed to rest for a minute to catch his wind. He sat down on the bar stool but he didn't want a drink. A ballplayer had to keep his body clean and tuned. No more booze. This was his second chance. He wasn't going to mess it up with booze. Next to him sat Wally Shaw. Wally was staring into the bottom of his glass, looking sour as usual.

"Hey, Shaw, how'd you like that homer?"

"Sullivan!" Shaw looked surprised then almost happy.

"How'd you like that hit, Shaw?"

"Listen, son. What do you expect me to say? I'm a *pitcher*, re-member?"

Ward laughed and that was the end of the movie. It was a lot of fun to go to the movies. It was fun to see Blue alive again and Shaw looking sour, and to see the ball real good and whale hell out of it.

The movies stopped after they took him off the medication.

His father often flew down to Louisville to see him. Until school opened in the fall, Gordie came along. At the Rhode Island School of Design, the kid would cultivate his great and mysterious talent for drawing naked people. In his junior year he grew a sparse orange goatee. It cost the old man a bundle for that portfolio of naked people and that drought-stricken goatee, but he acted like he got his money's worth. Sarah never did make it down to Louisville. She was always laid up on the shelf. She and her bed were like wallpaper and glue and that's where she stayed. Just too sick to bestir herself. The old man's lame excuses were embarrassing. He finally stopped trying to alibi for Sarah, and Ward was glad he did. Althy wrote him from Maine nearly every day on little sheets of linen paper in her spidery hand. Back in those days she was still living in the old house in Dunnocks Head, even though it took every penny she had. She spent the worst of the winter in Carlisle and lit out for Maine again at the first sign of a spring thaw. She wrote she was coming down early this year to help out when he was able to come home. Good old Althy. You could count on her to lend a hand among the maimed and injured. She had a talent for it.

On his last trip just before he went off to school, old skinny, four-eyed Gordie showed up with a package and a big grin.

"I bought you a present," he said, and laid it on the plaster cast that encased Ward's chest.

It was a baseball game, complete with the names of all the big league players on individual pasteboard cards covered with columns of red and blue numbers. It had play boards with all the possible base situations, and it had a sacrifice booklet, the last page of which showed you what happened if you tried hit and run. Dice came with it and little yellow tube-like dice cups. There was also a diamond printed in bright green and yellow on a piece of cardboard and red tiddledywinks to put on the bases to show where the runners were. The literature claimed that the game was a statistically accurate representation of the real thing, based on the performance of the players for the season involved. You could buy a new set of players' cards in the winter following each season.

"What do you think?" The kid was grinning from ear to ear.

Ward smiled back at him with his new lips. He wondered if they would stay numb like this forever.

"Thanks, kid. It looks great."

He no sooner said this than he fell asleep with the game box across his chest. He was weak, feeble, easily disposed to sleep. Sleep never felt so good, so luxurious. One second he would be awake and the next he'd go under again. He slept sixteen hours a day for the first month. The nurse would come in and wake him to help him shift from side to side and on to his back again so he wouldn't develop bed sores. He was weak as a kitten, and he needed help on and off the bedpan too.

He didn't have the strength to shift to his stomach. Besides he was scared. He didn't trust the nurse who helped him. She didn't look very damn strong. If he started to fall, she'd never be able to catch him. He was afraid he'd get halfway through the tortoiselike maneuver, lose his grip on the trapeze, fall to the floor, and shatter into a thousand pieces.

The cast cut across his chest just above his nipples and went down to his groin and buttocks. It encased all of his left leg except the five toes which were as ghostly white as fungi on the forest floor. The cast was hot and itchy. His skin was slimy. After a few weeks he'd catch a whiff of horrid putrefaction as he shifted around. It scared him silly. What if the damned cast cut off his circulation and caused gangrene? The only one-legged ballplayer he had ever heard of was Monty Stratton who had lost his leg in a hunting accident after the 1938 season. Of course there was Pete Gray who came up with the Browns during World War II and played a little outfield even though he only had one arm. None of this was good to speculate about. He was going to mend together into one piece again.

Mr. Coombs used to tell a story about Smoky Joe Wood. Smoky Joe was a great young pitcher for the Red Sox back when Mr. Coombs was pitching for the Philadelphia Athletics. At twenty-one or twenty-two, Smoky Joe won something like twenty-nine games. Everybody said he was the fastest, that he threw not baseballs but threw not baseballs but aspirin tablets. He was a hero. Everywhere he pitched crowds came to see him. One time, when he faced Walter Johnson, who was probably the best pitcher ever, the crowd was so big they roped off the foul lines and let the people right down on the field to watch these two giants face each other. Wood beat Johnson 1–0 in nineteen innings. Smoky Joe was just warmed up, it looked like. One day the following spring he slipped on the wet grass as he threw the ball. Something snapped in his shoulder. He had tremendous pain when he threw the ball. He could hardly push it up to the plate. Well, the old fastball was gone. He staggered through a couple of seasons just on plain guts alone. Finally the pain became so unbearable, he had to quit. There he was. He was out of the game. But he couldn't stand it. He went to chiropractors, special doctors, tried everything. He sat out the season, and he thought about it. He hung for hours from a trapeze he rigged in the attic. He figured if he stretched his arm it might help. But it didn't. He couldn't even lift his arm as high as his belt. That winter he decided he was a *ballplayer,* not just a pitcher. So he wrote to his old roomie, Tris Speaker, who'd been traded to the Cleveland Indians, and asked him if he could get him a tryout as an outfielder. Speaker arranged it for him and Smoky Joe made the team. He hit .366 one year, and then he quit the game forever. Because he'd proved what he'd set out to do. He wasn't just a pitcher, he was a *ballplayer.* Mr. Coombs' thin brown face glowed with the reflected glory of Smoky Joe's comeback when he used to tell that story. You could see he admired a man who wouldn't quit. Mr. Coombs himself put in some good years with the Brooklyn Dodgers after he'd burnt out his arm for Mr. Mack. He got through those summers on guile and grit. Smoky Joe's story was a good one to remember. Nobody or nothing could cut down Smoky Joe. And that went for Ward Sullivan too.

He remembered Elwood's last visit. *What's that sapsucker going to do if he doesn't play ball?*

Yes, what are you going to do, sapsucker, if you don't play ball?

When the doctors agreed Ward was well enough to travel the old man flew down to Louisville and rode back with him in the ambulance. The doctor examined Ward the day before he left.

"What do you think, doc?" asked Ward.

"I think you're doing okay," said the doctor. He was old and thin and remote. He acted like he didn't spend much time in this world. He had a scholarly, other-worldly quality about him. But he was supposed to be a good orthopedist. You can bet the old man checked him out.

"How soon do you think I'll be able to play ball again?" asked Ward. He had asked him the same question weeks earlier, and the doctor had shaken his head impatiently as if brushing off a salesman, as if Ward should not unsettle things by asking a question which didn't have to do with the current examination.

"How soon?" Ward repeated.

The old doctor looked at him. "I don't think I would count on that," he said.

We'll see about that, thought Ward. Soon as I get out of this turtle shell.

When he got home a rented hospital bed, complete with trapeze, sat in his room among his trophies. Althy, fresh from Maine, was there with a smile on her face. She was practically busting at the seams. Now she had two defectives to take care of. Her cup runneth over. She bustled around on her swollen old legs and puffed up the pillows.

"How would you like a nice, good homemade donut?" she asked.

About the time Althy and the ambulance attendants got Ward settled in the bed, Sarah burst into the room, dressed in sunglasses and her terrycloth robe even though it was five o'clock in the afternoon. She squirted tears everywhere.

"My poor baby," she sobbed. It was hard to hug a human tortoise. In the process she wrenched his head to one side. The cast cut into the flesh under his arm and hurt his neck.

"Let go," he said.

"Let go?"

"Yes, damn it. Let go of me, Sarah. You're pulling my head out of its socket."

"Jesus, I'm sorry. You poor darling. God, I don't know what to do. I never know what to do."

"He looks pretty good for a fellow who went through a windshield, doesn't he, Mother?" said the old man, trying to patch things up.

"He certainly does," she said.

They beamed at him. They seemed mighty proud of him.

"I have a terrible headache," said Sarah. "All this excitement."

"Why don't you go lie down," suggested the old man.

"Yes, I guess I had better," she said. She pushed her sunglasses against her nose and kissed Ward on the cheek. "I'll visit you later, darling. It's so good to have you home."

Althy said, "Do you want any help, dear?"

"No, Mother. I'm all right. Thank you."

Althy was beside herself. She had so many feebs and looneys to tend to she didn't know which way to run. She smiled at him brightly.

"Now," she said, "how about that nice donut?"

"Dad, do me a favor," Ward said, after Althy left to fetch the donut.

"What's that?"

"Just keep Sarah out of here as much as possible."

His father looked stricken. "Okay," he said. "If that's what you want."

"That sure as hell is what I want," said Ward.

They set up a table for all his paraphernalia. On it were the stainless steel bedpan, the porcelain-coated urinal which looked like a teapot with an elongated spout, the hospital johnny gowns, the towels, the toilet paper, the Kleenex, the enema bag, and the Dermicil. Althy kept the laxative there too. He suffered from constipation on and off and spent long hours in labor on the bedpan.

Althy rubbed the Dermicil on every part of his exposed flesh three times a day to stimulate circulation. As she rubbed in the lotion, she carefully checked to make sure he wasn't getting any bed sores. She wiped his ass for him. She shaved him so that he didn't get water down the front of his cast, making it soggy and uncomfortable. She washed his hair too but not often since there was more chance of water spillage. After a while they figured out that he could lay flat on his back with his head over the edge of the bed, and she could wash his hair with no risk at all. She clipped his toenails too.

Just above his buttocks, the sweat-soaked cast got soggy and caused a fierce, unbearable skin irritation. Althy called Dr. Torrill who came up and cut away a crescent-shaped, four-inch piece of the cast right in the middle of his back. Later above his right buttock just where the cast cut across, he developed another fiery rash. Althy came up with the idea of stuffing a Kotex between the cast and the flesh to stop the chafing. So in addition to all the other humiliations he underwent, he had his Kotex changed every day. Several times a day she helped him switch positions in the bed. Left side, right side, back, front. By now he had enough strength, dexterity, and guts to flip over on his belly. She brought him his meals and made sure he had plenty of ginger ale on the night stand. She kept those donuts coming. She made the best donuts in the world. He ate dozens of them, sprinkled with salt the way Granpa used to. She changed the sheets every day and sometimes more often if he had one of his occasional accidents. She stuck her head in the door two or three times a day to ask if he wanted company but he never did. His father brought him *The Sentinel* and *The New York Times* each night and *The Sporting News* on Sundays. Usually the old man ate supper on a tray in Ward's room.

The way it went was the old man would show up carrying a tray with two icy vodka martinis. In those martinis were two olives apiece, stuffed with almonds.

"Here you go boy, time to celebrate the day," he would say or something like that.

"Damn," he might say after a sip or two. "That's like drinking from a mountain brook."

After awhile Althy would appear with a trayful of dinner—plain delicious fare such as turkey breast and giblet gravy with a chestnut stuffing, or corned beef and cabbage, or baked beans and a family-invented cabbage salad with mayonnaise, chopped olives, and carrot shavings, an improbable but perfect compliment to the beans and fatback. And there was always an insulated pitcher of limeade full of musical ice cubes.

The old man was mainly a one-drink man in those days. After that one vodka martini, whether it was warm weather or not, he would go back to the iced limeade, his favorite drink, a habit he picked up from the Captain who drank it by the gallon as he sat out under the elms in the summer studying his books and journals. The old man loved the stuff. He called it "sublimeade."

"Have some sublimeade, boy," he'd say and slosh Ward's glass brimful again.

"Drink that sublimeade, boy," he'd say. "It's good for you. It'll mend your bones good as new."

At night Althy turned on the TV for him. Before she went to bed, she always came to ask if he wanted the channel switched.

When he was through watching TV, he pulled on the extension cord till the plug came out of the socket. The picture crumpled in a split second as though it had been sucked into the vacuum of outer space, leaving behind a slow-fading, silver starburst. He was usually asleep before it faded completely.

Once in a while Sarah slipped through the lines to visit him on the run. The average length of these visits was about thirty seconds, just time enough for a nervous smile and a fluttery wave of the hand.

"Hello, darling!"

Usually in sunglasses, hair wild, and clad in one of the old man's bathrobes she would flit into the room, give a zany, conspiratorial greeting, and vanish before Althy knew the difference.

Except for one time when she came in and stayed around for what seemed like six years.

"How are you tonight, darling?" she began, sitting down in the old man's bedside chair and smoothing out the lap of the ancient paisley bathrobe.

"Just about to go to sleep," said Ward.

"Well. I'll just visit a minute then. Your face is coming along nicely, isn't it? Have you seen yourself in the mirror?"

"Yes, Althy showed me yesterday when she shaved me."

"You look so much better," she said smiling nervously. "When you first came home you looked terrible, all puffy and blue with little railroad tracks running through your eyebrows and a thousand places."

"I bet I looked like I'd been in an accident," he said.

"Of course you did! Don't make fun of me. Why do you always make fun of me? You're such a joker."

"Yes, I'm a joker all right." He was damned sorry he was still in his plaster turtle shell. It made him feel claustrophobic with Sarah in the room.

"I'm so happy you're going to be all right. I was so worried at first."

"I'll be okay," he said.

"You'll look better when you have more teeth," she said doubtfully.

"I like applesauce and milkshakes," he said. "I can gum those donuts Althy makes."

"You make jokes, but are you all right?"

Damn the sound of her voice. Why did she sound serious and phony at the same time?

"Sure. I'm all right."

Then she really got into it. She was never satisfied to talk like normal people. She always had to give it an extra twist or two. She could go along pretty normal for a while, then she'd switch on her freaky side.

"I can never talk to you, can I?" she said for a warm-up. "I come in here and talk to you. I ask questions. You answer. I leave. I ask myself, what did I learn? The answer is always: nothing. We're not very close, are we?"

"No, I guess we're not," he said, hoping such agreeable answers would somehow blur the insistence of her questions.

"I ask myself: why?" she said. "There is no answer. I've even asked Carol. Carol has a theory."

"Sarah. There is no Carol. Don't come in here and talk crazy."

"You and your father say there is no Carol. But how can you be sure? I suppose you think there is no God, too. Isn't that right?"

"Don't come in here and talk crazy," he said.

"I risk being told I'm crazy because what I have to say is important," she said. She seemed perfectly sane. "Carol says everything is linked up. It is a mystery, but it is linked up. She says it began with the first Webster, the one who married the Indian squaw. Have you ever read about it in the old journals at home?"

"No, but I know the story," said Ward.

"He traded a powder horn for this woman whose name he could never pronounce. He got her to keep warm the second winter because he nearly froze to death the first winter. You can read about it in his journal. He had his children by her. He fought the Indians. He prospered. He called her Cora. He called his two daughters Cora, too, as if his imagination for female names failed him after that one effort. Later that Indian woman died under mysterious circumstances. She was tomahawked right in her own kitchen late at night while all the children slept, and he was away on a trip to Kittery. Nothing was stolen, and the children weren't hurt. He found the body. People were suspicious. Especially when he married a respectable white woman two months later."

"I know that story. Grampa used to tell me about it," said Ward, thinking: why don't you get out?

"Your grandmother and Aunt Dorcas saw an Indian woman on

the lawn at Dunnocks Head some summer nights. She comes back to see what we're up to."

"That's real spooky," said Ward but the hairs on his neck prickled. Damn this spook, he thought.

"Carol says it's all linked. Your great-grandfather, the Captain, was a hero. The Captain's ship burned in the Pacific, the work of a careless sailor. The Captain said it looked like a giant rose burning above the empty sea. They had only ten days' provisions in the little boats. But he kept most of them alive for forty-three days and took them over four thousand miles to safety. It ruined his health. He always had nightmares after that, felt uneasy about an act of heroism that should have made him proud. Why was that?"

"I don't know," Ward said. Where the hell is Althy, he wondered.

" 'I lost my way out there,' he once said to me. 'I never found it again.' I thought it was strange of him to say that. Do you remember how he used to sit out under the big trees in summer and read in the old journals, read the philosophers and such?" she asked.

"Yes, I remember that."

" 'Now don't you bother your grandfather,' Mother used to say. 'What's he doing?' I'd ask. 'I don't know what he's doing but you leave him alone, hear me?' That's what Mother would say. So I asked him. He was kind to me when I was little but he didn't like me when I got older because of Scott. I said, 'Captain, what are you doing out here all day, drinking limeade and reading books?' I'll never forget what he said. He said. 'It's how I prefer to spend my life, child.' I said, 'Doing what, exactly?' And he said, 'I'm looking for the answer.' 'The answer?' I said. 'Yes child. The answer,' he said. 'I'm trying to understand the meaning of life.' He had a lot to figure out, didn't he?" She smoothed the lap of that paisley robe again. Apparently she'd slept in it that day and it needed incessant smoothing.

"I tell you," he said. "It's late, Sarah. Why don't you give me another installment of this ghost story tomorrow?"

"Why don't you *listen!*" her voice was desperate. "His father was an illegal privateer in the Civil War. He almost brought the British in on the side of the Confederates. He had his choice of taking a commission in the U.S. Navy or hanging from the nearest tree.

Haven't you ever read the journals?" She seemed stupified at his
lack of education.

"No, but I know all the stories," he said.

"They're all linked in some mysterious way, Carol told me. Scott
went off and got lost in the war."

Did that hang together?

"I know, I know," he agreed.

"Do you know how much your cousin Scott loved Dunnocks
Head?" she asked.

"No, but you'll tell me," he said.

"Both Scott and I go back to that murdered Indian squaw," she
said. And now she was reciting hypnotically. She wasn't here
anymore. She was back there, where it counted. "It was our family
and its stories, his stories, and the old house his. And when the
Captain cut him off from that, it was the most horrible thing the
Captain could have done, and in a sense it was a kind of murder.
That's why Scott was lost, don't you see?"

That was it. He'd had enough.

"Get out. Will you get out? Where the hell's Althy?" he said,
trying to thrash about in his plaster tortoise shell.

"That's why he won the newspaper in the poker game. To be
at least as close as Portsmouth. So he could stare across the river
into the green ancestral dream," she said.

She wasn't talking normally. She was calm and steady enough.
But there was a quiet glitter to her words.

"What are you doing in here, dear?" asked Althy gently, as she
stuck her liver-spotted beak around the door.

"Talking. I'm talking to Ward, Mother. Telling him the old
family stories."

"Get her out of here, Althy," shouted Ward as he thrashed
helplessly about. He kept getting putrid whiffs of his own decaying essence.

"There's more," insisted Sarah excitedly, "Carol told me much
more. And it's all secretly linked, don't you see? Don't you begin
to see the implacability of God?"

"Come, child," said Althy.

"There's more—" insisted Sarah.

"Get her out of here! Get her out!"

"Come, come. Come away to your own room now," counseled
Althy and led away the glittering-eyed woman.

When the old man heard that Sarah was quoting Carol again he wanted to put her back in the sanitarium. But Althy talked him out of it. The old man didn't really want to do it anyway. He settled for Althy's promise that she would keep a closer eye on Sarah. Althy compromised too. She had to stand by while the old man sent for Terrill who knocked Sarah silly for twenty-four hours with one of his magic potions.

The next night the old man wanted to know all about it.

"She talked pretty silly, did she?" he asked.

"She came down here talking like a spook," said Ward indignantly. "All about the first Webster and the Indian squaw and the Captain adrift in the Pacific and Scott lost in the war—saying it's all secretly linked, because Carol told her it was."

"And you know where Carol got it?" said the old man.

"What?"

"You know who told Carol?"

"No. Who?" asked Ward.

"God. Carol talks with God. Didn't you know that?" the old man said.

"No. I guess I didn't."

"You think she's crazy?" asked the old man after a pause.

"Yes, I do."

"Yes, I guess she is," said the old man. "But you know, nobody would ever even notice if she didn't bring God into it. Plenty of people are crazy. You read the papers. Some fellow enters a house by stealth. His idea is he's going to rob the place. He is surprised by an old lady in a wheelchair. Surprised? Anyway he stabs her to death. Stabs her twenty times. That's in this morning's newspaper. Is he crazy? Then there's John Foster Dullness and Dimwit D. Eisenhower. Are they crazy? Throw a little God into their speeches and see what you think. By such standards your mother's a humdrum eccentric."

"You argue good," said Ward. "You argue too good. You're not trying to convince me. You're trying to fool yourself."

"Am I?" asked the old man.

"She's tried to kill herself half a dozen times," said Ward.

"I know. I know," said the old man. "I can't fool around. I can't afford to kid myself. You're right. But still I think she's all right."

"Okay. That's your business."

"Yes, it is," allowed the old man.

"Just keep her out of here," said Ward.

"I will," said the old man. "Have some sublimeade and cool off."

"Thank you, I will," said Ward.

Well, whatever the old man did, Sarah stayed out of his room after that.

Ward slept twelve hours a day. He didn't dream much. When he did he dreamed about baseball, seeing the ball real good, hitting it smoothly. Sometimes he woke in the middle of the night in the silent house and thought about his .386 batting average or about Blue and how beautiful she'd been.

One time he dreamed of Shaw, sitting alone in a corner of the locker room in just his high-waisted baggy blue boxer shorts, a gloomy outcast and token of bad luck and misery. In this dream, Wayne McLain was at the other end of the locker room, standing in just his jock, rubbing his hairy belly and convulsing the boys with his famous one-liners. *Hear about the man with five peckers? His pants fit him like a glove.*

Ward stood whole and healthy again in the circle of light around Wayne, enjoying the action. Somebody tapped him on the shoulder. He wheeled around and there stood Shaw wearing a hat with the brim turned down and a dripping wet raincoat. Rolled up and jammed in the torn righthand pocket of the soaked coat was Shaw's old gray glove, now rain-sodden and black. "I told you," he whispered hoarsely. "I warned you to guard your talent. . . ."

Ward jerked awake with a coppery taste in his mouth.

He took up smoking to while away the time. At first he just tried to blow smoke rings. Later he inhaled deeply and liked the dizzy result almost as much as his evening vodka martini with the old man.

He played the baseball game. He rolled the dice on the plaster belly of his cast. This edition of the game was based on 1954 statistics, the year the Cleveland Indians won 111 games, the most since the 1927 Yankees. It was also the first year since 1949 that the Yankees had lost a pennant. The Red Sox finished a distant fourth that year with a no-name infield and a no-name pitching staff. But the outfield was good with Jackie Jensen, Jim Piersall, and, of course, Ted Williams.

He carefully recorded each game, each play, in a notebook. Naturally he chose to run the Red Sox through a full season schedule. The 1954 Red Sox were not like the earlier great Red Sox teams, but it was fun anyway. He rattled the dice. They danced like Mexican jumping beans, tiny and frenetic with a hollow clatter on the plaster, the only sound among the glinting trophies, topped by straining miniature golden figures with gloves outstretched or bats in midswing. He kept complete statistics for the Red Sox as well as for the other seven teams in the league. It was scary how true to life the game was. Each little player card had its own personality. Just like in real life, you had people you could rely on, and people who would let you down every time. Jensen you could rely on. Piersall you could not.

He played the game for hours at a time. After he completed a 154-game schedule for the Red Sox, finishing with exactly the same won-lost record as Pinky Higgins, he went on to play a 154-game schedule for the Cleveland Indians, and he managed them to 115 wins.

He kept careful statistics. It was a great pleasure to keep good statistics. He worked on them late at night when the house was quiet. The little pool of light from his bed lamp fell on his notebook as he worked with the pencil and the average calculating book he'd bought through *The Sporting News.* Silence. Just the sound of his pencil and the sound of his head whirring. Sarah asleep. Gordie still away at school. Althy asleep. The old man asleep. Ah. Alone with just the game. In this manner he spent some of the best moments of his life.

About two months after he got home, Terrill came to the house and sawed him out of his forty-pound cast. Terrill pulled the plug on the bedside lamp and plugged in his cute little circular saw. He turned his back on Ward and started sawing the cast at the toes. He sawed with terrifying speed. Ward felt a sharp pain at his ankle.

"Awrgh!" he said.

But Terrill was already at his knee. When he got to his hip, he abraded him again.

"Slow down, damn it!" Ward shouted.

Terrill ignored him, quickly sawed him free to the top of his chest. It took him no time to saw through the other side. Terrill lifted off the top of the cast with the delicacy of an archeologist lifting the lid off the coffin of an old-time king. A tremendous sense of relief shuddered through Ward as the air wafted against his chest. Everything turned to gooseflesh. At the same time the

putrid smell of his body assaulted his nose. Terrill and Althy got
him out of the remaining jigsaw pieces of his turtle shell. Althy
stacked the pieces carefully on a chair like pieces of a broken
thunder-mug. What was she going to do? Use it for a puzzle some
winter night?

Well. *Ah!* He was out of his turtle-tomb. In the honest-to-God
light again. His flesh quivered and glowed in the mere air, goose-
fleshing as Terrill and Althy riffled slight breezes while they
worked over him.

The stink was awful. His leg was atrophied. It was a leg out of
the concentration camps, no more than bone and sinew, and
mushroom white. His knee was locked. He couldn't move it. The
whole leg was numb and hairless, the color of dead flesh, mottled
with blue veins. Oh my God, he thought, how you going to play
outfield or first base on a stiff leg?

"I can't move my knee," Ward said.

"That's normal," said Terrill. "Don't worry about it. We'll get
you to a physical therapist. The movement ought to come back.
Probably you'll have 80 to 90 percent mobility again."

"That's not enough," he said. "I don't settle for 80 percent. I
need it all back."

Terrill just looked at him.

"I'm a ballplayer," Ward explained.

"We'll get you to a therapist and see how it works out," said
Terrill.

The next few days he mainly slept. Althy washed his liberated
body and rubbed it with lotion. His skin was numb but it tingled all
the time. He kept her away from his hip and thigh. They ached
fiercely. He was surprised that he needed so much sleep. Maybe
getting the cast off had just knocked him out. After a few days, he
tried lifting his leg. Pain shot from the buds of his potato white toes to
his emaciated hip. He couldn't lift the damn leg at all. Good gravy, he
thought. How am I going to play ball with one half of me dead?

The old man hired a physical therapist to come in and tend to
him.

"This is going to hurt," said the therapist. She smiled. She was
a fat girl with a pretty face. She had very white teeth. She commenced to bend his knee. The pain was excruciating.

"Ow! Ow!" he cried.

"See," laughed Biscuit Pants. "I told you it would hurt."

"Damn that hurts," he said. "But that's all right. You go ahead and bend it. I'll do what I have to, to get it back."

"Okay," she said. "We'll work together."

Tempus fugit as the Captain used to say. The cast came off in November. Biscuit Pants came twice a week all winter and into the spring. She did a fine, if painful, job. Every day he did the prescribed exercises. After a while he found he could hunch around on crutches and then stagger around on a cane. He stayed on his feet as much as possible. Slowly, with much pain, the joint became flexible again. The leg took on muscle and strength and began to look like a part of him. He did exercises for his back muscles and stomach muscles, too, because they'd also atrophied. Biscuit Pants went away. Thank you, Biscuit Pants.

In the emergency room the night of the crash, the doctors had cut off his uniform, his cotton jersey, his belt, his jock, his socks, and sneakers. For some mysterious reason a nurse had retrieved the uniform, placed it in a paper bag, and handed it to the old man who took it home on the airplane. He naturally turned it over to Althy. For the last seventy years anything torn or dirty had been turned over to her. Althy, by means of thorough washing and ancient tricks of the trade, had reduced the bloodstains to modest faint bluish shapes, as innocent-looking and stubborn as the stains made by blueberries. She had sewn it together again by hand so that the cool desecration of the doctors was barely discernable. Her handiwork was a lot neater and less noticeable than the stitchwork the docs had done on his head for example. Yes, she had washed, carefully pieced together the ragged segments, and sewn them into an orderly identifiable garment again. She pressed the uniform and hung it in his closet in a plastic bag. To what purpose he wasn't sure. But there it hung, restored to a reasonable facsimile of innocence, gleaming darkly at him from its plastic chrysalis every evening as he did his chin-ups on the steel bar he had installed in the doorway of the closet.

Come May, he felt well enough to ride Gordie's ten-speed. It was a good conditioner, really worked out the stiffness. After a spell he rode to town and back without real pain. The hip was always pretty stiff but loosened up a little the longer he rode. The pain was wired to the hip socket in his left leg and ran down to the knee cap. As he worked the leg, the pain glowed hot as a light filament, went dull and numb, and then began to ache in the long bone as well as the two joints. But even though it hurt like hell, the hip socket seemed to loosen up.

The bike was a white Motobecane. It was lean and lightweight and skittish, equipped with Suntour derailleurs which moved through the gears beautifully. It was a keen machine. He liked pumping out of town up the hill toward the house. It felt good to work his legs again even if the one hurt like thunder. The lungs worked smoothly. His breath was no longer ragged or bitter with the taste of nicotine. He was coming back. He could feel it.

One evening that June the old man caught up with him as he wheeled the bicycle out of the garage.

"Where are you going with that thing? Don't you want to go down to the horses with me tonight?"

The old man was still in his white shirt, and his suit pants but he was ready to go play buckaroo.

"I thought I'd go for a ride," said Ward.

"Didn't you just go for a ride before supper?" asked the old man.

"Yes. I thought I'd go for another."

"Your leg must feel pretty good, boy."

"I'm doing all right," said Ward.

"Old Biscuit Pants must have done her job," said the old man. He leaned against the fender of his white Cadillac which was practically brand new but shamefully dirty. He'd even been known to carry bales of hay in the trunk.

"Yes. She did," said Ward. "She really threw herself into her work."

"Lucky she didn't break the leg, I guess," said the old man. "Doesn't the leg hurt when you ride around all the time like this?"

"Hurt? Hell, yes. It hurts all the time."

"Well, then," said the old man. "Why don't you ease up a little? Are you in a hurry?"

"Yes, I'm in a hurry. Don't you read the papers?"

The old man took a minute before he got it.

"You mean it's baseball season. Those grown boys are going ahead with the game without you."

"That's right," said Ward. "I should be playing for Boston. I would be if—"

"If what?"

"If my luck hadn't turned sour."

"So now you have to make up for lost time. That's why you're driving yourself."

"That's right."

"It's not enough to walk again," said the old man. "You've got to run, hit, and throw like you used to."

"Damn right. That's what I was made to do. That's what I'm going to do."

"Well, it's a real education to hear you talk," said the old man. "You mean nothing's going to stop you?"

"That's right, nothing."

"What did the doctor in Louisville say? That orthopedist. Did you ask him? Did he say you'd play ball again?"

"He said, 'Don't count on it.' "

"Don't count on it?"

"Yes, that's right. But I tell you what Elwood Flowers said. He said when I got out of that plaster turtle shell I'd be back on a ballfield in no time. Elwood is a ballplayer. He knows how ballplayers feel. That doctor was just a doctor. All he knows about is bones. He doesn't know about ballplaying."

"And ballplayers know about ballplayers like some men know about horses," said the old man. He was still leaning against the dirty car. He was going to get his suit pants all dirty but he didn't seem to care. Every night when he came home from work, he took off his tie and his suit coat, and considered himself ready to go down to the barn and work with the horses.

"That's right," said Ward. "Only forget about it. You're dragging it out so long, you're making it sound silly. The thing is: I know what I have to do. I know what's inside me. I'm going to play ball again."

"All right. I guess you know best. You work for it. But you remember—ballplaying's not everything. It just seems like everything."

"It's everything for me. Damned if I'll let this stand in my way." He socked his leg.

"Sure you don't want to play cowboys?" said the old man.

"Another night," said Ward.

"Well, all right, boy," said the old man. "Just don't hurt yourself." And he started down the long sloping lawn through the mild gray evening, heading for the stable.

Ward went down to see Albie Skinner, his old high school buddy, the manager of the town team.

"Anytime you're ready," said Albie. "We'd be happy to have you with us."

"It'll be a couple of weeks," said Ward. "I'm rounding into shape. It takes a while."

Albie studied Ward's face, the permanent fat lip, the scar tissue pink as bubblegum imbedded in his eyebrows.

"I'm surprised you're so far along considering what you've been through," said Albie. "Anytime you're ready we'll be glad to have you."

His left leg was slightly shorter than the right. He wore a lift in his shoe, that was all. It wasn't a real problem, except his lower back hurt a lot after he was on his feet for a while.

When Gordie got home from Rhode Island, they went over to the high school ball diamond every morning. Gordie pitched batting practice. Ward hired the next door neighbor's kid to go along and chase down the balls. It was good to have a bat in his hands again. The first pitch Gordie threw to him, Ward fell down trying to hit. Gordie crumpled to the ground and laughed and laughed, and Ward just lay there in the dust doubled up with laughter.

The bat felt good but funny. The ball, while not particularly fast, seemed to dart in and out of blind spots that never existed before. Things were trickier than they used to be. That's all right, he thought. I will catch on to this new way of seeing in a while.

In a few weeks he started to hit Gordie's junk pretty good. He was using his arms to hit with. His hips locked and lacked the old fluid motion. Sometimes his left leg buckled as he strode into the ball. But in time it would all come back. He figured he was ready to make the first move.

"Yes," Gordie said. "I think you're ready. You're hitting the ball pretty well. I think you're ready, really."

The kid didn't know anything about it. He couldn't throw a ball through a humid day but it was nice of him to knock himself out. Ward was as far as he could go with the kid. He'd have to finish rounding into shape against a little competition.

Albie put him over at first. He got through the first game against Newville without much trouble. He still couldn't stretch much but he finessed it pretty good.

The opposing pitcher was an old guy who'd been playing town baseball forever. He had a big roundhouse curve and not much else. Ward popped up twice and walked his third time up. Tommy Walker hit a line shot into right field. Ward, who should have made it to third easily, was thrown out on the relay by six feet. He walked again in the seventh, and Albie put in a pinch runner for him since he was the go-ahead run.

"No hard feelings," Albie said.

"That's all right," said Ward. "You're the manager." What the hell. He'd have done the same thing.

Next game they played at home against Boiling Springs. Big league scouts were in the stands, there to look over the Boiling Springs pitcher—a skinny seventeen-year-old righthander with a continuous black eyebrow that ran from ear to ear, little round eyes, and a nose like a parrot's. Ward watched him warm up on the sidelines. The kid was fast. Ward looked over the scouts: skinny old men dressed in Florida sport shirts with faces parboiled in booze by the sun. They stuck out in the bland crowd of staid and responsible people. No line of work attracted boozers like baseball.

Well, they're here to see the kid with the fastball, he thought. Let's give him a workout.

The first time up he struck out on three pitches. The kid was fast. The ball kept flicking in and out of the blurred edges of Ward's peripheral vision. The first pitch was a called strike, slipped over the inside corner. Ward didn't even see it cross the plate. The kid's fast, he thought and stepped out to spit. The kid knew who Ward was. Everybody knew he'd hit .386 in the Association, including the scouts. No doubt the kid was thinking what a feather it would be in his bonnet if he could handle a phenom like Ward Sullivan. The next pitch was out over the plate. Ward jumped on it and fouled it behind the wire mesh backstop right in among the decrepit scouts. The old men scattered. As the ball ricocheted among their folding chairs, they moved with the slow ineffectual panic of a bunch of hens being chased by a fox. Surprised they're sober enough to move, he thought. The kid's third pitch rode in on him. He lost the ball momentarily and then when he picked it up again it looked like it was going to miss the inside corner. By that time it was too late and he couldn't stop his bat. Strike three. Put that in your notes, boys.

There are two ways a pitcher can be wild. He can be wild out of the strike zone. And he can be wild in the strike zone, putting the pitches in there where you can see them too good. Usually a pitcher, if he was wild, was wild one way or another. This kid seemed to be wild both ways. The boy stood out there on the mound, twitching his shoulders, trying to shake off the psychological burden of those old scouts behind the backstop. From there, no doubt, he looked pretty good. Ward was pretty sure the kid was good enough to get a contract and pretty sure too that he'd never make it even to the high minors. It's no good to be fast if you're going to groove those pitches.

The next time up, Ward hit the kid's first pitch to straightaway center, over the wall. It traveled about 360 feet on the fly. The kid grooved the pitch, about belt high and right across the middle, a terrible pitch. As Ward swung he lost sight of the ball entirely, and it was just an accident that he hit the thing at all.

Well, it was very nice: all those people on their feet cheering him. But he felt like a cheat. He hadn't *hit* the ball at all. He was the lucky beneficiary of a pure accident. The team was waiting for him as he crossed home plate. They grinned, pounded him on the back, shaking his hand.

"Atta go, baby. Attago. Way to hit," they said.

He blinked, trying to clear his eyesight, but it didn't work. Everybody was pretty blurred. He looked out at the kid on the mound. The kid was staring at the ground, looking crestfallen. That pitch had cost him some money, maybe even a contract. And it was just an accident. Ward wanted to beat him, knock his brains in, but not this way.

The next time up the kid threw at him. Ward's hips froze, and he lost the ball again and it hit him right in the forehead, splitting the skin. The crowd moaned like a sick animal and fell silent as Ward sat down in the dust. For a moment, everything was clear again. His vision was perfect. Then the players moved in, including the kid pitcher.

"You all right?" he asked.

Now that he'd thunked him square in the head, the kid was

scared. The blood ran down Ward's nose and spattered onto the freshly laundered uniform.

"Yes, I'm all right."

"I didn't mean to hit you, honest," the kid said.

"Shit, man. Get away."

They helped him to his feet. The ballfield pitched first one way and then the other. Someone pressed a towel to his forehead to stanch the bleeding. I must make a great sight for the scouts, he thought. Albie and some others helped him away from home plate. As he staggered away, leaning heavily on the others and holding the towel to his head, he thought, well that is the end of that. I guess you're through fooling yourself now.

Gordie drove him over to the emergency room where the doc put six new stitches in his head to go with the thirty-eight he'd picked up the summer before.

E I G H T

A T T E N - T H I R T Y the telephone rang sharply. The sound produced in him the same gut-shock as the sudden descent of an
elevator. Ward swore, abruptly, harsh and sibilant. He waited, the
numbers in front of him dissolving into meaningless glyphs.

His room was dark except for the warm pool of light from his
gooseneck lamp which fell directly on his record book. He was in
the middle of the pleasure of numbers, the statistical shorthand of
mythology, the old beautiful summary of performance revealed in
naked, unforgiving arithmetic. Now he waited, poised blankly
above the baseball records, in the silence of the static, glinting
trophies, knowing who it was, who it must be to rob him of this
pleasure, the eggshell moment shattered. He waited while Althy
descended the stairs to his room. He heard her now, shuffling to
his door. Still, when the knock came, overloud and insistent, he
jumped again.

"Ward," she croaked.

Goddamn the voice. Goddamn the voices of old New England
ladies.

"Telephone. That girl's calling again," she cawed.

"Okay, okay," he said. "Goddamn. No peace and quiet around
here."

"Don't you grumble and swear at me," his grandmother shouted
indignantly through the door. "I didn't call you. I wouldn't call
you if somebody gave me the nickel."

"Okay, all right. *Cut.*"

He was on his feet now waiting for her to move off. When he
heard her shuffle off, he muttered, "Why don't you get a new
voice." He pulled open the door and moved quietly down the hall
to the family room. No sign of Sarah staggering around in her

164

pajamas and white terrycloth robe with that pathetic, beaten look on her soft face. At least that much was working in his favor.

He picked up the telephone. He heard the dull electronic babble of voices. Althy must be watching one of her idiot panel shows upstairs.

"Yes," he said, "What is it?"

The extension upstairs clicked, cutting the electronic babble in midshit.

"Hello? Is that you, Ward? This is Terry."

"Yeh, hi. I'm—I was in my room doing some stuff."

"Are you glad to hear from me?"

"You bet," he said.

"You don't sound glad."

This idiot line of questioning drove him nuts. She was always pulling this. It was part of her style, which in turn was part of a larger design of unanswerable idiot questions developed by females calculated to drive men either crazy or to some act of violence that could be held against them for the rest of their lives.

"What do you want me to say? That I'm not glad?"

"No. I would just like to feel that when I call you're happy to hear from me. That's all."

He said nothing. She'd led him into another one of those conversational dead ends that were her specialty. He wondered if she felt powerful when he said nothing as if she'd robbed him of the power of speech.

"I miss you," she said. "How come you haven't called me?"

"I've been busy. I work in that factory. I go see the old man at night. That's it. That's what I've been doing."

"I visited your dad again today. I went down to see him on my break. Did he tell you I introduced myself yesterday?"

"Yes, he did," he said. And thought: Why don't you stay out of it? The old man is dying and you're trying to score social points.

"He seemed happy to see me."

"I'll bet he was."

"He said the doctors say he can come home soon."

"Yes, that's right."

"We talked about you," she said. "He really loves you a lot. You can see it in his face when he talks about you. He says he thinks you're unhappy. He says he thinks you've been unhappy since that accident you had all those years ago. He said he wished there was something he could do to change it for you."

"Sounds like you had a nice little talk," he said.

"You sound mad," she said. "Did I say something wrong?"

"No," he said. "Nothing more than usual. I just don't cotton to the old man sitting around with somebody he just met discussing what a sad bastard I am."

"No," she said. "It wasn't like that. He loves you. He knows I'm —that I think you're special. He just wanted to talk to someone who cares about you too."

"I tell you," he said. "I suppose I should feel grateful to hear all this. But I'm not. There isn't anything wrong with me in the first place. And second, this sudden friendliness between you and the old man. . . . You walk in and introduce yourself as my girlfriend yesterday, and you're back there today working out solutions about me. There's something in all this I don't like."

"Don't be so touchy. It's nothing like that. We were just chatting and your name came up."

"Well, I don't like it."

"Okay. We won't talk about you anymore."

"Just leave me out of it."

"All right," she said.

"Talk about what you want, about the weather and such. Talk about yourself. But leave me and the family out of it."

"I'm sorry if I made you mad," she said.

"That's all right. Now is there anything else? I have some things I want to get back to."

"God, you're unpleasant," she said. "You're really working at it tonight."

"No, I'm not," he said. "It comes natural. Is there anything else we should cover?"

"Yes, there is one thing more."

"What's that?"

"How come I haven't seen you in over a week?"

"I told you, I've been busy."

Silence. As if she were weighing judgment. Guilty. Not guilty.

"Well, you could have called," she said. "Just a minute, to let me know how you were. Is there anything I can do to help?"

"No," he said. Yes, he thought. You can get the hell out of my life. You can stop calling here. You can stop pushing in on me.

"Would you like to come down?" she asked.

The old sleeping bat of biology stirred and flapped its wings once, deep in the branches of his soul.

"It's late," he said.

"It's not so late," she said.

"I've got some things to do here. Then I have to get some sleep. I don't sleep so well lately."

"You can sleep here, with me," she said.

The bat stirred again. Her bed was too small; it was just a double. He had a queen-size to himself right here. He could spread out in the big bed, find a way to get the hip comfortable. With her, they slept twined together like snakes. She liked to be close, she said. He would wake with her hot, stale breath in his face and a pain in his hip.

"No," he said. "It isn't a good idea tonight."

"Please, Ward," she said. "I need you. Please. Please do me this favor tonight."

"Look," he said. "I haven't been feeling so hot lately—"

She started to cry and hung up. He clutched the phone to his ear while the dial tone bored into his eardrum. He put the receiver down. Instead of relief, he felt frustration. Damned woman. Why didn't she leave him alone? He went back to his room. There was the pool of light, resting on the expectant record book. There were the trophies, glinting dully in the subdued light.

He started again. But it was no good. He couldn't get into it. She had ruined it. The pleasure of the moment was gone, and there was no way to get it back again. He closed the record book and put it away on the shelf of his closet, on top of the baseball game box just above the plastic bag containing the mended and neatly laundered uniform the doctors had cut off him twelve years ago. He put away the scoring sheets, and the perfectly sharpened pencil went back into the drawer along with the gum eraser. He looked at the clock. Quarter to eleven. He felt restless, uneasy. He'd done his exercises already, but he decided to do another series. It was good for him. To get into shape. To stay lean and hard. Ready. It was good to punish and discipline the body and let it know who was boss. Dressed in khakis and a navy blue T-shirt, he got down on the rug, hooked his feet under the bed and began his sit-ups. Soon his rhythmical breathing, like the expirations of a sea mammal breaking the surface of the water, filled the room. He fixed his eyes on the Hillerich and Bradley silver bat over the bed. Batting title, Carolina League, 1953. Hit .356. *Killed* that pitching. Twenty. Twenty-one. Twenty-two. Let's go, fifty. A second fifty. The body lean and hard. A lean body does its work. The body is kind of a temple. If you don't watch it, it becomes a garbage dump. Thirty. Thirty-one. He kept his eyes fixed on the silver bat. It glittered and winked as his body rhythmically rose and fell, the breathing harder now. Not much pain in the hip. A slight dull ache. Next the push-ups. In his head he heard the telephone conversation again. Her voice. He didn't even like her voice. Cheery all the time. Phony.

Would you like to come down?

No. The answer was no. He would not. She had asked the question with a determined cheerfulness in her voice. Bracing herself already for the refusal. It was enough to set his teeth on edge. No. He would not.

Thirty-three. The pain in his hip burned brightly now and his breath had lost its rhythm. It was merely ragged, like the hoarse gasps of a middle-aged man pushed beyond his endurance. He sank to the rug. He lay there till his breathing settled and the hot pain in his hip cooled down. *You can sleep here,* she said. He felt a nerve flutter in his groin. *Sleep here.* Bullshit. He wouldn't sleep anywhere. Not tonight. She'd ruined everything. He'd planned to work on his records. Wash out his underwear and socks as he did every night. And shave. Tonight was his night to shave. He shaved three times a week, slowly and meticulously. Pulling the skin of his battered face tight. Scraping the razor across it with more care than a carpenter planing a piece of wood. He performed minor skin surgery on himself every time. Going over and over his face with the blade. Eliminating every trace of a whisker. Reducing the face to perfect smoothness, whether you rubbed with the grain or against. It took him about an hour. It was something he did late at night, when the house was quiet. He found it a satisfying ritual. His skin and capillaries had toughened under the ordeal and he rarely bled anymore. Now all of his carefully structured plans were ruined. Because of her. Because her voice had got into his head and wouldn't let him go.

Slowly he rose from the floor. He went to his closet and got down the binocular case and slipped the strap over his shoulder.

As he started out the garage door, Althy's voice from the living room called out, "Ward? Is that you?"

He didn't answer. When he raised the garage door, the yellow car gave off a mirror gleam under dim overhead light. The windshield had the freshly satisfying perfection of a polished eyeglass lens. He saw himself in the glass, reflected back with fishbowl distortions—hollow-eyed, head undulating like an exotic marine plant—as he approached the car. Each day when he came home from work he checked the side panels and wiped them clear with tar remover. He washed the windows each day on the outside and the windshield both inside and out. In the confines of the garage the car looked enormous and powerful. He looked forward to washing it again on Saturday and seeing the water stand in amber beads all over the flawless broad hood. He would go over the chrome, really polish it up. He would use the upholstery cleaner. It always made the car smell new again. He would take the entire morning to work on the car, looking at it as much as working on it. As always it would make him feel good. It was really the highlight of the week.

As he went to open the car door, he spotted a fleck of tar he'd missed earlier tonight on a wipedown after visiting the old man at the hospital. He went to the workbench at the front of the garage, got the cloth and can of tar remover, and went to work on the hardly visible speck of tar. Satisfied, he put everything back neatly. He unlatched the heavy door and slid in, placing the binoculars on the seat next to him. On the first turn of the key, the car rumbled into life.

The car glided into the dark alley. He turned off the ignition and sat for a minute in the darkness. He could make out the shapes of trash cans, fire escape ladders, barred windows. The quiet darkness soothed him. He got out of the car, taking the binoculars with him. He came out of the alley between the courthouse and the bank, emerging into the bright light on High Street. There was no traffic at this hour, practically no one around. Nothing open, except Moffet's Bar and the all-night greasy spoon on the corner. Probably Otto, the cop, was asleep in his car behind the courthouse. He crossed over rapidly, and faded into the dark alley next to the church. At the corner he turned left, passed Mason's Jewelry Store,

slipped into the narrow passageway behind the clothing store and
jumped up for the ladder of the fire escape. On the second try, he
caught it and was on the roof in a minute. He crept cautiously
forward to the front of the building which faced Hanover Street.
It gave him a good view; from here he looked right down into her
apartment on the second floor of the white building across the
street. Crouching behind the parapet he brought up the binoculars. He twisted her into sharp focus as she sat reading a book on
the couch under a Renoir print that even he recognized—the one
of the overly pretty young lady at the piano. Terry was dressed
in a short-sleeved, red polka-dot shirt and jeans. Her bouffant
diffused the light from the lamp, the outer circumference glowing
pale white as the filament in a light bulb, grading down to dark
bronze at the curve of the skull. He watched her expression intently. She sat unmoving. Serious. Absorbed in the book. What
was it that could erase that perky smile from her face and keep her
attention like that? Too much make-up. He could see even by this
dim light that she'd gone too heavy with the blue eyeshadow and
liner. She overdid everything. He watched her carefully, studying
the angle of her head, her expression. She looked almost asleep,
looking down like that at the book. He saw how she curled her legs
under her on the couch. His groin fluttered as he studied the
swelling thighs, tight in the blue cotton jeans. He liked her legs.
She was too short, and they were too heavy, but he liked them
anyway. Careful. Careful. This is a scouting patrol, he told himself. This is no Peeping Tom trip. This is to study the terrain, to
figure out the pain and the pull, the why and the wherefore. There
are women everywhere. If I needed one, I could find one tomorrow. Tonight. No, this is to study and anticipate. Watch her. See
what she's up to. He studied her carefully, resting his arms on the
parapet, the binoculars screwed to his eyes.

   After a while she put down the book. He looked at the glowing
dial of his watch. Twelve fifteen. His heart started to hammer
against his rib cage. Careful, he thought. We're here on a mission.
This is no—

   The living room windows went black. He swiveled the binoculars
to the bedroom window. In a moment the light came on. Terry
leaned forward, apparently studing herself in a mirror over the

dresser that was out of his line of vision. A critical appraisal of the button nose, the too-wide mouth, the small chin, the big blue eyes. Nobody could take that face seriously. It was the face a toy manufacturer would put on a new line of dolls. Even at rest her face looked cheerful, a faint smile played at the corners of her mouth. She had the kind of face and figure that people say is "cute." The word really summed her up. She fooled with the front of her bouffant. The hand nervously picked at the bleached-out, stubborn hair. She spent probably a full five minutes fussing with her hair, looking at herself first one way and then the other. At the parapet Ward made a hissing sound of impatience and disgust.

At last she moved from the mirror and pulled her blouse over her head, her back to the window. He saw her narrow back and the white brassiere strap glowing against it. She turned to check herself again in the invisible mirror. As she did she reached around and undid her bra. She bowed and her apple-sized white breasts popped free. She hung the bra on the doorknob, kicked off her jeans. She was in her closet now reaching up on the door. She came away and stopped for another full-length glance in the mirror. She stood on her toes and looked over her shoulder to see the back of her legs, reached back and felt along her thigh, studying her body carefully. The vulnerability of that pose and the lovely line of her body made him ache. Careful, he thought. This is just a trick, one of old biology's tried and true stunts. She pulled on red silky pajamas with white piping. They looked good against her blonde hair and fair skin. She got into bed, fluffed up her pillow and reached up and turned out the light. He kept the glasses to his eyes, searching, probing the dark windows for clues. Nothing. He had learned nothing.

He found he was breathing hard, that the old pain under his heart had commenced again. He could go over there now and knock on her door. She would be happy to see him. She'd throw her arms around his neck and press against him happily. He could make it happen. It was up to him. He studied the blank window. He wondered if she would fall right asleep. Likely she would. What was there to keep her awake? She'd forgotten the telephone call, doubtless. She'd be oblivious to everything. Effortlessly, she would sink down into her heartbeat and respiration. She had disappeared into her sleeping flesh, leaving him behind to deal with the agonies of the wakeful. What would you expect? That

was what Shaw had tried to make clear about Blue. Be careful of
your talent, he'd said. There's a woman around. They get your
blood hissing in your ears and inflame your old injuries. They
headed straight for your talent. If it was drinking, they made sure
you didn't enjoy it anymore. If it was making pictures, they
nagged you for a good time. If it was playing baseball, they saw
to it that you were too tired to play right. No, he would not go over
there. He was through with women. He would do his job, take care
of the car, do his exercises, play the baseball game, and live a
simple life.

When he opened his eyes, he saw the stars. At first he couldn't
remember where he was. Sitting up, he discovered he was on the
roof of the clothing store. He looked across at Terry's apartment.
The windows were dark. He must have fallen asleep. His watch
said three o'clock. He got up stiffly, settled the strap of the binocular case on his shoulder, climbed down off the roof, and drove
home.

On his way to see the old man the next night, he stopped to get
a paper at the shopping center on the edge of town. The old man
might like a gander at *The Wall Street Journal.* "Well, well," he'd say,
looking at the stock quotations. "This is a real education."

When he came out of the store, Terry's apple-green VW was
parked next to his yellow Cadillac. She was sitting in his car,
goddamn her. A wave of blood surged hotly into his lungs. He
could see just the outline of her head, shaped like a light bulb. It
was her all right.

She was smiling as he opened the door.

"Hello," she said.

"What are you doing here?"

"That's a nice greeting."

"Who the hell do you think you are, just climbing into my car
like this?"

"I had to see you. I tried to get you to come down to my place,
but you wouldn't."

"Why didn't you just tackle me on the street?" he said, sliding
into the seat.

But she wasn't going to be deflected by sarcasm. "I had to see

you," she said. She studied him for a minute. "Don't you miss me?
Don't you ever want to see me?"

He just looked at her, and as he did her eyes filled with tears.
They spilled over and ran down her wide cheeks. She smiled and
patted her face with the back of her hand. "I miss you," she said.
"I miss you awful."

"Cut the tears," he said. "There's no reason to cry. Damn, don't
I hate it when you start to cry for no reason."

"I know," she said, sniffling. "I know you don't like it."

"Why do you do it then?"

"Because I can't help the way I feel."

"Yes, you can," he said. "If you want to."

"You don't like me, do you?"

"What—why are we talking like this, anyway?" he ran his hand
through his thick black hair.

"Are you interested in some other girl?"

That made him laugh, short and abrupt.

"Hell, no," he said. "I couldn't take the aggravation."

"I feel sorry for you sometimes," she said.

"Why is that?"

"Because you try so hard not to care about anybody."

"I tell you, it would be simpler that way, wouldn't it?" he said.

"I followed you from the hospital the other night," she said.

"When?"

"The other night. Two nights ago."

It surprised him. She was dumb but he didn't think she was
nuts.

"How come you did that?"

"I don't know. I had to work an extra half-shift. I came down
and there your car was so I just sat in my car. Pretty soon you came
out, and I was so lonely for you I just followed your tail lights all
the way home."

"That was a dumb thing to do," he said.

"Was it? Yes, I guess it was. Why do you think it was dumb?"

"Because what good did it do? I didn't even know you were
there. We didn't say one word. So what good did it do?"

"I know," she said. "You're right. It didn't do a bit of good. I'm
dumb sometimes."

"I don't like being followed around."

"I know it was wrong. I wasn't just tagging along to be close either," she said. "That was part of it. But I was really wondering if you would go right home or if you would go someplace else."

"And?"

"You went someplace else. You didn't go right home."

"Where did I go?"

"You went to see Avis and your brother. Then you went home. I thought maybe you had another girl. When you turned off Front Street, my little heart beat so fast until I remembered that was where Avis and Gordie lived. I know I did a bad thing."

If you weren't seeing one, you must be seeing another. That was the way their minds worked. They didn't think you had anything else on your mind. Because they didn't. So she spied on him, too. Well he deserved that, for acting like a fool.

"You can lay off that," he said. "I don't need anybody following me around, playing detective."

"I know," she said. "I'm sorry."

"Now. I have to get to the hospital. Have you got anything on your mind? Or are we just passing the time of day?"

She looked at her small hands folded in her lap. She had on a mint-green blouse with a round collar with little flowers on it and a pair of dark green slacks. Her fingernails were painted apple green to go with her outfit and her car. She looked very young.

"I'm pregnant," she said.

Somehow he wasn't expecting that. He figured when he had his accident he had ruined that capacity as well as everything else. But now as he thought about it, it seemed more fitting that God had smashed him up but left intact the curse for making babies. It was a good joke, now that life was over, for him still to be able to create new life. She was watching him. A waterfall of thought crashed through his head, but his face remained blank as a poker player's. I'm a damn fool to have let this happen, he thought. Now, by God, you have some real trouble.

"Well," she said. "I guess you hate me now, don't you?"

Suddenly the dam's broke, he thought. I have been holding things back, keeping things orderly. Now there is the old man's lady-paper will, Sarah acting crazy again, and this girl with a walnut of real trouble at the center of her.

"You picked a fine time for it," he said.

She began to cry again. It was all right to whip her with this.

She felt plenty of guilt, expected him to act like this. So why not? It relieved a little of the tension. But the fact was he had only himself to blame. He knew better than to get mixed up with her or anybody. A strong wave of nausea swept him as he watched her shoulders jerk with each sob.

The will lay in the drawer of his nightstand. Maybe the old man would ask him tonight if Sharfman thought it was all right. No doubt he would begin to wonder if Ward didn't say anything about it. He had to move fast.

"Okay," he said. "Okay. Don't cry so much. You'll wear yourself out."

She looked up hopefully at what sounded almost like a tender note in his voice.

"I can't get away tonight," he said.

He held her hand. Looked into her eyes. She looked so grateful and happy it made him want to puke.

"We'll go to Philadelphia this weekend. We'll stay down there a couple of days. Don't tell anyone yet. We'll just go down there on our own. Everything will work out okay. Don't worry."

He had to get to the kid and talk to him. Figure out how to handle Sarah. He needed time to think. Which was exactly what he wasn't going to get, it looked like.

Terry gave him a big hug. A nerve started throbbing in his neck. It was all he could do to keep from tearing her arms loose to turn off the electric pain. But he disciplined himself. He let her go ahead with the big hug.

What the hell was going on, anyway? Things were starting to speed up. That mysterious force which naturally opposes any man's attempt to live simply was working overtime to pull him back right into the middle of the mess. Now here sat this dumb foot doctor wearing four coats of green nail paint and matching eyeshadow, her blonde bouffant trembling with her effort to maintain a timid smile.

"Oh, Ward," she said. "I thought you'd be so mad. Everything will be just fine. I know it will work out fine. I was so scared to tell you. I thought you'd. . . . I know everything. . . . I love you so much. I know everything will work out just fine now."

Yes, he thought. Everything will be just fine.

N I N E

W A R D tucked *The Wall Street Journal* under the muscle of his arm like a baton. When he got off at four, he almost walked smack dab into Terrill.

"Damn! Where'd you jump from?"

"You charge off an elevator like a fresh bull entering a ring," said Terrill without particular force. He was a small bloodless fellow—slow, stiff, and geriatric before his time. His arms usually dangled motionless as two slack ropes at his sides and he walked as if his knee pans pained him all the time.

"Are you coming or going?" said the doc.

He had on one of those grayish-white wrinkle-prone laboratory coats he always wore on his rounds at the hospital. It hung slackly from the knobs of his shoulders and made him look even more nondescript. The damn thing was made of some material thin as one-ply toilet paper. It looked like you could stick your finger right through it.

"I'm just coming in," said Ward. "I'm glad I ran into you. Last night he was telling me how he couldn't get anybody to listen to him about limeade."

"Limeade? What's this about limeade?"

Out of one crumpled pocket flourished the twin ear plugs of Terrill's stethoscope like the stamens of a giant flower. He patted his pockets, hesitant, preoccupied. He seemed to be searching for a smoke. It looked like he didn't have any, as usual. Ward unrolled the sleeve of his black T-shirt and shook out a Camel.

"Obliged."

Terrill stuck the cigarette in his mouth and dreamily patted his pockets again: two pats on the right pocket, two on the left and then a tap or two over the left breast. This was code—universal, and known to all smokers. Ward handed him the matches. The doctor seemed startled to find matches in his hand. He regarded them quietly for a minute then with great difficulty he tore one loose and began to scrabble it against the emery board. It finally bloomed with a hiss into a small darting flame.

"He can't get any limeade here," said Ward. "He's asked about it. Nobody takes it serious. They offer him juice, soda pop. But he's really serious. The man is addicted to the stuff."

"I'll ask about it," said Terrill through the blue smoke. He really kicked up some smoke when he lighted up.

"Of course, you could always bring some in yourself instead of that booze you smuggle in here. That's just a rumor you understand."

"Is that so?" Ward grinned at him.

"I hear," said the doc to his cigarette—or was he contemplating the regrettable nicotine stain on the first two fingers of his right hand?—"there was some heavy drinking going on in Room 407 two nights ago."

"Miss Sims has no faith in the healing properties of a water glass of vodka," said Ward.

"I see you practice a little medicine," sighed the doc through the smoke. Behind the horned-rimmed glasses his eyes were baggy and bloodshot.

"Yes, I do," said Ward. "It usually goes: take two Budweisers and call me in the morning. For serious cases, I prescribe vodka."

"Miss Sims was upset," said Terrill. "She suggested that Security frisk you when you came in each evening. She says your father threatened to use his influence to get her fired."

"That's bullshit," said Ward. "The old man said he'd call Rogers Hollister and get him to get her to leave us alone. That's all."

"I know that without being told," said Terrill. "But I let her think she'd have to worry about that if she bothered you and your father again. I think she'll leave you alone."

"Good. Damn the bag anyway."

"Just don't get your father so drunk he falls out of bed and breaks a leg. Then it will be my ass."

"He's your one-drink man ordinarily. Then he moves on to limeade if he has any," said Ward.

"I take your point," said Terrill. "I'll look into it."

"How's he doing anyway?" Ward figured he better check directly. All he had to go on was what the old man told him. And the old man was not totally reliable anymore in this advanced stage of disease. That crazy will on the lady paper was proof. Plus those silly rhapsodies concerning the foot doctor.

"He's doing pretty well, all things considered," said Terrill. "I've been meaning to call you. I just stopped in to see him. He's worried about your mother. How is she?"

"She's okay," Ward said. "I guess I set him off the other night. She's been mooning around the place, mainly playing peek-a-boo with Althy. You know how she gets. It's nothing serious."

"He says maybe I ought to go up and take a look at her," said Terrill.

"She's no worse than usual," said Ward. "But he'll like it if you come up and listen to her chest and press her tongue down."

"You're not one of her big fans, are you?"

"I tell you, Doc. I know her from way back," said Ward. "There isn't anything wrong with her. You want to know what her problem is?"

"Yes, I'd be interested to know."

"She's damn mad," said Ward. "Nothing turned out the way she wanted it. She got so pissed she decided to go to bed and stay there till history rewrote itself."

"Is that it?"

"That's it," said Ward.

"I'll be out to see her tomorrow," said the doc.

"Good. Maybe you'll give her some new pills to play with."

"Maybe I will." Terrill pushed the button for the elevator.

"Wait a minute," said Ward. "I asked you how he was. You tell me: pretty good."

"That's right."

"Well, that's funny. He told me he was dying."

"He told you that?" said Terrill. The look was equal parts of disgust and fatigue.

"That's what he said. Now, is he dying or not?"

"This was a matter I wanted to discuss with your mother—"

"Sarah already knows, Doc. She's been saying he's going to croak ever since you made the diagnosis a year ago. You don't have to tell her anything. She gets her dope straight from God."

"You mean Carol who talks to God," corrected Terrill, perfectly serious. "Has Carol been using Sarah to talk about this?"

"You keep driving me off the track," said Ward. "Don't you have a straight answer in your black bag?"

"Just answer the question. Is Carol in the picture or not?"

"So far as I know," said Ward, "Carol has said nothing lately. Now you answer a simple question. is he dying?"

"The questions are always simple," said Terrill. "Your father tells me that. He says it's the answers that get complicated."

Terrill always let the ash crumble off his cigarette, Ward noticed. You'd always find little piles of gray powder on the carpet in Sarah's bedroom after the doc made one of his lethargic house calls. Now a gray powdery worm of ash about an inch and a half long fell away from the yellow stained fingers onto the crumpled and flimsy toilet paper coat.

"What is the answer?"

The doc's eyes wriggled like shapes in a funhouse mirror behind the thick lenses of his horn-rimmed glasses. His head up like that showed his scraggly throat and how old he was getting. He was concentrating. His turtle mouth, boney and lipless, fell open as if paralyzed with terrific geriatric concentration.

"The answer is he is probably dying. But I've seen funny things happen. Sometimes chemotherapy reverses the entire process. Sometimes, for no reason—no apparent reason—the disease goes into remission."

"Probably dying? Or dying?" said Ward. "Which is it?"

"You still looking for a simple answer?" asked Terrill. "All right. He's dying."

"That's what he said. I figured he knew what he was talking about."

"Those headaches and the dizziness he's been complaining about. That may mean the stuff's spread to his brain," said Terrill.

"Jesus."

"I don't know yet. We'll have to run some more tests," said the doctor vaguely.

"If he's going, I hope he goes quick," said Ward. "He's been dying slow for a year now. He ought to cut a break in the end."

"There's a chance things will change," said Terrill. "I want to keep him here longer, do the tests, and then maybe try some new treatment—chemotherapy—see how it goes, before I send him home.

"What's he say?"

"He says he'll think about it." Terrill turned around to look for the sand ashtray and flashed the small bald patch bleeding through the still black hair of his crown. The bald spot looked pink and soft as a baby's ass. He swiveled back, deciding to keep the cigarette for a few more puffs.

"Last night he told me he wanted to get out of here and come home," said Ward.

"Tonight he says he'll think about it," answered Terrill.

"What I want to know is how come when I asked you how he's doing you said: pretty good?"

"Because he's doing pretty good," Terrill was exasperated. "For a sick man he's doing pretty well. He's in no special discomfort. His condition is serious but there's a chance chemotherapy might help. Isn't that doing pretty well?"

"Since when is dying described as doing pretty good?" Ward wanted to know.

"There's a chance we can still help him," said Terrill. "I hope you will talk to him about this. Get him to see he's got nothing to lose."

"You still believe all that stuff they taught you in medical school, don't you?"

The doc looked at him.

"I still believe some of it. I'm slowly getting smart," he allowed wearily.

"Good. I'm a miracle of modern medicine myself. The docs practically had to reinvent me after that crash I had in Louisville. But I tell you. Whatever the old man sees, he'll see for himself. We were talking about it the other night. He told me a good story."

"He tells a good story."

"Yes, he does," agreed Ward. "He told me how he helped my great-grandfather out of a tight spot. He was ninety-six and your brothers wanted to chop off his leg for openers. His doctor said he might have a few good years left, minus that leg. He said to hell with that. He went for a sail instead."

"He went sailing instead."

"The old man helped him get out of bed, dress in one of his black suits and white shirts, and walk the path down to where his little catboat was tied up. And the Captain—that's what every-body called him—he got in the boat, and he sailed away."

"He just sailed away," said Terrill.

"That's right. He just sailed away. He said to hell with having a leg off at ninety-six, and he just sailed away."

I guess that's what you wish your dad could do, don't you? Just sail away?"

"It's up to him," said Ward. "I told him I'd do whatever he wants. He asked me to promise not to let anybody take away his say."

"I think the best way you can meet that promise," said the doc, "is to get him to agree to chemotherapy."

"I think you don't know what I've been talking about," said Ward.

Terrill studied him briefly. The baggy eyes sharpened momen-tarily, then glazed over again with fatigue. He pushed the elevator button. He went over to the butt can, took another drag, and delicately inserted the cigarette end in the sand which was pocked with other such leavings.

"I'll stop by to see your mother tomorrow night."

The elevator door jerked open spastically. Terrill shuffled in and slumped in his crumpled white smock against the far wall of the ill-lighted cab. Ward hated to ride in the damn thing. Its walls and railing, officially approved as suitable for the handicapped, smelled of human misery as surely as a subway train at two in the morning. Lots of times he climbed the stairs rather than taste the metallic hopelessness which oozed out of the walls of that sickly fluorescent box. The door convulsed shut, hiding Terrill from view.

Well, the doc didn't understand. He was probably insulted by the idea that there was some other way to go than what he, a doctor, suggested. Ward, being a miracle of modern medicine, figured he understood what the old man was up to. The old man had lost a few of his marbles. But he had enough left to figure out that there really was a choice. You don't have to say yes to this bullshit. Only if you want to. If somebody had leaned over Ward as they cut the uniform off him that night in the emergency room twelve years ago and said, "Listen son. We can patch you up and let you live half a life, or let you go now while you're on top," he'd have said, "Cut me loose." Well, maybe not. We always like to kid ourselves. Nevertheless, you like to think you'd have the courage to say, "Let's get it over with." Sometimes he felt like they'd patched up his carcass but left the ghost, the real man, dead in the ditch.

The old man looked pretty good again tonight. He was dressed in blue pajamas instead of the hospital gown and that alone made him look improved against the wedding-cake white of the bed, the walls, and the sheets. They exchanged the usual greetings and Ward tossed him the *Journal*. The old man folded back the last page of the paper to the stock quotations and made the thing into the customary three-fold wad.

"Your girl stopped by again today." The old man was being funny, maybe trying to rile him mildly by referring to the foot doctor in this manner.

"You mean Terry."

Again, in his head, he studied her from the rooftop, twisting her into focus in binocular recollection and learning nothing. Naked, but revealing nothing beyond the old tidal pull of sex. Seeing again the white breasts, pink at the tips as a rabbit's nose, pop forth as she bowed to the secret watcher beyond the window. Nothing. The naked body, the legs too short and thickly modeled, both magnetic and repulsive at the same time. The bouffant, under the light, electric white at the edges shading down to deep bronze. The solitary, unknowable doll's face bent to the book. The foot doctor home reading a book—a text on nursing?—below the corny Renoir print. Nothing. He learned nothing from this episode on the roof. Except that maybe he ought to step up his appointments before he got too weird. Maybe I'm going wacky like Sarah, he thought.

"Oh, I forgot," said the old man. "You need clarification. A description of any identifying scars, tattoos, and birthmarks is also helpful, I suppose."

"That's reasonably funny," said Ward. "How long does this part last?"

"Not long," said the old man. "You want some limeade?" He gestured at the coffee-brown insulated pitcher on the metal night stand.

"No thanks. Where did you get it, anyway?"

"Help yourself."

The old man took some relish in ignoring the question. "Now

let's get to these pajamas. How do you like them? Damn nice, wouldn't you say?"

His father's dark blonde fine hair with hardly any gray in it had been washed and combed and the damn pajamas which were new —by the look of the creases in the sleeves and across the front and the general stiffness of the blue cotton material—really looked good. He looked clean and happy and, if not well, at least convalescent.

"They look real good," said Ward.

"They make me feel good," said the old man. "It's a real education how good they make me feel. At home I just sleep in my underpants but after two weeks of this place and that hospital gown I was ready for some pajamas. I bet you wonder where I got these."

"I bet you'll tell me," said Ward.

The old man was satisfied by even this faintly sarcastic expression of curiosity.

"I'll tell you. Have some sublimeade and settle back. This person known to you, whom we have clearly identified—"

"You're the funniest fellow since Wayne McLain," said Ward. "Get on with it."

"Terry walks in here right after lunch. Almost the first thing she says is, 'You don't look very comfortable.' It surprised me. I *wasn't* very comfortable. The gown had been bothering me for a few days. Only I didn't know it. Until she told me. Then I knew immediately what the problem was."

"Pajamas," offered Ward.

"Right," said the old man. "Cool cotton pajamas. I talked wistfully of cool cotton pajamas. I told her about no limeade in this pesthole, too. And the matter of chemo-damn-therapy and more time and tests."

"You really blabbed," said Ward.

"I really spilled the beans," the old man confessed. "Damn. She *listens.* She hears you when you talk. You know how rare that is?"

"Pretty rare," said Ward.

"Yes, pretty rare. You fool. Humor me or not. So, she went right out and bought me pajamas, and she came in here with that package from Pomeroy's under one arm and a jug of sublimeade in the other."

"What a pretty picture," said Ward.

"It was lovely to see," said the old man. "She walks around in sunbeams anyway. She loves to do for other people. She told me they have a little refrigerator up there in Pediatrics. She bought a whole supply of frozen limeade, and she'll bring me a pitcher each day for as long as I'm here."

"I wish I'd known you were going to take matters into your own hands," said Ward. "I just saw Terrill in the hall and told him to scour up some limeade. He said he would. You'll have so much sublimeade in this place, it'll be running out of your ears."

"The beauty is how fast she moves once she's on to something," said the old man. "Besides, you can't have an oversupply this time of year. It's getting hot."

"It's getting hot early," agreed Ward. "It'll be good for baseball. Everybody'll be loose early."

"I wish the Red Sox luck," said the old man. "Keep me posted. I'd rather have it from you than the newspapers and TV."

"They'll surprise," said Ward.

"Anyway," said the old man getting back to the story of his pajamas. "That girl shows up with cotton pajamas. She gives me my first drink of sublimeade in two weeks. Discreetly she assists me with a sponge bath."

"Where is Miss Sims while this is going on?" asked Ward. "This is downright pornographic."

"She's too smart to come around," said the old man. "Terry gets rid of that Johnny gown and helps me into these crisp new duds. Somewhere in the process she decides my hair needs washing."

The old man put on his Ben Franklins and gave Ward a significant look.

"She's got strong fingers, boy. Her shampoo routine is almost as good as an osteopathic treatment."

"That's nice," said Ward.

"That's more than nice," allowed the old man. "I'm trying to pay you a compliment. You certainly found a nice girl."

"You're working hard at this," said Ward. "She's not my girl. I'm not looking for any women. I like to keep it simple, I told you."

"Well, boy," said the old man. "Even a blind pig finds an acorn once in a while. Call yourself lucky."

"I knew you two were chummy but I didn't know it went as far as pajamas," said Ward. "She told me you had a big conversation the other day, too."

He put his bad leg up on the chair.

"You don't like what you heard," said the old man. "What did she tell you?"

"She didn't say much."

"Which translated means, you're not saying. Because you don't want to talk about it. All right. Let's see here," the old man turned to the wedge of print he held in his hand. "Bath Industries up a quarter of a point. I wouldn't buy that on pain of death. Here's American Tel and Tel. What do you think?"

"I don't think anything about it."

"No, you don't," said his father. "Maybe you'll tell me what Terrill said."

"We talked about chemotherapy."

"Well?"

"He says it might help."

"Did he tell you it might not? Make me sick as hell too?"

"Kind of."

"What do you think?"

"I think I'm ready to back up anything you decide," said Ward.

"Fine," said the old man. "What did Sharfman say about the will?"

Ward experienced a hot pissing sensation, a scalding flood enveloped his crotch and thighs. Did I just piss myself? he wondered. I say I'm ready to do anything he wants, and the old man goes straight to the will. Is he just playing games with me?

Ward looked at him steady. Here goes a lie, he thought.

"He says it looks okay. He locked it up in his box."

"Good," said the old man. He raised his head to squint through his Ben Franklins up and down the rows of stock quotations in little jerky up-and-down motions sort of like a chicken makes.

"Fine," said the old man and turned the wad of newspaper over to the bond quotations.

"Did Terrill say he was going to see your mother tomorrow? I told him to get over there. Did you call him too?" still he looked at the page of newsprint.

"No, I was going to," said Ward. "But I went down to the horses soon as I got home. I let the mares out and fed that damn crazy stallion. Then I went up to the house and showered and ate dinner and here I am."

"I would like it if you would do a thing when I ask you, boy,"
said the old man, looking at him over the half-glasses.

"I was going to," said Ward. "Give me a chance."

"I rely on you," said the old man. "Don't let me down now."

Well now, you are a liar, he thought. You told the old man
Sharfman had the will and that everything is fine. Now you better
go to work and make sure everything turns out fine. Start with the
kid, he thought. Then move on to Sarah.

Ward drove over to the kid's place and knocked on the door. Avis
opened the door with a can of beer in her hand. She was dressed
in a red bandanna halter top, those carelessly patched cut-off
jeans, and leather sandals.

"Gimp," she said. "What are you doing here?"

Her black woolly hair framed the hemisphere of her forehead
in tight curls. The parenthetical lines of discontent around her pug
nose softened automatically at the sight of him. Automatically. He
had never noticed that before. But now it was plain she was one
of those people who is never happy at being alone. The last person
leaves the room, and her face goes out like a light bulb.

"Have a swig of beer," she said.

The cold beer stung pleasantly on his palate. Avis stood with her
sharp anklebones almost touching but her long-toed grimy feet—
you could see the strips of white under the crisscross of leather
straps and the rest of the skin gray as newsprint—splayed apart
on the stone doorstoop. The African pose, recalling old *National
Geographic* days on the floor of the study in Dunnocks Head, exag-
geratedly pushed the soft globes of her bandannaed boobs at the
streetlights and mellowed with soft shadows the Negroid curve of
her abdomen and hollow back. Again she brought to mind Lamont
Baltimore, the shortstop for Louisville back in the old days. He
handed her the can of beer.

"I thought I'd rescue the kid," he gave her his charming if
somewhat crooked and fat-lipped grin. "Get him out of your
clutches for a half hour and buy him a beer or two."

"Is that so. And leave me here with nothing to do, is that it?"

"Just for half an hour. I want to visit with him on a little family business."

"I see. *Family* business. Well, naturally count me out. Come on in."

Something warned him to just stand there and talk to her a minute more. So he said, "What's he doing? He up to his elbows in some picture of your ass?"

"Best ass you'll ever see," she smiled. "He's not here."

"Not here?" A little pain grabbed him under the heart. "Where is he? He didn't go see the old man, did he?"

"Hell, no," the ugly lines reappeared around her blunt nose. "You ever see him do anything he ought to do? He decided to go see your mother. He was feeling edgy about her. He had this tremendous urge to see her tonight. I said, 'Fine. I'll stay here and read the phone book.' I can't handle that spook. No offense. Come on in."

That pug nose was as shapeless as a plug of clay. It was little, with two round holes in the end of it, big enough to take two thirty-thirty shells snugly. Other than that it was just a plug of clay. Except for the lines on each side. Those lines, fading in and out, they were the real barometer of her internal weather. Right now, looked like a storm was coming up. He decided to ignore the invitation, effect a certain polite deafness. The fact that the kid wasn't here upset him. He was only half paying attention to her emotional weather.

"Damn. Why doesn't he stay put sometimes," he asked. His leg was starting to kick up too.

"You know him," said Avis. "He's as nervous as a girl going through puberty. I'm not sure he *isn't* a girl going through puberty. Come in for a minute."

"That's all right," he said. "Maybe I can catch him if I hurry."

"What's your rush? Come in for a minute. Now's your chance," she said.

"What chance is that?"

"Don't play dumb. Don't you want to get laid? Now's your chance, peanuts."

"That's a nice offer," he said. "What's second prize?"

"Don't give me that shit. You know you want it. I see how you look at me. You're always staring at my tits."

"You got *National Geographic* tits, that's why," he said, grinning. "They bring back memories of old magazines."

"That's pretty good, funny man," she said, but she wasn't laughing and the barometric lines around her nose showed foul weather ahead. "Come on. What are you worried about? Your brother? He doesn't give a shit. He can hardly get it up. Come on. Slam bang, and you're on your way."

"I'm on my way now," he said.

"You'll be sorry," she said. "I've got a beautiful body. I'm the best thing you'll ever get a shot at."

"That's right," he said. "So long."

He started to walk away.

Women of Avis' stripe said things like that. Nobody good he ever knew found it necessary or even desirable to make such outlandish claims. As he was considering this, a beer can bounced off his head.

"How'd that feel, shithead?"

For a second he debated going back up the walk and adding a little character to her nose. But, no. He had no time to indulge this bitch. He had to catch up with Gordie. She was entitled to feel a little ornery, he guessed.

He started walking again.

"I thought you were the family jock," she called after him. "I thought you were the big man."

He kept on walking.

"Why don't you go home and beat up on your mother? You're good at that. Big man. Go home and flog the dog, Gimp."

He opened the door of the yellow Cadillac.

"You and your brother eat shit!"

The kid had really picked himself a winner. Someday when he had more time maybe he would fix the bitch. He felt sorry for the kid. It looked like she was out to fix him one way or the other. Of course she could just take off if things were as bad as she said they were. But hell. That's the way she liked things. She wasn't happy unless she was making somebody miserable. Old Gordie fit the bill to a T, no matter how Avis complained. And this sweetiecake is a friend of the foot doctor's. It made him smile crookedly to himself as he considered how Terry would have reacted to that little scene Avis had just played out on the front stoop.

He drove along bathed in the green lights of the dashboard.

Well, boy. Even a blind pig finds an acorn once in a while. Call yourself lucky.

You tell me, old man. You're a good judge of women. But he had to concede that even though Terry was dumb and a pain in the ass, she wasn't mean and ornery like Avis.

He turned in the driveway, crested the hill, and saw the house ablaze in the night like a luxury liner at sea. The kid's little toy car, an old white Saab, was parked in the driveway.

Good, Ward thought. We have to get this will thing straightened out.

He was so hot to get at it he didn't even stop to wipe down the Cadillac.

The fact that all the lights were on in the big house should have tipped him off. But he was caught off guard, and the sound of Sarah's hysterical babbling struck him like a physical blow when he opened the door. Framed in the bedroom doorway at the end of the hall, Althy and the kid bent in frantic tableau over Sarah's bed. All he could see of Sarah was her naked feet, strangely passive in contrast to her wild and incessant voice. The kid spotted him and hurried into the hallway with an agitated expression on his face.

"Where the hell you been?"

His eyes popped and the cords in his neck stood out. He thumbed his glasses back into his forehead.

"Get in here and help us with Mother."

"What's going on?"

"She's—she's coming apart. She said she wants to kill herself. Althy discovered a bunch of sleeping pills and tranquilizers in that piano-shaped music box on her nightstand."

Ward remembered that music box. He was peeking in through the kitchen door the day Scott Prothero gave it to her. She kissed him on the lips when she opened the package and saw what it was. It played "Body and Soul."

Oh darling!

The old man knew where it came from too and never said a word.

"She said they were her pills," said the kid. "We had no right to take them away from her. She and I were sitting in the kitchen having a cup of coffee when Althy discovered them. Mother accused me of deliberately distracting her, so Althy could search her room. She says she doesn't want to live in a world with such despicable people."

"Shit," said Ward.

"She says she doesn't want Dad to come home. She says it's wrong for him to come home," said Gordie. "Listen, she's even mentioned Carol tonight. She says Carol told her not to let Dad come home."

"Goddamn her," muttered Ward and he started down the hall.

"Who?" said the kid. "Carol or Mother? What are you going to do?"

"I'm going to settle her down," said Ward.

"Careful. Don't overdo it," said Gordie, but you could see he was all for it, even relieved. "You got to take this seriously. She's beside herself. She's really been going at it."

Althy looked almost humpbacked bent over in her flowerprint housedress in an awkward effort to comfort Sarah who lay blubbering on the bed. Sarah's face squinched up in a soundless scream. She was catching her breath. She had on her crooked sunglasses with the pink frames and the old faded paisley bathrobe the old man was ready to throw out maybe twenty years ago.

"Now, now, dear," said Althy. "Don't act so upset."

"You tricked meeee!" Sarah went rigid in the bed, holding her fists against her breasts.

"I didn't trick you, dear," said Althy.

"You and Junior tricked meeee!"

"Hello, Sarah," said Ward. "What the hell are you pulling tonight?"

"Oh Ward! God, Ward!"

"That's right, Sarah. By God, you got it right off." He came around the bed. Althy moved back, a silent grudging concession that when things got bad, Ward was the only one who could get Sarah down off the roof. He sat on the bed, and she turned the sunglasses on him.

"Darling," she said uncertainly and groped for his hand. He did not offer it. After fumbling for a second, she gave up.

"What's this I hear about you giving Althy and the kid a bad time?"

"They lie to me," she cried. "I can take anything but lies."

"Now, Sarah," crooned Althy. But after repeating that fifty-year-old formula, Althy seemed at a loss as to what to say next.

"Daddy! Daaa-ddy!" Sarah went rigid and yelled out in her Baby Snooks voice. The hairs on Ward's neck stood up. "Daaddy's going to die," Sarah's voice was childish and very sad.

"Don't pull this shit, Sarah," said Ward. "You come back here."

"I don't want Daddy to come home," said the silly sad little voice. "It's bad. Daddy shouldn't die here. It's bad for me. I'm too little for death at home. Please. Please."

"You put that damn voice away," he said, the hairs still bristling on his neck. He grabbed her by the lapels of the old faded robe and shook her. Her head slapped around lax as a rope end.

"Ward!" said Althy. "You stop!"

The kid didn't say anything. He was too shook up to play the good guy.

"You listen, Sarah. Goddamn, you listen," he slapped her across the mouth.

Althy grabbed him by the ear.

"You hit your mother!"

"Get her off me, kid," said Ward. "Get her off me. I can't deal with her and this looney at the same time."

"Althy. Althy," the kid said. Althy let go. The kid, murmuring to her, backed her away to the far side of the room.

"Mean to me," the little voice sulked.

Ward slapped Sarah again, saw the spit fly.

"Goddamn you! Come back here," he said. Her head jerked suddenly. He figured she'd opened her eyes behind the sunglasses. He released the lapels of the old faded paisley robe.

"You listen to me," he said. "You listen, Sarah."

She was listening. She cocked her head slightly like a bird or a dog, so he knew she was back in town.

"I don't expect anything from you," he said. "You don't have to do anything. You just lie abed. It'll be all right. He'll be downstairs—"

"No," she whimpered.

"He'll be downstairs," he said. "We'll put him in the spare room. You don't even have to know he's around."

"He's going to die," she sobbed. She pressed her hands up under her sunglasses. Her body shook on the bed.

"Sarah, listen."

"I can't take it," she cried weakly. "Why does this have to happen to us? I told Dr. Walker there was no reasonable explanation for all this. For the rose of fire in the Pacific and the Indian woman on the lawn at nights and Scott lost in the war and you dead in the ditch—"

"Sarah—"

"No Freudian theory covers this. I told Dr. Walker. This is God at work. He has rolled a stone before the door of my soul and nothing can move it—not Freud, not anything, only God. I told him it was God who was implacable, not me."

"Sarah, Sarah," said Althy from across the room in a scared voice. "Let me get you a nice good glass of milk. It'll help to settle your nerves."

"Get out," Sarah said petulantly. "Let me talk to Ward alone. I want to talk to Ward."

When they'd gone out of the room, she said, "Don't bring him home. It will be very bad for me. I am not strong."

"You want him to die alone in the hospital?"

"We can't take care of him," she said. "Althy's too old for another sick person. I can't do anything. This weighs on me terribly. I feel it will crush me."

"It will be all right," he said.

"No," she shook her head. "It will not be all right. Don't you understand? Carol is very frightened."

"Don't start that business," he warned her. "I'll have Terrill come up here and put you through a triple loop."

"I don't *want* to start the Carol business," she said. "I want her to go away and leave me alone. She tells me terrible, terrible things. I can't stand it. I can't take these things."

"I tell you," he said, "Terrill wants to run some more tests on the old man. He wants to try a new treatment. It will be a while before he can even come home. So don't worry about it now."

She clutched for his hand.

"Will you talk about it again with me?"

"Yes," he said. "I will talk about it."

"Will you *listen?*" she gripped his hand urgently.

"I will try," he said uneasily. "Is that all?"

"No," she said quietly. "I have a secret to share with you."

"That's all right," he said. "I don't need any secrets. I'm dealing with too many mysteries as it is."

He stood up. His damn leg hurt like hell and so did the penknife pain probing under his breastbone. He wanted to go downstairs and work out the pain on the chinning bar, do his sit-ups. Then play a ballgame or two to smooth out his nerves. Boston versus Detroit was next up on the schedule. Ought to be an even match. But that wasn't in the cards, he knew. He had to get Sarah settled, then talk to the kid. He ought to call Philadelphia too. Get that squared away. He remembered he hadn't even wiped down the Cadillac. Suddenly things were getting complicated. It made him feel hot and sweaty all over.

"Well, I'm going to tell you anyway."

What was she going to tell him? A secret? She had some kind of a looney secret she wanted to share, as if it were a gift.

"You remember I told you about the Captain?" she said. "How we used to hear him rowing around in the fog at dawn out in front of the cottage at Birch Point?"

"Yes, I do," he said.

"Scott and I would sit at the window and try to guess where he would appear from the sound of the oarlocks. He would appear and disappear in the fog, and we would try to guess," she was smiling at the recollection.

"That sounds like fine sport. Is that all?"

"Sometimes the fog would open," she said in the glittering voice she used for memories, "and there he would be on the black glassy water with his oars poised, swept back like the wings of a bird, and he might be looking over his shoulder into the fog. The fog would close, and we would lose him. There would be just the sound of the oarlocks. You couldn't tell from the sound where he was because the fog plays funny tricks."

"Okay," he said. "Are you through? I want to go to bed."

"You didn't know him well," she said. "You were too little, and he was too old. He was a troubled man. He lost all our money, what there was of it. He had to sell a thousand acres just to put bread on the table. He felt responsible. He was a hero. He kept his men alive in open boats for forty days and brought them in safely to . . . somewhere. I forget."

"Hawaii," Ward said.

"Hawaii," she said dreamily. "He held them at gunpoint to keep them men. He had principles. He was religious. But it didn't matter. He still lost everything."

"That's too bad," Ward said. "Is that the end?"

"No, that's not the end. I think he blamed Scott and me. He thought we were the family's ruination."

"That's too bad. Go to sleep now," he said.

"Scotty ran away," she said. She sounded surprised.

"All right," Ward said resolutely. But what had he resolved? He stood up.

"The Captain needed him," Sarah continued in her glittering voice. "He counted on Scott to grow up and fix the business, manage things."

"And it didn't work out. Is that the secret?" he asked.

"No, it isn't. Sit down. Uncle Tyler gave away the bank. He was down there at the bank day after day reading Gibbon and Mac-Cauley and Carlisle and Ruskin. Anybody who walked in he'd give a handful of money to. He didn't know or care if they ever paid it back. He wasn't a banker."

"It doesn't seem like it," he said.

"He was smart enough though," she said. "He grew beautiful vegetables. The Captain loved those fresh greens."

"How about you go to sleep now?" he suggested. What the hell am I doing here sitting with this ding-a-ling when I have things to do? he thought.

"The Captain blamed me especially," Sarah said in a sad voice. "But it wasn't my fault. It wasn't my *fault.* Something had gone wrong before that."

"Is that the secret?" he said. Goddamn, didn't his leg ache now. He better get on the old bike tomorrow and ride out the kinks. Before he went down and picked up Terry. The body wasn't made to do nothing. It made you murderous to sit around. He wished some fellow would say something dumb to him on Monday at the factory, so he could punch him around the room.

"Do you know what I think?" said Sarah.

"No," he said. "I don't have the faintest notion."

"I think the Captain lost God somehow out there in the Pacific," she said brightly. "And he used to row around down there to Birch Point searching for him. To see if he could find him again."

"Is that the secret?"

"Yes, it is," said Sarah. She smiled.

"Mother," he said.

"You called me 'Mother,' " she breathed. "It makes me happy to hear you say that. It's been such a long time."

"I think you should go to bed now," he said.

"Darling."

"Come on," he said. "Jesus, we have to get some sleep around here."

He plumped up her pillows and freed up the sheet and blanket that she was lying on. It was a lovely L.L. Bean blanket. L.L. was one of the Captain's old duck-hunting cronies, and as L.L.'s fortunes had waxed, the Captain's had declined.

"One of the first laws of nature," the Captain opined one cool summer evening under the elms, "when someone climbs up, someone else must come down. There's a great natural balance in life."

"Where is Daddy tonight?" asked Sarah. "It's not like him not to tell me where he's going."

"Climb in," said Ward, holding the sheet and the blanket.

"I don't think I can sleep," said Sarah.

"You can't sleep?" he said. "Don't you have a book going? Why don't you try that?"

"I started *Anna Karenina* but I can't concentrate on it."

"I don't wonder. How about today's *Times?*"

"I like the papers. But they're such damn dirty things. The print gets all over my hands," she said.

"Do you want it or not?"

"Well. What about Sunday's edition? You still have that?"

"I guess so. You want that?"

"Just the book section and the travel section," she said.

He went downstairs to his room to fetch the paper. His hip stung as he jolted down the stairs, and that damn fist of pain throbbed like a bruise under his heart.

He came back with the sections she wanted.

"Here. Read a little bit and then go to sleep."

"Darling?"

"Now what."

"Nothing."

Did she want to tell him more about the Captain looking for God in the fog? Or how the ship burned against the empty sky like a giant rose? Or about Uncle Tyler's beautiful garden? Whatever it was, the expression on his face stopped her.

"Get some sleep."

"I will."

"Don't row around in the fog anymore tonight."

"I won't."

"Goodnight."

"Yes. Goodnight, darling."

When he came out of the room, Althy gave him a sidelong glare and shuffled in with a glass of milk. The kid accosted him, full of questions.

"Well? How'd you do, Svengali? How is she?"

"She's okay."

"What'd she say?" Gordie pushed his glasses back. "What did she want to talk about?"

"Let's go in the kitchen," said Ward. "I could use a drink."

"Good idea," said Gordie. "Any vodka?"

"Plenty of vodka," said Ward.

Ward got down the heavy squat crystal glasses and packed them with ice and then he poured the vodka to the brim. As he poured the vodka, the ice cubes gave off small restrained explosions. He opened the refrigerator and got out the bottle of olives, stuffed with almonds. Sarah was rowing deeper and deeper into the fog. He had better get Terrill up there tonight.

They sat at the kitchen table and took a few quiet sips. The clear liquid burned pleasantly in the back of Ward's throat.

I need this, thought Ward. This has been a tough night.

"Well," said Gordie. "What did she say?"

"Nothing." Indeed Sarah had said nothing that needed repeating.

"Come on. What did she tell you?"

The kid could be a real pain in the ass if he worked at it.

"Nothing, kid. Nothing worth repeating."

"Come on," said the kid. "What is this? What did she say? What's going on?"

Well, that's the way the kid was. Maybe he was a lot like Avis. Maybe they deserved each other. Ward looked at the four-eyed wimp.

"She's nuts, kid," he said.

Gordie paled appropriately in keeping with his artistic credentials. The kid, who never went to the hospital because he couldn't take it, and who usually managed to be somewhere else when Sarah really went looney, was full of curiosity tonight. He was afraid he might miss out on something. If the smell of hospitals made him queasy, a whiff of what really went on around the house ought to put him on the floor.

"She's telling me secrets tonight," said Ward. "She says the Captain lost God in the Pacific when the ship burned. She says the Captain described it as a giant rose burning against an empty sky. Then those forty days out there in the long boat. Somewhere out there he lost God."

"Poor Mother," said the kid.

"Rowing around out there," said Ward. "Pointing that pistol at anyone proposing cannibalism. Somehow he misplaced God, she says."

"And that's why the Captain sat under the elms and read all the philosophers. Is that it? He was hoping he could find a way back to that moment when he lost God."

"I can see this is right up your alley," said Ward.

The kid looked up, arrested.

"She's crazy, kid," said Ward. "She's been crazy for a long time."

"She's been doing pretty good lately," offered the kid. "She hasn't been away for five years."

"The old man knows she's acting funny," said Ward. "She's starting to show bad signs. She was talking about Carol tonight. Did you hear her voice?"

"Yes, that's when you . . ." the kid hesitated, "Slapped the shit out of her."

"That's it," said Ward. "It's funny farm time again. Unless we get to work."

He looked at his brother. The kid looked miserable. He glugged his martini, seeking solace. Well, he wanted to know didn't he? He wanted to be in the room hearing about the Captain rowing through the fog looking for God, and he wanted to be across town in the sunshine at the same time. He wanted Ward to slap Sarah silly till she put away the Baby Snooks voice and gave up on her plans to take a vacation in the dream country of 1923. At the same time the kid was horrified and probably secretly outraged as Althy was at the sight of a grown man punching his own mother around the room. Well, you son of a bitch, you can't have it both ways. The kid was just a paperhead, a reader of books. He didn't know anything about real life. He couldn't make up his mind whether he really wanted to. He was animated by electric notions of good

and bad which marched him all around the room like a tin soldier.
He didn't know from shit. And the old man claimed the kid was
his trustee, his businessman? Bull*shit.* Ward thought about that
will in the drawer of his nightstand, burning deadly bright.

"Look, kid," said Ward. "Terrill's going to say Sarah needs more
treatment."

"You think so?" asked Gordie miserably. The kid had had
enough. He didn't want to know anymore.

"Yes," Ward went on. "Carol's into this now. Pretty soon, we'll
have to do something."

"Well," said the kid. "Whatever Terrill says. I guess we'll have
to see what he says. Then I guess we'll have to do it."

The kid pushed his glasses back. His long blonde hair gave him
a girlish look as he sat there miserably hunched over his drink. If
the kid had enough money he'd never have to live in the real world
at all. He could lock Sarah up and paint pictures of Avis's ass till
hell froze over. Briefly Ward wondered how the kid would have
turned out if he'd taken a bath in a whirlwind of glass splinters
and landed on the road, crushing bones and tearing muscles that
would heal distortedly, tasted the snot-scented blood of near-
death.

You have to hand-feed a paperhead, Ward thought. Go easy, or
he'll bolt.

"Lucky the old man is leaving some money," he ventured.
"Otherwise Sarah couldn't afford a first-class sickness anymore."
Ward gauged his brother out of the sides of his eyes. "She'd have
to go into the fog permanently or get off her back and act normal."

Ward let that sink in. Then he laid down his first card.

"If he leaves me anything, I'm going to sign it over to Sarah. The
more money she has, the better chance she'll have enough. I sure
can't afford those doctors on my paycheck. I don't think you could
either."

He looked at the kid. The kid was in serious trouble. His head
was crunched between his shoulders, and he stared out the window.

"If the money runs out," Ward continued, "she'd have to go to
a state hospital. I don't think she'd ever come back. Do you?"

"No," said the kid. "She probably wouldn't."

"Neither do I," Ward said. "That's why whatever comes to me

I'm giving to her. Maybe you should think about doing the same, kid."

Gordie didn't answer. But the silence was fairly noisy. It was clear the kid had been thinking about the money his father might leave him. He was probably counting on it. No doubt egged on by Avis. The kid dreamed of giving up his agency job and sitting around and making pecker tracks all over canvas. He was hoping he'd end up with a few chips in his pocket, so he and the witch-woman could smoke pot and invite their hairy friends to dinner every night. But that game was over, and the kid knew it.

He sat there staring into his glass.

"Think about it," said Ward.

Althy came into the room.

"She's better now," she said. "She seems calmed down."

"Call Terrill," said Ward.

"Terrill?" said Althy. "She don't need a doctor now. She's all right now."

"Call him," said Ward. "Get him up here. Tell him what happened. She could use a good long sleep."

"That man doesn't do anything," she said crossly. "What does that fellow do?"

"You call him," said Ward.

The brown monkey eyes, the whites now mulled a faint beige with age, glared at him. He remembered how white the whites of Blue's eyes were, almost blue themselves, so coldly white. Silently he watched the wizened monkey face give up. Althy's jowls were sullen as she reached for the telephone.

It wasn't long before Terrill showed up, wrinkled and fatigued, his black bag dangling at the end of one lifeless arm.

"How is she?" asked the doctor.

"She's all right," said Ward. "She probably needs a good long sleep."

The doc came out in a few minutes.

"She'll sleep now," he said. "I'll be back tomorrow afternoon when she wakes up."

He put his bag down on the kitchen table. It gave off a heavy almost sickening smell of B-complex vitamins or something like that. He looked up at the ceiling vaguely. The reflection of the ceiling lights burned as two squares of white light on the lenses of his glasses hiding his dark morose eyes. He patted the pockets of his housecall suit, a rumpled charcoal gray that looked like it was purchased about the time the Captain turned over the bank to Uncle Tyler.

"What are you looking for? A cigarette?"

He seemed vaguely surprised by the question. Ward unrolled his pack from the sleeve of his T-shirt.

"Here, take one."

"Either of you fellows have a match on you?"

Ward handed him the matches.

"How about a kick in the lungs to get you started?" said Gordie.

Terrill looked at him with vague interest, exhaling a giant cloud of smoke blue as the smoke from a combustion engine.

The doc left soon after that. Or rather he didn't leave so much as he gradually diminished, retreating in a shuffle toward the general direction of the door, sighing, moving infinitesimally, dropping little piles of gray ash as he shrunk further and further from view.

"You think he's any good?" asked Gordie after Terrill had worked his way down the walk to the drive and had fallen into a revery while grasping the door handle of his late model Buick.

"I don't know," said Ward. "What difference does it make?"

"I don't know," shrugged Gordie. "Let's have another touch of the creature. Then I've got to go."

After another drink the kid was agitated. He started to shamble around the kitchen. Old biology had seized him by the gizzard.

"I got to get back to Avis," he said. "She hates to be alone."

"Have another drink," suggested Ward. Let the bitch sit there and fume, was Ward's idea.

"No. I got to get back," said the kid. His voice was edged with desperation, or was it panic? This boy is sick, Ward wanted to say. Terrill come back. Here is another exotic disease for you to poke around in.

"I got to get back," the kid said desperately. "Avis goes crazy if she's alone too long. You don't know how she gets."

The kid shambled around the kitchen silently debating the merits of another drink and then he left in a sudden rush, tootling down the driveway in his little white Saab.

Ward relaxed a little once everybody had cleared out. Sarah was pressed to the bed, ironed right down into the mattress by some magic potion out of Terrill's black bag. Out of the picture till moonrise tomorrow. Althy was downstairs in her room, probably listening to WBZ on the radio. The kid was racing down the Carlisle Pike, frantic to embrace Avis back in the alley. Ward had no more work to do down at the horse barn. The prospect of just sitting here and slowly sipping his ice-cold drink, feeling its healing magic steal into his blood was indeed pleasing. He contemplated his drink, taking satisfaction in the thought of those vodka-marinated olives and almonds he would crunch into a little further into the ritual. It had been a hell of a day. This silence, this being alone, worked on him like medicine.

A hell of a day.

Once in a while the old man's crazy stallion, Black Ace, would get loose. Althy would put in a call to the old man at the factory. In five minutes he would show up with a bunch of salesmen in double-knit suits, and, by God, it was rodeo time. Those folks, well intentioned but ignorant in the ways of horseflesh, would try to snare that stallion with handfuls of grass. They crept up on him. He arched his neck in powerful awareness of their timid approach. Careful, you fools, he seemed to say and went back to feeding. His teeth delicately snipped grass out in the freedom field, as the old man called the patch he hadn't yet fenced in. His jaws made a satisfactory crunching sound as if he were chewing a mouthful of peanuts. Those soft salesmen crept gingerly in his direction, through devil's paintbrush, chickweed, and grass, some of that stiff under their shoes as the bristles of a pushbroom. When they finally outraged his sense of territory and protocol, the stallion glared insanely, showing red at the corner of his eye. He'd snort, maybe give a blood-curdling scream and gallop a few yards toward a salesman. The glossy black muscles bulged in his chest and churned in his haunches and he held out his tail stiffly. He looked big as a locomotive. The man, usually fat, dropped the grass and ran.

"Where the hell you going?" his father would cry as all his salesmen ran off.

Eventually the old man, with the ineffectual aid of one or more of those salesmen, would get a rope over the stallion's head. And he would rassel the horse back into the front corral and eventually into his own stall. Black Ace was a mean son of a bitch. He'd never been saddle-broken. Ward once suggested that that might be a good idea.

"Nooo," The old man laughed. "Not that horse. We're not going to break him. We're just going to leave him mean and ornery."

"Why is that?" Ward wanted to know.

"Why is that?" the old man leaned against the fence and watched the stallion crop grass at the far end of the pasture, as far from the hand of man as he could get.

"I don't know," said the old man. "He's all right the way he is. He's mean, but he's the prettiest horse I ever saw."

You couldn't put the stallion in pasture with the mares. He'd chase them all day long. If there was a colt, he'd try to kill it. He was a crazy damn horse. When he got loose in the pasture with the mares or outside in the freedom field, times were desperate and matters were out of control.

Today was one of those days that made you feel like the stallion got loose. Everything was moving too fast. Sarah had picked a fine time to come unglued. He needed to get to her after he had the kid straight. But if she was going to take up residency at Dunnocks Head, circa 1923, that was going to be hard to do. He thought about the will. Maybe he ought to fire it, get rid of it. No, not yet. He'd lied to the old man. He'd slapped Sarah back into the present tense. He'd worked on the kid a little. He'd done all he could. Still it hadn't been much. The stallion was still loose in the freedom field. Tomorrow—

He stood up, almost knocked over his chair.

He still had that Philadelphia call to make. Damn! How could he have forgotten that? He took the number out of his wallet and dialed it. Somebody around the factory always had a name and number, no matter what the problem.

"Hello," said a tired voice.

"Dr. Brown?"

"Yes?"

"A friend of mine has a bad virus. I wonder if I could. . . ."

"What kind of a virus?"

"I don't know exactly. She's been trying to kick it for a couple of months, but she just can't seem to get rid of it."

"What's your name, please."

"Shaw. Wally Shaw. I was wondering—can I bring her in tomorrow night?"

"You don't allow yourself much room for error, do you Mr. Shaw?"

"I know it's short notice, Dr. Brown. But—"

"Be here at 9:30," the voice said, and then the line went dead.

After the essential call was out of the way, he decided to make the extra one.

"Are you all set to go away tomorrow?" he asked. Be nice, he counseled himself.

"Yes!" Terry was excited. "I'm all packed!"

"Good," he said.

What time, what time, she wanted to know.

"I'll go early to the hospital," he explained. "Then I'll pick you up about six-thirty."

"I can't wait!"

Her voice alone told him she was fairly jumping up and down.

Damn, he thought. What a time for this to happen.

T E N

THE WIND hurled sheets of water at the windshield as the yellow Coupe de Ville crawled through the blinding rain. Ward's guts churned as he peered into the fishtank world beyond the glass. Goddamned rain! Dr. Brown, the magic man, wouldn't wait. If they missed the appointment, he'd make them come back some other time. And how would he work that?

When things start to go wrong, more things go wrong. It's just like a landslide. One thing leads to another and pretty soon you have a mess on your hands. He went back over the day to see if he could detect the beginning of some subtle fissure that he'd neglected to his regret.

If you were going to live simply it took skill and a practiced eye. You had to go over your days with the careful hand of a horse dealer looking for flaws in an animal, things almost undetectable that might lead to grief later. If you did this regularly and if you learned from history, meaning other people's experience, as well as from your own mistakes, eventually you learned to read all the invisible signs of potential trouble. That way you could make your life work on simple terms. It sounded easy. But it took great skill. He was finding out it never worked perfectly.

Of course, it just wasn't the matter of a day. You could handle a day all right and still make a mess of things. You had to follow certain principles. If you didn't organize by the rules, you ended up in trouble. The real problem was getting mixed up with the foot doctor in the first place. You fool, he thought. Haven't you learned yet? You bring a woman into it, there's bound to be trouble. Just like old Shaw said.

He looked at Terry out of the sides of his eyes. She sat forward, trying to make out the road through the streaming windshield.

The car moved slowly, silent as smoke, a cocoon of leather and steel in the middle of the drumming rain.

"Boy, it sure is raining," she said.

You fool, he thought. The idea was to take care of the Cadillac, fiddle with the dials of the wonderful peanut sorter at the factory, and do exercises till the sweat ran down out of his black hair into his ears and his belly muscles glowed hot and his backbone died under protest. It was a good idea to read the box scores and, in the off-season, watch for the trades. It was okay to read the papers and see what the crazy world was up to. Play that baseball game and keep good records, that was okay too. It was a nice simple plan. Now why didn't you follow it? he asked himself. He gripped the wheel tighter and squinted at the pewter-colored rain. I don't know, he answered himself, truly puzzled. I don't know.

If it kept raining this hard he was going to have to pull off the road. He thought maybe he ought to find a telephone booth and call Brown, tell him they were going to be late. But she'd probably ask a bunch of questions. He could always tell her he was calling the hotel. She wasn't suspicious by nature, and he could probably lie badly and still fool her. He decided to stop at the next Howard Johnson's and call Brown.

Hello? he might say. Me and the foot doctor are running a little late.

The day had started off okay. He had a lot to do but he figured there was time to do it all. The minute he woke his mind began working like a machine gun mounted on a merry-go-round, spraying out thoughts in all directions. He jumped out of bed and headed for the bathroom, hobbling stiffly till the son-of-a-bitching hip started to work. He took a leak and put his plate in to soak. He didn't look at himself in the mirror. It was too early to face that. He came back into the room. He opened the closet door and did fifty chin-ups on the aluminum-plated bar. The first thirty-five were a piece of cake. He kept his eyes on that fifty-dollar ball glove on the shelf that Blue had not picked out for him finally but had paid for. He kept the glove soft and dark with neat's-foot oil, the perfect pocket curled like a shell around the giant pearl of the regulation-size ball. Be damned if he knew what he kept it for now. Or the uniform in the plastic bag. Or the spikes, all polished up and laid away like a museum piece in a shoe box with tissue paper.

He guessed it was like the fellow who keeps his army uniform all neat and pressed in the closet for twenty years. Till the material evidence of the uniform is at last the only thing left that convinces him he ever did anything except watch television and go to work.

He watched that glove with its secret history, his eyes fixed and glazed, as he steadily pumped out the last five chin-ups, working from a place beyond pain. He lay down on the throw rug and hooked his foot under the bed and began to do his sit-ups. He was thinking all the time.

In the drawer of the nightstand, as he pumped up and down, a piston of asthmatic flesh, lay the old man's will where it had burned now for two weeks. It burned in his brain too, like some radioactive trace material. Nine. No more shit. Ten. Enough numbers, enough bad news. He had sat on the bench for twelve years. No more. Thirteen. He would talk to the kid again, get him to agree that Sarah ought to name Ward executor in the absence of a will. The kid could go swab canvas. He could leave the preservation of blood, bonds, newspapers, shoe factories, whatever was left of the material translation of the old man's agony of days, to someone who really gave a damn about the tragic waste it represented—namely, Ward. In trade, Ward would take care of Sarah and Althy. And everything, so far as he was able, would stay just the way the old man would have wanted it. The minute the old man croaks, he thought, Sarah will come through with a miraculous recovery. She was just hiding out, waiting for it to be over. She was rowing around out in the fog because it was the best place to be.

I don't want Daddy to come home.

But before he was cold, she would hop out of bed, head for Maine, maybe Europe this time. She had been heard to reflect wistfully on the terrible deprivation of never having seen Venice. She would begin hemorrhaging money all over the map, getting rid of it in frenzy, bleeding it away in frivolity, in crazy frantic haste, till it was all gone, till the last nickel-symbol of the old man's quiet, patient accumulated vision of stability built on dollars and factories, had been torn down and the oceanic insanity which was Sarah's natural medium crashed in on them all. Pumping up and down, beginning to grunt with the effort, he saw her press her hands up under the pink plastic rimmed sunglasses.

This is God at work, he heard her say.

He has rolled a stone before the door of my soul.
It is God who is implacable, not me.

Gordie, as executor, could no more stop Sarah than one of those mares down in the barn could keep Black Ace away from her foal. Twenty-five. He was breathing like a whale, whistling a little through his mouth that was soft and shapeless now without the partial plate he'd left soaking in the bathroom sink. He had cashed in a bundle of teeth when he smashed through the windshield of Blue's Studebaker. He was used to having hardly any teeth in his head. The partials took care of that. He could chew his food good as anyone. But he never could get used to the stranger with the blubbery lips in the bathroom mirror. Thirty. Those teeth soaking in the sink cost him a cool thousand. He had tried to get the club to spring for it, but they wouldn't. The club had picked up the hospital bill but drew the line at paying out good money for what they described as "cosmetic purposes." You couldn't blame the club for weasling. He wasn't worth a shit to them anymore. The Red Sox had already blown a bundle on him for nothing. Thirty-four.

He was sucking greedily for air now, each time he breached above the dead bird of his sex. He fixed his eyes, slightly bugged with effort, on the framed copy of his first professional contract which hung over his bed along with the silver bat. He pumped out the last of the sit-ups.

He made his bed then in the prescribed manner, methodically folding the sheets at the corners, pulling the top sheet so tight that you could bounce a quarter on it. He went back in the bathroom, kicked off the jockey shorts he'd worn to bed, and threw them in the hamper. The kid said he wore pajamas to bed. Ward never wore anything but jockeys. Even in the worst weather all he needed was a thin blanket. If you were in shape, you didn't need a lot of clothes. Most winter days he wore just a windbreaker, no coat, none of that. He didn't go for mittens and hats, all that stuff Gordie had to hang on himself. In the winter the house was always too hot. Althy or Sarah was always fiddling with the thermostat. Both of them were thin-blooded. It was no wonder; they never did anything. Neither one of them had taken ten steps in an hour for the last twenty-five years. They kept the house hot as a rubber plantation.

"I can't breathe," he'd complain. "The sweat's just pouring off me. Look. I got on this little thin T-shirt. And look at me. I'm soaked. Look at me."

Althy either ignored him or said it was just comfortable. Sarah would sneak out of her bedroom and crank up the thermostat another notch if he didn't keep an eye on her.

He stood naked in front of the sink, his belly still aching from the sit-ups. He shaved slowly and deliberately. He lathered his face several times, going over his jaw and throat with the new blade until he was satisfied that the job was perfect. He hardly ever bled anymore now that his skin was used to it. Once in a while for no reason he'd bleed like hell. The blood would pop through his skin and stand in little drops all over his throat and chin. Maybe once every couple of months that would happen. The kid said he was nuts to spend half an hour or forty-five minutes shaving so he only had to do it three times a week. Why didn't he take five minutes a day like everyone else?

"Because this is the way I like to do it, peckerhead," he said to the mirror. It surprised him that he actually answered the figment question aloud. He laughed, embarrassed at himself.

The kid missed the point as usual. It wasn't a question of shaving three times a week instead of every day. It was a question of shaving *right,* getting a perfect job. But the kid wouldn't know what he was talking about, even if Ward tried to explain it.

After his shave he carefully rinsed the bowl, refilled it, dusted it with a little magic powder and put his plate back in to soak. He liked to soak it really good and kill all those bad breath germs. The kid sometimes got up close in his gooney enthusiasm for some picture or book, and his breath smelled a little suspect. He probably didn't brush his teeth enough. Ward actually carried a little fold-up toothbrush and some tooth string with him each day to the factory so he could brush after lunch. The kid's teeth were dingy when he smiled. He probably hadn't gotten around to realizing that, if you didn't brush regularly, food particles between your teeth and gums would cover each emphatic word you spoke with vegetable rot or worse, the highly acid stink of decaying meat. It was ironic that the kid should still have all his teeth, being so bad about dental care. Ward had always been fastidious about his teeth and gums. He didn't even have a cavity till he was seventeen. He had had a total of three up till the crash through the windshield, which had knocked out altogether or sheared off down to the gum about twenty teeth.

In the house, he used two toothbrushes and kept each one in a little plastic tube in the medicine cabinet. He'd use one in the morning and the other one before bedtime. That way the brush was always dry and the bristles always stiff. Everybody else he knew hung up a toothbrush right out in the open on the so-called toothbrush holder. He figured the smells of the bathroom would sink right into those toothbrush bristles. So he always put his brush in the plastic tube and stored it in the medicine cabinet. It was hard to understand why people let their toothbrushes hang out in the open.

He took the green toothbrush out of its case, sprinkled it with tooth powder. He never used toothpaste. If you wanted to get your teeth clean you used powder, not toothpaste. He scrubbed his remaining teeth thoroughly. He rinsed his brush under the cold water tap. He put the brush back in its plastic tube and placed it back in the medicine cabinet.

Ward bent to the mirror intently like a man examining his stamp collection. He plucked out with his fingers the few hairs which grew between his eyebrows. He glared into the mirror.

Hello, baboon. How's your ass?

He perched on the toilet seat to see the rest of his body. The torso was heavily muscled, his thighs, sinewy slabs of lean muscle that flickered under the white, almost phosphorous skin like muscle ticks in one of the old man's nervous colts. His knees were bony. You could see the left leg was skinnier. It was wound around with a network of scar tissue. The scars were a glossy blue-white like fish scales. In startling contrast to the hard white glowing flesh, in a wiry black nest, perched his short fat-barreled member. His dong pointed crookedly to his good right leg, repudiating the skinny left one. Years ago the kid had claimed that everyone dangled to the right because of the earth's rotation. Horseshit, Ward had said. It's true, Gordie had said sincerely. Even as a high school whiz, the kid always had a definitive pronouncement, no matter the subject. Why not on dongs? It was a trait common among paperheads. He had passed the kid's observation on to Blue as kind of a joke. She considered the matter for a moment.

Then she said, "What if you're left-handed?"

"Left-handed?" he asked in turn.

"Yes, left-handed. Does it dangle to the left if you're left-handed?"

"I don't know," he said. God help me, if the two of them ever get together, he thought. But they never did, did they? Some of these wishes that come true, they give you second thoughts later on.

Ward considered his reflection in the mirror. The old one-eyed pirate who took no prisoners. What a damned fool he was. He groaned in disgust.

"I'm pregnant," she had said and demurely looked down at her green fingernails.

Good gravy, he thought. How did I get into this, knowing what I know? Well. Maybe he could still make this come right.

He had no one but himself to blame, he thought, as he climbed down from the toilet seat. He fished his plate out of the lukewarm bowl, rinsed it in cold water. His teeth slipped into place with the satisfactory noise that a lock makes when you throw the bolt. He pulled the plug. The drain began to suck the water down greedily, burping and gulping.

The day still looked okay for openers. His thoughts were disturbing, but so far he hadn't detected any subtle fissures in the day itself. The sun was shining when he came upstairs for breakfast. Althy was rolling out some pie crust at the kitchen counter. Her birdlike claws slapped and kneaded the dough. She sprinkled flour on the wooden board. She used the wooden roller to flatten the ball of dough, transforming the golden wad into a large powdery wafer. She worked furiously, saying nothing to him as if his mere presence were an insult to cooks everywhere. It was plain she was still mad at him for slapping Sarah around. Usually he managed to avoid Althy. But this morning they showed up in the kitchen at the same time. This plainly was the first outright fissure.

Well, he was mighty hungry. Already the things he had to do were building up like high water behind the fragile dam of limited daylight. Otherwise he'd let Althy finish up and come back later. He had the car to take care of. He figured he'd go down and see Sharfman to get the law straight. He probably ought to mow a couple acres of grass. He had to tend to the horses, then get over and see the old man, then get back and pick up the foot doctor. He wanted breakfast whether Althy was mad at him or not. So he started fussing around the refrigerator, getting out the eggs, the bacon, the butter.

"What are you doing?" Althy demanded in an exasperated voice.

"What am I doing?" he said. "I'm in my own kitchen. Getting my own breakfast."

"Humph," she said.

"That's all right," he said. "You be mad. I won't bother you. Don't you bother me."

Word gets around, over the invisible telegraph wires that link people to people. If somebody starts out giving you a bad time, it seems like everybody you run into that day will do the same. That was another clue he should have seen but missed. A lot depends on how you handle that first person who starts after you in the morning. You give that person rap for rap and likely everybody else you run into that day will treat you civil.

He got out the cast-iron frying pan and started the bacon, three thickly sliced pieces, country style. It began to sputter lazily in the pan giving off a good smell.

"Turn on the fan," Althy said. "Turn on the fan. Don't come in here and stink up everything. If you're going to be here, do things right."

"All right," he said. He turned on the fan. "Don't get in an uproar."

Nobody said anything for a minute. Then he made a mistake.

"How is she this morning?" he asked.

"She's still knocked out," said Althy. "What do you expect? Didn't you tell that quack to drill her silly for twenty-four hours?"

"She can use the rest," said Ward. But he was already back-peddling, regretful of ever asking after Sarah. Generally, the less said about Sarah, the better for all concerned.

"Can she? Can she?" If an old lady can growl like a bear, that's what Althy was doing.

"Can she also use that punch across the face? Is that good for her too?"

Her old monkey face was ugly. She was so mad her eyes looked crazy.

"Don't start in on me," he said.

The old woman kneaded the dough furiously. "Your own mother!" she said. "A sick woman. And you treat her like she was some kind of animal that ought to be beaten with a stick. She nurtured you."

She wheeled on him suddenly, causing him to spill some of the crystals of the instant coffee on the counter.

"You know that?" she persisted. "Once you were helpless. You were once an innocent little baby, hard as that is for me to believe. And she helped you the best way she could, sick as she was even then."

"I'm not equal to your speeches this morning," he said. "I got a lot to do." He dipped the perfect sunnyside eggs from the pan to his plate. "Are you sure there aren't some missionaries back along the line?"

"There ought to be a missionary come and grab you by the collar and the seat of your pants and shake you till your teeth rattle. I never saw anyone treat a mother worse than you have."

He wrapped the tableware—the knife, spoon, and fork—in the paper napkin and stuck them in his back pocket.

"Do you want me to put a quarter in that pie plate there on my way out?" He poured the hot water into his cup.

"I don't want you to do anything except get out of my sight," she said. She sure could look ugly when she got mad.

So that's how the day started, with him being driven from the kitchen. Still he figured he had plenty of time to get everything done and get the foot doctor down to Philadelphia on time. He still didn't understand it was going to be one of those days when nothing goes right. It really wouldn't sink in till he went to see the old man. He wondered if Terry had spit the pillow out of her mouth yet.

He'd find out after a while. He cleared things away and ate breakfast at the little desk down in his room. Looking out his window down at the fields, he remembered with a start that he ought to bring in the mares and let Black Ace rage in the pasture for a while. He finished his eggs quickly.

Taking his coffee with him, he went down across the lawn, into the tall grass, along the balding elliptical path, in through the corral. It was a lovely mild morning, bright and sunny. No sign of rain at all. He opened the barn door of the low eggshell-colored building.

The smell of hay, oats, molasses, horseflesh, and ammonia all struck him at once and made him grin crookedly. The horses stamped and neighed, coming to life as the light flooded into the stable. He opened the stall gates, forked a little hay into the cribs and whistled the mares into the stalls. Between the slats of his stall which was like a maximum security prison cell, he patted Black Ace on his sullen nose. It was so dark he had trouble seeing the outline of the big horse. For Ward's trouble, Ace offered to bite him, his big flat teeth, going *click* on the unoffending air as Ward snatched back his fingers. The old man loved this mean bastard. He swung open the gate, and the horse exploded out of the stall. He kicked the gate, a show of lightning-quick invisible violence, rattling right up through Ward's forearms and shoulders clear into his neck bones. The animal, mean and big, disappeared from view out of the barn doorway.

Gone.

He heard the birds chirp innocently, where a moment ago the air was electric with his musky horse odor. A moment ago the horse had carved the air with his hooves and mean black bulk. Now the sunlight was innocent with the casual morning sound of innocuous birds.

Ward stayed at the fence long enough to finish his coffee. A couple of summers ago when they'd built the horse barn together, the old man had been solid muscle, mixed with a little healthy flab around the middle. He looked like he was going to go on forever, even though he was over fifty then. In Ward's head glowed a picture of the old man bent over the sawhorse. His bullneck was enflamed like a boil in the slashing sunlight. The sweat trickled down his broad glistening back as he sawed wood. A bead of sweat traced a dirty little road in the valley of his spine. He was plenty strong then. They worked hard all day on the weekends and after work every night. It was Ward who staggered around dizzy with exhaustion after a few hours of this, not the old man. His father enjoyed the work, luxuriating in the solid reliable strength of his fifty-year-old body, which, of course, was getting ready to serve up a joke or two.

While they worked, the horses drew near and curiously nosed everything. Ward remembered the time the chestnut hammerhead with lampblack stockings quietly sidled up behind the old man, looking away disinterestedly. When his father turned his back the hammerhead nudged the coffee can full of nails off the sawhorse. The old man chased her away, waving his hammer. She galloped a little ways off and stood with her hammerhead stolidly outlined against the blue ridge of mountains beyond. The old man had to laugh, the mare played it so deadpan. She stood with her brown elliptical haunches facing them, switching her coarse black tail. Pulling a moon. She craned her neck to deadpan the old man again as he, still chuckling, stooped to pick up the nails. "Damn you, horse," he said. He loved those horses. He loved every one of them. He didn't even ride them, he just watched them. He said it was his hobby.

Even then the cancer was in him somewhere, beginning its secret work.

The stallion sulked down at the far corner of the pasture.

"You are a mean bastard," he said softly.

So that was two.

Now both Althy and Black Ace had tried to kick him and he was barely out of bed. He should have been warned.

He walked slowly back up to the house, enjoying the molten warmth of the sun on his back. He took his breakfast dishes upstairs, got the riding mower out of the utility shed and bounced around on its iron kidney-shaped seat till his tailbone hurt. He cut the front lawn and the side lawn, about two acres altogether. Save the rest for tomorrow.

He backed the yellow Cadillac out of the garage and looked her over carefully in the bright sunlight.

In the other bay of the garage loomed the old man's brand-new 1967 white Cadillac convertible with barely 3,000 miles on it. It sat there like a splendid yet ghostly yacht, long and low with a black nylon top that sparkled darkly in the subdued light. It was a damn beautiful car. It'd been sitting there now for a couple of weeks. He decided to ask the old man if he wanted him to take the thing for a sail around the points of the compass from time to time. He'd ask him tonight. Maybe tomorrow he could take it out for a run.

He discovered he'd missed a few specks of tar yesterday on the right front fender of the yellow Cadillac, just beyond the wheel well. He cleaned that off. Doing stuff like that would keep a car from rusting out practically forever. He dragged the floor mats out and hosed them down in the driveway.

He got out the upholstery cleaner and sprayed that on the black leather seats, watched it foam up and wiped it with a clean rag.

The leather turned glossy and smelled new again. He didn't have to empty the ashtray. Even though he smoked he never stubbed a butt in the ashtray. He always had the window open a crack and he snapped the stub out the window. He didn't let anybody else smoke in the car—only himself. With the window down. To others he would say, "I don't allow smoking in this old car. I'm afraid she'll blow up." He'd make a joke of it. You had to have some rules. Otherwise people would accidentally miss the ashtray and stub out cigarettes on the dashboard or burn holes in the seats. If they wanted to smoke, they could do it someplace else.

He got the car cleaned up. And still, although he was beginning to feel uneasy, he had no notion that the dam of this day's allotment of hours and sunlight was going to crack and give way before the floodtide of the things he had to do and, more importantly, the kind of people he had to deal with.

Ward decided a little workout on the bike was in order. Besides, he had to see Sharfman down at the courthouse and get the law straight. Maybe he was barking up the wrong tree. He climbed on the white Motorbecane, slim and skittery, its handlebars curved gracefully as any antelope horns, and pumped down the driveway. The lightweight aluminum rack with its spring-loaded bar would hold *The New York Times* on the trip back. A simple fact like that gave him satisfaction. He was feeling good. He still hadn't caught on. The sky was starting to look disorderly. It had turned a dull gray. There was some kind of turbulence like boiling smoke, if you watched it close, coming in from the south. He rode on the uneven shoulder of the Merkleburg Pike for about a mile, the alloy handlebars palsied and cool beneath his hands. The highway was heavily traveled by a lot of farmers in a frenzy to get nowhere. They went whooshing by in dusty pickups with homicidal indifference, giving him damn little clearance.

He cut back into some greenly quiet residential streets and worked his way to Hanover Street. These quiet side streets smoothed him out, giving him the mistaken idea that things were going just fine. He worked his way to the old courthouse where Sharfman had his office. There were the sandstone Greek columns, pockmarked by the cannonballs of Jeb Stuart's artillery.

He wrapped the plastic encased chain around the railing to the public men's room in the back of the courthouse, looped it through his back wheel, clicked the lock home, and spun the combination.

He'd never forget the combination: 344. Some sweet batting average—in fact, Ted William's lifetime mark.

Sharfman had his office in a small dark airless suite in the southwest corner of the second floor. The walls had once been white but were now unevenly stained yellow after decades of absorbing the smoke from Sharfman's cigars.

"What can I do for you, son?" said the lawyer as soon as the amenities were over. This question spoken around a fat brand-new but unlighted cigar.

"Aren't you going to light it?" asked Ward, watching the man roll it around in his mouth.

"What?"

"I said: aren't you going to light your cigar?"

"Oh. No, I'm not. I give up smoking. My doctor said I had to. So I just roll it around and suck on it like a licorice stick. What can I do for you, son?"

"The old man is in bad shape. The doc says he's dying. I think he's got a will, but what would happen if he didn't?"

"Well, I'm sorry to hear that about your father. He's a good man. I hope you will say hello for me next time you see him."

"I will," said Ward. But not yet, he thought.

"Let's answer your law question first," said Sharfman. He swiveled in the chair so he was looking right at Ward and took the cigar out of his mouth.

Sharfman was a pyramid of flesh. The iron-gray crewcut formed the apex and the broad buttocks, planted in the creaking swivel chair above the courtroom chambers, provided the base. Between Sharfman's thumbs, hooked in the pockets of the tan linen vest which draped his fat gut, the pyramid was repeated upside down in small scale by his Phi Beta Kappa key, strung on a gold chain. The old man said that Sharfman was the only man he knew who wore his key horizontally. The gold chain stretched tight as a guy wire across his immense belly. The key did not dangle, it pointed.

"If the decedent leaves no will," said Sharfman, as if reciting slowly from a book, "the law provides that two-thirds of the estate is divided among the children. The surviving spouse receives the remaining third."

"Is that so?" said Ward.

"That's it," said Sharfman. "That's the law."

But Ward's mind was already racing on. It's so, he was really saying to himself. Everything I've done up to now was the right thing. The kid and I sign off, and Sarah appoints me executor and everything's safe.

"Well, he's sick," said Ward. "But you never know. Even the doctor sounds hopeful sometimes."

"I hope he makes it," said Sharfman.

"I thought I ought to check with you to see what the law is."

"Well, that's the law."

"I see it is," said Ward. "He hasn't got a will here with you, has he?"

"No, he doesn't," said Sharfman. "He ought to have one here but he doesn't. Maybe I ought to give him a call."

"Oh, he's got a will all right," said Ward.

"He does?"

"Yes, he told me he's got one. I just figured you would have a copy of it, that probably he'd have you witness it officially or something."

"I tell you something interesting about Pennsylvania law, son," said Sharfman.

"What's that?"

"A man don't need a witness to his will in Pennsylvania. He can just write it, and say this is my will, and sign it."

"And it's official?"

"It's official."

So that will, scrawled on blue paper, was every bit as much a legal document as a real estate title covered with fancy stamps or a divorce decree lettered in Gothic and full of Latin phrases.

"You say, he told you he's got a will?" said Sharfman.

"Yes," said Ward. "He told me that."

"I probably ought to have one on file."

"He told me he's going to send you a copy," said Ward. "Soon as he gets home from the hospital."

"Good," said Sharfman and seemed satisfied.

But then he said, "Why did you want to know what happened if he had no will?"

Again Ward experienced that scalding sensation of having just pissed himself.

"I just wanted to understand all sides of the question," said Ward.

"I thought you said he didn't have a will at first," said Sharfman, friendly enough.

"I said I thought he had a will, but what would happen if he didn't?"

"Oh," said Sharfman.

"He told me he has one," said Ward pedalling fast. "But I haven't actually seen it, and I don't know where it is. That still makes me *think* he has a will."

"I see," said Sharfman. "Well, you see that he gets a copy down here."

"I will."

"You say hello to him for me."

"Okay."

"Okay, son."

Maybe that's when he knew the day had exploded under the pressure of the floodtide of urgent human business. Or something urgent. Maybe invisible, inhuman, and uncontrollable. He'd gone about it all wrong. He should have gone to the library and looked the answers up in a book, instead of asking Sharfman a bunch of damn-fool questions. Maybe if he hadn't been distracted by his problem with the foot doctor he would have handled this thing right.

As he reached the shadowy portico of the courthouse the skies opened up. It was like a tropical cloudburst. The rain beat on the sidewalk fiercely. A haze of rain danced on the roofs of the cars parked at the meters along Hanover Street.

A fat lady ran toward him in ferocious slow motion, covering her head with a big red plastic purse. The expression on her moon face could have been mistaken for one of excruciating pain as if she were running through fire instead of rain. She slipped and fell down hard about five yards from the courthouse steps, landing on her side. Her purse slithered away. She sat up, her skirt above her knees and her legs sprawled apart, revealing a set of calves big enough to be the envy of any professional football player. She sat there with her head down, the rain battering her hairdo into her eyes.

Ward ran down the steps and fetched her purse. He was soaked instantly. But never mind. It was getting late, he was going to get wet on that bike. He might as well be a Good Samaritan in the process.

He hurried over to her, careful not to slip on some leaves that had been knocked off the trees in this rain.

"Here, lady, let me help. Are you—?"

He struggled to get her up. He could hardly budge her. She struggled fatly. She waved her big arms and jiggled her torso. Her mountainous legs remained spread on the pavement, but at last she found a way to get her feet under her.

"Goddamn near broke my leg," she said. She heaved to her feet and gave her skirt a tug.

"Are you okay?" he asked. His hair was plastered to his scalp now like hers was.

"I'll be black and blue for a month," she said. "Here, give me that."

She tore the red purse loose from his hands and gave him a swat on the chest with it. It made a surprisingly loud wet smacking noise like somebody doing a belly flop in a swimming pool. Then she turned again, covering her now sodden head with the red purse, and started up the courthouse steps.

"Goddamn jerkoff," he heard her say.

He had trouble getting the combination lock off the bike. He struggled and cussed over that, rattling and jerking the plastic encased chain in stupid futility till at last some rusty tumbler relented and the lock popped loose. The hard leather seat was cold and wet. At the shock of sitting on it, he squinched up to a pin hole. This is the way you get piles, he thought.

He pedaled the three miles out the Merkleburg Pike to the house. There wasn't much traffic moving in this cloudburst, but one time some damn fool in a pickup truck passed him going fifty and threw a blinding, cold, and what must have been a six-foot wave of water over him. Bleary-eyed and choking, he held on tight as the handlebars bucked. The skittery bike wobbled dangerously and almost pitched him into the steel guardrail. That's when he discovered the friction brakes were useless in this rain. It was just luck that he didn't kill himself. Eventually he got home.

He walked into the house, the water running off him, a streak of mud stippled in the middle of his T-shirt, the result of a steady spray of water off the back tire. Wherever he walked he left a shining path of puddle-deep water. Althy was standing in the doorway of the kitchen, with her apron on and a wooden spoon in her hand. She looked curious.

"Don't ask," he said.

He went downstairs and took a hot shower. Gradually the circulation was restored to his hands and feet, and his teeth stopped chattering.

By then, he was already running late. He was tempted to skip the visit to the hospital tonight. Maybe if he called him up, he could talk the kid into going over. He thought about the rain, how it made a day move slow when you had nothing to do but lie in bed. The old man would be waiting for him, expecting him to bring a copy of *The New York Times* since this was Saturday. What the hell. He decided to fit it in, even though he didn't have the time.

It was a good thing he did.

The old man looked awful. He had on his blue pajamas but they didn't look so fresh today. His eyes were hollowed and bruised looking underneath. He was generally pasty-looking. Today he really looked sick.

"Well," said the old man resignedly to the window. "I let Terrill talk me into that chemo-damn-therapy."

"I guess you had to give it a try," said Ward.

"I don't know. Maybe I should have just sailed away."

"No," said Ward. "You had to give it a try."

"I'm getting tired of this," said the old man. He looked pastier than ever and the circles under his eyes were big and dark. "I'm going through with this treatment business. Then I'm coming home."

"Good," said Ward. "You come home."

"I will. I'm tired, boy. I want to sleep in my own bed."

"I can understand that," said Ward. "I was happy to get back to my own room and out of that hospital in Louisville."

"Yes, but the trouble is: you never left your room after you came home."

"Is that right?"

"Yes, that's right. After twelve years you're still on the convalescent list. But we're making progress. We turned in the crank-up bed and Terrill sawed away the body cast. You're sleeping in a regular bed now."

"I see you're cheering up now that you've got me around to poke fun at," Ward said.

"I'm not sure I'm trying to be funny," said the old man. "Maybe I'm just ornery."

He sat there looking out the window. He was really down.

"You know Doctor Coffin didn't last long after the Captain sailed away," said the old man, no doubt thinking how clean and right if not painless it was to just sail away. "Your mother says their lives were linked."

"She says everything's linked," said Ward.

"The Coffins settled on Webster land early," offered the old man in proof of the family's intertwined destinies. "It was a Coffin woman the first Webster married after that Indian squaw died violently."

"That's new to me," said Ward.

"You ought to read those journals sometime," said the old man. "They tell you everything. Doc Coffin lost a grandson in World War II. So did the Captain. They'd gone to school together as boys. Known each other for—what?—over eighty years. Doc Coffin and L.L. Bean went fishing up on Mooselookmeguntik Lake the next spring after the Captain sailed away. The Captain maybe would have been among them, if he'd played by the rules. How he would have gotten in and out of the boat I don't know. But he, or they, would have figured out a way. On the second day of that fishing trip, which was the time when all those old cronies got together for their annual fish, the least of them with maybe forty years seniority, Old Doc fell out of one of the boats. He had on his waders. They filled up and dragged him right to the bottom like a pair of cement shoes."

In Ward's mind he saw Luther Coffin, arms outspread, boots filling, goggle-eyed, an ancient man, dreamily sliding down a mountain of silver bubbles, from the sun-shot green-and-gold shallows into the deeper reaches of pure and ever deepening green.

"I wonder," sighed the old man. "If the trout and pickerel were astonished to see the cagey old fisherman helpless at last in their element?"

"Life's funny," said Ward. "Two old men, known to each other all their lives, disappearing into the water at the end, just weeks apart."

"Yes," said the old man. "It's a real education."

It was urgent that Ward get going since he was running late,

especially since the rain, which hadn't let up a bit, would surely
slow them down. But he could not leave the old man now. This
recollection of Doctor Coffin's death and its relation to the Captain
and maybe his own death was, Ward sensed, the melancholy low
point of his father's day. Ward sat there with his bad leg up on
the chair and waited for the mood to lift. The newspaper lay
neglected and unread in the old man's lap. Once he started in on
the papers, he'd be all right. But before Ward could suggest that
he read and explain the headlines, the old man started in again.

"It's only Saturday," he said.

"That's right," agreed Ward.

"It'll be Monday before the rain stops," said the old man. "This
is going to be one of those weekends. It'll be Monday before your
girl visits me again."

"She doesn't work the weekends," said Ward.

"I guess she'll come see me Monday. I don't know. If you see
her, you tell her to come see me."

"I will."

"Why don't the two of you come together?" suggested the old
man.

Ward just looked at him.

"Not a good idea," said the old man. "I see that on your face.
Tell her to come see me."

"Okay."

"Damn this stuff," said the old man.

"What's that?" asked Ward.

"Damn this—oh, nothing, I guess. I'm just tired today. Fed up
by the whole thing."

"I'll bet you are," said Ward. "When you're ready, let's get you
out of here."

The old man looked at him. His face was yellow and hollow. His
eyes glistened. He looked unhealthy.

"I'm getting ready, boy," he said. "I'll be ready soon. I've had
about enough of modern science."

Ward was sorry to see the old man sunk down so low. Maybe
it was the rain, not just the chemo-damn-therapy. Or maybe this
evening he was convinced the whole therapeutic deal was a joke.

"If you see Terry, tell her I miss the shampoos she gives," said
the old man. He looked awful.

"You just saw her yesterday. You take on like it's been weeks."

"It's been weeks since yesterday," explained the old man. "Will you see her?"

"I don't know. Maybe," lied Ward.

"If you see her, tell her I may commission her to get me a new pair of pajamas."

"Good gravy," said Ward. "You're really sunk."

"You tell her," insisted the old man. "You tell her to come see me."

Ward did not like to leave him when he was so down, but he had to get going. He was late already. Now the object of all his father's melancholy rain-inspired affection sat next to Ward as the yellow Coupe de Ville plowed like an elegant stately old ship through the ceaseless rain.

Everything was falling apart.

The old man was dying.

Sarah was crazy as a loon.

This dumb girl was pregnant.

It was raining like crazy and they were going to be way late for their appointment. He hadn't even started to go to work on her, he was so upset with the way things were going with the old man. The old man was feeling so bad he probably wasn't thinking about the will. Still that didn't buy much time to figure out what to do next. Get this girl taken care of and then go to work, he counseled himself. You have serious work to do.

I'm pregnant, she'd said and looked demurely at her green finger-nails.

It was enough to make you puke.

She pretended she was sorry to lay this unfortunate news on him. But that was just an act. She was really happy as a meadowlark. No doubt she figured she'd worked him into a position where there was only one obvious and reasonable course of action for a gentleman. She probably took great satisfaction in that. Just on general principle, nothing made a woman happier than when she had a midget diver sounding the deep waters of her belly.

Good gravy, wasn't it a fine world to bring kids into. The papers described what a fine place it was. On the front page the politicians lied through their teeth and plotted patriotic bloodbaths. On the inside you read how this one threw her baby against the wall to make it stop crying and another one killed herself because of Elvis Presley, a young man she'd grown to adore by means of his records and news clippings. You were left with the idea that Sarah was just your average citizen. It made you turn to the sports page in a hurry.

But this woman was oblivious to the general conditions around her to say nothing of the specific conditions, such as the delicate balance of her blood pressure, the dangerous germs on her toothbrush, the endless hazards she ran just breathing, eating, and walking around. In this sad and miserable time, she wanted to squat and shit out another poor hopeless human being.

She was happy as a clam at high tide. Her face glowed. She looked prettier than he'd ever seen her. Her voice was full of a suppressed excitement. She was just waiting for him to give her some permissive signal, such as a mild chuckle. And then her laughter would peal out, she would laugh till she cried, probably to the point of exhaustion. She would dance all night if he'd feed the nickels to the jukebox. If he smiled, she'd smile back till her teeth broke. If he didn't hold her at bay, forgot, and made a faint gesture of affection, she'd be wrapped around his neck like a pet boa constrictor. She was just ready to bust out all over, which only made him madder. You could see it. Pretending to be sad about it, when she was really happy as a meadowlark.

You haven't got enough trouble, he thought. You had to take up with this idiot.

The rain ran down the windshield like molten pewter. He figured they were about fifteen miles from the Morgantown exit. Right around there somewhere was a turnpike Howard Johnson's and a pay phone. He would call Dr. Brown from there.

"Gee whiz," she said. "This old rain looks like it will never let up."

He gripped the wheel tightly, straining to see the road. Surely the stallion was in the freedom field tonight.

It is your own fault, he thought. You knew better. But you got mixed up in this anyway.

He remembered back to last spring when he had first met Terry. Against his better judgment, he had gone to one of the kid's studio parties.

The kid really kicked up a fuss about it.

"Come on," he said. "Help me celebrate my first one-man show."

The kid had just had a show in the community room of one of the local department stores, and he was all agog with himself.

"I tell you, kid," said Ward. "I have things to do."

"Bullshit," said the kid. "What do you have to do? Wash out your underwear? Take two hours for a careful shave? Play the baseball game? Do a hundred push-ups?"

The kid was getting pretty personal.

"Please," said Avis. "You never do anything. Why don't you break down one time? Frankly, I don't give a shit what you do. But it means a lot to your brother."

They kept it up for so long he finally gave in.

As he showered that night he regretted that this hot water which was pleasantly parboiling him, turning his belly and shoulders pink, would be the last true pleasure of the evening. He would have no time to begin that fanciful all-Boston World Series between the 1948 Red Sox and the Braves, which should have happened in real life but hadn't. There would be no quiet time with the record book under the golden goose-necked lamp. Instead he had a damn party to go to and a bunch of freaks to meet.

Dressed in a gray T-shirt that read "Candy Makers Union, Local 406," across the front in black letters, and a freshly ironed pair of khakis, plus a splash of the old man's aftershave, Ward shuttlecocked aimlessly through the warp and woof of beards and jeans, handcrafted jewelry, and plain, friendly female artisans. The heavy sweet smell of marijuana was in the air, mixed faintly with the body odors of these freaks.

There were a lot of would-be artists in the room, and they could have all used a shampoo and a shave. The girls were decidedly homely and had taken up serious occupations like growing herbs in apartment window boxes. They drank cheap sweet wine and camomile tea. One of them twanged a homemade dulcimer and gave nasal passage to some undecipherable song. B.O., bad teeth, and secondhand clothes were also in with these folks. He never saw such a bunch of phonies in his life. He'd like to have heard what Wayne McLain would have said about this crowd. And there was the kid, right in the center of it, just eating it up.

Through the interstices of pungent smoke, lank, dirty hair, and rank B.O., he got his first look at Terry Delaplane. This little blonde, her hair in a bouffant-style that was five years outdated, was definitely out of place. First of all she was all scrubbed up, clean, and neat. She wore a pretty little blue gown covered with the outlines of butterflies in white. Her neckline revealed the round edges of two nice apple-sized breasts. You wouldn't mistake her for pretty. But she was lively as she talked with Avis. Her cheeks were flushed with pleasure. She looked very fair and shiny-clean in her blue gown. Ward felt old biology stir within like a sleeping bat.

He put himself in Avis' line of vision so she would introduce him. Which she did. It was talk to this compact little albino or drift around the room and get high on the smoke. Besides she stirred him up. Good gravy, he was not completely dead. There, the old bat fluttered again. He decided to toy with the sensation a little, which he would mark down as a mistake later on.

"Delaplane," Ward said. "I knew a catcher, used to be in the Red Sox organization years ago. Any relation?"

"No," she smiled. "I'm afraid not. Are you a baseball fan?"

"Yes, kind of—"

"Gimp's the family jock," Avis said archly.

"That's me," he said.

Avis was too high-falutin' to give any time to sports. She figured if you played baseball you automatically must be stupid.

"Gimp played professional baseball," Avis explained to Terry. She was smiling and her voice was confidential as if she were sharing a private joke. Baseball certainly was silly. Compared to standing around bare-assed for an important artist like the kid.

"Did you play for a major league team?" asked Terry.

It was an honest question.

"No," he answered. "I never made the big time."

"Gimp went out one night, got drunk, and smashed himself up," said Avis. She trained her big breasts on him like a couple of mortars and smiled.

"Now he works in a peanut butter factory and makes fun of his brother."

"It passes the time," he said.

"I have to put out more dip," Avis said. "These creeps eat like a bunch of Comanches. You two enjoy yourselves." She retreated, breaking through the head-high layer of smoke that hung in the crowded room. The place was giving him a headache. Cold sweat popped out on his forehead.

"Is that how you got those scars on your face?"

"What's that?"

He was surprised to find her standing there regarding him in a
blonde study.

"Your accident. Did you get those scars in the accident that
ended your ball career?"

"Yes, that's right. I took a dive through a windshield."

"Oh, gosh."

"You know, it's funny. It happened the way Avis said. I went
out, celebrated too much. I wrecked a car and ruined myself. But
even though that's what happened, that's not the way it was at all.
Does that make any sense?"

"It does," she said. "I think I know what you mean."

Well, it didn't matter whether she did or not. He paused to look
at her fully. Yes, old biology was on the move. He could forget
about women for months at a time. Just go about his business
quietly. Then something like this would happen.

"Well, now you know about me," he said. "What about you?"

"I'm a nurse."

"That's nice. Where do you do this?"

"At Cooper Memorial."

"How come you're at this party?"

"Avis and I went to high school together. We've known each
other for ages."

"I feel like I know her pretty well too." He thought he'd try a
little humor. Girls like a little suggestive humor to get things
rolling. "She's been living with my brother for six months now.
He must have painted her forty times in the buff. In these paintings I've seen her naked as a jay from every angle. I found it
embarrassing at first. Now it's old hat. The kid is obsessed with
naked women. Do you think he's a sex maniac?"

She covered her smile with one small paw. When she took her
hand away he saw what she was hiding. One tooth slightly over-
lapped the other. She was mildly bucktoothed, probably a thumb
sucker as a kid.

"Avis has a neat figure," she said. "Gee. Anyway what's wrong
with the body? I think the human body is very pretty."

There she was, under her bouffant hairdo, her helmet of gold,
a regular defender of the arts. Her budlike mouth pouted under
this heavy burden. A frown ruffled her forehead. She was silly but
old biology didn't care. The muscles of Ward's chest tightened, his

palms were cold and sweaty, and his puffy smile stuck to his face overlong.

"I think he's just horny."

Ward gazed covertly at the mounds of her white breasts and felt the pulse-beat rise in his neck.

"Maybe he's kinky too," he speculated. "He'll probably paint Avis all trussed up in leather next."

She covered her mouth, giggled into her hand.

The gaze of her blue eyes invited him to do something about her. Those fine attractive apples were his if he had the appetite. She was a short number. She had a small waist if you went for that stuff. Her stubby legs and big hips suggested she likely would be fat someday. This little girl thought the human body was *pretty*. Well, hers wasn't; it was passable. He wondered if the verbal mating dance he had to go through, with all those "neats" and "gees," was going to be worth it.

In a few weeks he had the answer. She wasn't worth the trouble. She was okay like the rest. But she wasn't worth the bother. What woman was? Nobody had been worth it since Blue. And not even her, finally. If he'd known what was going to happen to him when he took up with her, how it would end in a shower of glass, her dead on the road, and him living a zombie life, he'd have said: "Thank you, Ma'm. No thanks."

Poor Blue. Every time the thought of her entered his mind, he tossed it out fast, like a man bailing water out of a sinking rowboat.

Sometimes he woke with a start in the middle of the night, feeling empty as a lightning-struck tree. Some instinct raised the bristles on his neck. Someone was in the pitch-black room with him. He could feel it. He could almost hear the breathing.

Was it Sarah, come to haunt him on some zany mission from God? He strained to see in the darkness. A faint suggestion of flowery perfume insinuated itself among the almost invisible golden trophies of enraptured miniature ballplayers and the hushed expectant furniture of the room. He shuddered as the cold realization hit his spine. It was *Blue*. Somehow she was there. The darkness was electric with her presence.

He would spring out of bed and click on the light to drive her away. He'd walk up and down the sleeping house, softly and harshly cursing to himself.

"Get away, damn you," he would mutter.

He walked the house.

"Damn you," he would whisper. "I can't help you. I can't help you. Just get away and leave me be."

If it was summer when one of these visitations occurred he might go out on the deck and stand there in his underpants and let the cold sweat on his body dry in the warm air. He'd look down at the silhouette of the horse barn where Black Ace slumbered and plotted violence in his boarded-up box stall and the mares' dreams were no doubt troubled by sudden apparitions of the stallion, bent on mayhem.

"I didn't want you to die," he'd say to the dark pasture. "I couldn't stop it. You can't hang around here. I can't do anything about it."

He would continue to walk the house and curse incoherently, turning on the lights as he went, driving her from each room.

When she was gone, he would lie down again in bed, his eyes squeezed shut. Slowly his trembling body would unclench. He would slip over the edge into sleep again. It didn't happen often. He had that to be thankful for.

He began to see Terry regularly, the way someone with corns might establish a steady appointment with a chiropodist.

"Hello, baby," she said. "Here's your martini just the way you like it."

Glasses click.

"Here's to us," she always said.

At first he thought it was a good idea to have this standing appointment two or three times a week. It was probably good for his health. She wasn't any problem at first. But then she started to get on his nerves. Even when she was trying hard to be accomodating, she made him mad.

"Whatever you want to do," she said. "I can fix dinner for us here, and we can just stay home and go to beddie early."

She'd press her lips together and waggle her head in a gesture that was supposed to be both cute and sexy. *Beddie,* for godsakes. What kind of talk was that?

She started to crowd him. A month hadn't even passed before she told him that she loved him.

"I love you," she said. "Do you love me?"

He didn't answer. The question was so stupid it didn't deserve an answer.

"No, you don't," she said sadly. "But someday you will."

Shit, he thought.

"I woke up yesterday morning," she said. "I could smell the smell of your body on me. It made me feel so good. Then later—there's something a man doesn't have. And that's the stuff, the stuff of love which sooner or later stirs and trickles in a woman. Do you know what I'm saying? And when it moves it feels so good, it's so private; it stirs in you when you're talking to someone or just sitting having a cigarette. And it's so nice."

Caressing his battered face, she told him, "I know you're going to hurt me. I know you're really going to hurt me." She stroked his cheek. "You're really going to hurt me."

Stuff like that made him mad. If she'd just let things go along nice and simple it would have been fine. But she had to ruin it, of course, by talking about love and holding his face in her hands and prophesying that he was going to hurt her.

He could use a night away from the house here and there. By then it was the fall of 1966. It was plain the old man was sick. Sarah had already tried to jinx things by predicting the old man's death and afterwards collapsing in tears. In December the doctors removed the old man's kidney. He improved dramatically for a brief time. He put on some weight and went back to work. But then it got bad again. The old man lay on the living room couch and the weight gain began to fall away. Getting out of the house helped Ward to forget his problems, which was a joke, because he was just making new problems for himself as it turned out.

In the theater of his head he could just see old Shaw sitting on the bench in the locker room, his blue boxer shorts hitched up over his belly, getting ready to pull on one of those black old-man over-the-calf socks he wore. He could see old Shaw's baggy eyes narrow to Mongolian slits.

You never learn, do you, son.

A statement, not a question. Trouble is the old son-of-a-bitch would be right.

In bed, the foot doctor was a thrasher. If she wasn't kneeing him in the small of his back, she was kneeing him in the groin.

"Oh, gosh. I'm sorry."

She wasn't like Blue. He could sleep with Blue. He could take the foot doctor's judo tactics for so long and then he would move to the couch and fall asleep almost instantly.

Alone. Ah, alone.

There was nothing like it for a good rest and feeling peaceful.

She woke up when he stirred. He remembered she put up a big fuss about it not long ago.

"No, no, no. I'll move over. I promise I won't bother you anymore. Please, Ward, stay here."

"Look, I'm tired as hell. You just stay here. I'll go on the couch, and we'll both sleep better."

She began to cry. It astonished him that at two o'clock in the morning she or any other woman would burst into tears over a silly thing. What was so important about sleeping together to the point of wakefulness and discomfort?

"All right, okay, okay. I'll stay right here. I'm not going anywhere. Stop crying."

"Oh, good!"

She held him tightly.

"Thank you, thank you."

"Okay. Okay."

What the hell was going on anyway? He couldn't figure it.

They'd made love then. Afterward she fell asleep right away. He lay there, stiff and cramped, moving gingerly so as not to wake her, trying to find a comfortable way to sleep with her. He wondered if that had been the time when they'd slipped up. Tricked, snared by her two o'clock tears.

"Women," he could hear old Shaw mutter. "They'll get you every time if you don't watch it."

He was unaware of the cigarette in his mouth till Terry pushed in the lighter on the dashboard. She was good at fussing over him. She fussed over the old man too. She had him fooled. Ward knew what she wanted. She was out to get married any way she could.

She held up the lighter for him, a small orange circle in the darkness. He cracked his window. The sound of the rain entered the car. The faint spray on his left temple felt good. His mouth went dry and acrid on the first puff.

"I'm sorry," she said.

She is sorry, he thought. She wants me to say it's fine she got knocked up, especially at a time like this.

He squinted against some approaching headlights. The electric eye on his dashboard automatically dimmed his own headlights. The lights cut a swath in the darkness to his left, revealing for a split second an expanse of slanting rain which struck the pavement with the violence of miniature detonations.

In the flash of light, the smoke from his cigarette swirled in a caul around his head and then spirited out the window.

He'd take a few puffs, snap the cigarette away, and close the window. He didn't want to take any chances on getting the upholstery wet.

"Gee, you're so quiet, Ward. Why don't you say something, honey?"

"I don't have anything to say," he said. "Don't you ever like it quiet?"

"What were you thinking about so long? You looked so serious."

"Nothing," he said. "I was thinking how good it was when everybody just shut up for a while."

That was like a woman, he thought. They wanted to know what you were thinking. They wanted to know everything. If you were going down the street to have the car washed, they wanted to go along. They watched you from the front window when you took the garbage down to the curb. They wanted to know where you were, what you were doing, who you were with, everything. They wanted to own you lock, stock, and barrel. She was crazy if she thought he was going to marry her.

"I'm happy, Ward."

"What?"

"I'm happy," she repeated. "I can't help it. I know it's a bad start, but we'll make it. I know we will, baby. I know I can make you happy," she finished quietly.

She was crowding him. They always crowded you. You couldn't be nice to them. They wouldn't leave you alone till you told them everything or knocked them around the room.

He snapped the cigarette away. He fingered the button for the electric window. It slipped shut.

"We're not getting married," he said.

Nothing.

Then she said, "What?"

"I said we're not getting married."

She looked at him in amazement.

"But you said we were going to. . . ."

"I said everything would work out okay. And it will because I've found a doctor."

"A doctor?"

"Yes, a doctor. One who will help you."

"You mean an abortionist?"

He didn't say anything.

"An abortionist? Is that what you mean?"

She began to cry.

His guts knotted tight. He gripped the steering wheel and looked into the blinding rain.

"I love you," she sobbed. "Doesn't that mean anything?"

It made him want to hit her. That would be the only way to get her to stop. But she surprised him. She didn't cry for long. She sat up suddenly and wiped the tears from her cheeks. She gazed silently out her window. The yellow Cadillac moved slowly through the rain. There was only the sound of the rain on the roof.

Then she said something. She spoke so quietly he couldn't hear what it was.

"What?"

"I said: let me out."

"Sure," he said.

"I mean it. Let me out of this car."

They can't leave you alone, he thought. They try every way they can to drive you crazy.

"Shut up," he said. "You just shut up."

"I won't let you kill this baby," she said.

"What baby? There isn't any baby. There isn't anything but maybe something the size of a walnut."

"No," she shook her head.

"Are you crazy? I'm giving you a way out. Nothing is going to happen to you. This man is an M.D. It's not like some butcher down on the corner."

"No," she said. "You're not going to hurt this baby."

"There isn't any baby," he said. "But there will be. What are you going to do? Wait till your mother finds out? What will she say? Do you think I'll marry you? If you think I'm going to marry you, you're crazy."

She looked at him squarely as if she were seeing him for the first time.

"I'm not going to marry you," he repeated.

"Let me out," she said.

He didn't answer her.

"Let me out of this car."

He didn't answer.

"You bastard," she said. "You're not going to hurt this baby."

He kept on driving.

She moved so fast he didn't have time to stop her. Suddenly he felt a rush of cold air and the fine spray of rain. He saw the open door and just the tail of her raincoat as she jumped. He slammed on the brakes. The Cadillac fishtailed. He jerked the wheel sharply. The car jolted onto the gravel shoulder of the road. The stones chunked the belly of the car. He hit the brakes again. The big car slid on the stones and lurched to a stop.

His heart beat against the bars of his chest as he tried to unlock his fingers from the steering wheel. At last he threw open his door and struggled out of the car. The rain instantly soaked him to the skin. He ran through the pounding rain to where the girl lay in the road. Lying on her side in the raincoat, she looked like a broken sack of potatoes. He knelt down beside her.

"You crazy bitch," he said.

He had run under a hundred yards but he couldn't catch his breath. He dragged her to the side of the road and sat down heavily in the mud. The rain marbled the blonde hair against her forehead. Her eyes were closed tight and her fist was pressed against her mouth as if to keep back a scream. He pushed the hair away from her face. Her skin was cold as snow.

"You crazy bitch," he repeated. But the words were hardly audible. The side of his chest began to ache.

He looked at her face. It was like cleanly chiseled stone. He cradled her head in his lap and bent over her to keep the rain off her face. She put her arms around him and held him tightly. He could feel her crying again, but he couldn't hear her. He heard only the rain, pelting the encircling darkness.

E L E V E N

THE RAIN beat in a pewter frenzy all around them. As it stung his shoulders and the cold spread down his spine, he felt the girl through her wet raincoat. She was alive all right, but was she broken? She remained slack under this investigation, no doubt interested in the results herself.

Clinging to his neck, her face hidden against his chest, she was sheltered from the direct passion of the rain, although it flattened her cotton candy hairdo down around her ears.

"Are you all right?" he shouted above the rain.

He thought she replied, without raising her head from shelter, her answer directed to his heart as it were. But in this storm he couldn't be sure he'd heard anything.

"What?"

This time she exposed her face to the rain and hoisted herself up and spoke huskily into his ear.

"I'm okay. I think."

"Can you walk?"

"I don't know."

He picked her up and staggered back through the slanting rain to the Cadillac. She was not heavy but it put pressure on his bad leg and he staggered as he carried her, her legs waggling about with the imbecilic aimlessness of a doll.

"Can you stand up?"

She put her nose into the protected recesses of his neck.

"I think so."

He set her down carefully on her feet at the back of the car.

"How is that?"

"I'm all right." She tested out a step or two.

"I'll get the blanket out of the trunk," he said, "so we don't get the seats all wet."

There in the trunk was the neatly packaged plaid blanket in its original plastic zip-up bag which he'd sent to L. L. Bean's for. Never had it been used and in fact it was never intended for use. It was supposed to ride around permanently in the trunk, neatly folded in its plastic purse, ready for emergencies that weren't supposed to happen. Now one had. He couldn't help but be disappointed, even disturbed. Ward unzippered the bag, full of regret knowing that he would never be satisfied with the blanket again now that he had been forced to use it.

With the violated blanket in one hand and his back hunched against the rain, Ward took Terry by the arm. She seemed undisturbed by the rain. Her hair was driven into her face. She pushed it back. But that was the only acknowledgment.

"Can you walk?"

"Yes." She gingerly tested her legs, swayed on his firm arm, but went steadily along with him to the door.

"It doesn't hurt much," she said.

"You're lucky," he said. "That was a bad stunt. You nearly killed yourself."

He opened the car door, began fixing the red plaid blanket on the bench seat of the car, draping it over the top of the back so the fringe hung down, tucking it slightly into the seat where the back and the seat met. The fringe on the other end hung down over the edge of the seat. He made sure he got it even. He did a neat fast job of it. Despite the aggravating circumstances, arranging the blanket neatly on the seat—keeping the fringe even, getting the plaid pattern straight—was the first satisfying thing he'd done all evening.

Terry waited patiently, oblivious to the beating rain. He turned to hand her into the car. Her blouse was soaked and clung to her breasts. The lacy pattern of her brassiere nubbled through the wet blouse above her breasts like some exotic notation in Braille. No doubt she'd picked out some fancy underwear to wear in honor of the historic occasion, which was supposed to turn out to be a marriage, not a death-defying leap.

"It was a dumb trick," he muttered.

She was settled in the car now. He could shut the door and that would be the end of it. No point in getting the car any more messed up. But he felt obliged to say this and wait for her answer.

"I know it was bad," she looked up. The harsh domelight emphasized the hollows under her eyes. "But you wouldn't let me out."

He closed her door on that remark and started around to the driver's side.

But you wouldn't let me out.

As if that was a sensible explanation for why some damn fool would jump from a moving car. When their bellies were activated, women didn't make sense at all. Or was it they made sense in some confounding way that men couldn't follow, in the manner whales were said to sing to each other in the ocean, using voices no man understood?

He reached over the seat and grabbed the other blanket, just a lap robe really, not a real blanket, of the type his grandfather had used in the old Dodge that he had to garage at Cousin Waterhouse's place because the Captain wouldn't even allow a car on the premises, much less ride in one.

He handed it to her.

"Take off those wet clothes," he told her, "and wrap this around you."

She took the blanket and looked at him, her blonde hair wetly dark and plastered around her face. Now that the bouffant had collapsed and her hair was troweled in dark waves on the curve of her head, you could see her nice cheekbones.

Terry's eyes grew big and filled with tears. She began to blubber. She dropped the car robe in her lap and put her hand to her mouth as if to catch or at least hide the awful invisible substance of her grief. Had he said something wrong or done something one degree more horrible? He was still too scared to figure it out.

"Don't cry," he muttered mechanically. His heart was still slugging against the bars of his chest. There in his head replayed the amazing picture of Terry being sucked out of sight into the boiling rain, just the flag of her white raincoat snapping brief defiance before it too disappeared into the darkness.

Was "take off those wet clothes" too bold a suggestion so soon after her death-defying leap? What was going on here?

"You're soaked to the bone," he explained. "You don't want to sit there in those cold wet clothes all the way back to Carlisle, do you?"

"No," she sniffed. The tears rolled down her cheeks. "I have other clothes in my suitcase."

"Good gravy," he said. "I forgot about your suitcase I'll fetch it for you."

He got out of the car hastily and trotted back through the rain which seemed to be letting up. Now he had some idea why she cried. Likely it was his insensitivity to the heavy symbolism of her luggage. Here she thought she was on some kind of honeymoon till his disastrous confession of the trip's real purpose, and he didn't have the decency to remember that a girl with such expectations would always carry some luggage. Maybe a whore wouldn't. But any respectable woman would.

He had just opened the trunk a few minutes ago to worry the blanket out of its plastic pouch, and had probably looked right at her powder-blue overnight case of molded plastic, no doubt a high school graduation present from her parents, a practical gift which likely she used for the first time on the class trip to Washington. Without question she had a complete set of the horrible stuff and knew where every key was to boot.

Yes, that was it. His damned insensitivity to her honeymoon luggage, her respectable and now ruined assumptions that had set her off. Although he couldn't be sure. You never knew about a woman for certain.

He opened the door of the car, saw she had already spread the lap robe so he could put the suitcase down without getting the back seat wet. She was thoughtful, he had to admit. Even though she was upset. Shaken up, maybe seriously hurt. She knew how he looked at things, surprised him sometimes, like now.

"There's your bag," he said. "Now maybe you'll get out of those wet clothes so you don't catch pneumonia."

The car was hot, the windows steamed up like a greenhouse. He didn't like that. It made a mess. She opened her door, pulled the seat forward and climbed in the back. Damn. They were milling in and out of the old car, carrying stones and mud on their shoes, treating the poor lady like she was a trailer at a construction site. He guessed it was the worst abuse the car had ever had. He wished he was home with the Cadillac safely parked under the carport so he could wipe her down. He couldn't wait till morning. He'd have to clean her soon as he got home. The whole thing was making him nervous. Don't get rattled, he counseled himself. If you do, you're liable to fly off the handle at the foot doctor and that won't do.

You've got to be nice to her. She might have internal injuries. Besides you've got to make up for this if you're ever going to get anywhere with her. He had already thought of a favor he wanted from her.

He snapped on the domelight so she could see. She opened her suitcase. Predictably, it was lined with some flashy blue silky stuff. Her clothes were perfectly packed and the blue silk baggage ribbons tied in bows held it all in place. Right on top was a black lacy nightgown. Probably there never was a young girl who went away with a man for the first time who didn't carry along a black nightgown. It was kind of a uniform, really. It meant you'd enlisted in the service of a particular man, the female equivalent of joining the army. The fact that it was on top gave him some idea of the seriousness of her expectations. She choked back a sob as she considered the nightgown, blatant and pathetic now under the domelight of this roadside reality. He felt sorry for her, he had to admit.

She edged the gown aside, careful not to mess up the clothes so neatly folded and crisp-looking you would swear she'd just bought them brand-new. She extracted some routine white underwear, a madras blouse and a pair of new blue jeans. Back to business as usual.

She unbuttoned the top button of her blouse. The lapels fell away like the white wet petals of a flower.

"You can turn off the light now," she said with a significant look which meant, *Get the point?*

Stupidly, he'd been sitting there looking at her as if she were going to strip in front of him and reveal those sassy breasts and the trim compact body which had made for all this trouble in the first place.

"Sorry," he said, and snapped off the light. Ward faced the highway again where the beams of an invisible car slid up the windshield like luminous dashes tracing a steady path across the videoscope of one of those machines that monitor vital signs in a hospital. The rain had slowed to a drizzle. The car sighed by, a faint melancholy sound, leaving behind the deserted almost indistinguishable road, a shadow of a hill, a sky as dark as a photo negative.

By the whisper of garments and the insinuation of zippers,

Ward sensed her movements as she worked free of her wet things, as she might call them, and in the tense darkness hurriedly pulled on her dry clothes.

"You ought to get into something dry yourself," she said. Her voice sounded relieved, even the sounds of the garments and zippers seemed more relaxed. She's almost finished, he thought.

"That's all right," he said.

"You'll catch a cold," she said. "You're human too." But she put some special English on her voice as if to suggest that all the evidence was not yet in.

"I brought along a paper bag for my laundry. You can put your stuff in it too. Here, wrap yourself in this blanket. I'm finished with it now."

"All right," he said.

She passed the damp blanket over the seat.

"Here," she said. "Here's the paper bag."

The bag was heavy and damp with her sodden clothes.

He pulled off his T-shirt, his sneakers, his white cotton socks, good hygiene for his feet. He unbuttoned his khakis and hesitated, aware she was behind him, maybe just calmly taking in his discomforture. Humiliated, he clabbered out of his pants, lifting up as little as possible, hunching down when he could. It was an act without grace. Even though the car was dark he figured she must be watching in silent contempt as he wrestled his wet khakis and lifted his ass to peel off the jockey shorts plastered to his hips. It was like sloughing off your self-respect. He felt better after he'd wrapped himself in the flannel-like consolation of the blanket and deposited the clammy socks, underwear, T-shirt, and khakis in the grocery bag. Still, sitting there as if dressed for a Turkish bath made him feel foolish, an easy target for ridicule.

"Okay," he said. As if to signal he was ready for the next humiliation, whatever it was.

"Can you open the door for me?" she asked.

He started to lean over to unlatch the door, then turned to her. "How would you like to lie down on the back seat?"

"No, I'd rather sit in the front."

"Are you sure? You could stretch out and relax back there."

"No, that's all right."

A little violence was bound to chasten anybody's manners and sweeten everybody's disposition. Women, who were supposed to be helpless and weak, had the uncanny knack for using violence, usually self-inflicted, to gain control over things. Even when in control, they acted like they weren't. This one, for instance, looked half-drowned, not like she was in charge of anything. But it wasn't only respect for her newly discovered talent for command which led him to suggest she take it easy in the back seat. Possibly she had truly injured herself. Subdural hemotoma, came to mind. Blue once told of a friend who had slipped on the stairs and hit her head. After a trip to the emergency room and X-rays, she was released by physicians into the custody of her family. She spent a perfectly normal day, went into convulsions at the dinner table, and was dead before the ambulance arrived. Subdural hematoma: a subtle invisible bleeding that suddenly kills you at dinnertime. Or some other kind of internal injury. God only knew what Terry had done to herself.

"Just lie down there and rest," he said.

She gave the front seat an impatient shove.

"I'm all right. Let me get in the front."

Naturally she wouldn't listen. He'd never met a woman yet who would.

Ward unlatched the door on the passenger side, assisting her as she pushed the black leather seat forward to climb out of the back into the front. The light came on when the door opened, giving him his first good look at her since they'd gotten in the car. She looked to be a sober-faced young lady with an unusually broad smooth forehead. Her rain-drenched hair was combed straight back along the curve of her head. He took in the discovery of her hair flat and wet against her skull and the perfect hemisphere of her forehead which was always hidden by cute wispy bangs of blonde hair, part of the bouffant baggage. She had the surprising air of a stranger. He couldn't recollect seeing her so unsmiling and subdued.

Bathed in the reflection of the green dashboard lights, they started back through the slow dream of rain, each numb in the aftershock of her death-defying leap. Ward wasn't even mad. Just numb. He seemed deep in thought, but his brain had ceased all but elementary operations. For a while he was content just to listen to the blood ticking in his ears. But after a while his heart slowed down and he got over being scared. His brain agreed to take up thought again. The first thing it did was to call him stupid. He should have known better. It was dumb to think he could just throw the foot doctor or any woman in the car and head for the abortionist's without a little discussion beforehand.

He had figured there was time enough to talk her into it on the trip down. But any sensible man would have known she'd find a way to provoke him till he just blurted out the true purpose of the trip, putting the matter beyond all reasonable discussion. Having already been double-crossed into honesty, he should have expected the unpredictable—some outrageous action on her part safely placing the matter, now beyond logical argument, in the country of the impossible. He could hear old Shaw now.

You never learn, do you, son?

Not a question but a fact.

Well, you have done it now, he thought. You let her get the best of you.

Gone. Sucked into the black night and the hissing rain. Just one patriotic snap of her white raincoat to punctuate the scene. An amazing picture. Nothing she could do could have shaken him more unless she'd cut her throat with a kitchen knife. It was strange business. He thought he had everything under control. That one thing at least was going to turn out right. But all she had to do was to fall down on the road, a simple but decisive gesture, to prove he was wrong again.

"I guess this spoils everything," he said. "But I still have a favor I want to ask you."

"What's that?" she asked miserably.

"Before I picked you up tonight I went to see the old man. He was feeling punk. He's on that chemotherapy."

"That makes you sick," she said. "But it makes the cancer sick, too."

"He talked about you," Ward said. "He enjoys your visits." He could barely keep the amazement out of his voice. "I know you don't owe me any favors, but I know he sure would appreciate it if you would still go see him."

There by God. I've done it. I asked her for a favor, he thought. It wasn't like him to beg for anything, not from her or anybody else.

His problems were his problems. And he was proud he kept them to himself and worked on them as he could. But it wasn't fair to wreck one of his father's few remaining pleasures, even if it called for extraordinary measures like crawling a few feet on his belly.

His father was crazy about Terry. Anybody could see that. He painted her in glowing terms, describing for Ward her wonderful singularity. You didn't have to be smart to see that the old man was in love, in the pathetic way sick people pick out a green willow tree, a person who glows with the riches of good health— clear eyes, good blood, clean kidneys. Having those riches gave Terry a wonderful ignorance of what it is to be washed up. Since she didn't know, it meant the old man could forget it too when she was around. Being neither young woman nor green willow tree, Ward couldn't do that for him. In fact, when his eldest son was around doubtless the old man not only couldn't forget, but was reminded. He read the awful news in Ward's battered face. He found the horrible signs in the boy's aching, imperfectly mended body. But Terry refreshed like a sweet balm. She was the old man's original discovery, effortlessly dispensing affection and comfort as if no shortage of these commodities existed. It was natural the old man should be a little childish where she was concerned. Although offering no permanent cure, she could be relied on for shampoos and pajamas. He sulked on the weekends when she was off-duty. Through her, Ward guessed, the old man had deluded himself into thinking the last of the dying would be no more complicated than taking a spoonful of castor oil.

Terry didn't answer for a minute. They coasted smoothly through the subsiding rain. He watched the quicksilver trails made by the erratic progress of the water down the windshield.

Then she said, "I don't believe you."

"I know it's asking a lot," he admitted.

"Don't you know seeing your Dad has nothing to do with you?" she asked.

"Okay, good," he said.

Did that mean she'd still go to see him, bring him the pitchers of limeade that he relished, wash his hair with her strong fingers?

"I don't understand you," she said. "Don't you think a person does anything nice for somebody just because they want to?"

"Yes, I guess so," he sounded doubtful. Indeed, he was sure the only reason she visited the old man was to pick up points.

"I *like* your father," she insisted. "He's a wonderful man. I'd visit him no matter what. It has nothing to do with you."

"Well, I appreciate it." He honestly thought it was mighty nice of her.

"Stick your appreciation up your ass."

You could have knocked him over with a feather. Now there was one thing about Terry that he did genuinely admire, apart from her being so clean and neat. And that was she never used any bad language. But she was full of surprises tonight.

"I never heard you talk like that before."

"You never heard a lot of things," she said.

The conversation lapsed then, and he was left to deal with the furious confusion still buzzing in his bloodstream. Nothing seemed to be going right anymore. He couldn't carry off a polite thank-you without it blowing up in his face. What was going on here? he wondered. What's gone so wrong that you can't get anything to go right anymore? The big car glided through the slow dream of rain. What am I feeling? Ward wondered. Am I feeling anything? He listened for signs. Sometimes the pain in his chest told him things. Occasionally revelations ticked in his blood, streaming in secret passage through the surgical impromptitude of his vessels and organs, tapping out messages that got past his head. But no messages were on the wire tonight. So far as he could tell, he was feeling nothing except just plain tired.

You are just a cat.

The voice in his head was Blue's. He saw her clearly now. She looked troubled. She had discovered something new and disturbing about him. He remembered vividly—as he remembered everything—what it was. He'd told her he'd rather not make love the night before he went on a road trip. Starting the trip that way helped his concentration, he claimed. She looked at him, and she said:

You are just a cat.

"A cat?"

"Yes. You hurt people. You hurt me so casually. In the name of your body. You want your body to be in perfect harmony with your talent. Isn't that what you go for?"

"I guess I do," he said.

"And you have no idea of the price you make me pay because I love you."

"This is not a big deal," he said. "I was just stating a preference. It's not important—"

"But you hurt and hurt," she persisted. "It isn't even malicious. It might be easier to take if it were. It's just your body, the balance between it and your talent, that you worry about. You're just a cat."

"I don't understand," he said.

"You're a cat disguised in ballplayer's body," she said.

"Why is that?" he still wanted to know.

Why did he even *want* to know? Blue had a way of provoking him into questions for which he wanted no answers.

"Because you don't know yourself," answered Blue. "You're a cat trying to become a man, and you're having trouble. You don't know what you feel anymore. You can't connect discomfort or pleasure with people. Only with whether you are hot or cold and if your belly is empty or full. You don't know where the people fit in. You're a cat," she finished. "You're just a cat trying to become a man."

Maybe Blue was right. If he hadn't acted like a cat tonight maybe Terry would be in Dr. Brown's clutches now. Instead they were headed home with nothing done. And things a lot worse off.

To hell with it. He decided to think a little baseball. He would take a little holiday from his troubles and think about the game. He couldn't figure out exactly the reason for the depth of terror he felt when he saw the tail of Terry's raincoat disappear in the rain. The heart always hammered violently when you were eye-witness to mayhem, accidental or otherwise. It was natural. But not this terror. When he saw the raincoat snap from view he thought: *No. Not you too.* Thought it so spontaneously, it didn't even amount to thought but to some electric secret buried in the brain. Perhaps he was just tired of the terrible. Wearied by all kinds of death, both the slow and the sudden variety. Maybe that's all the message meant. Already pooped out, like a little kittycat. Just now he'd decided to do something about the dirty tricks life pulled on you. He hadn't been back in the game for long, and yet so quickly he was showing signs of serious fatigue.

That's what comes from being out of shape. If you decided to get tangled in the business of ordinary life, you had to be in condition specifically for that business. You can be in shape to ride a bicycle but that doesn't mean you can play basketball. Each thing requires its own kind of conditioning. And for a long time, he had not trained for the ugly business of everyday life. No wonder he was bushed.

How are you going to get anything done, he asked himself, if you fold up every time somebody jumps from a moving car?

He would take a little break and think about the game, let it ease the ache of his poor head.

What he would do is start a series between the 1949 Yankees and the Red Sox. Now that was nice. He could do that and forget all this cat business and Terry and the walnut and the old man and the chemo-damn-therapy. Let a three-game series be the deciding factor in the pennant race. Give history a chance to rewrite itself. This time, the right way. If the Red Sox won the series, they, not the Yankees, would be the American League pennant winners. Then he would play them against Brooklyn, the National League champs, and just see if Boston, given a second chance, couldn't become champions of the world.

So in a fugue of daydreaming and baseball, he drove Terry home.

Some people, had they seen the two of them, might have found it curious to see a young woman, properly dressed, enter a building on the main street of town at one o'clock in the morning followed by a man with a slight limp wrapped in nothing but a colorful blanket. On the other hand, it seemed fitting to Ward that he should look like an undeniable fool, the punishment being suitable to the crime.

It was not till she stood outside her door with her latch key in hand, just extricated from the jumble of female junk that yawned dangerously from the open maw of her purse, that he asked her another question just to confirm what he already knew. But he was curious to know if she knew what she'd done, or whether she'd relied solely on female instinct.

"What I want to know is why you did it?"

Terry seemed surprised.

"Did what?" she wanted to know.

"Why you jumped," he persisted. "You could have been killed."

"If I had, you could have just taken the body down to your friend. He could have performed an autopsy to make sure the— what?—the little walnut?—wasn't kicking anymore."

"Don't be so fresh. Just answer the question."

"What I want to know is why *you* did it," she said. "Did you think you could just carry me down there to your abortionist friend? That I would just go along with it?"

"I didn't mean it to work out this way," he said. "I lost my temper. I'm sorry. I was going to explain to you on the way down. So you'd understand that it would be best all around if—"

"No, no," she shook her head vigorously. "I'm not going to listen to you. Don't you know anything? I *love* this baby. I thought we could both love this baby together. That it would make us both happy—"

How could she misunderstand him so completely?

"It's just a bad time—" he began.

"I love you," she said fiercely.

He looked at her blankly.

"That doesn't mean anything either, does it."

"Let's not get into it now. I'm so damned tired I can hardly stand up. You just go in there and lie down—"

"Nothing means anything to you, does it?" she persisted. Her blue eyes widened on the sudden revelation. "You lost your baseball career and your girl in that accident. Ever since it hasn't been worth getting up in the morning, has it?"

"Look, don't get started. I already told you I'm sorry."

"Why are you so important to me?" she asked him angrily. "You've got more stitches in your head than Frankenstein. I look at your poor hurt face, and I just melt all over. But it's silly. You don't give a damn about anyone. Well, I don't need you either. You hurt me, Ward. You hurt me very bad. I don't want to see you anymore."

"Wait a minute. Don't get so upset."

This was getting out of hand. He had to stall for time till he could think what to do next.

"I'll have this baby by myself," she was saying. "I'll love it enough for both of us. I'll tell you one thing. This baby will be a happy baby. Let go of my arm."

"Wait a minute, will you."

"I gave you my love and it didn't mean a thing. Let go of me!"

"Now just a—" he got out before she conked him with her purse on the nose, a tender organ, having been broken in three places in the accident. Since then it was sensitive as a funny bone even when lightly tapped. But she gave him no tap, she walloped him good, and he blacked out momentarily as he thundered into the hallway banister.

He came to on the cold linoleum under the naked, hurtful light bulb just as her door slammed shut. As he sprawled on the floor his blanket had fallen away, revealing grounds for immediate arrest and imprisonment, had any public-spirited citizen have happened along just then. He covered up and, pulling himself up with the aid of the railing, painfully got to his feet. It was the second time in less than twelve hours, he noted, that a woman had attacked him with a purse. The whole tribe seemed to have turned against him.

This is one damn fine mess, he thought groggily. He dabbed gingerly at his vibrating nose to see if it was leaking blood, which it was. She had just told him he carried more stitches than Frankenstein's monster. This might be taken for a sympathetic observation, and sympathy could buy him the time to figure out what to do next. But that momentary hope perished immediately when she slugged him, apparently bent on embroidering the surgery which already decorated his face. The damn nose really hummed. She was pretty mad, that was for sure. One fine mess, he thought.

He drove home and, too exhausted to work on the car, went to bed. It had been a bad day no matter how innocent its beginnings. Looking back he could see those subtle fissures of impending trouble, even downright bold patterns. In the space of eighteen hours an old woman had chased him out of his own kitchen, forcing him to take breakfast in his room, a crazy horse had tried to shatter the sad integrity of his poorly mended bones, a fat woman in a rainstorm—a complete stranger—had whomped him with her purse when he'd tried to be helpful, a lawyer had caught onto his game or at least might remember later what had happened in his office and ruin everything, a foolish pregnant girl had jumped from his car risking death and so took charge and destroyed all possibility that anything would go right that day. Plus the old man was in a bad way. He had noticed lately that the days seemed to turn out even worse than they used to. As he fell asleep he wondered if he could count on this decline to go on indefinitely, and if it did, how in God's name would he be able to get out of bed and face the day by the time he was, say, forty. How, for example, did Althy brave the mornings at close to eighty? She must have some kind of secret, he decided. He did not sleep well.

The next morning he did a bunch of extra sit-ups, chin-ups and push-ups, working the body extra hard to make up for yesterday's failures, the way he used to take extra batting practice in the old days when he turned in a bad game.

Fresh from the shower he passed silently by Althy's open door, still stark naked, and entered the downstairs family room where he picked up the telephone. It was probably a mistake to wake Terry like this. Then again, if she was half asleep maybe she'd be reasonable. The telephone rang once, twice, three times.

"Hello?" a sleepy midget voice answered.

"Hello—" he got out. With a sob she cracked the receiver down in his ear. Standing there, naked and battered, he stared in outrage at the black mouthpiece with its silly pattern of holes like the head of a sprinkling can. He dialed the number again. This time he got a busy signal. No doubt she had taken the thing off the hook. He decided to wait a minute, then dial once more. It would give him time to rehearse again. He had to sound sincere when he finally connected. And that required practice. He had to practice being sincere and serious. It was hard to take the foot doctor seriously. One reason was the way she talked. *Panties* instead of underpants, *kissy* instead of kiss, *beddie* instead of bed. How could you take anyone serious who talked like that? He had rehearsed once or twice in the bathroom mirror that morning after his shower.

"Hello, Terry? You all right?" he asked the mirror sincerely.

He even worked on his facial expression because even if she couldn't see him, the performance had to be authentically complete for his voice alone to be convincing.

Call her. Get her on the phone. Ward didn't have any great plan in mind. He would just go slow and not act like a cat. He would apologize, claim temporary insanity. He would ask her out for a pizza, offer to take her to Walter Juneau's place. Walter, a family friend who owned a bar and grill just down the street from Terry's, made the best pizza in town. Ward was ready to hold her hand. She liked that stuff. He wouldn't mention the walnut. He'd resume his appointments. Eventually he'd work something out.

He dialed her number again. Still busy. Probably she'd buried the phone under the seat cushion in the chair beside her bed.

Feeling discouraged, he went back to bed.

Ward was tired out. Things were getting complicated. The

whole business wore him out. Normally he jumped out of bed in the mornings, not exactly cursing and swearing with that abundance of energy characteristic of the old days, but up fast and about his business. But for the last week or so, he found he could barely crawl out of bed. Maybe it was the change of seasons.

Bullshit, he thought. Don't bullshit yourself. You just weren't ready for all this, and now you want to go to bed like Sarah and forget the whole thing. Well, bullshit. Come on, he thought. Don't pull this. Get going. You don't have time to fool around.

He sprang out of bed so fast his bad leg buckled when he hit the floor. He did an extra twenty-five chin-ups on the chrome-plated bar just to prove he was ready to face things again.

He put on his clothes. The fresh T-shirt and the khakis with the razor-sharp creases automatically made him feel better. He washed out his underwear and socks and hung them on the rack to dry in the bathroom. That made him feel better too. He was getting things done.

The next thing was to clean up the Cadillac. He folded the blanket in the original way so it fit neatly into its plastic bag. He put it back in the trunk. He hosed down the floor mats. Hooking up the tank vacuum cleaner the old man kept in the garage, he cleaned the floor of the car. Luckily the car made it through without any real damage, a small unlooked-for miracle since everything else was going wrong. Just a few pebbles and a couple of flecks of mud. He used the spray can of spot remover to get a minute smudge of dried mud out of the carpet on Terry's side. Presto. Gone without a trace. He filled a bucket with warm water using a mild liquid soap and swabbed the white sidewalls with a sponge. He never used one of those harsh pads. Do that, and you ruined the sidewall. This way took longer but it kept the whitewall smooth and perfect as brand-new. After he was finished the car looked just fine again.

The old man was wrong about the rain. The day was clear as a bell. Clouds piled up in the west and counter-balanced hard blue sky in the east. The breeze showed off, dying away, then gusting in a sneak attack from a foreign quarter before melting away again. It was sunny, one of those days you look for.

Ward began to feel hopeful. Weather had that effect on him. Put the sun in the sky and he began to think things would turn out right. Maybe the worst was over. Your troubles are bound to peak sometime. After a while they slack off, like everything else. Surely things had to get better after a while. Who knows? Maybe now.

He went down to the horses, brought in the mares, and let out Black Ace. The horse bolted out of the stall so fast as to be practically invisible. The horse did not offer to kick him. At least not that he could see. Another good sign. He considered breakfast, but decided not to risk running into Althy or maybe Sarah since the day was off to a fair start. Breakfast seemed a fair trade for a good start.

Feeling so good led to his first mistake that day, for he decided to take the old man's white convertible for a spin. He drove out to Merkleburg and north of town along the stream, all the way up to the paper mill and was considering going all the way to Pine Grove Furnace when he was overtaken by some bad feelings.

This car he was fooling around in, this damned beautiful hardly-used white convertible, likely would outlive his father. Outsurvive, say. If that was a word. Just a damn piece of junk really. And it would be around looking racy long after the old man was nothing but dust. Like those collections of hundred-year-old campaign buttons you read about in the papers which in a sense play the final joke on those big important politicians, dead and long since forgotten, survived by these pieces of stamped tin in the felt-covered display boxes. When he thought of that, he had no heart for driving the beautiful car anymore and he turned around and started back for the house.

Coming down alongside that stretch of the stream before the railroad crossing where the shallow rapids ran white over the rocks, he decided to go down to Terry's and see if he couldn't patch things up.

After he put the car away, Ward took the Motobecane down off the ceiling hooks he'd installed so as to save the tires and generally keep it safe from someone accidentally running over it, and he pedaled into town. As he went along his hip loosened, an additional pleasure, and the sun felt warm on his face. So far so good, he thought.

As usual, as soon as Ward hit town he cut off Hanover Street and worked his way through the placid green maze of side streets lined with lovely old brick houses with white painted woodwork and screened porches, tall dignified hedges, brilliantly emerald in a show of early season vitality. Surrounded by forsythia bushes and situated in the sunlight of such a spring day, those houses lied convincingly that nothing bad had ever taken place inside. It was a nice pretense to entertain briefly as he pedaled without haste through these quiet orderly streets. Wouldn't it be nice, he thought, if fresh paint and well-behaved shrubbery could keep out trouble.

He came onto High Street winding his way, through heavier traffic now, to the combination tobacco shop–poolroom where he ordinarily bought the papers. Inside he paid for *The Baltimore Sun.* The *Sun* would have the best coverage of last night's game. Probably a few pictures of the action.

On the sidewalk out front of the shop he opened the paper to the sports section and discovered without surprise that the Red Sox had lost 4–3. Bill Rohr, the Red Sox starter, had only lasted three innings, giving up six hits and four runs, the killing blow a bases-loaded two-run single stroked by Davey Johnson. Boston had pecked away against McNally and closed to within a run till Drabowsky came on in relief and closed the door. But today is another day. Let's consider the pitchers. Today's pitchers were Lonborg vs. Palmer. Lonborg was pitching good so far. He seemed to be finding himself this year. Palmer, as always, would be tough.

Standing there on the sidewalk, he read the whole account of the game, satisfying himself as to each detail. He examined the boxscore as carefully as an auditor might go over a set of books. Sometimes he toyed with the idea of going down to see the Red Sox play in Baltimore. It wasn't all that far away. And the roads were good. Somehow he never got around to it. The last time he saw the Red Sox play in person was the day he signed his contract —fifteen years ago, just before they shipped him off to the Carolina League. He guessed he liked reading about the games just as well as watching them, maybe even better. Take the boxscore. A baseball game could be neatly summarized in a boxscore like nothing else in life. The game itself might be full of action, loaded with painful suspense and unpredictability. Anything could happen. Watching a game on TV drove him crazy. It worried the hell out of him. But now the boxscore, whether the result was good or bad, was the boxscore. Unchangeable and unarguable, no longer subject to the dice roll, a boxscore he could accept peacefully. Better to read the papers where it was all laid out in simple terms, instead of being tortured by the actual event as it unfolded, the result still anybody's guess.

Ward cycled to the square, turned left onto Hanover and glided past the old church where George Washington had once worshipped on his way to put down the Whiskey Rebellion. He swooped down the alley to see if Terry's apple-green VW was parked in the lot behind the apartment house. It was. He circled around to the front, his free wheel ticking, one foot dangling free of the toe clip. He tethered the lean graceful bike to a parking meter, wrapping the chain around the back tire and the frame and scrambled the combination tumblers.

Now properly dressed, he climbed her stairs for the second time in twelve hours and rang the door bell. He felt foolish standing in the hall. A milk box, the dull color of an armored car, stood sentry by the door. At the end of the hall, a drift of old newspapers had collected in the corner. That's all there was out here. Just him, the milk box, and the old newspapers. A small sign in the middle of the gray door said:

GET OUT OF VIETNAM.

He knocked on the door. He made a fist. Bam! Bam! Right in the middle of it just below the anti-war sign.

"Who is it?" asked a small frightened voice behind the door.

"Hey," he said to the gray door. His voice echoed unnaturally in the hall. Come on, goddamn it, he thought.

"What?"

"It's me."

"Go away."

"Come on. Open up for a minute. At least talk to me."

There was no reply to this.

"I pedaled all the way down here on my bike."

"Go away."

"Look, I'm sorry about last night. I handled it all wrong."

Silence.

"Are you all right?"

"What do you mean?"

"Are you okay? You didn't hurt yourself jumping out of the car? Sometimes it doesn't show up for a while. You should see a doctor. Let him check you out."

"No. I'm all right," she said. "Now go away."

"I'd be happy to take you over to the emergency room."

"No. I said I'm *all right!*"

He was baffled by the disembodied voice and the unsympathetic door. Then he said, "I'd appreciate it if you would go see Dad today. He was really down yesterday."

"Yes. I will," she said. "I'll go this afternoon. If you promise to go tonight." She must have been leaning right against the door. Her voice came through the wood small and reasonably clear.

"Right," he said. "We wouldn't want to run into one another and actually talk face to face."

"What?"

"You didn't hurt yourself, did you?"

"What?"

"Come on. This is a hell of a way to talk. Why don't you open the door?"

"Go away!"

He went away. To hell with her, he thought. I'll get her later. She can't pull this on me. So, feeling oddly hollow and dispirited, he pedaled home.

Be patient, he counseled himself. This is going to take some time. You made some bad mistakes, and now it's going to take a while before you get it straight. But we don't have the time, he answered himself. Of course we do. We've got the time. We just hang in there. Take our time. We'll get this worked out.

If you can't do one thing you can do another. That's the way you have to look at it. As he hung the bicycle back on its hooks, he considered a visit with Sarah. He had urgent business with Sarah. He didn't know whether she was up to it or not. You have to get her past the question of the old man's coming home. The dying part. That part has got her crazy. Get her past that. Get her to think about herself. Or at least think about herself in a different way. See if you can't get her to consider what to do next, after the old man dies. Because, he thought, this is the last piece of the puzzle. If she will make me the executor of the estate, then we're home safe. Life would go on, less valuable than before maybe, but it would go on. No major changes would take place. They would continue to live in the house, three of them now, instead of four. He'd tend the horses, paying special consideration to the arrogant stupidity of the hammerhead mare and to Black Ace's swollen ego, the old man's two favorites. He'd hold on to the house, too big or not. Everything would go on as before. That would be something anyway. It would not be like having the old man around but it would be something. If they sold house and horses, the old man would be deader than ever. If Sarah would agree, Ward would orchestrate this politic response to death's latest incursion, and everything would turn out all right. He had to convince her. And soon. Time was running low. Should I try it now? he wondered.

He stood in the hallway, his head cocked to one side, thinking it over. Should I try it? he wondered. Yes, he decided. Why not. If you can't get one thing right, maybe you can another.

He decided to talk to Althy first to see if Sarah was making any sense this morning. There was no point opening himself up to a long visit with Sarah if she was still crazy as a loon.

He found Althy downstairs in the family room, watering her pots of African violets. They held no charms for him. Their hairy purple leaves and strong vegetative smell made his skin crawl, rankled his nose. His grandmother tended those grotesque jungle weeds as if unaware of the long catalog of their faults.

"Good morning, Althy. How are the violets coming along?"

"Good morning yourself," she said.

She held a small green watering can with a long spout in her gnarled liver-spotted hand as she absorbedly watered the plants in their terra cotta pots, dipping and lifting and swinging the small watering can in conservative arcs. The morning light shined coolly through the windows and fired the edges of the leaves, the purples and greens, transfigured the hairy convoluted plant stems into a velvet filagree of smoldering gold, the earnest morning glow forcing a modicum of grudging beauty from the damn things.

Well, get to it, he urged himself.

"How is Sarah this morning?"

"She is better," said Althy not looking up. "She had some nice chicken broth this morning. She's been to the bathroom. She said she had a lovely movement."

"A lovely movement?" he grinned crookedly. "What are we talking about? Beethoven? Wait a minute. I'll get the kid on the phone."

He wasn't funny, so far as Althy was concerned. She took the homely details of nursing seriously. Taking care of the sick was no joke to her.

"How is her head?" he asked too bluntly.

"What do you mean?" This time she did look up, the sagging jowls of the ancient face tightened warily, the eyes watery, but alert.

"I just wondeied if her mind was clear, that's all."

"Of course her mind is clear."

"I just wondered," he repeated. "Sometimes her mind tends to wander. It's hard to talk to her sometimes."

"Why? What are you up to now?"

"Nothing. I just want to talk to her sometime. We have to make some plans for the future."

"Well," she said. "You keep your plans to yourself. Let the future take care of itself for now. You know how upset she is about your father. Don't you add to it."

"I don't intend to. It might even ease her mind if we worked out how to handle things before Dad is gone."

"Never mind," said Althy. "You leave her alone. Don't trouble her with that. She's got enough to deal with, without you getting her upset."

"All right," he said.

"Leave her alone."

She looked him dead in the eye.

"Okay," he said. "I'm glad I asked. I don't want to talk to her if it might upset her."

"Just leave her alone."

"Right," he said.

Well bullshit on that, he thought. That would be fine if we had all the time in the world. He decided to finish the lawn, and give Althy's vigilance time to subside.

He got out the iron contraption, an ancient heavy riding mower, and clattered through the uncut lawn, bouncing uncomfortably on the iron kidney seat. He cut sparkling wet dark-green swaths in the lawn filigreed with dew. By the time he finished, he guessed Terry was probably at the hospital, dispensing comfort and limeade to the old man. Briefly he considered jumping in the car and getting over there and catching her as she came out of the hospital. He could pull the same trick she had the other day, trapping him as he came out of the newspaper store. But likely such a stunt would backfire. You have to be patient, he counseled himself.

He wiped a million spears of wet grass from the blades of the mower, put it away, and took his second shower of the day. He worked on his baseball records and waited for Althy to settle into her afternoon routine of television game shows.

On the pretense of a visit to the bathroom he limped by her door, open just a crack, out of which issued the excited garble of the TV. He gave her another fifteen minutes to really settle in. She tended to get sleepy in front of the TV and dozed most afternoons away as one peppy game show host after another dispensed freezers, TV sets, sofa hide-a-beds and lawn furniture in an unending frenzy of witless largess that lasted all afternoon, every weekday.

Sarah's door was closed as usual. It was almost two o'clock but no doubt she was still behind the door drifting through dreamland on the great warm barge of her bed, the curtains of the room drawn against the light.

He knocked gently on the door. Nothing.

He knocked again.

"Sarah?"

Nothing.

He opened the door. Just as he figured, the curtains were drawn. Sarah lay flattened in the twilight, her covers up around her neck. Her sunglasses smashed against her pillow at a devastating angle.

But she was awake. She sat up as if startled, yet delighted by his unexpected visit.

"Darling!" she said. "A surprise visit."

"Didn't you hear me knock?"

"Yes," she laughed. "I heard you. I thought you were Mother. If I'm quiet she goes away. You see, I like to be alone. I'm very close to thinking things out."

"Well, I don't want to interrupt," he said.

"No, no. That's all right. Here, come sit by me. I like to have you visit."

She patted the bed at her side, wiggled over to make room for him. He would just as soon sit on the chair, not right next to her like that. She'd probably want to hold hands too. She always wanted to hold hands.

"Isn't it funny?" she said. "We don't seem to have much in common. Not even much affection, at least not on your side. Yet you have a very calming effect on me."

She gave his hand a squeeze. He did not return the pressure. It

would be nice, he thought, if she took off those sunglasses sometime.

"How about some light in here?" he said. "Want me to open the
drapes?"

"I like it this way," she said. "It's peaceful in the dark. It helps
me think."

"How are you feeling? Althy says she got some chicken broth
down your gullet this morning. She says that signifies some kind
of improvement."

"Mother believes all questions of emotional health are answera-
ble in terms of food."

Sarah patted his hand. He thought he would like his hand back
now, but he didn't know how to reclaim it without offending her.

"I am not well," she said bitterly. "I am not at all well. And you
know why."

"No, I don't know why."

"Yes, you do," she laughed. "Don't tease me. I *know* you do."

"No," he said. "What is it?"

"We have lost God," she said. "That's why everything has gone
wrong."

"Oh," he said.

"It is not a simple matter to find Him again," she said. "It is very
complicated. It is just not simple."

"Suppose we talk like this another time," he offered. "Let's talk
about regular life."

"This whole place and time is bad."

She gestured with a knobby hand. Her hands were old looking,
congested with veins. They looked slightly arthritic. She was still
good-looking for her age if you could forgive the frog neck and
the lines fine as threads in a spiderweb which radiated in all
directions out of the bridge of her nose. But her hands looked
almost as old as Althy's.

"You have too much time to think," he said. "What you need
is a routine."

He believed that. The thing was to concentrate on the routine
—the perfect shave, the Sunday papers, the fifty chin-ups ex-
ecuted with the discipline of a dancing master. Nothing can beat
a routine. When you ask yourself: okay, what comes next? you
always have an answer. She didn't have a routine, and that's why
she'd gone looney.

"I have to get out of here," she said.

"Out of where?"

"Out of *here.*"

Violently she indicated with her forefinger the room or the bed or maybe her own body.

"You have to get off your ass," he said. "You can't lie there and think about your troubles all the time."

"No, no. You don't understand," she shook her head hopelessly.

"Yes, I do. Nobody can do what you do without feeling bad. You can't just have all that time on your hands and not end up feeling sorry for yourself."

"Perhaps you're right," she said. She dropped his hand.

"Sure, I'm right."

"If you think at all, maybe you're in trouble," she said.

"Could be," he allowed. "But I didn't say that exactly."

"I hate life!" She spat the words passionately.

"No you don't."

Why did he want her to deny it? He didn't know. It was just automatic.

"Yes I do," she insisted in an ugly voice. "It is so bitter. It is such a joke."

"Well, it's funny all right."

"Yes. Yes. So goddamn funny, don't you think? I've got to get out of here."

"You'll be all right," he promised. "What you want is somebody to take care of you."

"He's coming home. You don't *understand.*"

"You'll be all right. He'll be downstairs in the spare room. I told you that. You'll never know he's around."

"No." She shook her head.

"No what?"

"It will not be all right. Why don't you listen?"

"I listen all right," he said. "I hear all you say. But you don't hear me. If he dies, you'll need somebody to take care of you. He's always done it, and now you will need someone else."

"Althy will do it," she said. "She's always done it. Not him. She'll do it now."

"No. That's not what I mean. I mean the old man provided you with everything. He looked out for you. Now you'll need someone else to do that."

"He will leave me money," she said. She searched his face in sudden panic. "There'll be money, won't there?"

"Yes. Plenty of money, all right. But you'll need someone to manage it for you. You're no good about money."

"Yes, I am too. How do you know anyway? Why are we talking like this? Daddy's not dead."

She was slipping into her little girl voice, the one that was rightfully hers in 1923, so he hurried on.

"No, he's not. But we have to plan ahead, Sarah."

"Why are you torturing me with this?" she cried.

"Okay. I'm through. We won't talk about it anymore. Just take it easy."

"I've got to get out," she said desperately. "It's almost as if God is telling me to go somewhere where I can hear the message."

"Just relax. Don't get yourself worked up."

"Talk about nice things," she said. "Help me."

"How about some ice water," he offered.

"You said we would talk some more. You said you'd talk to me before you brought him home. That you would *listen.*"

"Yes. I said that."

"But you don't mean it," she said.

"Yes, I do."

"No, you don't. If only you would listen."

"Look, we'll talk some more. We talked too much for now. Let me get you a drink."

He got her a big glass of orange juice with ice cubes in it and put it beside her bed.

She didn't seem interested.

"Don't you want the drapes open?"

She didn't answer.

He left her there, still propped up on her pillows, dissolving like a lozenge in the artificial twilight which she found so comforting.

T W E L V E

THAT NIGHT, as always, Ward went to see his father at the hospital. He drove toward a lilac sky which paled quickly and flooded with dark blue. The world around him dissolved in this solution of dark color. Ward turned on the lights of the big car and drove on.

The ancient Cadillac soughed through the dark in pleasant, smooth passage. The purl of the engine was so faint it was practically a figment. The dummy who designed this car was no dummy, Ward thought. He felt beholden to some remote wizard, maybe in the mold of Edison, whose engineering genius provided such driving pleasure to a few lucky Americans.

Driving the big car smoothed him out. Ward began to feel good, a condition brought on, really, by feeling nothing. He sank into the car itself. His pores sponged up the green glow of the dash lights. Bathed in the soothing phosphorescence of the instrument panel, Ward watched the road smoothly flow toward him, widen, and disappear beneath the classic sculpture of the car's front fenders. The Cadillac steered itself without effort on his part. Steadily and hypnotically it continued to reel in the highway. His body pumped away quietly at its automatic tasks; mucose valves opened and closed, fluids squirted through contracting vessels, while his brain lay dark and, for the moment, undisturbed.

That good feeling evaporated after one look at the old man. Tonight the old man really *looked* sick. The bruises under his eyes were glossy and blue. His skin stretched tight across his cheekbones. The parenthetical lines from his nose wings to the corners of his mouth were carved deeply into his yellow skin. Overnight it seemed his hair had taken on the dry, unhealthy look of so much excelsior.

"Well, you see," Ward said putting his bad leg on the chair.

"You were wrong. You thought it was going to rain all weekend and here today was a fine day, wasn't it? Clear sky—" his voice trailed off. The old man didn't look interested in the weather.

"Feeling bad?"

"God."

"I brought you the *Times.*"

"Thanks."

"I guess Terry came to see you today, didn't she?"

A trick question, calculated to get his father to brighten momentarily and relieve some of the bad feeling that had climbed like a forty-pound monkey onto Ward's back at the sight of the old man's glum and sickly face.

"Yes, she did."

His father glowed a little at the memory, but then his haggard face dimmed and left him looking old and sick again.

"Did you two have some trouble?"

"Why? Did she say—?"

"No, she didn't say anything. She just wasn't herself."

Ward didn't take it up. At least she knew how to keep a thing to herself, he thought.

"You ought to be nice to her, boy. She's good folks."

The old man shut his eyes and lay back. The white pillow made his drawn face look even more yellow.

"God," he said again.

Sarah once said that *God* was the most hopeful word in mankind's vocabulary. Here in this room on his father's lips, it was the most hopeless too. Ward didn't know what to say. He felt bad for his father. He wished somebody was responsible for this, so he could grab him by the shirt front and sock him around the room. The old man took the silence as a form of criticism so he amended that one syllable summary of his exhaustion with a promise or maybe an apology.

"I'll feel better tomorrow," he said.

Ward didn't stick around long. His father was too sick and tired to tolerate, let alone enjoy, any company. He relegated him to the good offices of the newspaper, hoping his pain would bleed into the newsprint. The stories about napalm raids on remote jungle villages and earthquakes in Patagonia might sponge up his own troubles and provide a few minutes of distraction. Ward left it up to *The New York Times* to accomplish what he couldn't do tonight, and maybe, in truth, could never do again.

couldn't do tonight, and maybe, in truth, could never do again.

He went home, did some sit-ups, and hit the sack. Ward didn't sleep much that night. At three he woke, turned on the light, and smoked a couple of cigarettes. He kept a ceramic ashtray in the shape of a catcher's mitt on his night stand. Below, on the open shelf, he stored the two cartons of smokes he bought every pay day at the discount store, one of his regular stops. Having things set up that way made it convenient for smoking in bed on those nights when he couldn't sleep. He lay there, his legs wrapped in the bed sheet, his head propped on the headboard, and the ashtray on his chest. Probably he looked uncomfortable but he didn't feel bad at all. Likely it was his troubles that made him wakeful, so he made a point of not thinking of anything particular. He just lay there watching the smoke coil in the lamp shade and stream out the top like smoke out of a chimney. He took a good deal of pleasure in just looking around the room. For instance, that dresser scarf of white Irish linen that Althy had embroidered made such a nice field for his collection of gold trophies which seemed to wink at him from across the room. And the polished sweep of his desk top, his baseball notebooks stored neatly on the shelves below. Something about orderliness seemed to give him special satisfaction. The drapes were closed. The green curtains seemed to vibrate extra bright as if hoarding the meager light from his bed-side lamp. The corners of his room were thick and secret with shadows. Yes, it was a cozy room. Ward lay there smoking, enjoying everything around him, taking care not to go into anything too deeply. At five o'clock he got up and got ready for work.

That week each evening he tried to reach Terry. Twice he got through but as soon as she heard his voice, she hung up. Other times the phone just rang, unanswered. Either she was out, or not answering. It was getting serious.

One night he went downtown, jumped up for the fire escape ladder, and climbed to the roof of the clothing store across Hano-ver Street from her building. With a sinking sensation, he discovered the windows in her apartment were dark. No doubt she was out someplace, maybe in the company of some fellow who believed in babies.

On Saturday he got out the bike and pedaled to town just before noon. Ward was so agitated he didn't even stop at the store first to get the paper and check the sports page. He pumped directly to her place, chained the spidery bike to a parking meter, and clumped upstairs.

By God, he thought. This has got to end. It's making me too nervous.

He rapped sharply on the gray door, beating a tattoo on the "Get out of Vietnam" sticker. If she doesn't answer, Ward thought, I'll break down the damn door. He was convinced somehow she had developed the magical knack of knowing when he was ringing her telephone or knocking at her door. She was in there, of course, maliciously being quiet as a mouse till he gave up and went away. The idea made him so mad he got dizzy. He had forgotten to circle around back to see if her Volkswagon was in the lot, but he was sure she was home. Be damned if she was going to get away with just letting him ring her telephone and rap on her door to no account. He'd had enough of this shit.

Just as he was ready to assault the door again, it flew open.

"Okay Gimp. What's up?"

By God, there was Avis. Standing in the doorway, sleep sodden, an astonishing if surly reincarnation from an old *National Geographic.* Dressed in a crummy brown corduroy bathrobe, she stood, with her feet splayed apart and wedged into blue mules.

"What are you doing here?" he wanted to know.

"I *live* here," she said.

"What do you mean you live here?" He tried to look past her into the livingroom. "Where's Terry?"

"Just stand there, big boy. Don't try to throw your weight around with me."

Now that she'd brought up the idea maybe he ought to push her on her ass and go in there and flush out Terry for himself.

"Some people will take your guff, but I won't," Avis said.

"What the hell are you *doing* here?"

"I live here, for the time being," she smiled emphatically. "It's a good thing, too. Terry can use the company. I've had it with your brother."

"Good," he said. "I wish you both luck."

"Creep," she said. "You and your brother are both creeps."

"Where's Terry?"

"He never even took me to a movie for the last month." The recollection struck her as a fresh insult. "I can't remember the last time he took me out to dinner. Do you think that's fair?"

"That's between you and the kid. Let me talk to Terry. It's important."

"Sure," she said. "What you have to say is important. What I have to say is nothing. That's the way it is with you men. His idea of sex was once a week. Does that make any sense?"

"Jesus, Avis. Keep it to yourself, will you?" The last thing he wanted to hear about this morning was the kid's sex life.

"I'm a young woman, for Godsakes! What am I supposed to do?"

The excitement of this situation inflated her pug nose. It looked like a dusky nob in the middle of her round face.

"All that son of a bitch ever wants to do is paint. Is that fair?"

"Look," he said. "Just ask Terry to come out and talk to me for a few minutes"

"She doesn't want to see you, Gimp. What's it take for you to get the message? You call on the telephone, she hangs up. You knock on the door, she says go away. You're slow, Gimp. She's had enough of your shit."

"Since when do you do her talking?"

"She's fed up. You treat her like your stupid brother treated me."

He had the idea she was pretending to more knowledge than she had. What if in a weak moment Terry told her she was pregnant? Avis' natural medium was trouble. She would surely see a pregnant girlfriend as a first-class chance to stir things up. The notion made him sweat. He didn't need any more complications.

"Just let me talk to her." That sounded like he was begging a favor so he amended it.

"This is none of your business," he told her. "Stay out of it."

"To hell with you," she said. "Get lost!"

She slammed the door.

GET OUT OF VIETNAM.

It took a second for his eyes to refocus on the slogan. The pulses twitched in his trembling arms and legs. He breathed against the gray wood; the door gently refuted his warm breath back into his face. Silence inside the apartment. If Terry was home, actually home, Avis would be sounding off about how she'd told him off.

Surely Avis wouldn't be able to wait till he went away. She'd start to blab right off.

Therefore, it must be that Terry wasn't home. That made sense, didn't it?

He cocked his head to listen better. He'd be damned if he'd press his ear against the door like some heartsick wimp.

Get Out Of. . . .

Silence. Nothing so nerve-racking as silence sometimes. Slowly down the pitched, narrow stairs he went, favoring his bad leg. The son of a bitch had throbbed like a toothache the last few days. He felt bilious and headachy. It was getting to be a hell of a mess.

He went around back. There was the apple-green Volkswagen. The sight of that car made him feel bad for a second. But it didn't really prove Terry was home, letting Avis do all her talking for her. She was probably out getting groceries. Or at the hairdresser's getting her hair spun into a cloud of cotton candy. He hoped so, anyway. She wasn't the kind to let some bully take over her life, was she?

Ward felt pretty low. He decided to have a beer at Walter Juneau's bar and think things over. Walter's was just up the street from Terry's apartment. If he stayed close to her place, there was always a chance he might run into Terry. They might get to talking on the street the way people do and—who knows—fix it up right then and there. He waited for the light to change at the corner, wheeled the bike, ticking like a live thing, across the street, and chained it to a parking meter outside the bar.

Walking into Juneau's was like entering a movie theater just before the show started. He felt disoriented and a bit dizzy and then in the darkness things began to take shape. Walter, for instance, loomed behind the bar opposite a silent patron. The light over the pool table spilled a dim path to the bar between tables, forlorn in the early afternoon.

"Ward, you son of a gun!" said Walter.

"Hello, Walter!"

"Ward, you son of a bitch. It's about time you come to see me."

Without asking, Walter drew Ward a Genessee draft and set the glass in front of him.

"How is Gordon?"

"Still in the hospital, Walter. They've got him on chemotherapy. Makes him sick as a dog."

The beer tasted good—cold and coppery.

"Too damn bad," Walter shook his head and stubbed his cigarette. "Such a good man. He doesn't deserve bad luck. How's your brother?"

"He's okay, Walter,"

"Crazy kid," Walter said. "Still paints pictures, I suppose?"

"Yes, he does,"

"Still paints nudes?"

"Yes. Nothing but naked ladies."

"I could use such a picture over the bar."

"You couldn't see it, Walter. You keep it too dark in here."

"Yes, but I'd know it was there. I could light matches and show my favorite parts to close friends."

Over the bar there were two backlighted scenes, one of hunters and bird dogs in the field and another of fishermen boating a pike. Under the shielded fluorescent light the felt cloth of the pool table glowed emerald green, the balls centered in a colorful wedge ready for the next break. Small boxes of blue chalk were scattered haphazardly on top of the long metal light shade.

Ward drank a little more beer and felt himself begin to relax.

"Gordon is a very fine man," Walter said. "I ought to go see him."

"He'll be home soon," said Ward. "We'll come down to see you."

"Wonderful. That would be wonderful. You tell Gordon I said hello. Bring Gordon in here. Tell him I will feed him and make him well again. I'll make steaks and potato skins and that cabbage salad Gordon taught me to make. We'll eat well. We'll all feel better. Will you tell him that for me?"

"Yes, I will, Walter."

"Good. Have another beer. You're a slow drinker."

"Have one with me, Walter."

"All right, son. Since you ask."

No sooner had they settled this matter when the door opened and Gordie shambled in.

"Here comes Too-loose Lautrec," said Walter. "Hello, Junior. Will you paint a naked lady for the bar?"

"Bastard!" Gordie screamed.

"What the hell is wrong with you?"

"You bastard," repeated Gordie.

Behind his glasses, Gordie's eyes were watering. He said slowly, amazed and outraged, "You are a real bastard. Do you know that? I'm glad I saw the bike, so I could stop. Tell you to your face what a bastard you turned out to be."

"Easy, kid. What's the problem?"

"What's the problem, big man? I'll tell you the problem. Avis left me, that's the problem."

"Jesus Christ," said Walter.

"That's too bad," said Ward.

"And you, you bastard. She told me how you were always trying to get in her pants. You son of a bitch! You had your own girl."

"Oh, God," said Walter.

"She told me about the last time. How you grabbed her by the tit and tried to throw her down on the couch. You disgusting son of a bitch! You're supposed to be my brother!"

"You dumb shit," said Ward. "She's got you so buffaloed—"

"You bastard!"

With a sob the kid threw a punch which grazed Ward's chin and landed on his shoulder. Gordie fell into him, knocking Ward off his stool. Another slammed to the floor. Ward's hip struck the pool table.

"Bastard!"

The kid had gone completely crazy. He swung again. Ward ducked and grabbed him, turning him around by his blue chambray shirt. Pieces of it came off in his hands. He punched his brother in the mouth, and his glasses flew off. Collapsing on the pool table, Gordie broke the neat wedge of balls with his head. The three-ball dropped into the corner pocket. Other balls exploded on the floor like rifle fire, and rolled thunderously across the floor. Ward had his brother by the throat. The kid tried to swing. Ward blocked with his shoulder. He banged the kid's head on the table. It was amazing how good it made him feel.

"You damned fool."

Gordie struggled and tried to throw another punch. Ward whacked his head on the table again, mainly to get his attention.

"I'll let you up if you act sensible."

The kid opened his hands and let his arms flop back.

"Okay," he gasped.

Ward let go and stepped back cautiously. The kid jumped up.

"My glasses."

The solitary customer in the green cap at the end of the bar handed over his glasses. Using both trembling hands, the kid fumbled them back on his face. He stood there, most of his blue shirt hanging down around his waist, the collar still buttoned around his long neck.

"I ought to punch you in the mouth."

"You already tried that," said Ward.

"It's a nice day," suggested Walter. "Why don't you boys go outside and fight in the sunshine?"

"Are they brothers?" the fellow in the green cap asked no one in particular.

"It's not your fault," said the kid. "I know she's a bitch. I can't help it. I'm crazy about her."

"Shut up. You're making a damn fool of yourself."

"I don't care," said the kid.

"Think of Walter."

"To hell with Walter."

"To hell with you," said Walter.

"I can't help it," said the kid and covered his face.

"Get out of here," said Ward. "Don't make a fool of yourself."

The kid dropped his hands. His eyes blazed crazily.

"If you ever touch her again, I'll kill you!"

The door slammed shut behind him. The customer in the green cap picked the bar stool off the floor and thoughtfully sat down on it.

Ward helped Walter find the balls for the pool table.

"I'm sorry, Walter."

"It beats television," said Walter.

So much for Saturday.

Sometimes when things go bad, they just get worse. The next week he tried again to reach Terry several times. But Avis always answered the telephone.

"Yeah?" she demanded.

He didn't even bother to ask for Terry. He just hung up.

Once she answered, giggling, "Delaplane Hall. Who in the Hall do you want?"

Hilarious female laughter in the background.

He hung up. It was enough to make you sick.

He ran into Terrill one night at the hospital.

"How's the treatment working?"

"I don't know," said the doc. "It's too early to say."

"I don't think it's doing a damn bit of good."

"Oh? Where did you say you studied medicine?"

"He looks bad," said Ward. "His hair's turning gray. He's losing more weight. He's weak as a kitten. He says it makes him real sick."

"It's too early," said the doc.

"To hell," said Ward. "Look at him."

"Who's the doctor around here?" asked Terrill.

"It's bad enough," said Ward. "I can't see making him suffer."

"It could save his life," said Terrill. "You want to try for that, don't you?"

"It's not working," said Ward. "You know it, and I know it."

One night Ward sat by his father's bed reading the papers as his father dozed, his hands folded in his lap. The interlaced fingers and knuckles looked frail and yellow. With his mouth open, and his Adam's apple bobbing like that, he appeared to be about eighty years old.

Let's see. Time to concentrate on the sports page. The Red Sox winning steadily. Playing good ball. About the only thing going right. Ward tried to read, but he kept looking up at the old man and at that lump bobbing around in his throat and at those frail hands folded in his lap. Good gravy. How he's gone downhill, he thought.

The old man opened his eyes and chewed a bit to get the saliva flowing again.

"Terry never mentions you anymore," he said.

"Is that so?"

"You must have had a good fight."

Ward said nothing.

"You're off her list, boy," said the old man.

When Ward didn't reply, his father said, "I hate to see it."

That's the way it went.

Well, I'm not getting anywhere this way, he thought. But he didn't know what to do.

The next Friday night he was down in his room lying on the bed smoking a cigarette when Althy knocked on his door and called his name.

"What is it?"

He was reluctant to get up and open the door. His idea was just to hide out in his room and think things over. He didn't want to deal with anybody tonight. He was after a little peace and quiet.

"You better come out," she said.

"What for?"

"Your mother."

"What's wrong?"

"She's not feeling well."

That was code for "Sarah is acting crazy." So he got up, pulled on his khakis, zipped up the canoe shoes he used for slippers, and went upstairs.

He knocked on Sarah's door and then went in.

"Hello, Sarah."

She lay on her side facing away from him. He walked around the bed and sat down in the chair.

"It is hard," she said.

"Is it?" he said.

"You don't know. You think I'm merely weak. But that's not so."

"Why don't you sit up for a minute."

She allowed him to plump up her pillows and get her settled.

"You want something to drink? How about some limeade."

He had laid in a stock of the frozen juice against the day when his father came home. He was glad to go out to the kitchen and mix up a batch, happy for a few minutes in which to collect himself. She didn't sound good. Her voice had that slow-motion quality which signaled bad trouble. She sure knew how to pick her moments. The last thing he needed right now was to have Sarah fall out of her tree.

He carried the glass into the bedroom.

"Thank you!"

Sarah was much too grateful really. Maybe her exaggerated show of appreciation was meant to be ironical. To make him feel bad for the sins of past neglect. He battled a mixture of anger and discomfort, which was nothing new. Around Sarah you never knew what was going on for sure. You always asked yourself: What is she up to now?

"It is a blessing to be unaware of the godly or the diabolical," she said.

"Yes, indeed," he agreed with her.

Althy came in.

"Ward fetched you a cool drink. How nice!"

His grandmother said this as if a cold drink might be the solution to everything.

"I am one of God's pincushions," said Sarah.

"Are you?"

"The sun and the moon go through me like knives. The sound of children playing may be Mozart or screaming machinery, but never simple."

"I think you're tired out," Althy fretted. "You worry so. You don't see anyone. You never get out of that bed except to go to the bathroom. No wonder you don't feel well."

She searched Ward's face anxiously to see if he agreed with the diagnosis.

"I'm so glad you're here, darling."

Sarah squeezed Ward's knee, the only accessible part of him since he'd been careful to position himself in the bedside chair.

"I am getting messages," she said confidentially. Her hand fluttered up to straighten her sunglasses.

"What kind of messages?"

"They are not altogether clear as yet. But it's apparent I can't stay in this house any longer. I must get out. He will interfere with the messages. I know this. I've been told."

"Who told you what, Sarah?"

"Please don't laugh at me," she said. "I know you'll laugh when I tell you this."

He waited.

"I believe I'm getting messages from God."

"Sarah—"

She laughed.

"I know that sounds crazy. I knew you'd laugh at me. It *is* crazy, actually. I don't deny it."

Ward turned to Althy.

"How long has she been like this?"

"She just started feeling so bad today."

"Just today?"

"Well. Yesterday a little bit too."

Sarah ignored them both and continued with her explanation.

"The ancient prophets went about telling people that God talked to them. In those days, people wanted to hear what they

had to say. Times were different. You might say people were
ignorant or superstitious then. Or you might say that in those days
people really believed in God with all their hearts."

"Sarah."

"They wanted to know Him with all their hearts. So they found
ways that are closed to men now. They were delighted to talk to
someone who claimed to have spoken with God."

"What does God say to you, Sarah?"

"You shouldn't encourage her," said Althy.

"What does God say, Sarah?" he repeated.

She didn't seem to hear his question.

"Let's just say I'm a little psychic," she was saying. "That has
a semi-respectable sound to it, even in the age of science. What
a dreary time! What a dreary time you have to live through,
darling. The next pillar of fire man sees will likely be a hydrogen
explosion. It surely won't be God leading his people into the land
of milk and honey."

"Get Terrill," said Ward. "I think she could use a good night's
rest."

Althy didn't make any trouble about it. He sat there for the next
half hour while Sarah calmly documented Old Testament conversations with God.

He went out in the hall when he heard the doctor come in.

"What's up?" said Terrill.

"This business about Dad is getting to her," said Ward. "She
hasn't slept for a couple of nights. She says she's been talking to
God."

"Oh?" Terrill was interested. "What does He say?"

"She doesn't know," Ward said. "She says the message isn't
clear yet, but when it is revealed everything will be simple enough.
Then, she says, she will know just what to do."

"Maybe at that point," said Terrill, "she'll be interested in going
partners in my practice."

They went into the bedroom.

"Oh, Jesus," Sarah said when she saw the doc. "Who called
you?"

"Now, Sarah," said Althy.

"Why can't you people leave me alone?"

"How are you feeling, Mrs. Sullivan?" sighed Terrill, slowly
sinking into the chair beside the bed.

"I'll be downstairs if you need me." Ward had to get out of there. Nothing was going right. What he needed was to hide out in his room and think things through. Seemed lately there was no chance for any peace and quiet. His hip hurt as he jarred down the stairs. Get on the bike, he thought. Go for a long ride. Get loosened up before you freeze in your tracks.

He opened the door of his room.

"What do you say, Gimp?"

There was Avis, in his bed, the sheet wrapped demurely above her breasts and held in place under each arm. She was clearly naked. Her clothes lay in a little wanton heap on the floor by the bed—the cutoff jeans, a flowered halter from an old bathing suit, sandals, and right on top, a pair of red bikini panties.

"What the hell are you doing here?" His eyes must have goggled right out of his head, because she giggled at just the sight of him.

"Surprised?"

"Get out of here," he said.

"I thought I'd give you another chance."

"You get out of here," he said. "I had enough trouble for one week."

"I hear Gordie tried to knock your block off in some bar. I'd loved to have seen your expression when he came after you."

"How did you know that?"

"He *told* me of course. He came right over to the apartment and told me. As always he was distraught about it."

"Thanks for setting me up."

"Don't mention it. How about getting laid? You must be pretty ripe by now. You haven't seen Terry for over a week."

"I'd have to be plenty ripe to look at you twice. How did you get in here?"

"Are you kidding?" she snorted. "You people never lock a door or close a curtain. I just walked in."

"How the hell did you get up here?"

"I borrowed your little pussycat's car. I told her I was going to an exercise class. You appreciate the irony?"

"I don't appreciate any part of this."

"Come on. It's no big deal. What's a piece of ass between friends?"

She leaned over and unzipped him.

"Your fly's open," she giggled.

He must have jumped back a foot when this happened and then a foot forward when the knock came at the door.

"Ward?"

It was the kid.

"Oh, Jesus," Avis whispered. "You're in the soup now."

"Hey, Bro. Open the door."

"Is that you, kid?" said Ward, stalling for time.

"I want to talk to you, buddy," Gordie said sincerely through the door. "I'm sorry about what happened at Walter's—"

There was a thud overhead followed by a stringy scream which he recognized as his grandmother's alto. Ward hit the light and plunged out of the room, past the kid, who stood there with his mouth open. As he thundered up the stairs he heard scuffling sounds and thumps from the hallway above.

"Sarah!" Althy wailed.

Framed in the doorway to Sarah's room, Terrill crawled, blind as a mole, on the carpet. His glasses were gone, his eyes reduced to slits. There was blood on his cheek.

Althy beat on the bathroom door. She looked at Ward wildly, trying to put all her urgency into one wordless glance.

"She's locked herself in," she gasped. "She wants to hurt herself."

"Help Terrill," Ward told the kid who had humped up the stairs after him.

Ward pounded on the door with his fist.

"Sarah," he shouted. "You open up."

"Get away from here! Get away, all you bastards!"

"Open the door!"

"Sarah!" Althy sounded broken-hearted.

"Move, Althy."

"What?"

"Get away from the door."

He threw his shoulder into it. Sarah screamed. She kept on screaming as he crashed rhythmically into the door. At last the frame splintered. He piled into it one more time, and the door exploded open.

"Get away!"

Beside Sarah on the floor, as she knelt in front of the toilet, was the music box—that miniature piano Scott Prothero had given her before disappearing into the war, and in which according to Althy

she squirreled away her magic pills. Sarah held her hands over her
ears and screamed.

Gordie was right behind him.

They made a grab for her.

She threw the only thing at hand, the music box, which hit
Ward in the shoulder.

"Get her!"

"Get away from me! Leave me alone!"

"Help me, kid. For Christ's sake, don't stand there."

Together they half-carried, half-dragged her, kicking and struggling, back into the bedroom. Terrill was erect now although leaning at a radical angle in geriatric defiance of the law of gravity. He
was adjusting his glasses to his face. The frames were bent and his
cheek was scratched, as if he'd run into a cat or a screen door. An
exclamation point of blood punctuated his limp collar. He looked
bored by the whole thing.

"Get her on the bed," he muttered.

"You bastards!" cried Sarah.

They held her down while Terrill fumbled around in his bag,
breathing asthmatically. Sarah began to blubber. Her eyes looked
terribly naked.

"My glasses," she cried. "I want my glasses."

Althy found them in the hall and fitted them to her face.

"How many pills?" asked Terrill.

"None," said Althy. "She couldn't have had any. I took them
all away from her."

"Humph," said Terrill. "She was just sitting there in front of the
toilet bowl with her music box and no pills?"

"She must have forgotten," said Althy. "She kept the pills hidden in the music box. I found them the other day. She must have
forgotten."

"No pills you say," asked Terrill, still too tired to look interested
in the answer.

"No. No pills," Althy said.

"A phantom suicide attempt," said Terrill. "As real as the real
thing."

He plunged the hypodermic into the amber vial, holding it up
to the feeble light and drawing the contents slowly into the cali-
brated plastic chamber.

Everyone watched Terrill silently, except Sarah whose sunglasses were directed at the ceiling.

"Everyone's dying," sobbed Sarah. "They're part of your life, part of you. They keep dying. What do you do?"

Nobody had an answer.

"Hold her down," said Terrill.

He pulled up the sleeve of the faded bathrobe and neatly inserted the hypodermic into the faint blue marbling of her arm. Slowly he squeezed the contents into her rigid arm. Although tensed, Sarah did not struggle. Perhaps she was preoccupied, listening to the voice of God. Terrill seemed to take forever. But almost at once, following the doc's painfully slow injection, Sarah dissolved right into the bed, going limp under their hands.

In the kitchen everybody wanted a drink except Althy. She kept shuffling back and forth between the kitchen and the bedroom. The doc settled for a shot of scotch.

Terrill slumped at the table. He fooled around with his empty shot glass; taking off his glasses, he shut his eyes and squeezed the bridge of his nose. Nobody was talking much.

"There is a nice private hospital on the other side of Elizabethtown. We better put her in Hazelwood for a while."

"No," said Althy. "I'll look after her. She'll be all right."

Terrill looked up.

"She needs psychiatric attention, Mrs. Rideout."

"That's fine. Recommend a psychiatrist. Ward will see that she gets to her appointments. She's better off at home."

Terrill looked at Ward. "It's amazing how many resident physicians you have in this household," he said tonelessly.

"Althy," said the kid. "You better listen to the doctor."

"I know my daughter," insisted Althy. "She's better off at home."

"Well, you talk it over, folks," said the doc, getting up. "Let me know what you decide."

They all stood up. Terrill handed Althy his empty glass.

"We will," said Ward. "We'll let you know."

"We've already talked it over," said Althy. "She's staying home."

"Relax," said Ward.

Terrill shuffled off, sighing, dangling his black bag at the end of a lifeless arm, diminishing slowly down the walk. Althy went off to Sarah's room.

"I'm tired as hell," said Ward.

"One more drink. Then I'll go," said Gordie.

Ward got fresh ice cubes, poured the vodka. It tasted clean and powerful. Some of the tenseness eased in his shoulders.

They stood in the middle of the kitchen, each lost in his own thoughts, drinking the vodka.

"I didn't expect to crash one of Mother's suicide attempts—even a fake," said Gordie. "I just came up here to tell you I was sorry about that business down at Walter's."

"That's all right," said Ward.

"I'm just crazy about her, that's all."

"Okay," said Ward. "Forget it."

"I acted like a fool, and I'm sorry. I know she's a liar. She was just trying to make trouble."

"Good for you," said Ward. "Now just drink your drink and forget it."

Althy stuck her head in the door.

"Don't tell your father about this," she said.

"We'll talk later," said Ward.

"You boys have to stick up for your mother."

She looked around the room for support, got no sign, and left.

"Poor Mother," said Gordie, looking at his drink.

"Come on, kid. Finish up. I'm so tired I can hardly stand up."

"You feel a refreshing breeze in here?"

"What's that?"

"I said: do you feel a breeze."

"No. Why?"

"Your fly's unzipped, dummy."

Ward looked down, nonplussed. Yes, indeed. His fly was open. He zipped up.

"I must be getting senile," he said.

Gordie grinned.

"Come on," Gordie said. "This is me remember? I know what's going on."

"Well, kid. It's hard to explain."

"What's to explain? I know you had Terry in your room."

Ward just looked at him.

"Hell, her car's right out here on the driveway. You don't exactly have to be Sherlock Holmes to figure it out. I guess I shouldn't have come right down and knocked on your door like that. But I felt so bad about last Saturday I didn't stop to think."

"Are you finished? Let me take your glass," said Ward.

"I bet you jumped a foot when I knocked on the door."

"It's been a long day, kid."

Ward gently pushed the kid in the direction of the door. After he finally got Gordie out the door, Ward turned out the lights and went downstairs, taking it easy not to jounce his bad leg.

He held his breath as he opened the door to his room and snapped on the light. But Avis was gone, leaving behind a rumpled bed. That girl couldn't even lie on a bed without making a mess of it.

He was so damned worn out by all the shenanigans of the last two weeks he lay down without taking his clothes off, very unusual for him, and fell right off to sleep, never even waking up till ten o'clock the next morning.

T H I R T E E N

T H E K I D began to faint the second he stepped across the threshold of the hospital. Next to the glass box where the receptionist was obliged to sit like a Nazi war criminal, the old man sat with a grin on his face, but he looked awful. Terrible. Still he was grinning above his check sports coat. Happy to see his sons and to get out of the place. Grinning somewhat like a fox eating shit, as Wayne McLain might say. Sitting there, more dead than alive, trapped in the dying garment of his body. The kid's legs turned to rubber the minute they came through the door. He swooned in slow but still locomotive descent in the general direction of his smiling father, groping past confetti-colored nagahyde chairs and plastic settees. This ocean he traversed was polished granite, liquid black as the onyx stone in the old man's pinky ring. Chances are, if the kid sank to the floor he was liable to crack his skull. Not a good thing. Therefore, as the kid slid down to meet his fate, his big brother grabbed him by the long bone of his upper arm. A broom handle, a book reader's arm. Yet Gordie seemed surprisingly strong. Throwing him around Walter's bar had not been easy. Leverage, Ward guessed, from all those long bones. The kid was a collection of gears and levers, a walking demonstration of the laws of physics.

"Here," said Ward. "Careful, you goddamn girl. You'll fracture your skull."

The old man found it funny. Indeed they both laughed as Gordie, glowing like a watch dial, sat down in a cold sweat on a plastic settee and put his head between his knees.

"Come on, Nancy." Ward gave him some time to collect himself. "Can you make it to the door?"

Gordie, still green and sweaty, raised his head from his knees and gave the question serious consideration. Yes, he nodded. He thought he could. He looked so solemn and yet so dog-sick, his father and brother had to laugh again.

"Let's give Jocko some more time," suggested the old man. "Never did like hospitals, did you, Jock?"

So, counting his brother, Ward brought home two convalescents that day. It had been a good move to use the Cadillac convertible for this job. When his father saw it gleaming at the curb in the hospital drive, he smiled in a way that made clear the car was not merely shiny metal but another member of the family. They threw his bag in the back, put down the windows and took off, Ward at the wheel, the old man next to him, and Gordie in the back seat. The breeze was mild and lovely. They rode down Front Street next to the brown shallow river flecked with winking gold in the sunlight, reached the tunnel of cool shadows cast by the elms and buttonwoods in the riverside park, turned onto the Harvey Taylor, and as the damp river wind came with new force in his father's window, headed west toward Carlisle.

In the fresh air the kid revived to tell a joke about a pawn shop parrot, which his father found amusing.

"Ah," said his father, holding his head up the way a dog does when he's enjoying something in the air.

"You like this?" asked Ward.

"Damn right, I like this."

At home, he stood on the edge of the drive and as the breeze flapped his pleated pants against his emaciated legs, he looked all around. Took it all in, including the trees, most of which he'd planted, knew by name, nourished, and loved. The pin oaks were tall and strong now and periodically plugged the sewer line. Collectively, the pin oaks, the tulip trees, and the pines, all conspired to attract the damn birds who pooped up the cars. But it made no difference to him. My, my, he seemed to say, so this is home.

Gordie took his bag in the house. Still the old man, the breeze slapping his pant cuffs, just stood there like a dog on the scent of something big.

"I see the horses aren't in the field," he said.

"Good gravy. I guess I forgot to put them out in all the excitement this morning."

"Come on, boy. We'll let them out now."

They walked down the green slope of the lawn and went single-file through the tall blonde grass. The path curved right, no doubt the kid would say, owing to the rotation of the earth.

When they opened the barn door a warm mixture of smells—mostly horse droppings and hay with a little molasses thrown in —hit them. The animals stamped and snorted, aroused by the sudden light and, likely, the presence of men.

The hammerhead lolled her chin on the stall gate, gazing stupidly at them. Ward swung up the wooden crossbar and pushed open the doors leading to the pasture, letting in the pale light which jumped through the doors and sprawled on the iron ground.

Leaning his hip against the stall gate, his father put his arm around the mare's neck and with his free hand stroked the mare's nose. She didn't like all this attention one bit. No sir. Bits of yellow straw, fine as splinters, clung to the hair of her gray lips as she struggled to get free. If a horse can look embarrassed, this animal did.

"How is the pony's nose today? Glad to see your papa home? Your soft nose feels glad. Yes, it does. It feels glad. Yes, yes. Good pony."

The horse struggled against this embarrassing display of love and affection.

In his dark stall, the black stallion screamed and began to crash against his door.

"Quiet, you beast," said the old man.

He let go the mare who sank her head from sight in relief. Damned two-legged stallions, always trying to kiss your nose, she seemed to say.

As his father approached, the stallion stopped punishing his gate. Almost invisible through the slats, the horse gleamed silky in the darkness, except for the glowing coal of his bloodshot eye.

The old man chuckled at the stallion's sudden change of character.

"What an obedient pony," he mocked. "You black devil. Look at that, boy. See him try to stare me down. Come here, horse."

The old man ran his arm through the slats into the dark stall, pressing the side of his face to the wood in order to reach the animal. He stroked the crazy beast. He seemed to be soothing a shadow, nothing more. Hardly visible, the horse remained electric and motionless as the old man combed his flank.

"Yes, yes," his father assured the horse, as if in answer to some anxious question put to him by the creature that only a man gifted in the ways of horses could understand.

"Yes," agreed the old man again.

The stallion seemed to accept this answer and remained motionless, his main interest at this moment appearing to be the rhythmic application of the old man's hand.

His father broke the spell by pulling his arm back into the light. "Let's put the mares to pasture," he said.

The black horse didn't like this. He screamed hysterically at the sudden withdrawal of the soothing hand and began again to slam against his gate as they opened the other stall doors. The bolt-lock and hinges sang out like the clang of a horseshoe ringing a stake.

Ward kept his eye on the gate which bulged like a diaphragm in spasm as the horse kept socking into it. Some day, when they were least prepared for it, the door was going to explode off its hinges and that horse, big as a building, was going to be in the runway with them, making the most of his sharp hooves to kick the stuffing out of somebody he didn't like at the moment. He noticed his father paid no mind to the stallion but just went about opening the gates. The mares, more sensible on this question, nervously clattered past the big horse's stall as quickly as they could and made for the sunlit pasture.

At the corral fence they stopped to watch the horses mill around the bathtub.

"How's your mother taking all this?"

"All what?"

"Me coming home. Is she upset?"

"She's all right."

"She doesn't like it, I'll bet."

"No, she doesn't. But too bad."

"She hates this."

"This?"

"Yes. *This.* Life's too messy for her."

"That's really too bad," said Ward.

The old man leaned on the fence. Then he said, "Terry said she'll come to see me."

"That's good."

"She didn't know how to say it. But I guess she'd like it better if you weren't around when she visited."

"Is that so?"

"You really did it, boy. Whatever it was."

Ward was tempted to say "too bad" to that too. But instead he said, "Well, what do you want me to do. Take a room at a hotel?"

"You don't have to do anything fancy. Just make yourself scarce when she's around."

"I'll do that," Ward said. "I'll be happy to do that."

"Good."

The old man looked at him. The smell of horse manure was in the air. A fly crawling on the lip of the bathtub, apparently at the end of his days, fell into the water, buzzed feebly on the surface, and then stopped as if not up to any pretended interest in survival at this point.

"You still don't see it, do you?"

"See what?"

"She's a fine little girl. Good to people. Loving and giving. You could do worse, boy. Much worse."

"You talk like somebody's maiden aunt," said Ward. "The only thing you talk about anymore is boys and girls. What happened to World Events?"

"We're down to basics now," said the old man.

"I like it better when you discuss the front page of the newspaper. At least that shows class."

"I see you won't listen," said his father mildly. "I wouldn't try, except I don't have any time for fooling around."

"Well, don't lecture me," said Ward.

"I'm dying, boy."

It was hard to argue with that.

"We tried chemotherapy and everything else. We all know it didn't work."

Well, he was right of course. But you don't say "you're right" in a case like this. Somehow it seemed unfair for a man to have to live so long with the knowledge he was finished and not a damn thing he could do about it, except to go on patting his horse's nose and looking over his trees and shrubs. Ward leaned against the fence and watched the horses drift off.

"Look at those horses," said his father after a minute. They had drifted down pasture and they bent in graceful arcs in the yellow grass. "They sure are beautiful."

"Yes, they are," allowed Ward.

"You don't belong here," said the old man. "This isn't your country. I made my peace here. But you. Hell. You aren't *in* this place. Understand?"

The old man was tracking fast. First he described what a jewel Terry Delaplane was. Then went right on to his next favorite subject which was that Ward ought to clear out. Really, it made Ward a little indignant the way his father kept after it. No question, the man was trying to kick him out. What had he done wrong, anyway?

"You and your mother suffer from being in the wrong place at the wrong time."

"I can't say I like that comparison," said Ward.

"Your mother talks about being lost in history. Living the wrong life."

"Living the *wrong* life. Hell, she's not living at all."

"Are *you?*" asked the old man. Said so softly, it shocked Ward, as if the question, asked so quietly, gave it an extra jolt.

"Or are you just dreaming, boy."

"I'm doing okay."

"You're doing shit. Wake up. You've used up most of being young. But you still have a chance. Do something."

"I'm doing fine."

"You're smart. But the trouble is, you're dumb."

"Thanks for the advice," said Ward. "How about we go up to the house now."

Before his father answered the hammerhead had time to clop back to the bathtub and stick her nose in the rusty water. The fly, on its back, spun lazily in the whirlpool made by the mare's lips as she dreamily slurped the water.

"You grieve too much, boy. The bad luck works on your mind. Be careful. You'll end up like your mother."

"That's bullshit."

"Maybe," said the old man. "But you're not doing anything either. That's what sinks you in the end."

They started back up the hill.

"Look," said the old man, pointing. "See those horses from here. Aren't they beautiful?"

Ward was too damned mad to look at any more horses.

You don't belong here, his father had said.

If I don't belong here, he wondered, where the hell do I belong?

Maybe he would get out, if the old man kept it up. He didn't
have to take a bunch of guff. If his father didn't want him hanging
around anymore, okay. He could always get a room in town. He'd
be glad to give them the slip. He was getting sick of the whole
bunch.

"Look, look," his father said by the rhododendrons.

What was he carrying on about now? Ward looked but there
wasn't anything to see, so far as he could tell. He was sick to death
of his father raving about how he ought to get out. Change his life
and everything. Hell. It was a good thing he lived at home, what
with the groceries to get in, horses to tend to. Somebody had to
chase down that crazy stallion when he broke loose from time to
time. Who would do that, now with the old man so sick? Not to
mention the seven acres of grass somebody had to mow. Ward was
sick and tired of the whole thing. He expected Althy to get on his
neck. But now even Terry put her two cents in from time to time.
And here was his father, a man to be trusted and relied on, a fellow
who all his life had pretty much gone by the rule of live and let
live, coming at him all the time, with endless advice and dark
predications about how Ward ought to do something. Enough was
enough, as his grandfather used to say.

"I'm tired boy." The old man was standing next to the rhododendrons, making no pretense now about his fatigue. "Pooped
out. You know, I'll tell you a secret. Maybe you can guess it."

"No, I can't."

"I'd rather not see your mother. I'd like to rest up first. Give her
a chance to get used to having me back in the house."

"Five will get you ten she won't be around, anyway," said
Ward. "Of course, we can always go in through the lower level."

The old man looked at him.

"The spare room?"

"Sure. If you want."

"Good idea. Let's go."

Maybe I'll just pack a bag and go off some night, Ward thought.
To hell with them. How would they like that?

In the sunny spare room basked a miscellaneous collection of
furniture, including the kid's blistered student desk and his old
bed. In the soft pine of the headboard Gordie, as a boy, had carved
naked women and flowers. At the time Ward had been scandalized

by such vandalism. But, wouldn't you know, the old man regarded
the result as a work of art. Indeed even Ward could see now that
it was almost beautiful. Now. Some fifteen years after the fact. It
made him wonder if he was some kind of a slow learner. On the
far wall was a bookcase full of the old man's books. Some Utrillo
prints garnished the ivory walls. They too had been in Gordie's
room when he was a boy. The kid once said Utrillo's family had
to lock him in his room to get him to paint. It was no wonder,
Gordie said, when you looked at the results.

At the foot of the bed humped a solid old sea locker with rope
handles that had sailed around the world with the Captain in the
last century, having come south with Althy one fall on a last
voyage of sorts, where it had been refinished for Sarah by a nice
man on Pomfret Street. Alone, late at night in that room, the
furniture might start to talk to you. If it did, it would have quite
a tale to tell. Especially that old sea chest.

The old man sat down heavily on the bed.

"Son of God," he said.

"Ah. Books," announced the kid who breezed in as Ward was
helping his father off with his shoes. Huddled inside his overpow-
ering sports coat, he looked tired and blearyeyed.

"Get those shoes off, boy."

"I'm trying. Stop thrashing around."

"I'm cranky as a little kid. I want to take a nap."

"Hey, Milton!" The kid pushed his glasses back and peered at
the bookcase.

"Can I borrow some of these, Dad?"

"Sure, Jocko. Take what you want. Hell, I don't read them
anyway."

"Let me help you with that jacket," Ward suggested.

"Good," the old man said. "I'm dog tired."

"Get me a hanger, kid."

"What?"

"I said: get me a hanger. So I can hang up his coat and pants."

"Oh. Sure."

The kid displayed excessive bustle to show he was really with
it.

"We'll start with your pants. You just unbuckle your belt, and
I'll pull your pants off. You won't even have to get up."

"Good. I'm too damned tired," the old man said. He was already sagging toward the pillow, wanting to put his head down in the worst way.

Ward handed the pants to Gordie who straightened and smoothed them along the creases as best as he was able. His brother didn't seem to have any talent for fine details.

"Now your coat," Ward said to the old man.

His father sagged toward the pillow.

"Help me. I'm all tangled up."

He couldn't get his arm out of the jacket, he was so tired. Ward helped him get out of the thing, always a kind of straightjacket for a tired man. He was surprised at the unnatural brick-hard feel of his father's back and the prominence of his shoulder blades. Although why he should be surprised, he couldn't say. After all the man was very sick and had lost a lot of weight. Why should it be a surprise if he didn't look or feel the same?

Some people as they go downhill seem to sink into themselves like houses whose walls fall in, creating an unexpected density of mass. While others grow frail and featherweight and practically blow away. They seem to burn up in an invisible fire. It looked like the old man fell into the first category. Probably Althy would come under the second when she started to give up the ghost. Then again maybe she would, at the right moment, just slip off to Lake Mooselookmeguntic and in the fashion of old Doc Coffin, slide beneath its untroubled surface to join the pickerel and lake trout in the clear spring-fed water. Or just sail away like the Captain. As the old man should have, instead of waiting around to fall in on himself like the shell of a burnt-out house. Goddamn Terrill. We never should have listened to him. Never should have listened.

After having struggled free of his coat, his father began to scrabble at the covers.

"Don't you want to take off your shirt?"

"I'll take it off later. Just let me get into bed."

Still holding the jacket, Ward lifted the blanket and sheet with his free hand as the old man crawled in.

"Ah," he said and closed his eyes.

Gordie had the pants on the hanger by now. Of course, he had them all twisted, like they'd just been put through a wash ringer.

"Give me those," said Ward.

"What's wrong?"

"Don't you know how to fold a pair of pants?"

"What's wrong with the way I did it?"

"Here. Hold this coat."

Ward took them off the hanger and started to take the belt out. The old man opened his eyes.

"Leave the belt on those pants, son."

"You can't fold a pair of pants so they hang right with a belt on them."

"That's all right. I like the belt on them. Saves me time."

"Here, kid," Ward handed back the pants. "Fold them any way you want to."

"Feels good to be in bed," said the old man.

"You need another pillow?"

"No, I'm fine. Thanks."

"I'll get you another one from the linen closet. Maybe you will want to sit up after a while."

The kid hung up the coat and pants in the closet and drifted back to the bookcase.

"You have any Ruskin?" he asked.

"I used to. But it disappeared."

"How about some limeade?" said Ward. "I got a batch made upstairs."

"I've lost some books, moving around," said the kid. "Avis loaned some to her friends. They never bring them back."

"How does that feel?" sympathized the old man.

"Terrible. Just terrible."

"When I was young, I made the same mistake, loaned books to some degenerates who had never learned the moral imperative for promptly returning borrowed books."

The kid laughed. This talk about books was getting silly, it seemed to Ward, when there were things to do. For example, he still didn't know if his father wanted a glass of limeade or not.

"I sold a bunch once," said the kid. "Did it in a fit of pique over my deplorable taste in literature."

The old man and the kid chuckled. What the hell was so funny? Ward decided he'd go get the pillow instead of standing around.

"I swear. Some books just got off the shelves and *walked* away," the kid was saying. "They became despondent as the result of neglect and one night slipped out of the house."

What kind of a conversation was that anyway?

As Ward stood in front of the closet door, tucking one end of the pillow under his chin so he could draw one of Althy's hand-embroidered cases over it, they laughed again.

What with Sarah acting so damned crazy and now the old man talking like a wimp, there was hardly any point to staying around the house. Hell, he'd be better off in some rented room close to work. He didn't need this aggravation all the time.

You don't belong here, his father had said. By God, he was probably right. Why don't I just pack a bag and get out? Let him figure out a way to get that lawn mowed, those horses out to pasture, and a daily copy of *The New York Times.* Who needed all this grief anyway? No sooner had his anger clarified his thinking than another entirely different idea popped into his head.

It suddenly occurred to him that maybe his father was trying to make the world over in a hurry. To set things straight, as it were. That would explain a lot. After all, he was a dying man. He was at that stage of his disease where he was willing, even desperate, to take the world for what it ought to be, not for what it was. Therefore, the foot doctor was the perfect cure for a has-been ballplayer.

Ward plumped up the pillow.

Therefore, if his oldest boy left home his spoiled life would put out new sprouts.

He started back down the hall, carrying the pillow under his arm like a football.

Therefore the kid was a merchant prince in the bud.

When the old man asked how Sarah was, he already had the answer—never mind what Terrill or Ward or anyone might tell him. There is a balance in nature, as the Captain once observed, using himself and L. L. Bean as examples. If the old man was in decline, Sarah must be on the rise.

Yes, Ward believed that was it. All this talk about getting Ward out on his own and Terry's many virtues and the kid's hidden talent for business—that was all a condition of the disease. It was a relief to understand that, and it calmed him down. Whereas he'd been mad five minutes ago, he felt this revelation before the linen closet door made quite a few things clear.

His father sat up, and Ward propped the pillows behind him. "Thanks, son."

"Why don't you go get him some limeade?" Ward suggested to the kid.

"You want some limeade?"

"Sure," said the old man.

The kid shambled out eagerly.

Ward kept on thinking about this new idea as he unpacked the old man's suitcase and put the clothes away in the dresser. Except for the top drawer which contained Althy's supply of greeting cards for all occasions, a box of stationery, and a neat pile of Christmas wrap, all the drawers were empty, and his father's small supply of black socks, boxer shorts, and ribbed undershirts all fit in the second drawer with plenty of room to spare.

Yes, this new idea of his explained a lot. His father didn't need facts anymore. He would remake the world along the right lines using whatever was handy. He would be more wrong than right from here on in, and you would have to take what he said with a grain of salt and keep your own counsel.

Looked at in that way, he was sure his father, had he been healthy and in the right frame of mind, would expect his oldest son to take certain actions. For example, you can't have a sick man in charge of a large estate, making decisions that would damage his own long-term interests, to say nothing of his true intentions. What Ward was doing—this business about the will and even how he was handling Terry—some people would say was wrong. But if Ward was doing something wrong, then it was for the right reasons. He was sure of that.

"Enjoy your nap," he said.

"Thanks, son."

If a man gets sick, his son is supposed to help him out, isn't he? When his father had handed him the will, Ward had just instinctively hidden it away. Now it seemed to him he'd known the right thing to do before he even knew the reason why.

As Ward started up the stairs his brother came bouncing down with the glass of limeade in hand.

"Guess what?"

He couldn't seem to say anything without making a game out of it.

"What, kid?"

"Terry's upstairs."

At the sound of her name, his heart constricted into a fist and started to beat a tattoo on his breastbone. His member twitched in his pants like a comatose creature stirring at a sweet note from some magical lute. What is this anyway? he wondered. I'm getting along fine. Let's not start anything, he counseled his body, as if it were a thing separate and apart.

"She says Dad told her to come over this afternoon. He made her promise, she says."

No doubt the old man saw her as a welcoming party more official than his children—one beat-up and gimpy, as Avis might say, and the other just a dreamy flamingo with his nose always in a bookcase. Terry, on the other hand, was the fresh-faced innocent who could transform this dreary homecoming into a festive occasion. It was simple to explain, once you caught on. The old man gave her leave to perform magic and so Terry did, easily and unfailingly. Ward was sure his father would want to see her— now, right away—no matter how exhausted he was.

The kid, however, was thinking other things.

"Does she know about you and Avis?" he asked in a hoarse conspiratorial whisper.

"Kid, I thought you'd wised up on that score."

The kid fell back a step. "I'm sorry. She's just a liar. A troublemaker."

Gordie confessed this in a halting voice, as if the simple truth was being wrung out of his guts. He was still having a bad time without Avis, that was certain.

"Don't talk stupid then," said Ward. "Where's Terry?"

"In the living room."

"Take that glass of limeade into the old man. I'll go get her."

"Take it easy on her. She's pretty nervous."

"Don't worry. I'll be gentle as a. . . . Just take that stuff in there. He's waiting for it."

Ward rocked upstairs, favoring the bad leg which never seemed to let up aching these days. Careful now, he counseled himself. You have to go slow. Or she'll bolt. But even as he talked to himself in reasonable terms, his body glided along in the grip of an irresistible pull toward the living room. Like a witching stick, you might say, bending toward secret waters. Well, it made him feel both low and excited at the same time. Because when it came to women, he supposed a man, thanks to old biology, was doomed always to be a fool.

In the living room, Terry sat tensely on the edge of the couch under the big mirror. As a result, Ward saw every side of her at once as if she were the subject of some goony but fascinating painting that the kid might pull off. In her hands she nursed a white cup and saucer, coffee no doubt offered by Althy in a show of hospitality. Terry's bare arm extended from her dark plaid sleeveless blouse in a compelling curve to the delicate white cup. It was the first thing he saw. That arm, curiously naked, surprisingly handsome, glowing in the afternoon light which poured in the windows. Bare-legged. Wearing an A-shaped denim skirt that went well with the plaid blouse. Her hair, softly golden, fixed simpler than usual. He could see her from every angle, thanks to the mirror. She was completely still, the cup and saucer resting in her lap, her head bent, everything adding to Ward's impression that he'd stepped inside a painting. Careful, he thought when he saw her bare legs. He was grateful for the knifelike pleasure that cut through his gut at the sight of them. But angry too for being so weak. Careful now, he thought. Remember what's going on. It's just old biology, out to get you again.

But wait a minute now. If he was honest he had to admit it wasn't her bare legs or gold hair or the sunlight on the fine curve of her arm that stirred him up. No. It didn't even take that much. Maybe it didn't even take the mention of her name. Perhaps all it took was for her to be somewhere in the neighborhood, that was all. Possibly any second, even if the kid had said nothing, his member would have leaped like a lake bass and his damn heart doubled like a fist to beat on the gates of his chest. Had he—a man who prided himself on living sensibly and staying clear of trouble —had he come to this? If so, it was a sad commentary on human nature, one that actually humiliated you to admit you were a member of the species. Yessir. He was afraid he was fighting more than the foot doctor. He was up against all of nature. Good gravy, it was enough to depress anyone.

Luckily she ruined his sense of doom right away by fluttering half out of her place and rattling the coffee cup when she became aware of his presence in the same ocean of afternoon sunlight.

"Oh, gosh!" she said putting her hand to the round neck of her blouse. "You scared me."

"Yes. It's me again. The boogie man."

It's lucky she's a dope, he thought. Otherwise I could make another mistake.

"I'm sorry," she said.

"How have you been?" he asked. "You look good."

Indeed she did. He guessed it was the new hair style or maybe the no-hair-style that did it. She didn't have any nail polish on either.

"Look. I wouldn't be here except for your Dad. It's embarrassing. But he asked me—"

"I know. Relax."

"He asked me to come," she persisted. "I wouldn't let him down for anything."

"I know that too."

Indeed he did. It had the ring of simple truth about it. Before, he'd thought she was just trying to pick up points by making up to the old man in his dying days. But now he knew what she said was the pure truth. Somehow it didn't surprise him. Today was certainly the day for learning new things. Or was he finally discovering what was obvious to everybody else? He was beginning to suspect he was one of those people who get the news late. He looked suspiciously at her bare legs and felt himself twitch again. Was this one of those times when a man would agree to anything, swear to the truth wedged in any lie, just so long as a female said it? Tend to business, he counseled himself. This is serious.

"He's tired. But I know he wants to see you. I'll take you down. He's in the spare room."

"Oh. All right." Just the way she said "oh" told him she knew all about Sarah. And maybe really understood how important she was to the old man at this time in his life.

"I wouldn't be here at all," she said. "If it wasn't for him. I don't *want* to be here."

"Well. Since you are, maybe we should talk."

"I don't think so. I'd better see your Dad now."

"Just give me a few minutes after you visit with him."

"No, I don't think so."

"I miss you," he said. Surprisingly, after he said it he discovered it was true. And of course it was a lie at the same time. Without question, he was tending to business. But it was also true he was feeling the pull of those secret waters too.

"I miss you like fire," he said.

She gave him a look so pained and direct it was all he could do not to jump back a step. He had to admit to some shame, as if he'd been caught torturing a poor dumb animal.

"If I thought you knew what you were saying—" she choked on the unspoken words that followed.

Move fast, boy. Here's your chance, he thought—in unconscious imitation of the old man's method of speaking

"I know what I'm saying all right. Just talk to me afterwards. I tell you, it's tough without you."

It was true or half-true, wasn't it? Something was going on here which he didn't feel he quite understood.

"I don't know," she said. "I made up my mind to give up on you. I don't like to go back on a decision like that. But I miss you so much." Her eyes were full of tears and her face turned rosy. Really he had to say she looked kind of pretty.

"Don't get worked up," he said. "Just do what you think is right. But think about it, will you?"

"Okay."

"I'll take you down to see him now. How long do you want to visit?"

"He's tired. Maybe I'll just stay twenty minutes or so."

"Fine. I'll take you down. Then just give me a few minutes."

"Don't push me," she said. "Give me a chance to think."

"All right," he said. "It's up to you."

When Terry entered the room his father's face brightened, and he held his arms wide open.

"Sweet girl!"

"Hello, Gordon."

"Come here, sweetiecake. Let me give you a hug."

She practically threw herself into his arms. They carried on like a couple of kids. If Ward hadn't been so dumbfounded, he would have left the room right away. People who carry on like that ought to be left to their privacy. But they didn't seem to mind. In fact, they paid no attention to him at all.

"Ummm," he heard Terry say.

They rocked back and forth in each other's arms. His father had his eyes shut.

"Oh, you feel good."

"You do too. How are you doing?"

"Tired, gorgeous."

"Here, you settle back. Let me straighten out that pillow."

"It's all right, sweetie."

"Here, come on now. Let me help out. Don't go John Wayne on me."

That made the old man laugh.

"You sweetheart."

Well, now. Ward got out of there so they could bill and coo in private. It was amazing how they got to be so crazy about each other so fast. But he understood. Especially on a day full of flickering revelations like today. Given the old man's condition it was natural. Damn sad. But natural. Ward had to admit he was glad the old man had had the good luck to find himself as the object of some warm and generous female attention at this stage of the game. But he couldn't help wishing that people could learn to knuckle on to each other without looking so damn silly in the process.

F O U R T E E N

W A R D ' s bad leg shot out electric branches of pain from his hip to his knee as he jarred up the steps. Dark photographs in white mats and black frames rose along the wall. He rocked past the Captain's picture, the old gentleman dignified in a gunning jacket, a shotgun balanced in the crook of his arm, his legs blotted out from mid-thigh to his boots by a big black Lab. A picture with a dark funereal background of a slim and pretty column of a girl in a white silk gown, her rich black hair piled on top of her head: *Sarah.* He better look in on her, he thought. First see what the kid was up to. Then check in with Sarah to find out if there were any messages from God. Discover how she was holding up under the terrible strain of the old man actually at last being inside his own house, if only in the spare room downstairs.

Ward found his brother out on the sundeck.

"Dad glad to see her?"

"He sure was."

"He looks bad."

Gordie whispered this. His eyes got big as if with the effort.

"What are you whispering for?" Ward asked him indignantly.

"Shhh. I don't want Althy to hear."

Indeed they were standing in front of the open kitchen windows and heard her slamming around pots and pans, making more racket than a Chinese band. Gordie motioned Ward to the other end of the deck.

"What's eating you, kid?"

"She's bad. She's as bad as I've ever seen her."

No need for him to explain who "she" was.

"You think so?"

"I took her tray in," Gordie said by way of explanation. "You better see what you think. I believe it's time for Hazelwood."

"I'll check her out."

Which is what he was intending to do anyway. The kid was always a few beats behind.

Ward knocked on Sarah's door.

Nothing.

Lately whenever he knocked on doors a dumbfounded silence usually followed. Only with difficulty could people bring themselves to answer a knock at the door these days. No doubt a sign of the times.

I will know just what to do when the message is clear.

He wondered if Sarah had heard from God today. Maybe the message was: go to the bathroom and perform a pantomime so everybody runs around in circles and worries about you when there's more important business to tend to. Was that it? Still you couldn't just ignore it. The kid could be right. Maybe a few weeks on the farm was what she needed.

"Sarah?" he called.

He pushed open the door. It took his eyes a second to adjust to the dark. Sarah seemed to be awake. At least she was propped up on her pillows with her pink-rimmed sunglasses on as usual. One hand pressed the old paisley robe to her chest, making her appear to be suffering from a case of heartburn, perhaps over a recent message from The Great Beyond.

"Hello, Sarah."

His mother didn't answer. She just sat there, bleeding into the surrounding shadows.

"How are you feeling today?"

He came around the bed and sat down in the chair. It took her that long to say, "You brought him home anyway."

Said it so quietly in that glittering voice of hers that it raised the hair on his neck.

"Yes, he's home," Ward said. "He won't be any trouble. You won't even know he's around."

She laughed.

"I knew he was in the house. I could feel it, without you telling me."

She trained the pink-rimmed sunglasses on him, flashed a coquettish smile which was so obviously calculating he might have laughed if its effect hadn't been so grisly.

"You never listen, do you?"

"I listen."

"If you listened perhaps you would hear God."

"I doubt it," he said.

"Oh yes," she said. "Anyone can. It's just a matter of really wanting to. First you must have patience. You need a quiet room and lots of time. God must see that you are willing to listen. He speaks to you at first in a tiny voice as if over a faulty telephone connection from far away. Later his voice will fill your head. Your head becomes merely a cave to embody God's voice."

"That's interesting, Sarah."

"You think I'm crazy." She cocked her head at him like a bird. "I know it sounds crazy. But it doesn't matter what you think. I don't mean that unkindly. What matters is what God thinks. I must do what he tells me. Only that way can I save this family. I have heard the message, clearly this time."

"That's nice," said Ward.

Sarah's hand fluttered up to adjust the crooked pink-rimmed sunglasses. She patted her hair and flashed him another coquettish smile.

"It is much much simpler than I thought. I should have guessed. The Bible is full of stories of sacrifice. I have lost everything in life. Everything and everyone I valued. I asked God why he was punishing me, punishing all Webster blood. Once the Indian squaw appeared to me in a dream. I asked her as well. She would not answer."

She looked tragically at her hands.

"How about some orange juice?" Ward asked.

"It is so hard to do God's work."

"Relax, Sarah. I'll bring you some orange juice."

Her creepy talk made him nervous. Wouldn't it be nice, he thought, if all these zanies stood in line so you could deal with them one by one instead of all at once?

"In my dreams I see God," said Sarah. "He sits before a rolltop desk. He wears a green eyeshade and sleeve garters on his stiff white shirt. He smokes a pipe. He looks like the old Captain."

"Well, it's nice that he looks familiar. That way we can spot him in a crowd."

"*Listen,*" Sarah said.

Everybody wanted him to listen these days. They said "listen!," meaning "shut up." They wanted him to shut up and stand still so they could slap him with a few facts. He was becoming a good listener, he decided. Everybody was so crazy, he didn't have any choice. Especially with Sarah. Thanks to her, he was refining the art to its highest degree, to the point where he listened to everything she said, could repeat it all practically word for word but actually *heard* nothing, no part of it whatever.

"*Listen,*" she said in that glittering voice that made the hairs on his neck stand up. "Beyond God a low window opens onto a mild gray summer evening. Mild and lovely such as I remember from my childhood in Dunnocks Head. Down the field I can see the *Arzamas,* the last ship, sitting on the ways. Do you remember that old ship?"

"Yes, I remember."

Yes, he remembered. Two old men in black suits. Both lean and white-haired. Maybe the old Captain standing on the edge of the field in the shadow of the house, he too in a black suit, only his coat laid in a neat bundle on the vivid green grass at his feet. No bigger than Keats, the kid said. Against the black butterfly of his vest his shirt glowed pure white.

Come on, Colby Jack! Show this rube your good stuff!

The black tails of Mr. Coombs' suit coat flapped as he slipped through the notches of his wind-up, moving jerkily as a figure striking an anvil on a Swiss clock. And the ball on the bright air, not fast, but heavy. And Ward, a boy of promise then, whaled hell out of it. The old men cackled delightedly when the ball jumped off the bat as if repelled by the wood, the boy now master of some secret law of physics known only to him and God. The ball rose in the light, winking like the evening star. It plummeted suddenly, with violent speed as if heavy as a shotput, a little white pea hurtling onto the deck of the half-built ship which wallowed in the tall weeds.

You little gnat! You hit that one a country mile!

And the special silence that followed. The old men looking at each other significantly, acknowledging this boy had the special gift too.

"In my dream," Sarah went on, "a giant transparent rose of billowing fire hovers over the decaying ship. It is the ghost of the giant rose of fire that consumed the Captain's ship that time in the Pacific. That holy fire that made him a hero and broke him as a man."

"I tell you, Sarah," he interrupted, because hearing Sarah talk in that glittering voice about her dream of God just made him feel he had to get out of there and settle things fast. "I told Althy I'd take the old man's dinner down on a tray. I'll be right back."

"*Listen!* You can't leave," Sarah insisted. "Don't leave, please. You must hear this. Someone must listen to me."

There it was again. The customary insistence that he should listen. Why did he have to do all the listening?

"*Listen.* You must listen."

"Make it fast," he said.

"God turns to me," Sarah continued. "His head is framed by the billowing rose of fire. Even though, beneath his green eyeshade, he looks like the Captain, I am sure He is God. He smiles. And He tells me the truth. It is simpler and more horrible than I suspected."

"What does He tell you?"

"The truth."

"Good."

"The truth is far simpler than I imagined. It is there for all to see."

"All right," he said.

She smiled.

"Your cousin Scott once said that people will do anything to keep away the truth."

"Why is that?"

"The truth doesn't set you free. It haunts you. It sets you in chains no anvil and hammer can break. The truth is terrible, more terrible than we can stand. Only God makes it possible."

Silence. End of Divine Broadcast. Ending on a puzzling note since what God makes possible could be either the terrible suffering or the courage to withstand it. However, he would be happy to wait for God to clear up this problem in a later transmission.

"Is that it?" he asked.

After a pause she said, "Yes."

"Fine. I'll be right back."

To that she replied, "God is a stern taskmaster."

"Lie back," he counseled her. "Take a little nap. I'll be back in a jiffy."

"Gordon's dead," she sobbed. "After all my prayers."

Sarah put her hands under her sunglasses. The sunglasses bobbed on her knuckles. Her mouth trembled.

"He's not dead, Sarah."

"Good as dead," she whispered.

It made the hairs on his neck stand up.

"I have to go to the bathroom," Sarah announced in a determined voice, composing her hands in her lap.

A call of nature right in the middle of divine revelation. Isn't that the way of things?

"I'll get Althy to help you," he said.

"Are you sure?"

"Of course. Althy's just waiting out there in the kitchen to help out somehow. She's practically pacing the floor."

"God's truth—" Sarah began. Her voice trailed off. He waited to see if this was the beginning of another divine broadcast. But apparently not.

Althy sat at the kitchen table, a cup of coffee laced in her gnarled fingers.

"Junior took your father's tray down to him. I hope that girl lets him eat."

Althy tucked out her lip as if the foot doctor's presence was an offense against decency.

"I'll take care of her. You listen to me."

"What now?" she asked him indignantly. She puckered the liver spots on her forehead into a frown. Even though she was pushing eighty, Althy's hair was just now turning gray. Her eyebrows were still jet black.

"She's acting funny, Althy."

She looked at him quick with those monkey-bright brown eyes, the brown smudging into the whites now with age.

"I want you to stay close to her."

"I don't need you to tell me," she said. "Haven't I always tended to Sarah? Long before you showed any interest?"

"Fine," he said. "You just do it now. Do it real good."

He trailed after her angry back as far as the bedroom door. She steadfastly ignored him. Sarah lay deadweight on the bed facing the door, her face mashed into the pillow, her sunglasses in a crash dive. He watched the old woman coax her up.

"Hello, dear," murmured Althy, bending stiffly over the bed in the twilit room. "Do you need Mother's help?"

"Yes," Sarah answered in a small pathetic voice.

"Here. First, let's put back the covers."

"Yes."

"Here are your slippers, dear."

Althy bent for the slippers, staggered slightly. She was still bright and mean as ever but she was getting a little feeble. A couple of weeks ago she'd been knocked down by a tulip. He'd been outside fooling with that iron Frankenstein of a lawn mower and looked up and there she was on the ground, like a sack of beans, down by one of the flower beds. He thought she'd had a stroke. He got down there on the double. She was just lying there, face up on the ground, as if peacefully contemplating the big fluffy clouds passing overhead. Till he entered her line of vision. Then she frowned and sat up.

"Goddamn it," she spat out.

"Are you all right?"

"Of course I'm all right!"

"Here, let me give you a hand."

"Take your hands off me! I can get up myself!"

Althy got to her knees okay but then she was buffaloed. Angrily she let him hand her up to her feet. He asked her what happened.

"I was pulling on that tulip there," she said indignantly, "and the damn thing pulled back."

If he'd laughed out loud, Althy probably would have hit him with the garden trowel she still clutched in her hand.

"What were you doing just lying on the ground when I came up?"

She looked at him fiercely, as if his question were an invasion of privacy.

"I was just lying there, resting," she said. "Is that a crime? I was going to get up, if you'd have left me the hell alone."

She was mad as a hornet, but, he figured, not so much at him as at the indignities age sometimes lays at your feet, tough old bird or not.

He watched her fuss over Sarah. She's getting old, he thought. That damned tulip reminded her, and it's really made her mad.

"Now where's your robe, dear?"

Sarah sagged on the edge of the bed in the faded robe the old man had discarded twenty years ago. She was wearing yellow pajamas. The toes of her fat white feet looked like the buds that sprout on potatoes.

"I already have on my robe," Sarah said dreamily.

"Not that old thing. I'll wash that. Let's put on your nice terry-cloth. Here it is. Under this pile of things."

Althy helped Sarah out of the paisley robe and began to bumble her into the fresh one. Her daughter, a boneless lump on the edge of the bed, seemed unable to help herself.

"There now," said Althy, fumbling the robe onto Sarah's rubbery arm. "That's a girl. Now the other arm. Do you feel all right?"

"Yes."

"You're not dizzy or anything, are you?"

Sarah suddenly sat up and looked at Althy. She wrapped her robe around her tightly.

"Why did you push me down the stairs?"

"Push you down the stairs?" Althy's wattles trembled at the shocking idea. "Who pushed you down the stairs?"

"You did, I think. I lost the baby because of that."

"Sarah," Althy straightened herself up. "I did *not* push you down the stairs. You fell."

"Well, if you did, it was a terrible thing to do."

"No, Sarah. No. I'm not going to let you think that way. I'm your mother. I did not push you down the steps."

"I could have been happy, except for that," said Sarah dreamily.

"Stop talking nonsense and take my arm."

Well now let's see, Ward thought, as Sarah sagged against her old mother. That puts it about 1929. The year Lefty O'Doul hit .398, 32 home runs and batted in 122 runs for the Phillies. Sarah had quite a season herself. It was the year she turned seventeen, ran away with her cousin Scott on the night of her high school graduation, and was found several months later by a kindly Irish policeman wandering about Kenmore Square in Boston dressed in nothing but a raincoat borrowed from some Negro hotel maid. And when she was fetched home on the train by her mother and father, old Doc Coffin discovered in a routine examination that she was pregnant. Then she managed to fall downstairs and lose the baby. Although from time to time she still seemed to be pregnant, carrying a child—person—something—named Carol, in what now, after thirty-eight years, had to be the longest pregnancy in history. Yes, 1929. That was it. If Sarah had to be out of town at this moment it was at least nice to know where she was in her travels. Together mother and daughter crawled in terrific slow motion across the disorderly room, moving with the elaborate deliberateness of a pair of drunks.

Ward left them then, certain he knew just what to do next about Sarah. The kid was in the kitchen having a touch of vodka on the rocks. Before Ward could tell him a few weeks on the farm were in order, the kid piped up.

"I talked to Dad. I told him about Mother and what Terrill said. He agreed she ought to go to Hazelwood for a little while."

"You talked to him already?" Ward's surprise showed.

"Yes, I did. Okay?"

"Sure."

"Good. I just thought we'd better move. I called Terrill. The people from Hazelwood will be here first thing tomorrow."

"Hell, kid."

"What?"

"When you start to move, you really move."

"I just figured we had to act fast."

It was amazing how the kid had suddenly materialized out of thin air. He'd really hit the ground running.

"Was Terry there when you told him?"

"Yes, he wanted her to stay while we talked."

"What'd she say?"

"She told him he'd better do it. She convinced him it was the smart thing to do, not me."

"I guess I better break the news to Althy."

Gordie thought about it for a second. He took a sip of his drink and thumbed his glasses against his forehead.

"We'll tell her in the morning. I'll come back before they get here, and we'll tell her together."

"Maybe we better tell her tonight. Give her time to get used to it."

"No. She's not going to get used to it. The less time she has to think about it the better. The first thing she'll do is harass Dad. We don't want that."

"No, we don't," agreed Ward.

"We tell her in the morning," said Gordie. "They'll get here about nine. I'll be here at eight."

"Okay, kid."

Ward couldn't help breaking into a fat-lipped grin. His little brother was really taking charge. It would be interesting to see if he actually showed up in the morning. He wasn't famous for being an early riser.

"Persephone," the kid said. His eyes glazed over as he thought about it.

"Persephone?"

"Yes. Old Pluto's bride. I always thought of Mother in connection with that story. Six months in the sunlight while the delighted earth flowers. Then six months with old Pluto in his underground kingdom. And the earth turns brown and sere."

"Not this time," said Ward. "The good weather's back. Only she's crazier than ever."

"Well, anyway. Everybody agrees she ought to be in Hazelwood for a while. Look, I've got to go."

"Too busy to stick around, huh."

"I said I'd be back in the morning. Avis told me she'd meet me at Walter's so we could talk a little bit."

"Good for you, kid."

Gordie grinned happily and pushed his glasses back. His long hair was drawn tightly back from the blonde block of his high forehead into a neat ponytail which touched him like a golden finger between the shoulders, gently tapping on his clean khaki shirt adorned with epaulets. His madras slacks were freshly laundered, his crepe-soled shoes looked almost new. Yes, all spiffed up, going to see his girl. Avis—with her moon face and little turned-up nose which was all nostril, her small suspicious brown eyes, her Captain Marvel eyebrows—would no doubt greet him in traditional costume, sandals and cut-off jeans revealing her ass cheeks. Perhaps she'd have on one of his old white shirts thrown over the bikini top that almost contained her big breasts. If the kid got that far—and he would—he would no doubt discover she wore red bikini pants, maybe the same pair she wore when she visited Ward two weeks ago. Naturally the kid would return unabashed to Walter's, never giving another thought to his baby act in front of them all. Avis and the kid would engage in animated conversation. She would tell him what a shit he was. The kid would ask why. Avis would give him several examples. No doubt the kid would suggest they make up in bed. Avis would go along with the gag, saying it didn't make any difference to her, and besides she could use a piece of ass. Likely the kid would show affectionate tolerance by not getting mad. They would then leave, probably go across the street to Terry's apartment, and fall into bed. Gordie would hump away happily and afterwards fall asleep with his thumb in his mouth, dreamless and warm, curled around this crazy woman. Yessir. His brother was a wonderful piece of work. He'd found his trouble. And it looked like he'd never be happy without it.

As he watched the kid dart down the driveway in his little toy car, Ward had a moment's uneasiness. In the theater of his head, Avis giggled and hugged the sheet to her breasts in self-congratulatory delight as he stood there with his fly unzipped.

Trying to make a damned fool out of him. Doing a pretty good job too. She was out to make big trouble. The more she could make, the better she'd like it. That night, except for the intervention of Sarah's phantom suicide attempt, Avis had almost produced more trouble than anybody could have handled. Still, she had collected the basis for enough innuendo to drive Gordie into a frenzy, if she wanted to. What *did* she want anyway? No telling what. She was a woman, mad and pissed off, as unpredictable and wanton as a tornado, liable to touch down anywhere and just tear hell out of things. Oh, the poison she might pour in the kid's ear if she got a chance. Damn, why can't things be simple? he asked himself.

Ward padded down the hallway. Terry unwrapped herself from the old man's embrace when she heard his step along the hall.

"I have to go now," she said holding his father's hand. "I'm sorry your homecoming wasn't nicer."

"Thanks for coming, sweetie. Sorry I wasn't better company."

"Silly, you're always good company."

She kissed his forehead and smoothed back his hair.

"So long, gorgeous," the old man said. A word right out of his youth, used by tough guys like Bogart to summon or dismiss their movie women in the hardboiled 30s. The words the old man used, even the worn out terms of endearment like "gorgeous" and "ace," seemed to fit him right.

Ward and Terry walked down the hall, troubled by each other's company. *Easy,* he counseled himself. *Easy.*

"Come on in here for a minute," he said. Ward led her through

the family room right past the astonished eye of the TV set into
his bedroom.

"Sit down for a minute," he said.

She sat down on his bed. He pulled the chair over from his desk.
He figured he couldn't have gotten her to come to his room like
that if she hadn't been preoccupied with thoughts of the old man.

"Your poor dad. He comes home and right away your mother
has to go to the hospital."

"It's the best thing," Ward said not thinking about it, looking
at her bare arms and her bare legs below the blue skirt. "She's been
getting worse for a long while now. Maybe a few weeks on the
farm will snap her out of it."

Terry's face turned rosy with emotion.

"I feel sorry for your father," she pouted. "I feel sorry for you,
too."

"She's really sick this time."

He was not really listening to what Terry was saying, but secretly studying her bare legs and the flush of color on her neck.
Her toes were jammed together like typewriter keys in her beige
sandals. She jams her feet into shoes a size too small, he thought.
Why is that? The top button of her plaid blouse was unbuttoned.
He could see the dark glint of a delicate gold chain in the warm
shadow of her throat.

The old familiar pain in his chest ached like a bruise. He swal-
lowed dryly, his pulse beating in his ears. How do I do this? he
wondered. He had to figure a way, a natural but not too obvious
way of getting her to let him hold her close and thereby work some
of the old magic which might lead to the restoration of those
regular appointments that, sooner than later, he hoped, would
permit him to talk some sense into her. Again he wondered as the
blood beat in his ears if he was as clever as he thought he was or
if old biology was merely back in the saddle again. Was he in
control, moving with the grain, or just improvising pathetic excuses while being swept away on a secret tide beyond his understanding?

Nobody was saying much. But electric messages darted through
the air. He hardly breathed. Still he was locked in some airless
insistent dialogue with her and half strangulated by some insup-
portable anaerobic tension.

"Is Avis still staying with you?" he asked for something to say, just a delaying tactic since he already knew.

"Yes."

A thought puckered the foot doctor's brow. "She says terrible things. She said one day you reached under her skirt and tried to pull her panties down."

"She's a troublemaker," he managed

"She hates you, Ward."

He took her hand. She didn't seem to notice.

"No, she doesn't," he said. "She's just crazy."

"She doesn't talk about Gordie," Terry was amazed. "She talks about you. She says nasty things."

"You ought to get rid of her." He let their clasped hands drop so they rested on her warm skirted thigh.

"She doesn't have anyplace to go," Terry said.

"You can't trust her."

Indeed even as the kid humped away deliriously, what was Avis whispering into his ear at this very moment? The thought made Ward go cold.

"I know. But she needs help."

What the hell kind of answer was that? You kept around somebody you couldn't trust because they needed help? Where did she get an idea like that? You poor jerk, he thought. If you only knew what your girlfriend is really like.

"To hell with her. What about us?"

"Us?" she looked surprised.

"Yes, us."

Careful, he told himself. He looked sincerely into her eyes.

"I miss you like fire. I'm sorry about everything. Can't we get back together?"

"Oh God. If I thought you knew what you were talking about . . ."

"I do," he swore. "I really know."

". . . I'd take you in my arms right now."

Suddenly he lost his theme. He would recollect his reason for this maneuver later. But at this point, his hands took on a life of their own. They moved under her skirt and gripped her warm thighs. He stroked the silken center of all his troubles. She collapsed in his direction with a sigh. Her blue eyes fluttered shut.

Her rosebud mouth fell open like a bullethole. Her rosy face grew wider and wider till it blurred and went dark against his own. Her urgent mouth was juicy and sweet-tasting as an apple.

She tugged at his belt while he searched for the elastic top of her panties. What amazed him was how wonderful, warm, and soft she felt beneath her skirt. Ah, he thought. He had to bend awkwardly to keep his lips to hers. He was afraid if they unlocked and opened their eyes, she'd recollect herself and rush from the house.

She unzipped his fly and held him. She stroked him, clawing down his pants at the same time.

They crashed onto the bed. He kicked off his khakis and underwear, considered rising to fold them neatly, but thought better of it. Sky blue underwear—he saw that now, her pants dangling from her ankle, as he lifted her back. He quivered like a witching stick over secret waters.

"God," he groaned.

"I love you," she said in his ear.

Luckily, being otherwise engaged, he wasn't obliged to reply.

They rocked in one another's arms. The old bed grumbled.

"God," he said again.

Afterwards he lay and watched her pull on her sky-blue pants with a sudden graceful flourish of her skirts. He caught a momentary glimpse again of her pale-peach thighs and firm backside. How pretty the whole momentary action was, he thought, like something in a dance.

"I bet you think I'm awful now," she said.

"No, no," he protested sleepily. He wasn't sure he could get up. His bones had turned to slush.

"I'll bet you do."

She tucked in her plaid blouse.

What a pretty thing to do, he thought.

"No," he said again.

"It's just that I love you so much. I wanted you so much."

"So did I," he said.

"I'll be strong from now on," she said.

"Don't be strong. Let's work it out," he said drowsily.

"Get under the covers," she said for an answer. The professional nurse took over now. And just as she had done for his father, she got him all smoothed away in his bed.

His body—flesh, bone, and blood—began to flake away in living crystals and drift off grain by grain on some sweet secret outgoing tide. My, my. How good he felt. Relaxed. Even hopeful. For the first time in a long time. She kissed his slack hand. He remembered that. A fitting tribute to pay a perfect fool. He flickered into the room again and found it empty except for himself. He didn't care. So what? Just as she had left him, skillfully and professionally placing him smack in the middle of the bed with his hands crossed reverently on his chest, he melted into the bed, died into a deep sleep so numbing and luxurious it seemed he'd never find his way back to daylight.

He dreamed. He was rowing in a fog that boiled thickly all about the small white skiff. The stern flickered in and out of sight, the fog was so thick. The oarlocks, grinding under his hands, made the only sound, monotonous and magnified, the cry of a sad jackass. Condensation lay like small glass beads on the plank seats. So thick afog was it he couldn't see the black glossy skin of the ocean beneath him. He glided on the ghostly fog, sometimes looking over the gunwhales as if all of creation now was fog and he the only thing drifting in it, accompanied only by the haunting creak of the oars in the oarlocks.

The wet blades rose. Long glutinous strings of water snapped into glittering beads and spattered somewhere in the boiling fog. The white oars waved above the boat, white like the boat, poised overhead as graceful as wings, then dipped and disappeared in the dense fog. Sometimes though, the fog's fabric tore and the oars dug into the black undulant skin of the ocean before rising again in graceful repetitive arcs.

A pink *aurora borealis* pulsated on the fog ahead. The rosy wall opened and there, in a stretch of open water surrounded by mountainous fogbanks, was the silhouette of a burning ship, consumed by a towering rose of flame. In the next moment, he was magically transported to the ship itself. Unsurprised to find himself in the Captain's cabin, he pulled gently at the Captain's sleeve.

The Captain didn't seem to notice. His head was bent in rapt absorption over the open book before him on the chart table. Delicately hooked about his ears and over his nose were eyeglasses rimmed in spider-thin gold. Corrugations of well-fed flesh were arranged along his jaw and around his firm but studious chin.

Ward looked urgently at the pink part in the Captain's wavy white hair.

"The ship is on fire, Captain," Ward said quietly. He was scared. But for some reason he felt obliged not to show it and to talk slowly and calmly to the white-haired old gentleman who looked to be, in his black jacket with its circle of gold around the sleeve cuff, no bigger than a good-sized monkey.

"Captain. The ship is on fire," he repeated. He put special emphasis on the word *fire.*

The Captain looked up, the pools of light in his lenses shifting like liquid.

He smiled. His teeth were white and even, obviously artificial. He pointed to the page of the open book.

"It is here, right here in this passage, that I lost God," he said gently.

"Captain. The fire," Ward spoke as if reminding him of an appointment.

The Captain seemed to rouse himself. He laughed gently and patted Ward on the hand.

"No, my boy," he said sadly in exactly that strong fine voice Ward remembered so well. "We must resign ourselves to the long boat."

Fiery pieces of rigging crashed to the deck. The poles were naked, the lines on fire. From the hatchway the fire glowed as bright as the open mouth of a coal furnace. Ward tossed a cedar bucketful of water at the nearest fiery clump, but the fire leaped up as if the water were kerosene. The Captain was right, of course. They must resign themselves to the long boat. Ward stepped forward in the billowing black smoke to fetch the Captain, still in his cabin, pondering the text before him. Suddenly, staggering blindly along the deck, he plunged through a skylight ringed with fire.

Ward was plummeting with deadweight velocity through a glittering shower of glass toward darkness when he heard the sad, rending scream of a peacock. He sat bolt upright in the quicksilver light of early morning and discovered he was in bed. The terrifying yet melancholy cry of the peacock came faintly from above followed by clumsy scuffling.

Sarah, he thought. *Sarah. She's. . . .* He leaped out of bed and found without surprise that Terry had folded his khakis neatly on his chair. He pulled them on, reeling groggily, tugging at each stubborn trouser leg. He staggered up the stairs, still half-unconscious. The door to the bathroom was half open.

He plunged into the bathroom and immediately slammed to the floor. It was slippery, wet with something. Reflexively he fell into a hook slide and slid right into Sarah and Althy who were on the floor. Both round-eyed with terror, they seemed to be struggling to get away from each other. Althy's wrinkled arm, crooked at the elbow, the arthritic hand splayed on the floor, was covered with a thin red sauce. Sarah's white robe was stippled on the collar and down the front with the same thing. Apart from them over by the tub, a pair of scissors ribboned with red glimmered unnaturally bright against the dark sheen of the floor. Ward's eyes fairly bulged out of his head. He could not get enough of looking at the gleaming scissors, which were surrounded by a small round haze of light as if pulsating with incandescent energy. The room echoed with noise. Still, for all the confused thrashing, he seemed to have lots of time to goggle at the scissors.

That's blood, he remembered thinking as he turned to see Sarah's thunderstruck, haggard face. His ears at last registered the "no, no, no, no—" that Althy was wailing. He did not remember the rest. He was left with this picture, startling in its clarity, of the two women on the floor both on their hands and knees, facing each other, their heads hanging down in complete exhaustion.

A gap followed this picture. He must have blown a circuit about here. He remembered no sensations within that small capsule of time, although he knew he had continued to function. The lost minutes lay encysted in his memory. Someday, whether he wanted it to or not, the cyst would dissolve and he would remember. In the meantime he could only guess as to what had happened. He believed the two women fell silent. The room lapsed into a silence as concentrated as that of an operating room. But he couldn't be sure. He had no idea what he did in that silence. The next thing he remembered was Althy sitting at the built-in vanity. She held a towel to her arm. He was staring at the cluttered shelves of the medicine cabinet, unsure of what had brought him here.

He found he was studying a can of Foamy with a picture of a

lemon on it. The old man's shaving cream produced a little shock of anger in him. Where was the old man when he needed him? Why didn't he come in here and help? It was only then that he remembered that his father was mercifully tucked away in the spare room, probably still asleep.

Althy sat dourly at the vanity as he worked with scissors and tape and gauze. His fingers were steady as a surgeon's. He felt nothing as he bandaged up the lacerations in the slack flesh of her old woman's arm. *Good. Good,* he thought. *I'm getting through this just fine.* While he did this Sarah sat on the floor and studied with apparent interest the sunburst pattern on the trash can. He helped Althy into the living room and settled her on the couch.

"I'd like an aspirin," she said quietly.

She had her head back on the pillow and her eyes shut.

"Here, put your feet up," he said. "I'll get you the aspirin."

He unlaced the brown oxfords and removed them. Her ankles were swollen, puffed over the edges of the sturdy, high quarters of the square-toed shoes. When he took them off, a kind of rounded puffy design remained stamped in the flesh just above her ankles. He lifted her feet onto the couch; the harsh texture of the flesh-colored support hose she wore chafed his hand slightly. Her swollen legs, the skin tight and shiny, lay straight and unmoving on the couch. She seemed to have shrunk inside her flowered housedress.

He fetched the aspirin and a glass of water. Although the carpet was thick and her eyes were shut, she reached out for the glass unhesitatingly. She glared near-sightedly at the two white dots of aspirin in her cupped hand before putting them in her mouth. Then she lay back on the pillow and squeezed her eyes shut again. "You better see to your mother," she said.

Sarah was right where he left her on the bathroom floor. The morning light poured in the window and enveloped her in a bright shaft. She knelt on the floor, like a figure in a religious painting. Her head was bent down; the once pitchblende hair was shot through with gray. Turned toward him in profile was the finely handsome nose and the high intelligent forehead.

When he offered her his hand, she was startled and annoyed as if he had interrupted a complex cycle of devotional prayers. She adjusted her sunglasses. She puckered her lips indignantly and gathered her terrycloth robe around her. She refused the offer of his hand. "No, thank you," she said primly. Nevertheless he trailed after her to see that she got into bed all right.

"Here. Sit by me." She patted the bed. "Hold my hand."

Ward sat down on the bed and allowed her to take his hand.

"I've done nothing wrong," she said brightly. "I only did what God told me to do. Now perhaps we will all be happy again."

"Isn't that a nice thought," he said.

She squeezed his hand.

"We had such happy times when I was a child. From my bedroom I could see the sun sparkling on the Reach in the mornings. It was a beautiful room. Wasn't it wonderful how we all lived together in the Captain's house?"

"It certainly was."

"And the Captain was really the daddy. All the rest of us were his children. Even Daddy and Mother and even Uncle Tyler who was a foot and a half taller than the Captain, and Aunt Dorcas and Scott and I—all of us his children. And we were all so happy. It was wonderful."

Sarah smoothed the light blanket across her lap. Her hands seemed full of independent nervous energy beyond her control. A hand fluttered up to touch her hair. She smiled brightly.

"Happy, happy times. As you grow older of course you must learn to obey God. Do you remember the piano in the front parlor?"

"Yes." He was not sure how God and the piano came together but he was sure she would tell him.

"I took lessons on that piano," she said. "I was not musically inclined. Miss Porter, who also worked at the telephone office in Bath, came to the house on Thursday afternoons to give me lessons. The lessons were a terrible nuisance, I thought. But now they seem part of the happy time. I even remember the words to a tune she had me practice."

And Sarah sang for him in a high sweet voice:

> *Papa Haydn's dead and gone*
> *But his memory lingers on.*
> *When his mood was one of bliss*
> *He wrote jolly tunes like this!*

"Isn't that lovely?" she asked him, clutching his hand.

"It's very pretty," he said.

At her request he adjusted the curtains against the morning light and left her smiling to herself in the shadows.

F I F T E E N

So old pluto locked Sarah to his breast again, this time unseasonably, and carried her off to his dark kingdom. And all she had for a trousseau was her memories of 1929.

By the time Gordie arrived, Dr. Terrill's Buick and the ambulance from Hazelwood were already in the driveway.

Ward held open the screen door.

"Hello, kid."

"What the hell's going on?"

His brother goggled at a bloody towel lying in the hallway.

"Jesus," he breathed. "What happened?"

For an answer, Ward jerked his head in the direction of Sarah's bedroom. He unrolled the pack of cigarettes from his T-shirt sleeve and lit up. He had kind of a lump in his throat anyway. He was getting through this okay. But it was just as well, given his sudden incapacity for speech, that the two fellows in the bedroom were performing a pantomine that explained everything.

The two men in hospital jackets were lowering Sarah onto an ambulance litter. She was unconscious. The kid gaped at the blood-spattered terrycloth robe below the serene face. As Ward and Gordie watched, the aides covered her with a gray blanket and began to strap her to the litter.

The young doctor caught sight of them, an impromptu audience, standing at a loss in the hall, and came out briskly wearing a friendly smile. He had pale thin hair and a round head. A little downy moustache of fawn-colored hair hovered like a moth above his well-shaped, almost pretty, mouth. He had the comfortable beginnings of a double chin. You could tell he was soft as an eclair in the middle. He looked like he had never played any kind of ball as a kid, probably always sat around the house with a book in his lap.

"I gave her a sedative," began the young doctor. "She'll be all right now."

"What happened?" repeated Gordie.

"She tried to dice up Althy with a pair of scissors," Ward said.

"Jesus! Mother hurt Althy? What the hell for?"

"I don't know, kid. She said God told her to."

"We'll find out why when we have some time with her at Hazelwood," confided the doctor. "Your grandmother's all right, incidentally. Thanks to your brother's temporary patch job. Dr. Terrill's looking after her in the living room."

"God." Gordie looked in the direction of the bedroom.

"Don't worry," said the doctor. "She'll be okay."

The man evidently believed in the miracles of modern medicine. Pump the old broad full of Valium, give her a few electro-shock treatments, and in a few days she'll be good as new. You'll be able to use her for a mailbox or make her into a lamp for the den.

As advertised, Terrill was in the living room finishing up with Althy, who still lay on the couch. Her face was white as a parachute and the liver spots on her forehead had darkened, like the bruises on a piece of fruit. She looked like a sick old lady, as if her faith had drained away, along with her color.

Terrill had outdone himself in bandage work, this neat construction of gauze and tape traveling from the apex of her withered deltoid to just above her wrist.

"Are you all right?" asked the kid.

"I'm fine. Where's your damned brother?"

"Lie back, Mrs. Rideout," said Terrill. "You stay calm till the other ambulance gets here."

"Where's Ward?"

Ward sat smoking in a chair across the room. He didn't answer. Althy clutched the kid's hand.

"Junior, don't let him do it." Althy said desperately. The kid seemed startled by the expression of shock in her watery old eyes.

"Lie back, like Dr. Terrill said."

"Don't let your rotten brother do it."

"Just calm down, Althy," Gordie patted her bony hand.

"Don't put me off. I'm not an old fool. I know what I'm talking about."

"All right," the kid said. "Tell me about it."

"Your mother," she cried. "Your brother has signed a paper to put her into that Hazelwood place."

"Well—" the kid began. He ducked his head and pushed his glasses back on the high bridge of his nose.

It was all right if the kid did not tell her that he and the old man were also sponsoring Sarah's latest trip to the farm, that the decision had been made yesterday, and that the real pity was it hadn't been made the day before. It was too much territory to cover with the old woman lying carved up on the couch, and besides, there was no sense in her getting mad at everybody.

"No," she said. She shook her head slowly, emphatically.

In the frame of the doorway behind Althy appeared the young doctor and the two aides with the wheeled litter containing Sarah. They disappeared quickly, quiet as cat burglars.

"She's not crazy. She wouldn't really hurt anyone. She's terribly upset. I know she's sorry for what she did."

"Lie back," said the doc. "The rest of you, get out."

Ward and Gordie fixed up an English muffin and some orange juice for their father. They went downstairs and woke him up and told him what happened. The first thing Gordon Sullivan remembered was what that doctor at the sanitarium in Massachusetts had told him thirty-five years ago, about how Sarah's self-directed violence might turn outward someday. The ancient prophecy fulfilled, he said. He slumped on the edge of the bed. The news seemed to make him tired. He didn't say much. Nobody said much.

Pretty soon another ambulance arrived.

"Take your hands off me," Althy said. But they made her lie down on the litter and, completely defeated by these persistent technicians, she permitted herself to be raised off the ground like the Queen of Sheba and carried off to the shiny new emergency van which squatted in the driveway, looking more like a bread truck than an ambulance.

Gordie left to resume negotiations with Avis. She had agreed to meet him for a drinkie-poo at the Jimmie Wilson. When everyone had cleared out, Ward was surprised to see it was past two o'clock. Time for his medicine. He got down the bottle of vodka from the cabinet over the refrigerator. He packed the big squat glass with ice, added two olives stuffed with almonds, and filled it to the lip. The first sip shuddered down his spine and he shook it off like a

wet dog. Awful stuff. Silence pervaded the house as he sat at the
table by the kitchen window. Silence. A silence that was uncanny,
pure unnoise devoid of human presence. As soon as he was properly fortified by this drink he resolved to go down and check on
his father, see how he was holding up. Take him his mineral oil.
Maybe he'd like a cup of tomato soup and a ham and cheese
sandwich.

The events of the past few weeks left him reeling with fatigue.
Now, sitting at the table, he could hardly keep his eyes open. He
had had trouble following the drift of that simple conversation
with the kid doctor. He had seemed to drowse through Althy's
accusations. As he had disinterestedly watched his father trying to
absorb the catastrophic morning news, Ward felt himself fading
pleasantly into the wallpaper. It was the old Webster technique,
raised to a high science by Sarah, for avoiding the consequences.
So what? he asked himself, crunching one of the olives. Who
wanted to know what was happening anyway? And who in hell
would want to face the consequences? The vodka helped to slow
things down and smooth him out. With a little application no
doubt, he could become a regular drunk.

He finished the rest of his drink. The ice cubes clinked against
his dentures. Out the kitchen window, in the distance, the break
in the mountain ridge called Kings Gap was blurred in a haze of
humidity. The sky looked hot and milky. Carefully he set the glass
down on the table but made no move to get up. The house
crouched in quiet expectancy. He had plenty to do. But he couldn't
remember what. What should I do? he wondered. Try as he might
he couldn't think of anything.

Doc Terrill kept Althy overnight at the Carlisle Hospital to get
her sewed up and to keep her "under observation," as he called
it. She ended up with twenty-six stitches, an impressive number,
but by no means the family record. Terrill was kind enough to
drive her home himself the next day. So when Ward got home
from work, carrying a hot paper bag which contained the evening's proposed meal—some take-out chow mein for him and the
old man—plus the newspapers, he was pleasantly surprised to find
Althy reinstalled in the kitchen and a meat loaf in the oven. Althy
emptied the paper bag of its toasty-warm little white cartons of
steamed rice and crunchy dried noodles, the little rectangular plastic extrusions swollen with bilious-looking bubbles of soy sauce,

and the bigger box containing the main course of nondescript vegetable glop. She opened and inspected each article with what he thought was marvelous restraint but obvious contempt.

They never did eat that stuff. It congealed in its boxes in the refrigerator for a few days, and then disappeared.

Now that she was down to one patient, Althy concentrated all her nursing skills on his father. She insisted that they move the old man back upstairs, into the more comfortable master bedroom now that Sarah was "away," as she delicately phrased it.

Gordon Sullivan was not a good patient by her lights. He liked to read the papers. Reading, in her patients, disturbed Althy. She figured if you were reading you must be desperate for something to do. The only person she ever let read unmolested was the old Captain and then, really, only out of doors under the elms. The Captain, of course, had a serious purpose. In a sense his reading could be called work, and therefore, excusable. When Althy caught Gordon with the papers she'd come in and sit down for a chat, determined to lift the heavy burden of boredom from his shoulders. The old man put up with it, got rid of her as soon as he could, and went back to the stock quotations.

He wouldn't eat much either, claiming that he wasn't particularly hungry. He drank his milk from a tin measuring cup which he said made it taste sweeter and colder. You could see his Adam's apple bob in his skinny yellow neck as he raised the cup. He often settled for a cup of milk and an orange for supper. Sometimes he didn't even finish the orange.

"Look at this! Look at this!" Althy, scandalized, shoved under Ward's nose a thick brown plate, glazed the color of a country egg, on which a few spit seeds were pasted and a couple of sections of the beautiful jewel-like fruit still wobbled.

There was a faint odor about his father now, nothing Althy could wash away by means of the daily sponge bath she perpetrated on him despite his feeble protests. Could odors follow you around from place to place? If so, this was the faint, sweetly rancid smell familiar from the old days, the same odor that subtly threaded the air in the old Captain's room, Ward remembered, just before that wizened little monkey sailed away so many summers ago.

Terry, he noticed, did not come to the house to see his father as she had promised. It was too bad to get the old man's hopes up like that and then ruin them. He had expected better of her. Then too he had considered her proposed visits his best chance of talking some sense into her. One night at the supper table he mentioned his disappointment to Althy and, as usual, got more of an answer than he wanted.

"It's too bad Terry let Dad down," he had said. "Promising to visit and then not showing up again."

"Hell, that's all you know," said Althy. "Don't you know nothing?"

"I know everything," he grinned. "I just lack the facts."

"Well, let me supply some," she said. "Terry visits your father every day."

"She does?"

"Yes, dope. Every weekday after lunch."

"What did she do, give up her job?"

"She works the second shift now."

Well, he had to hand it to Terry. This new schedule solved her problem. If she couldn't be "strong," as she might say, then at least she could make careful plans to avoid him. He admired the simplicity involved in her solution and was troubled by the thought that nobody had bothered to mention her visits but had just let him stumble over them himself. A person's family ought to show more loyalty than that. On the other hand, maybe his father and grandmother thought whatever was going on between him and Terry was his business and therefore what he knew or didn't know about her comings and goings was his business too.

"That young lady's a real nurse," Althy had declared. As if she were sharing new information with him.

"She'll do anything," Althy rhapsodized. "She'll change the sheets just as nice and quick as you could want. The other day she did the laundry for me. She always stays for a cup of coffee and a little chat after her visit with your father. Such a nice sweet girl."

Althy, her coffee cup arrested in mid-air, stuck out her chin and glared at him through her trifocals.

"How did she ever get interested in you?"

How indeed.

He kept trying to reach Terry by phone, using the coin box in the hallway at work on his lunch hour, but Avis always answered saying, "Yeah?" and he, immediately depressed by that stupid animal grunt of a question, quietly hung up without a word.

One day though Terry actually answered. He was dumb-founded.

"Hello? Hello?" she repeated with growing suspicion.

"Don't hang up," he managed to croak at last.

To which she said, "Are you all right?"

"Why?" he asked searching for a possible clue to sympathy.

"You sound awful."

"I'm all right. I just want to know why you won't see me. I thought when we got together the day Dad came home –I thought maybe we could patch things up."

"Ward."

"What's that."

"I'm trying to make a new life for myself," she said in an even voice. "I feel sorry for you. I'll even admit that I still love you. But I don't want to see you. I'm doing what I can *not* to see you. So please don't call here again."

He stood there with the dial tone boring into his ear. It sure made him feel low.

If Avis wasn't hanging around the apartment all the time, it might be easier. He couldn't just go down there and beat on the door till Terry answered with that witch hanging around. He wondered whether the new note of cool self-possession in Terry's voice meant that old Avis had cooked up some wild story, maybe about how he and she had pumped away obliviously one night in his bedroom while on the floor above them, others, including the kid, dealt with Sarah's phantom suicide attempt. *Isn't that a riot?* he could hear Avis say. *I mean I wouldn't tell you about it all except I know you can't stand the creep anymore.* Good gravy, the whole notion made him go cold all over.

Things were getting desperate. The next day at work as he was thinking of all the hoops he would have to jump through to get things right again, a numbness began to steal over him. He knew the signs; they were familiar. Ever since he had catapulted through the car windshield in Kentucky, he had suffered from this malady sporadically. "Sinking spells," Althy called them. "Ward's having one of his sinking spells again."

Think baseball, he thought. Think baseball. The Red Sox are playing tough. Doing okay. Making Leonard Koppett look dumb. He lifted another 100-pound sack of peanuts and carried it on his shoulder up the midget ladder to the mouth of his wonderful peanut sorter. He could hardly move his limbs. It was like the central power supply was slowly fading and pretty soon it would peter out altogether, leaving his body helpless and juiceless in mid-motion.

Think baseball.

His joints were starting to petrify.

Think baseball, he thought. Think baseball.

Harry Hooper, Duffy Lewis, Tris Speaker, Smoky Joe Wood, Gardner at third. Who else on that 1912 team? Ruth. No, not till 1914.

He grabbed another sack of peanuts and climbed the ladder slowly. With his pocket knife he cut the red stitching at the top of the burlap sack as it rested on the edge of the machine. He dumped the peanuts into the hopper. I got to keep moving, he thought numbly. His body temperature seemed in decline already as the perfidious flesh prepared to slip out of gear and lurch to a stop.

By next morning his face had cooled into an expressionless mask, hard and immobile. He examined it in the mirror, feeling it gingerly with his stubby fingers. It was smooth and set as concrete. Even the parenthetical lines around his mouth were gone, as if filled in with putty. His gray eyes were flat and lifeless.

With effort he was still able to move around the factory. That afternoon after work he took the old man a jigger of mineral oil which he promptly threw up. He didn't even raise his yellow face from the pillow. The bilious vomit rolled soundlessly out of the corners of his mouth, down both sides of his thin face, soiling his pajamas and the bed clothes.

"Kaaa," the old man said, deeply embarrassed, but he had no words. He was too weak even to raise his head. He just lay there and said "kaaa" like some Arab.

As he cleaned up his father with a damp washcloth and helped him into the fresh pajama top, Ward could hardly move his fingers or arms or bend at the waist. His father just looked straight ahead at the wall through all this. Althy was nowhere around. Maybe she was downstairs watering those ugly African violets of hers. Whatever. It was okay. Ward could handle it. In fact, he wanted to do it in order to force breaks in the mysterious adhesions that slowly had been putting a lock on his joints for the past few days. I'm getting through this just fine, he thought as he folded the washcloth and scrubbed the other side of his father's yellow face. Still he noticed, on his way to the laundry room to deposit his father's soiled pajamas, that he walked with a kind of Franken-stein lurch.

Downstairs, Ward sat on the edge of his bed and felt his guts turning to cement. I haven't got time for this, he thought. To keep his fingers from petrifying to his thighs, he struggled off the bed and attempted to change his T-shirt. Only with great difficulty did he manage to claw it off his back, open the drawer, and pull the fresh one over his head. Keep moving, you baboon, he told him-self. Ward's stiff fingers tangled in the material as he wrestled his gray union T-shirt down the length of his torso. I've got to help the old man. I've got to catch up with Terry, he recited to himself to keep the sand out of his brain. He dropped his khakis to smooth out the wrinkles in the material across his can. It took the last of his strength to hitch up his pants again and button his fly. He toppled over onto his bed and sank into a deep sleep.

Once he had been offered a new future by Mr. Levin, the per-sonnel manager at The Distelfink Peanut Butter Company. The machine Ward operated at the factory sorted the good peanuts from the bad peanuts. It was a big complicated piece of machinery sensitive to changes in barometric pressure. It had a lot of gauges, petcocks, and dials. It was also expensive so they didn't want any dummy running it, and maybe wrecking it. They gave him an intelligence test to see if he could handle the job. For some reason, Mr. Levin gave Ward the test that candidates for army officers' training take. Levin told him that he wasn't expected to pass it, but to just do as well as he could.

In a week he was called back into the office. For a minute Levin just sat there behind his green metal desk and looked at him. Levin wore glasses. He was boyish-looking, but was going bald in front, so he had taken to combing his coarse black hair from left to right to cover it up.

"What are you doing in a peanut butter factory?" he finally said.

He had an expression on his face like the old man's when he discovered that Ward could read at the age of three. Ward didn't answer. It was bullshit time again. There was nothing to do but sit through it. He knew what the man would say next, knew he meant to be kind and helpful. It would be like the old man wan-dering around the house saying, "I can't understand it, I can't understand it" when it finally sank in that Ward had no intention of going to college. It would be the same thing as the guidance counselor back in high school. *Yes but you really ought to consider. . . .* All he had to do was sit there patiently. In a few minutes it would be over. Yet he wanted to smash Levin's neatly arranged, lineless face and shut him up before he could say any more wonderful and complimentary things about his marvelous native intelligence.

"You know you have the mental ability to go to college?" Levin snorted contemptuously at his own failure to express the situation adequately. "Hell," he said. "You could do *anything*. Even brain surgery, if you wanted."

That's right, you goddamn clown. Tell me all about it. Ward wanted to hit him to get him to shut up. He couldn't help it. He wanted to sit there calmly and let the words run off and not let any of Levin's kindly disposed advice and curiosity aggravate him, but it was all he could do to keep from jumping up and knocking the man right out of his chair.

"Would you be interested in our management trainee program?"

"No," replied Ward. "I wouldn't."

Mr. Levin thought he was offering him a big chance. It was all right. He is trying to be helpful, Ward counseled himself, so don't get on the man. But what did a fellow like Levin know about it? As Levin talked on about management opportunities, Ward traveled back in memory. A line drive jumped off his bat and caromed off the third baseman's chest into short left. Ward made it all the way to second, standing up. In the theater of his mind, Ward crouched in a cloud of gnats in center field on a hot humid southern night. The little bandbox of a ball stadium was cramped and dimly-lighted. The lazy drone of the crowd of good-natured Okies was a major ingredient in the warm soup that washed over him, made up in equal parts of humidity, dim light, and crowd noise. At the crack of the bat, Ward turned and raced for the wall, instinctively sure by the mere sound of the ball coming off the wood where it would go and how far it would carry, fully confident he would get to the wall before the ball and make the catch look easy. And he did just that, intersecting its flight at the perfect instant, spearing the white blur of the batter's best shot about knee-high on the dead run, revealing, almost too fast to follow in that split second, a part of that marvelous gift which nobody could learn and certainly nobody could share. The crowd clapped and whistled and stomped appreciatively and Ward, exercising the privilege of talent and the natural contempt of youth, ignored them completely.

Levin kept on talking, an intense fellow. He smoothed his hair sideways on his head. Too fat for his green double knit suit, Levin seemed to take his work seriously. Ward wondered why, briefly.

But Ward wasn't diverted long by such useless speculation. His head, which seemed big as a movie screen, flooded with the picture of the beautiful Bluette Fingers, not merely the beauty queen he had bargained for but an unsettling woman of complicated emotions and the author of unanswerable questions. Yes, lovely. He lost himself again in her beautiful face, the rich dark hair, the stupefying movie star smile, the long stirring legs. "Hello, traveler," she seemed to say. "Welcome back." Ward remembered how people gasped when he walked into a place with the tall lovely girl on his arm. Bluette knocked people breathless, won their dazed admiration, but left them feeling sad for all they'd missed and would never have. She was almost too beautiful, to the point where it might be a hazard to your mental health if you had the misfortune of living in her neighborhood. But he was the fellow. This dazzling, heartbreaking woman was his girl. "Welcome back, traveler," she appeared to say and as she held out her arms, the screen darkened and there was Levin smoothing his hair again and making another serious point.

It had been a good life. A little short, but a good one. He wasn't settling for any management trainee shit after that.

"Think about it," Levin said.

"I don't have to think about it," said Ward.

He walked out of Levin's office and back down on the floor. After this interesting meeting, Ward got the job tending to the wonderful peanut sorting machine and Levin, who'd taken such a sincere interest in Ward's future with The Distelfink Peanut Butter Company as the result of his test scores, left him pretty much alone. But once in a while Ward would look up from his work at the peanut sorter and catch the personnel manager, gazing at him from a safe distance. Caught in the act, Levin would look away quickly and walk off, but not before Ward saw the look of puzzled disappointment in his eyes.

On Tuesday night Althy tried to rouse him but couldn't. The watery image of her old face rippled above him, and he heard the faraway caw of her crowlike voice. She brought him tea and toast but they cooled untouched on the bedside table.

Ward glided into deepening shadows until at last he came to rest on the bottom of some lightless, uninhabited interior ocean. Here was the slow delight of nothing. No dreams or voices or objects of any kind, nothing but a cold black heavy sleep. Periodically he seemed to regain buoyancy and he would feel himself grow light, breaking loose silently from the suction of the utter bottom of this place, and slowly rising into an aqueous twilight of considerable activity where fuzzy balloons swam into sight and were sometimes distinguishable as faces. Sounds abounded here, sometimes as riotous as those in the birdhouse of a zoo, but mostly the sounds pumped slowly as molasses, voices slurring into baritone registers on a dying tape recorder.

Suspended in this zone, which rippled and pulsated with golden light between dim and shadow, he sometimes heard the noises die away altogether and found himself surrounded by animated pictures without words, like old-time silent movies except the motions of the people in his head were slow and graceful, not herky-jerky. There was Blue jumping up and down at the ballpark, that dark shiny hair in tumult about her glowing face. Yea, hero.

And the ball. Gleamings of the bright ball coming toward him slowly. He actually followed its spin and distinctly saw the suture-like red thread stitched in the horsehide as it moved in a graceful flat arc toward him. The ball in slow motion was so beautiful in its simplicity, it was breathtaking.

There were pictures too—though no words—of the old Captain, that little monkeylike man in his nineties. Just an old man dressed in his black suit, wearing one of his shiny hard white shirts, going "ha-ha-ha-ha," cackling the way he did over the cribbage board. Even in this dream, the air was spiked with the smell of a slightly damp Labrador retriever. Yes, that too because the Captain always had a black Lab named Lucky underfoot and even when he didn't, the smell of the dog mixed with the old man's odor and one scent became the same as the other, both of them smelling like moderately clean dogs. This pleasant smell was bonded to the woodwork in the study and on rainy days it would seep into the room like a ghostly presence even years after the Captain was gone, and so the presence of this scent now seemed perfectly natural to Ward, as the old Captain's perfect false teeth gleamed beneath his moustache and he cackled with delight over his cards.

These pictures would fade and Ward would dive again, plunging secretly inside himself beyond every thought, sound, and image.

After two days Ward became aware of the light glinting off his trophies. He began to enjoy the body-made warmth of the bed and the silence of his room. The blood stirred along his veins and arteries, sluggishly at first but with a definite quickening rhythm. As he lay there, too weak to move, getting reacquainted with the everyday objects of his room—lamp, dresser, trophies, student desk—he slowly flexed his fingers, truly a simple but wonderful feat.

This is Sarah's game, he thought. Not mine. He could just lie in bed and Althy would bring him tea and toast till the world shut down. Between thoughts, which were spaced far apart, Ward followed a patch of sunlight, a fugitive crab nebula, as it moved slowly across the ceiling.

This is not my game, he thought. This is not my game.

That night Ward got out the baseball game with the little brown packages that looked like pay envelopes and contained the players' cards. He set up the big pasteboard cards which showed what happened after you rolled the dice. He rattled the dice in the dice cup.

"Come on," he whispered to the players' cards.

The 1964 Boston Red Sox had finished eighth in a ten-team league but they were still the Red Sox and if replaying a full league schedule with them yielded melancholy results, that was life. Johnnie Pesky, whom Ward remembered from his own days in spring training, was the manager that year. Pesky was a good baseball man who deserved a kinder fate. Ward, of course, would have played for this team, and if he had, it was possible that Dick Stuart might have been traded, maybe for some pitching—who knows. Frank Malzone was over at third base and Yazstremski was installed in center, still with a few things to prove before he replaced Ted Williams as the man the fans loved to hate. Young Tony Conigliaro was looking good. That year he hit .290 and twenty-four homers. On the pitching staff Bill Monbouquette—Ward had played with him in the minors—was the staff leader, but fading fast. Felix Mantilla came over from Milwaukee that year and hit thirty home runs playing part-time. *Felix Mantilla,* for Godsakes. Moose Radatz was at the top of his game that season. Big, ugly, and bespectacled, Radatz came out of the bullpen and threw thunderbolts. In short, a bad team with lots of good fellows.

Ward brought his pitchers' records up to date. It was no surprise to discover Radatz led the staff with an ERA of 2.31. He was wonderful, that fellow. He ignored the mediocrity around him and hummed that ferocious fastball past everyone. If he kept going good in this table top replay, who knows, the Sox might even finish in the first division.

After careful preparations, Ward pitched LaMabe in the first game of a doubleheader against Buster Narum of Washington, a team that lost 100 games that year. In the second game he pitched Dave Morehead opposite Bennie Daniels.

The small dice, one red and one white, popped out onto his desk blotter and lay with astonishing clarity against the green field, shouting coded results: *Base hit to right! Pop-up to the catcher!* Ward made neat entries in his scorebook. As the game went along, the scorebook reflected its ebb and flow and the climax seemed to be foreshadowed by a mathematical certainty. He liked that.

On Friday Ward spent the whole day in his room playing baseball. He came out for meals and after lunch he drove downtown to get the papers. But he avoided the old man's room and was careful not to bait Althy. He was coming back. But he was still fragile.

By the time Gordie stuck his head in the room that night, Ward was feeling okay again.

"Hi."

"Hi yourself, kid. What's up?"

Gordie was wearing a dark-green Tyrolean hat and a gold corduroy jacket.

"Althy says you're feeling better."

"Right. Must have had a virus."

"Want to play a game?" Smiling like a goon. He had spotted the baseball game on the desk.

"No thanks, kid. Where's Dad?"

"He's on the sundeck. Althy's trying to keep him from reading the paper."

In a customary nervous gesture, Gordie thrust the package of cigarettes under Ward's nose. Putting aside the sports page of the *Times,* he suffered his brother's match lighting ceremony in which he, as usual, darted the match forward as it still flared with sulfur so you felt lucky if this nice gesture didn't result in setting your hair on fire. Ward lay back on his pillow, spewing smoke.

"How's he look?"

The kid's pale, mobile face jerked around. It was message enough without words: the old man looked awful

"I tell you what," said the kid. "Let's get the hell out of here for the weekend."

"What?"

"Let's take off. We can both use a change. We haven't done anything together in years. What do you say?"

"Where the hell would we go?"

"To the Jersey shore."

"The Jersey shore!"

"You make it sound like it's Timbuctoo. It's only three and a half hours away."

"Who the hell wants to go to the Jersey shore?"

"It's *nice* this time of year. Nobody around, the beaches are deserted, no carnival atmosphere. You'll like it."

The kid was serious.

"You're crazy, kid."

"Shit, man. Take a chance. Do something different for a change."

"Are you serious? With the old man sick as a dog?"

"Do you think he'd mind?" the kid smiled. "He'd be happy if you got away for a few days. He'd be all for it."

No doubt the kid was right. But still Ward said, "I can't do that."

He couldn't exactly think why he couldn't. It just didn't feel right.

"Come on. Cut yourself a break. I tell you, this Avis thing has me half crazy. I know you've been going through hell with Dad and Mother. And probably with Terry as well, although you'd never admit it. We could both use a few days on the beach."

"Hell, kid. This is early June. You can't swim this time of year."

"Who said anything about swimming? We'll take the bikes. We'll sit in the sun. I'll do a little painting. Nobody will be around. We'll have the place to ourselves. Come on, what do you say?"

The whole discussion was making Ward nervous. The damn kid was boxing him in.

"Not in my car," said Ward. "We're not loading any bikes in my car."

"We'll take Dad's car. We'll put down the top and give it a run. He wants the thing driven around. That trunk's big as the ballroom at the Waldorf. We'll take the front tires off the bikes and stick them both in the trunk. No trouble."

"Jesus, kid—"

"I tell you what."

"What?" replied Ward feebly. Gordie was a whirlwind once he got started.

"If Dad says go, you go. Okay? If he shows the least hesitation, we forget about it. All right?"

Well, maybe a little time away, Ward thought. Weakened from the exertions of his dive into that secret interior ocean, he had to agree that maybe a few days on the beach was just what he needed. Come back fresh and pour it on.

"Okay, kid."

"You'll do it?" said the kid gleefully. "You mean to tell me you'll actually get off your ass and go someplace?"

"Well, let's see what Dad says."

But they both knew what he'd say. Who was Ward trying to fool? Nevertheless he rocked upstairs to see the old man. His father was out on the deck in a chaise lounge, actually reading the paper now that Althy had apparently despaired of exorcising, by means of sociable conversation, that desperate melancholy that drives men to drink or to the printed page. The old man looked tired and thin but quite comfortable, even swank, in his blue striped seersucker bathrobe with white piping, his new blue pajamas with big round mother-of-pearl buttons, both the product of one of Terry's recent shopping trips. A mild breeze ruffled his father's graying hair and rattled his paper.

"You know what damn crazy Gordie's suggested now?" he asked his father.

"No. What?"

Slowly Ward shook his head to demonstrate his utter disbelief. "He thinks we ought to go down to the shore for the weekend."

The old man just studied him over the top of his Ben Franklins.

"Can you imagine?" Ward shook his head again. "With the way things are around here?"

"Everything's fine around here," said the old man. "Stop worrying. Go ahead. It'll do you good."

"Hell, I don't need to go to the shore. I get plenty of rest right here." Ward squinted at the broad lawn below. "That grass is getting tall."

"The grass can wait," said the old man. "Go. Get out of here. Have a good time for a change. Althy will take care of me."

"You sure? I don't mind sticking around."

"Stop worrying for Godsakes," his father said, "and get out of here."

S I X T E E N

NATURALLY, Gordon Sullivan thought it was a good idea for his sons to use his car on this trip to the New Jersey shore. He seemed to think it was a plus if the car had some miles on it. Actually it was a plus if it just stayed in the garage, practically brand-new and hardly ever touched, was Ward's idea. There was no figuring how other people thought.

The kid rushed home to pack and make a reservation at a motel he knew about in Brigantine.

Ward packed his gym bag: a change of underwear, a black T-shirt, a new pair of gym socks still in the plastic, his swim trunks, a beach towel, his shave kit together with his two toothbrushes, and a tan windbreaker. It took him five minutes. It would take Gordie at least an hour and a half. He would have to run around in circles first. Gradually he'd wind down and be able to think what to pack. Naturally this would include a couple of carefully chosen books, a sketch book, all his painting junk, and last, and certainly least, some clothes. There was a fair chance Gordie would forget to pack his underwear or socks and with that in mind, Ward threw in an extra pair of each. Since he had a little time, Ward sat down on his bed and had a smoke. He looked around his comfortable room. He truly regretted leaving it, even though it was only for two nights. Except for spending half the night at Terry's from time to time, which didn't really count, he guessed, he hadn't spent a night away from this room in twelve years. Christ, he was as bad as a baby. No wonder the old man wanted to kick him out. Still, even though he kind of kidded himself about it, the idea of being away made him a little nervous.

When Ward stopped at Gordie's house on the alley, he noticed the place was dark and pinched. Strange to say, it no longer looked like a happy place and when Gordie came out with his famous pansy suitcase in hand, he was moving fast, as if to escape from its altered personality. This suitcase they placed on the back seat. It was the same fag bag of brown cloth with yellow and red stripes which Gordie had carried flagrantly back and forth on the train to Providence in his college days. In the mammoth trunk they carefully layered Gordie's ten-speed, sandwiching an army blanket in between, over the top of Ward's. Actually the kid's bike was one he'd bought for Avis. It was maroon, a girl's model.

"Are you actually going to ride that?" Ward asked him

"Sure. Why not?" the kid answered cheerfully.

Ward just shook his head sadly. The boy had no sense of decorum.

They took off in the old man's big convertible. It was totally dark by now, which reminded Ward of the old days when Sarah and the old man used to put him and Gordie in the back seat with pillows and blankets and drive straight through the night to Maine. It was nice to fall asleep listening to the traffic and watching the headlights slide across the padded ceiling. When they woke up the next morning they would be close to Boston. At age eight, Ward had found something especially satisfactory and predictably miraculous in that development. Maybe because of those memories, he had always found night driving a pleasure. His brother slumped in the corner of the front seat. The long slats of his thighs were jammed against the dashboard. He did not look comfortable at all, and Ward suggested he crawl in the back and stretch out.

"That's all right," Gordie said. "I'll keep you company."

In a few minutes he dozed off. His head rolled around on the flexible white stalk of his skinny neck. Once, when Ward glanced over, he saw by the dash lights that the kid's mouth had fallen open. A silver line of drool ran from his lip to the collar of his shirt. His eyes were half-closed, showing new moons of glassy white eyeball. He looked like a damn zombie.

The kid was already enjoying his trip to the shore. The poor sap hadn't slept well at all since Avis had walked out on him. It was good to see him catch some shuteye, even if he did look a little obscene.

Gordie was still asleep when they pulled up in front of the motel, which was completely dark except for the light in the manager's office.

"Wake up, kid. We're in paradise," Ward said when he came back with the key to the room.

"We here already?"

"Yes. Short trip, wasn't it."

They parked the car and grabbed their bags. The wind was damp and blustery, full of a clean salt smell. They stumbled along the damp cement around the wickedly slurping pool where the reflection of the full moon swam and collapsed in spasms like a phosphorescent jellyfish.

They climbed some solid wooden stairs, the kid sleepily bumping his bag along the steps and railing. They went along the moon-washed balcony. After some scrabbling with the key, Ward managed to open the door to the room. They plunged past the beanfart smell that hovered around the little gas range by the door into a room crowded with two double beds, two nightstands, two Danish modern chests, a formica top kitchen table and chairs, and other odds and ends. There wasn't enough room left to swing a cat. The plaster walls had been boldly troweled and resembled cake frosting. All this was lighted by one feeble bulb hidden behind a flat frosted piece of glass dangling from the ceiling.

After a few preliminaries—Ward noticed the kid didn't even bother to brush his teeth—they fell into their damp lumpy beds. The wind buffeted the window, a comforting sound as Ward grew cozy under his blankets. In nothing flat he was out like a light. And surprised to find it bright daylight when he woke.

Ward showered. He pulled on his swim trunks, black T-shirt, and sneakers. He put on his mirror-like sunglasses and looked in the mirror. Ta-da! Vacation Man strikes again.

He left the kid still knocked out, arms and legs like a collapsed deck chair, with half his bed covers on the floor. At the end of the balcony, Ward smoked his cigarette and looked around. The air was nice. The bright light danced on the walls. On the horizon the dark ocean bled into the pale blue sky like ink onto a blotter. The vulgar pool, fluorescent blue, was still deserted. It was surrounded on three sides by rows of redwood chaise lounges minus cushions. Seaside fossils. On the ocean side of the pool deck a string of plastic palm trees rattled in the breeze.

Looking south down the curve of the silver-gray beach, he spied the domes and minarets of Atlantic City. The practically invisible smoke from his cigarette streamed away horizontally, a glow of orange eating rapidly at the cigarette paper in the steady breeze.

"What a beautiful day!"

The kid exploded out of the room thumbing his prescription sunglasses into place.

"I'm hungry as hell." Gordie rubbed his hands together. "Let's get the bikes out and find some breakfast."

They got the bikes out of the car. They forced the skinny tires through the brake blocks and fitted them into the slots of the front forks, tightening the quick-release levers. The bikes were lifted off their front wheels and the wheels spun to see if they ran free.

"Come on, come on. Let's go. I'm hungry."

Gordie danced around irritably as Ward carefully checked the clearance of the wheel through the brake blocks of his brother's bike.

"We don't want to hurry this, kid. If this wheel comes off, you'll have a hell of an accident."

"Well, hurry up. I'm hungry."

The damn fool.

Down the crumbling street they wobbled, careful to avoid the sand which drifted over the curb in places and made baby sand dunes in the road. Slowly they pumped along, turning into the broad cement street which ran through the middle of the one-story business section of the town, Ward starting to pick up the pace now as they glided by a brick post office, a grocery store with a dirty window, a real estate office, a bar with a bamboo front.

At a drugstore where stacks of papers from New York and Philadelphia, held down by rocks, flapped in the breeze, they stopped to buy the *Times,* which Ward fitted neatly into the spring-loaded aluminum carrier, and then they started out in search of breakfast again. A dirty orange chow dog, his tail tightly rolled on his back, crossed the cracked cement ahead of them. Plainly, it was a town where, in some seasons, a dog could cross the road at high noon in complete safety.

At the end of the ramshackle street, they found a restaurant where for ninety-nine cents apiece they wolfed down a breakfast of two eggs, bacon, and toast.

The cafe curtain at the big plate glass window was made from the same red check material as the tablecloth. Behind the counter, next to the big silver coffee machine hung a sign which read:

KIDS WITH PARENTS
UNDER TWELVE EAT FREE.

Coffee was ten cents extra. But the waitress, an unsmiling girl of seventeen or so, who wore her black hair parted in the middle, shyly dispensed volumes of coffee without asking if they wanted more. She had them down as tourists, Ward guessed, and she clearly knew what to do about them. Tourists always wanted more of everything.

After breakfast, they pedaled briskly back to the motel. Naturally, Ward was out front setting the pace. The kid, on his girl's bike, kept lagging behind.

"Slow down!" he yelled. "Let's enjoy it! Why do you ride so damn fast?"

"Doesn't do any good if you crawl along like an old lady!" shouted Ward. He kept on pedaling, pedaled a little harder in fact, grimly deploring how the kid could never seem to make a serious effort at anything physical. By the time they reached the motel, they were both sweaty and ready for the beach. Naturally, in addition to the folding chairs and beach towels, they had to drag all Gordie's painting paraphernalia along.

The ocean was so blue-black it looked like you could fill a fountain pen with it. They sprawled in the sun. Gordie pinned a piece of watercolor paper to a composition board and unscrewed the lid of a plastic bottle containing water which he poured into another plastic bottle that he'd cut down and made into kind of a bowl. On a white enameled butcher's tray he squeezed out colors —yellow, ultramarine, burnt umber. Dipping a big flat brush in his homemade bowl, he whipped up a blue sauce on the butcher's tray and quickly covered the upper half of the paper. On the lower half he dropped in a gray tone with yellows and browns in it. Using the same brush, he began to build the ruined pier that staggered into the water just ahead of them. The kid could certainly paint. Ward sprawled in his beach chair and watched his brother with interest. His cigarettes and matches were rolled in the right sleeve of his black T-shirt in case he wanted a smoke. He felt the sun on his biceps, felt it boring into his thighs along the hemline of his dark blue boxer trunks. If it got much hotter he would cover his legs with his beach towel. From behind his mirror-like sunglasses, he scanned the beach while the kid painted away. This was all right, he decided, and unrolled his cigarettes.

A fat man with large hairy tits wallowed past in a red bathing suit worn at half mast. He had a paper bag of bread crumbs. He threw the bread crumbs in the air. Like circus performers the gulls swooped and dipped to gobble the bread in mid-air. He moved off down the beach, tossing bread crumbs, a cloud of gulls wheeling in the bright air above his head

A bowlegged old man, string hair flapping in his face, staggered by against the wind. He wore sunglasses with round black lenses. His skinny arms hung motionless by his sides as his legs churned unsteadily in the sand. His bronze boxlike chest was tufted with thick white hair. The yellow boxer trunks he wore rode high over the bulge of his belly.

A gull, his gray wings neatly folded, walked stiffly on the sand. Not far away a ripe lady in a black tank suit sat on a beach blanket while two little kids ran down to the waves and back, carrying pails and shovels. The blanket was littered with red and yellow plastic toys. It looked like it had taken a direct hit from a mortar shell.

"What a relief to get away," said the kid.

He was right there.

"I thought I was going to have to cancel at the last minute. I got a call about a plumbing problem in one of the houses."

"One of the houses?"

"Right. But I got hold of a plumber friend of mine. He'll take care of it."

Gordie continued to slap paint on the paper. The picture of the beach really looked good now. He was talented. No question. It was a shame he wasted his time painting naked people when he could paint like this.

He added more water along the horizon in the picture so the ocean would bleed a little into the sky. But in the breeze, the paper dried so fast it was hard for him to make a line soften and automatically give the effect of distance.

"What houses you talking about, kid?"

"Those houses I bought. Don't you remember?"

"No, I don't."

"Well, I found these shacks over on the West Shore about three years ago. I must have told you about this."

"I don't think so."

"I was looking around," said Gordie, still painting away. "So the real estate guy showed me one of these little ranchers. Eleven-five with five hundred down, seven percent mortgage. Total monthly payment—principal, interest, insurance and taxes—seventy-nine dollars. Thirty-year mortgage."

Gordie looked at Ward over his shoulder and grinned significantly.

"So?"

"So I didn't like the place. For me that is. I rode around the development. Half a dozen of them were for sale. I asked the real estate man why. He said he didn't know for sure. He thought people figured colored people would move in."

"At that price it figures," said Ward.

"So I decided to buy," the kid said.

"Why?"

"Well. A West Shore location, close to Harrisburg. A lot of building going on. Blue Shield expanding. Lots of jobs. It seemed like a natural. So I borrowed $1,500 from Dad, and I bought three of them."

"Three of them!"

"Right. I got lucky. I rented them right away. For $125 apiece. So I figured. Hell. Why not take the plunge? I borrowed another $1,500 from the bank against the equity I had in the first three houses and bought three more."

"So far you haven't spent any of your own money."

"That's right. I rented the other three places fast too."

"Hell, you're in debt over $60,000, and you're not even thirty."

"But I clear about $260 a month on those places."

"That's awful rash, kid. You could get wiped out. What if you lost your job or something?"

"It doesn't have anything to do with my job. Those places pay for themselves."

"It sounds dangerous."

"But it isn't. Let's say you could find a stock for $3,000 that would pay $3,120 a year. Would you say that was a good deal? A dividend of over 100 percent a year?"

"Sure."

"Well, that's what I found. See, I only invested $3,000 in these places. It's true I owe $66,000 or something. But I've only got $3,000 in them. And it isn't even my money."

The kid seemed to be proud to be the bearer of this stupendous amount of debt.

"I don't know, kid. It sounds a little slippery. My idea is you buy a thing and pay it off."

The painting was almost finished and Gordie bent to the paper, a delicate brush in hand now, to put on the finishing touches.

"Those things have appreciated in value about 15 percent since I bought them," he said over his shoulder. "Which is actually 300 percent on my equity. And, hell, we haven't even talked about the tax break. I hardly pay any income taxes at all."

The whole thing made Ward dizzy. The kid painted in his name on the bottom right of the painting and put "A.W.S." after it.

"American Watercolor Society," the kid said proudly, turning around to grin. "I just got the word. They've accepted me."

"Great," said Ward.

"It's a great honor," said the kid. "Besides, it doubles the price of my paintings."

He put a precut white mat around his picture. It was a hell of a nice picture.

"What do you think?" asked the kid.

"Now that's a nice picture, kid. Why don't you paint those all the time? Instead of those naked women?"

"Well, from a purely commercial point of view, I should. But people are the thing. You can tell the spiritual condition of the age by checking to see how artists treat nudes. Or if they even paint them."

"Is that right?"

It was a wild idea, one you'd expect the kid to come out with.

"It's true. When a civilization feels good about itself, people are in the center of its pictures. Like in the Renaissance. But when things go bad and we lose faith in ourselves, the nudes get ugly or disappear altogether."

"How about that."

The kid was plenty smart in a bookish way. It was fun to sit on the beach and listen to him carry on about nudes and the Renaissance. He was a little sappy, but he was quite a guy too.

Gordie started to pin another sheet of paper to his board.

"You going to paint another one?"

"Yes, I thought so."

"Guess I'll go up and watch the ballgame. I've had enough sun."

"Hell, you didn't even take your T-shirt off. Come on. Get with it. Take off your shirt and drink it in."

"You better come in a little while yourself. You're starting to get red."

"I never burn," the kid said. "I'll be along soon as I whip out this next one."

The game on TV was the Yankees, Ward's favorite team to hate, versus the Cleveland Indians. What a bunch of wimps. He fell asleep in the sixth inning. By the time he woke up, it was over. He never did find out how it came out. Not that he cared.

When he woke up the kid was on the other bed. His face was red as a lobster.

"Well, you wouldn't listen," he said to him.

"I never burn," said Gordie. "I just tan. Only not this time."

"I told you, you damned dink. Why don't you listen?"

"I got the chills. Man, my skin is tender all over."

"You're not going to believe this, but I've got the answer."

"What's that?"

"Milk of magnesia."

"No. I'm not going to believe that. I don't need the poops on top of everything else."

"You don't drink it, stupid. You swab it all over yourself. It draws the sun poisoning out of your skin."

"You're shitting me."

"That's all right," Ward said. "It works. An old relief pitcher down in Louisville told me about this remedy. It works."

As indeed old Shaw had when one day after a weekend at the country club pool with Blue, Ward showed up so damn miserable he couldn't even put on his uniform.

"Milk of magnesia," said the old relief pitcher. "Milk of magnesia. Slap it on you. It draws the poison."

And it did.

So now Ward said to his brother, "I'm going to do you a favor, son. I'm going to run out and buy you some cotton balls and a giant bottle of milk of magnesia."

"Well, good luck," moaned the kid, turning over and hugging his blankets.

Along with clouds and the buildings across the street, he and the bicycle wavered on the uneven surfaces of storefront windows as he pedaled along the cracked and heaved slabs of the town's almost deserted main street. Brightly lighted in the dusk, the drugstore floated empty like a ship mysteriously abandoned at sea. Ward found the stuff he was looking for and handed his coins to the cadaverous teenager behind the counter. The store's serpentine marble soda fountain top, the round little tables of white marble surrounded by chairs with wire backs twisted into heart shapes, reminded Ward of Mr. Johnson's drugstore back in Dunnocks Head. Mr. Johnson, ancient even then, was probably dead by now like everybody else, he decided.

When he got back to the room, he woke Gordie up and applied the goop to his back.

"Boy. It really feels cool."

"Isn't that amazing?" said Ward.

Indeed it was truly incredible that anything Shaw had suggested would actually work.

In an hour or so, after they watched the news, Gordie felt good enough to go out for dinner at a little Italian restaurant they'd spotted on their morning bicycle ride.

The murals in the restaurant—depicting gondoliers and gondolas, wrought-iron balconies shaded by awnings striped the colors of the Italian trident—were so bad Gordie sat with his back to the offending wall. Nevertheless the humble scent of oregano was in the air, and they were not surprised when the meal turned out to be delicious. One bottle was not enough for Gordie. They had to have two bottles of Broglio, admittedly a smooth lovely Chianti, with their spaghetti and meatballs, garden salad, and hot garlic bread.

"This trip is on me," he said after a few glasses of wine.

"Why should you pay for everything?"

"Well, I'm really having a good time. Besides, guess what happened this afternoon after you left?"

Ward had to grin as the kid fell into his habitual interrogative style of conversation.

"I don't know. What happened?"

"That fat lady with the kids. Remember her? She waddled over and fell in love with the painting."

"How much did you get?"

"Two hundred bucks."

"Nice going. You can pay for the trip."

The kid laughed and refilled their glasses with the Broglio. The old man was right, as usual. This four-eyed crane seemed to have an inherited talent for making money. So why, Ward asked himself, are you standing in the way? Because if I don't, he answered himself, everything will change.

"Want some dessert?"

"No. You go ahead."

The kid was still skinny. He could get away with that stuff.

"I think I'll have a beer for dessert."

"Don't get gooned up."

"God, it feels good to relax," said the kid. "Thanks for coming along."

"I guess we both needed a break," said Ward.

Gordie looked at the bottom of his glass.

"Poor Mother."

"Let's make a deal," said Ward. "Let's not talk about it. Let's just take a break."

"Good idea."

The kid didn't have one beer for dessert. He had three. He told Ward a funny story about some female pen pal in France he had had when he was in college. He wrote to her in French, and she wrote back in English—for practice. That was the idea. But the kid got carried away. He began to make romantic suggestions, he said, since French was such an appropriate language for that kind of stuff. Really, he was just practicing. But Monique took him seriously. Pretty soon she was proposing that she come to the states to visit him over the Christmas holidays. Since the kid already had a live-in friend, things were getting awkward. But he didn't know how to handle it. "It never occurred to me to be honest," he said. He found himself faced with the prospect of meeting Monique at Logan Airport within a matter of a few weeks. Things were desperate.

"How did you get out of it?" asked Ward.

"I wrote myself out of the script," said the kid. "I got a friend of mine to take down a letter. I can even remember the opening line. It went 'Dear Monique—I am Philip Westover, Gordon Sullivan's roommate, and I am sorry that it is I who must tell you of the tragic accident that befell Gordon just after he received the wonderful news that you were flying over to spend Christmas with him.'"

They both laughed like hell. Only the kid could get himself in a pickle like that and figure out such a weird solution.

Gordie had had his choice of deaths. It was wonderful, he said. He thought about it overnight and decided that since she knew of his prowess as a swimmer, it would be death off the high diving board. He had his friend write, "I know Gordon was too modest to tell you this himself, but he was in training for the next Olympics, and everyone here felt he had a good chance for the gold."

They really cracked up. They cackled like a couple of fools, clutching at the table cloth and drawing sidelong glances from the other patrons. The kid said the letter ran ten pages. It was all he could do to get himself to stop inventing wonderful things about himself to put in it.

"Didn't you feel bad about it?" asked Ward.

"Hell, no. I got out of a tight spot and gave her the most romantic memory she'll ever have. I'll bet she still has those letters, including the last one. Tied with a ribbon and in a tin box at the top of her *armoire*."

Ward finally got him out of the restaurant and into the car. As they pulled away from the curb, Gordie said, "Let's stop at the liquor store and get a bottle of vodka. Have a night cap."

"We don't need a night cap."

"We might want a drink tomorrow. Come on. It'll take two minutes."

"It's probably closed by now."

"What time is it?"

"Five of nine."

"Well. Let's see," said the kid.

The lights were still on in the liquor store, and one customer still stood at the counter.

"We're in luck," Gordie said.

Ward parked the big car and they went in. The customer, a tall thin Negro wearing shades, a dirty raincoat, and a white porkpie hat with a black band, looked up from the store's brochure and stared at them coldly. He was probably six-ten.

The old guy in the gray cardigan behind the counter smiled.

"Gentlemen, what can I do for you tonight?"

Before Ward or the kid could answer the fellow's question, the Negro spoke up.

"Hey, man. I was here before these cats."

"Oh, I'm sorry," said the old guy. "Have you decided, sir?"

Here is a nice little man who wants no trouble, thought Ward. The black man balled his fists into his raincoat pockets. His face hardened into a coffee-colored mask, his eyes hidden by the sunglasses.

"Yeah, man. I've decided." The Negro's voice took on a hard edge. "Forget the wine. Gimme a bottle of Johnnie Walker. Black Label, man. The best."

He flashed a smile at Ward and Gordie as the old guy ducked behind the curtain.

"Damned porch monkey," muttered the kid.

"Shh," said Ward. "Just relax."

"What you cats whispering about?" asked the tall Negro in a slow menacing voice.

"Nothing," said Ward. "We're just talking."

"I told him," Gordie said, "that I thought you were pretty rude."

Not till his brother slurred this out did Ward realize he had a drunk on his hands.

"Yeah, man? You think I'm rude?" The Negro stuck out his purple lip.

"Yes, I think you're rude," said the kid prissily. "We know you were here first. It's fine if you get served first, but you don't have to be rude about it."

"Shit, man," said the Negro to Ward. "Who is this dude? Where he learn to talk like that?"

"He's had a few drinks," said Ward. "He's just running off at the mouth."

"Hell I am," said the kid.

"Keep him under control, man."

"Shut up, kid. We don't want any trouble. Sorry, buddy."

"Keep him down, man," replied the Negro.

The clerk reappeared.

"Here you are, sir." He looked a little nervous, as if he'd overheard their conversation. He bagged the bottle and rang up the sale.

"That will be six dollars."

The Negro stood there, his hat tilted down over his sunglasses, his fists balled in the pockets of his raincoat. He smiled slowly. In a sly voice he said, "Now gimme the bread in the register, man. Nice and slow. Everything's cool. Nobody gets hurt. You dig?"

He picked up the bagged bottle of scotch and held it by the neck. At the same time, from his raincoat pocket the fellow produced a ridiculously small nickel-plated pistol. The tiny gun looked damned silly in his huge mitt of a hand.

"Of course. Of course," said the storekeeper.

"What the hell's going on?" the kid demanded indignantly.

The Negro swung around. The pistol glittered in their direction.

"Shut up, kid." Ward actually squeezed the kid's arm.

"Hey, man," said the Negro. "You get him to shut his mouth. *Now.* Hear?"

"Right," said Ward. "Shut up, kid."

"That gun's a fake," whispered the kid.

The hold-up man swung the gun back on the clerk who was now taking the money out of the register and stacking it in a neat pile on the counter.

"Careful with that gun, mister. You don't want to hurt anybody."

"Shut up, Dad. I handle the gun, you handle the money. You dig?"

"Certainly. Certainly."

"Now I want you cats behind the counter with ol' Dad here."

The Negro waved the gun at them, his finger on the trigger, a careless, dangerous gesture.

Ward started forward in meek obedience. He froze as he heard the kid's voice. "Why don't you stick up some rich guy?"

"Say what?"

"I said why don't you rob somebody whose got some money?"

"Shut up, kid."

"Really," said the clerk. "It's all right. I'm insured. Let's not make trouble for the man. He has a gun."

"Get you ass behind that counter!"

"Come on, kid."

But the kid didn't move.

"Why don't you wait till the bank opens in the morning and really make a score?"

The Negro went wild. He danced around nervously squeezing his little gun and shouting.

"Who *is* this motherfucker, man? Shut him the fuck up before I do!"

"Don't be stupid, kid. Do as he says."

"Really, it's all right," said the storekeeper nervously. "I've learned to expect a certain amount of this."

"Expect this! You're a damned accessory," said the kid. "Don't take this lying down."

"Open you mouth agin and *you* gonna take it laying down! Shut him up, man! He making me damn nervous!"

It was getting tense. The goddamned kid was acting crazy. He was driving the hold-up man to do something he didn't want to do.

"Cut the shit, kid. Get behind the counter."

The clerk patted the stack of money on the counter. He smiled at the dancing Negro.

"Here take the money, mister. Take it and go with my blessing."

But the bandit didn't even act like he heard. The gun in his hand wavered and glittered in the kid's direction.

"Keep that skinny motherfucker under control, man. Else I'll give him a new asshole!"

Quick as a wink, the kid reached over and jammed the thick wad of bills into his jacket pocket. The black man's mouth fell. His palsied gun flickered up and down on the kid.

The clerk moaned softly.

"There," said the kid. "What are you going to do about it? Kill all three of us? Shoot me—and my brother and this man will jump you."

He sounded awful damned confident.

"You're dead, man." The Negro shook his head sadly. "You're dead. I ain't got no choice."

"Take it easy. The kid's been out in the sun too long. He doesn't know what he's doing."

"I do too," the kid said indignantly. "Go rob a bank. Leave the little guys alone."

Without meaning to, Ward found himself standing in front of the kid.

"Put that bread on the table!"

"Fuck you," said the kid.

The quivering gun suddenly glittered to attention as if it had an anger of its own, pushed now past endurance. Ward found himself staring thoughtfully into the lethal eye of the now steady pistol which seemed to have grown in size. Good Christ, he thought. I'm dead.

The kid suddenly bounded past Ward in a wild gazelle leap right into the arms of the startled Negro. And Ward, shocked and horrified, sprang forward too, convinced that in a split second his ass would be thoroughly extinct.

"I've got insurance!" he heard the owner cry.

The gun exploded. The blast rang in Ward's head. Something wet and hot was on his cheek, and the roar seemed to echo in his head. The man staggered backward, Ward and Gordie clinging to him. The man was so tall his head seemed unreachable. In a panic Ward swung wildly and hit the door jamb. A numbing pain surged up his arm. As he clung helplessly to the tall Negro, his arm dangling uselessly, he was aware of a powerful mixture of body reek and sweet cologne. I'm dead, he thought again. Even the man's smell added to his sense of hopelessness. He waited for the final explosion.

To his amazement, he saw the kid had his fingers around the man's neck. The Negro's sunglasses had been stripped from his narrow face. His mouth was open and spit was on his lips. He looked horrified. The kid was growling something and choking the shit out of the man. The pistol barked again. Ward winced involuntarily. The hot acrid smell of gunpowder mixed with the reek of sweat and cologne. The owner yelped, high and piercing, almost like a dog.

I'm dead, Ward thought and dropped to the floor. He looked up. The Negro was trying desperately to tear the kid off him. The kid's head was buried in his collar. He had his arms wrapped around the man's body. The man looked scared. His eyes were wide. His mouth was twisted open, and he was screaming like a banshee. He dropped the pistol and the scotch. The bottle made a modest little plop as it broke inside the paper bag. It began to pee an amber puddle on the floor. With a final wrench the tall Negro, with the kid's head still buried in his neck, pitched backward through the big window in a crescendo of shattering glass. The man lay on the sidewalk screaming. Gordie still clung to him. His head was bent as if whispering some rapturous secret in the fellow's ear. The Negro's sneakers kicked spastically on the cement. He kept on screaming. Gradually the howls became hysterical words.

"Get him off! Get him off!"

The screams were soprano, out of control, almost sobs.

Ward and the owner ran outside. Gordie and the Negro lay in

a circle of broken glass. A big ugly stain was spreading on the right side of the kid's windbreaker.

He's been shot! thought Ward.

He bent to the hysterically screaming man and saw that the kid, apparently unconscious, still had his teeth clamped on the Negro's delicate ear. His hands still loosely clutched at the man's throat. The Negro hammered at the kid's back with his fist.

"Get him off!"

Ward rolled the kid off. The front of his jacket was soaked with blood too.

"Call an ambulance," said Ward to the clerk.

"What the hell is wrong with your friend?" moaned the old guy wringing his hands. "Look at this mess. Why didn't he let him take the money?"

"Look," said Ward. "You get your ass in there and call an ambulance."

The Negro screamed out in pain again. A spasm shuddered through his body. His sneakers kicked the pavement in an ugly dance.

"Roll me over, man! Help me, man. For Chrissake."

Ward turned him halfway over. Under one shoulder blade in the middle of a dark blot the size of a dartboard the end of a big sliver of glass stuck out.

"No! Jesus, man! No! No! Don't move me no more!"

"You got a piece of glass in you."

"Yeh? How's it look."

"It's bleeding a lot."

"Don't touch it!"

"I'm not. I'm just looking."

He lay there quietly on his side his eyes closed, his nostrils flared. His ear looked in bad shape.

"Who was that fucking maniac anyway?" panted the Negro.

"He's my brother," said Ward.

"Don't he know no better than to jump a man with a gun?"

"He thought it was a fake."

The man actually laughed, soft and musical, and ended with a cough.

"Fake," he said mildly. "Next time I'll have to get me a sign."

Gordie moaned.

"Don't move, kid."

He had blood on his mouth and chin, but it was the Negro's blood, Ward was pretty sure.

The kid's eyes opened wide. He tried to sit up, clutched himself, and fell back.

"Take it easy, kid."

"Jesus." He closed his eyes. And opened them again, seemed to see Ward for the first time.

Ward took off his windbreaker and stripped off his T-shirt. With his good hand, he unzipped the kid's jacket and balled up his T-shirt on the inside.

"Here, hold that against yourself."

"Okay."

He laid his windbreaker over the top of the kid.

"How you feeling?"

"Okay, I guess." Then the kid said, "We got that hoon, didn't we?"

"You got him, kid. You were a one-man cyclone."

"I thought it was a fake."

"Wrong again," said Ward. "Just take it easy. The ambulance will be here in a minute."

"Am I hurt bad?"

"Hell, you're all right."

Tears pricked in the corners of Ward's eyes. He was pretty sure the kid was bleeding to death right there on the sidewalk.

"I don't want to die," said the kid.

"You're all right," said Ward. "Hell, you can't die now. You're a hero."

"I got too much to do," the kid said. "I haven't got time to die."

At last the cops and the ambulances showed up. The liquor store and the pavement pulsated with red and blue light from the cop car's rooftop revolving light. A crowd came out of the shadows to watch silently now that the ambulances and the cops made it a safe and legitimate scene of disaster.

Ward rode along in the ambulance.

The kid clutched Ward's broken hand. It hurt like hell. The sweat popped out on Ward's forehead. Of course the kid didn't know it was broken. He was just holding on.

"Ward."

"What is it, kid?"

"You wouldn't remember me as just a dumb jerk who jumped some boon with a gun in a liquor store, would you?"

"Hell no, kid. You're a hero."

"I thought it was a fake."

"It makes no difference. You have more goddamned guts than anybody I ever saw."

"You think so?"

"Damn straight."

Don't die, kid, Ward thought. The kid clutched his hand tight. Don't die. God, don't let him die. Goddamn you, God. Goddamn you, you son of a bitch. Don't kill the kid. Let the kid alone. Let him be all right. Listen, God. You son of a bitch. What do you want? Let him alone. Kill me, you fucker. But let the kid live.

SEVENTEEN

YOU CAN'T HAVE SO many things go wrong and not wonder if somehow, unwittingly, you have interfered with the basic
order of things.

So it was not surprising that each morning, Ward cautiously
stuck his head out his motel room, using the cast on his arm to
hold the screen door open a crack. He squinted against the cool
dance of light on the white wall of the motel and sniffed the salt
air for clues to he-knew-not-what mystery. Safe and peaceful. No
Negroes with guns seemed to be prowling the place. Everything
normal looking, except for that peculiar luster common objects
had taken on since Gordie had been shot in the liquor store. The
quietude of early morning seemed in friendly league with the
delicately bobbing light that splashed the balcony railing. Satisfied, he ducked back inside.

Automatically that week he woke at dawn, startled awake by
the hushed retreat of the ocean at that hour. Even the furniture
seemed dumbfounded by the sudden stillness. So he got in the
habit of sticking his head out the door to see what was going on.
Nothing ever was.

Dressed just in swim trunks and tennis shoes, the cast making
him clumsy, he ran on the beach. Maybe two miles out and two
miles back. Sand stung his legs like fleas as he scuffled along. The
air was cool, but sweat poured out of him, turning the edges of his
cast soggy and staining the elastic band of his blue swim trunks
almost black. By the time he climbed the cement steps to the pool
deck of the motel his breathing was no longer located in his chest,
but in his head, and he seemed to be exhaling raggedly through
his ears. He had thought he was in pretty good shape, but this
running business was something else. It proved again that you

could be in condition to do one thing, but that didn't mean you were prepared to do another.

Although he took comfort in familiar thoughts like this, the week he spent alone at the motel had a special unreality for him. Even the flatware in the little restaurant he frequented for break-fast looked strange, if not beautiful, and he hesitated over these instruments some mornings, no longer sure how to use them. Some days he found himself stopped in the middle of a busy sidewalk, lost in puzzling reverie. With a jerk, embarrassed, he'd discover himself standing like a dope right there in plain daylight while others milled past and some looked at him curiously. Dis-mayed by the sad realization that he no longer knew what his intended errand was, he would seek out a place to sit down—on a bench or in a sandwich shop—and wait for his original purpose to drift back into his head, which it did, mysteriously and quietly as fog. That is, if he did not consciously try to recollect the nature of his errand. If he did that, it wouldn't come back at all.

The Negro's gun kept going off in his ears. Once it happened while he was standing in line at the check-out counter in a grocery store. He jumped straight up in the air and looked quizzically around him to see if others had heard the explosion too. Appar-ently not. The skinny old lady in line behind him clutched a head of lettuce to her chest and stared. He raised the heavy cast and touched his burning cheek, the one that took the powder burn that night in the liquor store. The scab was crusty now. I must be going crazy, he thought.

In the night he was given to cold sweats and dreams about the Negro with the gun. The tall bandit pointed the little silver pistol at him and smiled. He fired, jerking bullets out of his little silver gun as if shaking down a stubborn thermometer, blasting away at pointblank range. Ward hopped and jerked, his limbs alive with involuntary dance, and awakened in his bed to discover it was, after all, just the same old dream he'd been having all week.

Naturally the way he found to combat this strange new unreal-ity of simple facts and objects was to take up a regular routine. But the gunshots still went off in his head at unpredictable times, and his face commenced to twitch, a cold sweat spread between his shoulder blades under his T-shirt, and his ears rang. Sometimes he'd have to hold onto something, like a telephone pole or a mailbox, it made him so dizzy.

"Shot!" Avis cried when he called her from the hospital. That was the first time the pistol shot rang out in his head. It seemed to rocket down the telephone wire and pierce him in the ear. He all but tumbled down right there in the telephone booth outside the emergency room, but instead he steadied his buckling knees by pressing his back against the wall and sweatily submitted to her questions.

"When? Where? How bad is he? Is he okay?"

"I don't know. It just happened a few minutes ago. He's in the operating room now."

"Oh my God! Where *are* you?"

"The Jersey shore."

"The Jersey shore!"

A new range of alarm entered her voice at this news, as if she had momentarily confused geography with anatomy and had concluded the Jersey shore was an especially bad place in which to get shot.

"We came down to get away for a few days." Ward laughed bitterly, a sound even to his own ears close to grief.

"What happened?"

"Gordie got shot by some guy trying to hold up a liquor store."

"Oh my God!"

"We were in the store. This guy whipped out a gun. Gordie decided he was going to stop him."

"Oh God! The *dope!*"

It seemed this was going to be the universal opinion. The kid had done something rash and foolish, nothing anybody with any sense would undertake. Gordie proposed in one semidrunken thoughtless moment to be a hero. Nobody would thank him for it, certainly not the owner of the store. The best he could hope for was kindly disposed pity from close friends. Unless he dies, Ward thought. If he dies, they'll love him. Everybody will see he is a hero. Knowing how people are, he figured they would conclude the almost accidental act must have been important if he'd gotten killed in the process.

"The *dope!*" Avis said.

That about covered it.

Ward slumped against the wall, a clammy sweat crawling across his belly, his eyelids beating rapidly against the echo of yet another reverberating gunshot in his head, and considered the hopeless impossibility of ever explaining just what it was his crazy brother had done.

He's a real hero, he could have said. But Avis, familiar with disaster, had no understanding of what might pass in a pinch for bravery. Only the final catastrophe of death could certify the kid's heroism for her.

Having now realized that what the kid had done was beyond normal understanding, unless of course he explained it by dying, Ward clearly knew what to do next. He had to get off the telephone and concentrate on the kid. Avis, greedy for facts, would keep him on the line for half an hour and in that time, the kid would bleed to death. In a panic he felt his desertion. He had to get off the phone and back in that waiting room and bend all his strength to the single thought: *Don't die. Don't die.*

"Look," he said, "I've got to get back, see how he is. Ask Terry to go see my father. Ask her to stay there till I call. Is she there?"

"No, she's at work."

He'd forgotten about the night shift.

"Call her at work," he said. "Tell her. She'll know what to do. I'll call back as soon as I know something more."

And so he broke away and went back down the hall to the emergency room, where behind the glass in the nurse's station, the radio played senselessly, a throbbing little box of static and fading stations. As he pushed open the door to the corridor that served as the waiting room, two middle-aged black women stoically seated on similar errands, looked up at him, saw he was in trouble same as them, and lost interest. He plugged the Coke machine with coins and sat down to wait.

The women seemed to be experienced waiters. They sank down into themselves, leaving behind shapeless bodies wrapped in bright-colored cloth. The radio tortured him. It dribbled and sputtered and smeared what should have been the pure solemn air with idiot sound.

Nobody was around. The nurses were all off somewhere, no doubt helping doctors attend to emergency cases. Nevertheless, he felt deserted. He wanted someone to come and talk to him about his brother. They didn't have to bring him news, good or bad. Just give him a connection, provide some relation between his sitting there on the hard metal chair in the hallway, beaten about the head and shoulders by the stupid radio, and what the doctors were doing to his brother. He swigged his Coke and waited. Squeezing his eyes shut, the dark liquid still bubbling in his mouth, he visualized his brother on the table and talked to him.

Don't die, he told him. What the hell do you want to die for? Don't die. You've got your whole life in front of you, peckerhead. You got to help out anyway. I can't do everything myself. Somebody has to help me take care of things after Dad's gone. So just don't lie there and take the easy way out. Don't I know you're a hero? Isn't that enough? Come on, kid, don't die.

If that was praying, he was doing it.

The new cast weighed heavy on his damaged arm. His hand throbbed with little electrical shocks as if independently reliving its shattering collision with the door jamb in the liquor store. Beneath the rough plaster his hand seemed swollen with blood, about to explode and splatter all over these black women and the walls of the waiting room. He rested the pulsing arm on his knee.

"Mr. Sullivan?"

A young doctor dressed in a green gown and cap, his preformed paper surgical mask pushed to one shoulder, beamed at him. A thick dark moustache made his smile seem especially wide, even a little fanatical. Ward found himself shaking the fellow's hand awkwardly with his good left hand.

The doctor smiled on. Good news, plainly.

"Your brother's going to be okay," said the doctor.

"He's okay?"

"Yes, he's fine. The bullet missed his vital organs. It came close to his spine but he's in good shape. It was a low-caliber slug so it didn't tear him up too much. He's lost quite a lot of blood. But he'll be all right."

"Good," Ward said. "That's wonderful."

Indeed it was.

"We'll keep him in intensive care overnight," the doctor said. "Just routine to make sure he gets maximum attention. In a day or so, we'll be able to move him to a regular room."

"Good," repeated Ward. "I was really worried. I thought he was a goner."

"You think he was torn up," said the doctor, "you ought to come back around midnight. I mean, we get some *real* cases in here some Saturday nights."

It was amazing how far you could get on just a change of

underwear or two. Every night when Ward got back from the hospital he washed out his socks and underwear and hung them from wire hangers on the shower curtain rail to dry out over the tub. On Wednesday morning, dressed in just his swim trunks and canoe shoes, he drove to the laundromat and ran his entire limited wardrobe, including khakis, through the washer and dryer. While this was going on, he sat outside on a bench, read the papers and took in a little sun.

His father wanted to send money but Ward said no, he didn't need any. Gordie insisted he live off the proceeds of the seascape. That was nice, and Ward agreed he'd use what he needed to get along. But the room rent was low (he'd worked out a weekly rate with the owner), and he ate cheap, buying a few things to stock the little refrigerator under the counter.

The time went fast. In the mornings he ran on the beach. Then he showered, careful to dangle his plastered arm outside the plastic curtain, and followed with exercises on a bamboo mat the owner loaned him. He figured he might as well stay in shape. Usually he showered again after this. Of course, he had the Motobecane, his by forfeiture, which he kept along with the other bike in the room. This he rode slowly to breakfast, careful not to get sweaty again. Over a slow breakfast of bacon and eggs, an English muffin, and lots of coffee, he read the New York and Philadelphia papers, his only extravagance.

He liked to live simple, prided himself on how far he could make a dollar go, how little he needed in order to be satisfied. When this was all over, he'd give Gordie most of his money back, taking satisfaction in the look of amazement and maybe even respect that the kid would flash at him in that moment. His brother may have inherited the old man's Midas' touch, but in the same circumstances he would have bought himself extra clothes, eaten out all the time, gone to movies, bought books and art supplies, and never thought to work out a weekly rate at the motel. Somebody had to be a saver, a conserver.

The afternoons he spent at the hospital with his brother. The kid was coming along fine. Ward usually grabbed a bite to eat right there in Atlantic City and walked the boardwalk till it was time for evening visiting hours.

By Wednesday he was in the errand business. Gordie sent him

out to buy a copy of something called *Under the Volcano,* which no bookstore or drugstore in Atlantic City had in stock.

On Thursday afternoon he was dispatched to find a sketch tablet and pencils of a certain softness. He found those, as well as magazines that Gordie requested.

Every night when he got back to the room he gave the troops at home a jingle.

Every night Althy asked him, "What do I tell Mr. Levin at the factory?"

And every night Ward answered, "Tell him I'm still sick."

Now they both knew that in peanut butter factories the truth wouldn't work. You couldn't say, my brother's been shot and I'm going to hang around till he gets better. After all there were those jars of peanut butter to produce and a man off the line, a man with an especially important job like checking the nuts, why, that put a serious crimp in things. At The Distelfink Peanut Butter Company, people got half a day off to bury their closest relatives and, here, the kid wasn't even dead. So this situation required a little lying but it didn't make either of them feel any better about it.

Still Ward found it easier each night to tell her to repeat the lie and Althy, a prisoner of conflicting loyalties, felt trapped into doing it. If a man had a job to do he ought to do it and not let people down. On the other hand if a fellow had a brother shot full of holes, he had a responsibility there, too. Since she accepted his nightly instructions in a grim silence, he guessed loyalty to family had won out over a fellow's responsibility to a peanut butter factory.

The job had receded so rapidly in just a few days that it seemed twenty years ago that he had worked at a job in some factory sorting the good peanuts from the bad ones, spending all day watching the dials of his wonderful electronic sorting machine, carrying big bags of peanuts up the midget ladder, slitting the dotted red thread, and watching the bag release its contents into the machine's wide-mouthed hopper with the surge and subsequent relief of a pent-up bowel. How did I do that for twelve years without going crazy? he asked himself. Naturally the question scared him and he tried to push it aside. After he got off the telephone he had to go up and lie down on his bed for fifteen minutes before he could get up and do his nightly laundry.

These troubling thoughts were no doubt the product of having too much time on his hands and not enough of a routine to take it up, he decided, lying there looking at the circular designs on the shadowy plaster ceiling of his motel room. This can happen, he realized, when you get away from home. He asked himself how he was going to get along if he kept thinking like this. If you didn't have that job, how would you earn money? he asked himself. Himself had no answer. It came to him that he had only held one job in his life, besides playing ball, and that was working in the peanut butter factory. Good gravy, he thought. Get ahold of yourself before you go and do something foolish. This kind of thinking did indeed make him sweaty, but not for long, as every morning the sun popped out of the ocean like a cork bobbing to the surface, and during the daylight hours, he always managed to keep busy.

Of course, there was the other telephone call too, which he made to Terry around noon each day. She got the benefit of last night's news, sort of like the morning paper, and then he had his late edition phone call to home in the evenings after he got back from Atlantic City.

Terry now was willing to talk to him on the phone. She didn't give him any of that don't-call-here stuff. But at the same time she made it plain this was a new deal, a matter of people conferring on a question of mutual interest. Ward looked forward to those conversations. She always had some little piece of good news to report. He found that incredible. He hadn't heard any good news from anyone for so long he didn't suppose anybody had any to give anymore. Everybody had gotten into the habit of talking like the six o'clock news, an understandable development. But Terry told him that she'd found a good buy on cauliflower and made a batch of her special cheese and cauliflower dish and carried it up to the house, and his father had declared it, secretly when Althy was not around, the one thing that had tickled his appetite in weeks. Even though scared, she said, she had tended to the horses, feeding the mares and the stallion and letting them out to pasture by turn. She was so happy and relieved when Mr. Volmer, the neighbor, took over that job. He listened quietly, smiling to himself at these tales which were interesting in their own right but more importantly made him feel like everything was okay at home. Terry even took Althy down to Hazelwood twice, and she said she was happy to say that Sarah was very much improved and had a nice sunny room and all the people seemed very nice and really took an interest.

These reports had his undivided attention, although sometimes he got lost in the sound of her voice and missed some of what she said. But really he did not worry too much about what she said, trusting it was all to the good anyway. Her voice had changed and this new voice, belonging to someone more confident and grown-up, was what fascinated him and took his mind off the content. She didn't sound like the same girl to him anymore. That wasn't all bad, even if it did make him feel like a stranger. In fact, she sounded a lot more interesting than she used to.

One night, after he'd listened for a while to this new fully grown-up voice, he finally worked up courage to say what he had been trying to say all week but couldn't because he didn't exactly know who he was talking to anymore, and besides, words like this never came easy to him.

"Thank you for your help," he said.

"I am happy to do it," she answered.

If she'd seemed dumb and silly not so long ago, he figured it must have been because she had loved him and that incapacitating emotion had stripped her of every dignity and even immobilized her native intelligence. Now she had come to her senses and in so doing regained her competence or maybe discovered it for the first time—he wasn't sure.

As he pulled off his socks and thought about the situation, he was sorry in a way. It's no good for anybody's ego when someone gives up on you. It's like they discovered it was all a piece of deception anyway, that you were never what they thought you were, and their letdown and disappointment sends a chill through your blood; you're bound to feel a little like a cheat. Despite that palpable tinge of regret, he had to give Terry credit for wising up. He was nobody for her to waste her time on.

He washed out his underwear, put his teeth in to soak, and went to bed.

In this manner the week went along in orderly fashion and he could say—although he would have been too ashamed to admit it, considering the circumstances—that the time by and large passed pleasantly. In fact, for him this visit to the shore had ironically reverted to its original purpose. If he had been honest when his father asked him almost nightly how he was doing, he would have answered, "Great." But propriety held him down to a low-key "okay."

On Saturday the doctor said that come Monday, this lad could head for home. Although Gordie would need another four weeks or so in bed to recuperate, he could do that at home as well as anywhere. When Ward relayed that news along the wire it caused considerable jubilation in Carlisle.

"Landsakes," said Althy and "thank God," said his father.

What has he got to do with it? Ward thought. But that foxy old phantom, who in Sarah's vision wore a green celluloid eyeshade and sateen sleeve guards and looked like the old Captain, had seemed real enough to swear at the other night when the kid brother got himself plugged.

"We'll come down and help you bring Gordie home," said Terry.

"What for?" he asked. "I can handle it okay."

"With your arm in a cast? Don't be silly."

Her tone said the matter was settled. Fine. He wasn't going to argue. His objection, if his question could be called an objection, was more automatic than real. In his head a picture flared of Terry's swinging skirt and pale-peach thighs and compact little butt as she, with a quick and dance-like gesture, pulled up her sky-blue panties. This, arguably, was an image out of ancient history now, but nevertheless, behind the mirrored sunglasses his eyelids fluttered as if beating back the burning picture itself and, for some reason, the roof of his mouth began to tickle. These physical sensations were accompanied by a mixture of feelings—sorrow, he guessed, that he was still old biology's patsy, and regret, too, that he'd probably seen the last of those sturdy little legs.

On Monday, grouped together around Gordie's wheelchair— Ward at the right side with his brother's fag bag in hand and the old hospital aide at the push handles behind—they peered out the glass doors of the hospital lobby.

"You feeling okay?"

"Sure. Fine."

The kid looked kind of peaked.

"Keep that blanket wrapped around you. You don't need pneumonia on top of everything else."

Had Ward remembered to tell Terry to bring along a pillow and blanket? Yes, of course he had. He remembered now. He shifted his grip on the bag and looked out through the doors. He could always put the suitcase down, but no point to that as they'd be here any minute.

The hospital aide looked like a man used to pointless waiting. Bald and sad-faced with a tiny network of purple veins mottling his cheeks, his small-skulled head was balanced on top of a spinal curvature that made him look like a pile of blocks about to tumble over.

So they waited, three kinds of halt, maimed, and crippled, just inside the door with nothing left to say to each other, watching for some immediate sign of rescue. Just then the green VW shot into view and stopped on a dime with a motion comic and abrupt like a car in a movie cartoon.

"There they are," said Ward. "Let's go."

They started out. Gordie leaned ahead in his wheelchair as if supplying momentum to his forward progress. The old aide guided him through the automatic doors, the man dipping at the push bars in a slow swaying dancelike shuffle to compensate for the unlucky way in which nature had stacked his body.

Indeed there they were.

The door on the passenger side swung open and a well-shaped leg in a gray high-heeled shoe planted itself in the driveway. Now that ravishing leg was the first thing Gordie had seen of Avis in almost two weeks and that alone must have nearly killed him. Avis emerging from the car was really an astonishing sight. It was the first time Ward had ever seen her dressed up. Her glossy black hair was piled on top of her head, which, combined with her pale complexion, round face, and high arching eyebrows, gave her an almost oriental beauty. She wore a gray shirt-waisted dress which quietly complimented what, after all, was quite a figure. After a man has been nearly shot to death it seems unfair that his girl-friend should get all dressed up to come see him before he is fully recovered.

"Damn you, Gordon Sullivan!" she cried and smudged the tears on her cheeks. If a woman can hug a wheelchair and the man in it both at the same time, then Avis can be said to have done just that. She knelt and embraced man and machine and cried silently against Gordie's chest while he grinned with pleasure. For a second it looked like she was going to pick up both man and wheelchair and carry them off.

"You did this on purpose," she sobbed.

"Now, now," he heard his brother say.

"I let you out of my sight for a minute," she complained, "and you nearly get yourself killed. Why the hell didn't you take *care* of him?" And she shot Ward perhaps the most venomous look he'd ever experienced.

"Here now," said the kid. "I'm all right."

My, my, how things change from day to day.

Terry on the other hand came around the back of the car clad in a blue oxford cloth button-down blouse, blue jeans, and a pair of light brown saddle shoes with pink soles. Not exactly the regalia fitting a significant occasion. There is always a message in the way women dress. If you can read it right, you know just where you fit in—or out.

She came up alongside Ward and they both stood there watching the reunion, which was now being played out almost completely in mime—an affectionate hand on the cheek, another stroking the hair, a smile designed to speak volumes, and so on.

"I can see," he said to Terry by way of greeting, because Ward could see no way of commencing a conversation with her except in the middle, "that if a fellow gets shot to hell people are liable to take him seriously."

"Don't be so cynical," she said. "She loves him. She really does. It's just taken this for her to get it straight."

"That's what I mean," said Ward.

The three of them bundled Gordie into the back seat of the Cadillac convertible with pillow and blanket.

"How are we going to do this now?" Ward asked.

"I'm driving him home. You ride along with Terry."

There you go. Avis would drive home the invalid of the week, while he took his ease in the back seat. Thus she would do penance for former wrongdoing and demonstrate her revised opinion of Gordie in the process by actually driving a vehicle without surcease, except for rest stops and gasoline, for three and a half hours. Don't be cynical.

They decided not to try to keep together on the road, since Avis said she was going to go very slow and stop often to make the trip as easy as possible on Gordie.

"Okay," Ward said. "We'll see you at the house."

"No, you won't," said Avis. "Your grandmother has her hands

full now. I'm taking him back to our place where he belongs. I'll take care of him."

"Are you sure you want this kind of trouble?"

"He won't be able to paint for four weeks," Avis answered. "I've got the son of a bitch right where I want him."

On that bloodcurdling note, they separated, Avis the beautiful getting in the Cadillac convertible. He supposed she might look like some gangster's sweetheart to those passing her on the road unless they got a glimpse of the four-eyed stork in the back seat.

Terry put the key in the ignition switch of the VW and, turning to Ward, looked at him steadily.

"No fooling around, now."

He returned her gaze. Nothing in his expression, he supposed, revealed just how hopeless and sad those words of hers had struck him.

"I'm not going to fool around."

"Okay," she said. "I just want an understanding. I'm just doing a favor, that's all."

"Fine," he said. "That's fine with me."

She turned the key and the engine gnashed its teeth. Then she wrestled the shift. The VW clashed gears and jumped forward down the driveway and bounced over a series of invisible bumps out onto the highway. The engine rose punily as Terry manipulated the damn thing—car—through a series of punishments each accompanied by a forward lurch. The car rode like it didn't have any springs. Each crack in the cement jarred through the soles of his feet and snaked up his tailbone into his spine. They swerved around a corner, and, stiffly, his head and body strained after the lost inertia, him trying not to come too close to Terry for fear even accidental contact like that might be part of her definition of fooling around. Ward was prepared to be scrupulous even if it meant defying the laws of physics. He was amazed to see that the speedometer showed only forty-five. The little green car seemed to be hurtling over the road at a terrific rate, shuddering but undaunted by a series of shocks caused by nearly invisible imperfections in the road.

Out of the sides of his eyes, Ward slid in a look at her. Terry, doll-like even in this little bubble of a car, peered straight ahead over the top of the steering wheel, all business, her head tilted ahead slightly, her lips parted in concentration revealing the milk-white tips of her moderately bucked teeth. She looked completely ready for any shananigans the road of shifting concrete might try to pull, demonstrating total mastery over the little car as it angrily bucked and kicked its way out of town and onto the expressway which would head them east, toward Philadelphia.

Outside raced the marsh reeds, tall and silvergreen, stretching out like a wheatfield to the horizon, the marsh broken in places by dark estuaries where a boat or two pulled on anchor lines. A shadowlike shack here and there in a desolate clearing. The skeleton of a cabin boat lay half-exposed in the reeds, like a sea beast that had crawled onto the mud to die privately. Telephone poles whipped past. Up in the blue air a few brilliant gulls glided on wind currents which flowed in invisible channels with the driving force of rivers. Their normally snow-white wings, stationary and curved like boomerangs now, seemed overlaid with a faint blue cast, as if the birds, gliding so long in the upper air, had taken on some of the color of the sky itself.

The angry snarling of the engine filled the car and made conversation impossible. The sound soaked into his face, destroying his chances to keep up a pleasant expression, and battered his eyes till it began to hurt to look out on the blur of scrub tree and marsh anymore. It assaulted any words he might try to string together in his head, for it seemed to him he had something to tell her, something new, something she might find interesting, but the relentless drone of the little motor made it impossible for him to figure out what it might be.

So they darted along down the road, in the grip of the combustible tyranny of the outraged engine. Ward was more and more convinced that he had somehow fallen out of time during his stay at the shore and, as a result, much of what he might have had to say to Terry had become, just by sheer dint of time and distance, total nonsense.

They stopped for coffee at a Howard Johnson's on the Pennsylvania Turnpike, having twitched and jolted along together for two hours without attempting so much as a word above the admonishment of the engine. Stiffly, their muscles still cramped, they headed in separate directions for the restrooms, agreeing to meet again in the neutral precinct of the lunch counter for a cup of coffee. At that point it seemed he had nothing to say, had only one object in mind, and that was to get home and go to bed and somehow drag himself back to work in the morning. But at the lunch counter, as he fiddled with his spoon in the cup of coffee, it came on him unexpectedly. Something ballooned in his mouth, causing his teeth to pry apart, and these words fell out, onto his powdered donut, as it were. "I'm sorry," he told her in little better than a hoarse whisper.

"What?"

Terry looked at him warily, not certain what he was up to now. Given past experience, it might be anything.

For a second he was as puzzled as she was as to what those words intended to ask forgiveness for or what they were meant to explain. Then other words ballooned on his palate, escaped his teeth, and he was curious to hear what would follow next, hopeful if he talked some more he might understand what he was trying to say, even if she didn't.

"Sorry," he said. "I know I gave you a bad time. It's funny. My idea was to live quietly. The more I tried, the more complicated things got."

"You aren't trying to live quietly," said Terry. "You're trying not to live at all."

"Maybe," he said. "Maybe. All I know is the more I went after it, the more berserk things got. I know I caused you a lot of grief. I want to make it up somehow. You want that baby; I think that's too bad. But that's your business. I'm not going to try to stop you."

"That's damn nice of you," she said.

"Maybe I didn't say it so it sounds right. You said when we started out today no fooling around. Well, I can tell you I'm through fooling around. What you want to do is your business. It always was. I'm just saying, now I know it too."

"Thank you," she said and moved as if to get up. He put his hand on her arm, withdrew it quickly as if from a hot stove. He didn't want to interfere with her, offend her, and he could certainly understand how touching her, if she didn't want to be touched, was a damn physical insult, as outrageous as a slap across the face.

"No, wait," he said, "Let's not go yet. Nobody can talk in that damn car. Let me finish, now that I've got started."

"All right," she said, subsiding into her place.

"I thought you were just dumb," he said. "But you're not. You're good. I don't think I could tell the difference before."

"Thanks."

"You know when Gordie was lying there on the pavement I thought to myself: that's it; there he goes—the last person on earth."

For the first time she seemed interested, not merely cautious.

"What do you mean?"

"I mean I thought: if he dies, there's nobody else left. Althy is old, my Dad is just about finished. Sarah is living on the farm, circa 1920. I thought to myself: well, now you have what you want; you're all alone at last. It didn't feel very good."

"You're so dumb. I could have told you that."

"I know. I know you tried to. It scared me, I can tell you. This is stupid, I know. But let me say it anyway. Maybe you and I ought to work out something together."

"What?"

"I mean you're going to have this baby. Maybe you could use some help."

"Are you talking about marriage?"

"No, not exactly. I don't think I could handle anything like that. But maybe you could use somebody around the place to help out. I'd pay my share, help out with the baby. We could see what happens."

"Ward."

"What's that."

"It's time to move on."

"I know," he said. He wanted to add that's what he was trying to do, but he suddenly felt breathless.

"I gave you my love and it didn't mean a thing to you."

"I know," he repeated, acknowledging that she had told him that before, in the hallway after the failed trip to Dr. Brown just before she slugged him with her purse to punctuate the gravity of her statement. Maybe that's why it sank in that time.

"You can't just give and give and not have it accepted," she said.

"Yes." He knew that too.

"I feel sorry for you," Terry said, "I do love you still for some reason. God, I don't know why. But it doesn't matter anymore. Past a certain point you have to make do with the way things are and not kid yourself."

"It's still possible we could work something out," he suggested feebly.

"No we couldn't. I'm sorry, Ward. I want this baby to myself now. I don't want to gamble. I know I can love him enough, give him everything he needs to be a good child."

He looked at her.

"There's a baby forming in me, Ward. He's in a hurry. There isn't any time for other stuff."

She smiled when she said this, but he knew damn well that smile wasn't for him.

"I'd like to help out," he said.

"I don't need any help. I'll get along just fine."

"Let me help in some way."

"I don't—"

"Anyway you say. Call on me. Will you?"

"If I need help, I will call on you."

"Thank you," he said, absolutely sure that this little girl would never need any kind of help he could offer.

E I G H T E E N

THE NEXT THING Ward did came naturally enough. In the morning, without thinking about it, he got out of bed, put on his clothes, and started for town on his bicycle.

He pedaled along the Merkleburg Pike in a ripe humid silence, periodically overwhelmed by an occasional car or truck screaming down on him like an aircraft in a powerdive. It would explode past, setting off a whirlwind of roadside trash—bouncing coffee cups and swirling hot dog wrappers—and spraying gravel over his legs and bicycle. As he swayed in a warm blast of gasoline-scented air, the vehicle shrank rapidly, almost comically, before his eyes, penetrating the distant road ahead with the whine of a high-speed drill. Then up rose the weed-rank quiet of the surrounding fields again, and Ward steadied and cycled on, conscious only of the need to get to town and get the job done now that he'd made up his mind.

Even though it was humid, the wind of his own going kept him comfortable. By now he was used to the cast on his arm and rode along without difficulty. It was never too hot to ride the bike. The old hip kicked up a little bit. Jagged and sharper at the socket, a little dull current of pain ran down as far as his kneecap. But nothing serious. Soon he was riding down South Hanover Street, past the striped neckties and pastel shirts on display in the window of Hobart's Clothing Store. He glided past the pockmarked columns of the courthouse and cycled around back where he chained his bike to the pipe railing of the stairs leading down to the public convenience.

When he entered Sharfman's office, he found the attorney pasted to his chair, working amid a welter of paper on his big oak desk.

"Young Mr. Sullivan," said Sharfman, by way of greeting. As

he turned, the paper he'd been writing on stuck to his hand. Attorney Sharfman was chewing vigorously on a stump of a cigar and spewing smoke in several different directions.

"I see you took up smoking again."

"Be damned," said Sharfman. "A man dies anyway. What's up, son?"

"Found this," Ward said, pulling the papers out of his belt. "Looks like his will."

"Well, well. Finally found it." The pieces of blue ladies' paper still in hand, Sharfman turned a little in his creaking swivel chair. Ward got the full view of his ponderous belly, the heavy, pensive lip and the iron-gray crewcut.

"Where'd you come across it, anyway?"

"It was in his stuff, in his bag from the hospital. We just never bothered to unpack it till now. I asked him last night if this was his will, and he said yes and told me to bring it down here."

This will be my last lie, thought Ward. Won't that be nice?

"Fine," said Sharfman. "I'll call him now."

"He's pretty sick," said Ward.

"I know," said Sharfman. "But this is important."

Naturally, his father confirmed everything on the phone. Why had he worried at all? Of course his father would swear to what he said. The attorney did a lot of listening. He listened so hard that the sweat ran out of his crewcut and down into his collar. When he hung up, Sharfman said, "Your father said he doesn't want you to hang around town after you finish here. He wants you to come right home."

"Okay."

Now Sharfman might think those were instructions you gave a twelve-year-old boy, not a man in his thirties. But these directions, simple and clear beyond a shadow of a doubt, suited Ward just fine. It was nice, if not a relief, to have others such as his father tell him what he should do even with respect to simple things. It went without saying that more complicated matters were best left in the hands of those who seemed eager to deal with them. Or perhaps they were best ignored altogether in the interest of maintaining the natural balance of things.

"How'd you hurt your arm?" Sharfman asked.

"I punched a door jamb by accident."

"You still punching doors at your age?"

"Some of us are slow learners."

"Have a cigar," Sharfman suggested.

"Thank you," said Ward dropping the offered cigar down the front of his T-shirt. Who knows? Maybe the old man might want to smoke a cigar sometime.

Ward stopped at the news store in the shopping center on the edge of town to buy a *Wall Street Journal* for his father who would enjoy looking through the numbers in the back. Then he pedaled back out the Pike, taking the grades easily, not killing himself, going along at a steady relaxed pace but keeping a weather eye out for maniacs in automobiles.

He went right to his father's room and found him sitting up in bed, looking brighter and more chipper than he had for weeks. Even some of the yellow seemed to have faded from his face.

"Hey, boy."

"Hey, Dad. How you feeling?"

"Feeling pretty good. What's this?"

"*Wall Street Journal*. Thought you might want a gander at it."

"Oh. Hey. Thanks. So you got the will down to Sharfman?"

No overtone. No undertone. Just a statement.

"Right."

Nothing more than that. Not: how come you didn't take it right down there when I gave it to you nearly three months ago? No questions. The old man had lived a long time with Sarah and knew the true futility of questions.

Instead he repeated, "I'm feeling pretty good."

"That's good," said Ward.

"You decide not to go to work today?" asked his father.

"Yes, I did. I decided not to go tomorrow, too. In fact, I decided not to go back at all."

"Well, it's a real education," his father smiled. "Wonders never cease, do they? Did you call to check on your brother this morning?"

"Yes, I did that. He was still asleep. Avis says the trip home pooped him out. He *looks* all right though, she says."

"Good," said his father. "Good. Well, since you're a free man, how about you taking me for a ride? It looks like a nice day out there."

"Are you sure you ought to?"

His father just looked at him.

"You mean there are some things I shouldn't do at this stage? What would they be? I'm curious. I'd like to know what it is I ought to avoid."

"You want to go for a ride."

"Right. You going to take me?"

"Yes. I'll take you all right."

"Okay, then. Get me some clothes."

In the dresser Ward dredged up a clean white shirt, jockey shorts, and V-necked T-shirt, and black socks, the only kind his father had ever owned. He even wore them with his one pair of bermuda shorts. In the closet he located a pair of pleated navy-blue slacks with a black leather belt still in the loops. From the rack on the closet door hung a colorful row of knotted neckties. His father never unknotted them. Instead he slipped them on and off over his head, tightening and loosening them in some notion of time-saving he'd picked up somewhere. Ward guessed leaving the belt in his pants was the same idea.

Ward helped the sick man out of his short cotton pajamas and into his clothes. He fetched a pair of black wingtips from the closet, the kind his father had always favored. It was a thirties style but had never faded in popularity with the old man, like the Vaseline hair tonic he still used, that close-up made him smell a little like hard-rock candy. Some habits you just don't break.

"I don't want to wear those things," his father said, meaning the shoes. "I want something more comfortable on my feet."

"Well, put on the socks anyway while I look around. What about a pair of slippers?"

"Slippers? You mean those woolly-lined leather slippers that Althy gave me? It's summertime, you know."

"Well, I don't know what you want."

"Come over here and help me with these socks. My damned fingers won't work right."

Ward rolled the black over-the-calf hose over his father's white toes, strangely cold in all this heat, and pulled them up his marble-white hairless shanks.

"There. How's that?"

"That's fine. Now what about something comfortable?"

"How about my canoe shoes? They're comfortable. You want to wear them?"

"Bring them up here, let me look at them. I tell you what."

He was dressed now in the crisp white shirt and baggy navy-blue pants, with his black-stockinged feet dangling over the side of the bed.

"Reach up there in the closet and see if you can find that Stetson hat your mother gave me two Christmases ago."

"What?" Ward looked at him smiling. *What are you up to?*

The old man smiled back. "Reach up there and see if you can find it."

"Good gravy," said Ward. "We're going for some fancy ride, aren't we?"

Ward found the creamy cattle baron's Stetson in its black round box at the top of the closet. He took the virginal hat out of the tissue paper and handed it to his father who put it on his head with real satisfaction.

"Ah," he said. "How's that look?"

"Looks good."

It made his face look thinner and the circles under his eyes darker.

"All right. Where are those canoe shoes you promised me? Let's get *going.*"

Suddenly the old man was in a big hurry.

Ward got him the shoes. He put them on, wiggled his toes critically and decided they were all right.

"You want some help?" Ward asked when his father wobbled as he stood up.

"I'll be fine. Just let me lean on your shoulder."

They started out into the hallway, weaving like two drunken cowhands. Althy was in the kitchen, her back to them, busy at something. Ward started to speak but his father held up his hand, Indian fashion. *Just keep going,* he signed. *Just go on.*

So they crept down the hall and out into the double garage where the two Cadillacs sat side by side.

"Which one do you want to take?"

"I'm not going to ride around in that antique of yours," his father grinned. "We'll take mine." He spoke in a jailbreak whisper, apparently worried that Althy would catch them.

When Ward opened the car door for him, the old man threw himself on the black leather seat. Ward backed the big convertible out of the garage and on down the driveway they went to the highway. No sign of Althy. A clean getaway. The old man touched

the control button and his window slid out of sight with a faint
electric whirr. The humid breeze smacked him in the face and
twiddled the wings of his shirt collar. He took off the Stetson and
put it on the seat next to him as gently as if it were an egg.

"How you doing," Ward asked him.

"I'm doing just fine."

"You want the air conditioner on?"

"No, no. I want some fresh air. I'm tired of having my air
conditioned."

"Where do you want to go?"

"I don't know. Anywhere. Just drive around."

They went south on the Pike and just outside Merkleburg cut
onto an old road that took them to the half-dozen houses of Craigs
Head.

An iron bridge spanned the Yellow Breeches creek here, and as
they crossed over his father said, "Let's stop for a minute."

Ward parked next to an old shed painted egg-white. A fisherman in waders, up to his knees in the stream, cast his rod, flexible
as a buggy whip, within the shimmering grid of the bridge's
shadow. Ward's father opened his door and got out. His clothes
bagged on him as he stood there, thin as a stick watching the
fisherman, looking around, taking things in. The katydids buzzed
lazily in the forenoon heat as the old man stretched and looked up
at the haze that had bleached the sky and turned the surrounding
hills blue. Along the creek, the leaves of the buttonwoods were dry
and dusty. His father's baggy shirt was pressed to his skinny chest
by the damp breeze.

"This is nice. It's been a long time since I've been out this way.
You have a cigarette on you?"

"Yes, I've got a cigarette. You want one?"

"Yes. I'd like one, thanks. I haven't had one in probably six
weeks. This seems like a good day to have one."

Ward shook out a pair and they lighted up. Leaning together
against the side of the white Cadillac convertible, they smoked
their cigarettes and watched the stranger cast his line, working the
shadows and the edges of the current of the brown fast-moving
stream.

"This is all right. Too bad we don't have something to drink."

Ward stopped in mid-motion, his cigarette pinched in the circle
of his thumb and forefinger.

"Something to drink?" He smiled. *What are you up to?*

"Yes, something to drink. I haven't had a drink in days. I'd like something to drink I believe," his father grinned back almost shyly. True confessions.

"Aren't you getting tired?"

"No, I'm not tired. I'll let you know if I get tired. Why don't we go find a State Store?"

"Okay. But I better call Althy to let her know what we're up to, so she won't be worried."

"That sounds reasonable," his father said.

They drove into Boiling Springs. Ward left his father sitting in the car, smoking a cigarette, and watching the swans glide along the pond, while he crossed the road to call Althy from the old stone tavern.

"What in hell do you think you're doing?" she hollered into the telephone.

"It's all right. He's with me," said Ward.

"Terry and I have been worried sick. What are you doing with that poor man out there?"

"It's okay. He just wanted to go for a ride. That's all. I'm just taking him for a ride like he asked."

"That man is *sick.* Don't you know that? He ought to be home in bed."

It was hard to figure why it was okay for a dying man to be on his back at home but not all right for him to be out riding around.

"It's okay. He's with me," said Ward and hung up on her.

He bought a six-pack of Budweiser, a pack of Camels, and went back out to the car.

"You check in?" his father asked. But he didn't sound interested.

"Yes. You want one of these?"

"Yes. I'd like one of those."

His father pulled the tab off and glugged a little from the can. He held up the can and looked at it like he'd never seen one before. His face was patchy with prickly heat; he looked tired but happy. "I still want a real drink," he said, the voice bluff, trying to cover his embarrassment.

"Fine. We'll go back to town and get you a real drink. You want to stop at a bar?"

"No." The old man was definite. No dark bar with a few sad strangers.

"Just stop at a State Store and get a bottle," his father suggested. "We'll just have a drink as we go along."

Pretty soon the milk-dipped spires of the town loomed wanly in the humidity. Ward drove the Cadillac under the cool shadows of the maple trees along Hanover Street and parked in front of the State Store.

"You want something particular?" Ward asked.

His father sat on the black leather seat in his baggy clothes stroking his cream-colored Stetson like a lap dog. "No, just anything. Get something you like. Here."

He pulled a twenty dollar bill out of his baggy pants.

"I don't want you to pay all the expenses on this ride."

Ward went inside and bought a bottle of Wolfschmidt's vodka and a bottle of Johnnie Walker scotch. Next door at the corner grocery, he purchased a jar of big Spanish olives and some plastic glasses. When he came back to the car the Stetson was on the front seat, and his father had crawled in back.

"I'm tired," he explained. "I'll just take a little nap." He looked gray and very sick again.

"Sure you don't want to go home? You don't want to overdo it."

"Just drive around," his father told him. "I'll be okay. Why don't you put the top down?"

Ward put the top down. The hot sun socked him in the head. He wished he'd brought his sunglasses. He drove under the cool maples again out to the Gulf station near the War College, filled up the car, and bought a five-pound plastic bag of ice cubes, putting a quarter in the Arctic ice machine they had there. He made himself a martini, sitting right there at the gasoline pump. Wasn't this a filling station?

His father sat up.

"Where's my drink?"

He opened the door, climbed out painfully, and got in the front seat.

"You ready for one?"

"Yes," he said. "Never mind. I'll make my own. You just drive."

Ward drove along as his father fumbled the ice cubes out of the plastic bag, dropped a couple of olives into the plastic glass, then poured the vodka.

"Ah," he said on the first sip. The collar wings of his white shirt were flapping in the breeze and the sun was full in his face.

"Ah," he said. "That's not bad. All this ice is going to melt though. Pull over here."

They were just riding up and down the side streets of Carlisle with the top down, sipping their vodka martinis like a couple of farmers in town on Saturday morning. Right now they were in front of a variety store on Pomfret Street. Ward went along as his father wobbled around the aisles till he found what he wanted— a picnic chest, enamel blue with an aluminum lid. They put the ice cubes and the olives and the beer in the chest.

"There. That's better. Now, I want you to stop at the bank."

Ward looked at him. *What are you up to now?*

They drove back down to the square and parked in front of the Farmers' Trust. Ward went in with him. Mr. Morris, the teller, was surprised to see his father.

"Why, Mr. Sullivan. How are you?"

"Good, Jim. Feeling better. I'd like you to take care of this."

He finished filling out the withdrawal slip.

"Any particular way, Mr. Sullivan?"

"Hundreds will be fine, Jim."

The teller reached into his neat little drawer of bills, drew out some slim brand-new packs of one-hundred dollar bills, and counted out twenty on the white marble counter. The old man folded them, nodded to Mr. Morris, and shoved the money into his pants pocket. They walked outside.

"What's all this about?" Ward said as they slid into the hot leather seats. His father's face was thin and drawn but he was smiling, and he looked happy.

"Well," he said. He looked even yellower in the sunlight. "I thought we'd just keep riding around for a while longer. I'm enjoying this. We might need some gas money or something."

"Two thousand dollars for gas money. You have any place in mind?"

"Oh, I don't know. What do you think?"

"I'll go anywhere you want to go," Ward said, cards on the table.

"Well, as a matter of fact there is a place I'd like to go."

"Where's that?"

"I'd like to go home," his father said.

"Pardon me?"

"Maine," he said. "Why don't we take a little ride up to Maine? I haven't seen the Kennebec in ten years or better."

"You sure you want to do this?"

"Yes, I'm sure. What do you say? Or do I have to get another driver?"

"I'll do it. But are you sure?" Ward looked at the sick man. "Are you sure you want to do this?"

"Look, son. You drive. When I tell you to stop, you stop. When I tell you to talk, you talk. We'll make it all right."

"Okay," said Ward. "When do you want to start?"

"We've already started."

"But we don't have any clothes. They'll be worried at home."

"We can buy what we need, and we can call them. But we'll call them later, not just now. Let's stop at Sears on the way out."

At the flat hot shopping center on the edge of town his father said, "Put the top up. The sun's giving me a headache."

Looking haggard, he opened a can of Bud but was hardly able to get it to his lips.

"I'll just sit here," he said. "I want you to go in there and buy a pillow, a pillowcase, and a light blanket."

The old man sat there for a moment, his lids so heavy he could barely keep his eyes open. He turned wearily toward Ward. "Anything else you can think of? Anything you want to bring along?"

"No, I guess not."

"Okay then. I'll just lie down here and wait for you."

When Ward got back with the things, his father stretched out on the back seat with his new pillow and blanket. By this time he wanted the air conditioning on. Ward left the car running in front of the Giant Market so his father would stay cool as he ran in for a few things. He was still asleep when he got back with the bag of groceries. Ward made up the sandwiches, ham and cheese with mustard and butter on rye bread, wrapped them in Glad Wrap and put them in the picnic chest along with the dill pickles and cans of ginger ale he'd bought. He put the sticks of butter and the mustard in the chest too. When he got out and put the chest on the floor of the back seat, the old man never stirred. Then Ward drove toward Harrisburg, picked up Route 22 at Colonial Park and headed through the iron-red farmlands of Lebanon County. Outside Allentown, his father said in a deathly whisper, "Pull over, boy."

Ward pulled the car off the road at the first place he could. The old man got out slowly with his pillow and blanket, climbed over the guard rail and started up the mild grade of a grassy hill. Ward watched till he disappeared over the crest, grabbed a couple of cans of Bud out of the back, then followed. When he caught up with him, he had spread his blanket in the grass on the far side of the hill away from the highway noise and was fast asleep. Ward sat down on the blanket beside him and pulled the tab ring off a can of beer. He looked at the sky. The humidity was letting up; a pale blue glimmered through the soup now. It was probably four o'clock, about four hours or so of daylight left. They would have to call home pretty soon before everybody went out of their minds. He hugged his knees, drank his beer, and watched his father sleep.

Think baseball, he thought. Think baseball. In 1926 the Detroit Tigers had an outfield. Heinie Manush batted .378. Harry Heilman hit .367, and so did Fats Fothergill. Fothergill earned his nickname. He was five feet ten and weighed 230. He moved like a freight train down the rails, but he played for twelve years and hit .323 lifetime. Yet nobody ever heard of him. Maybe it was the best hitting outfield ever in the game, although there have been many.

At a gas station on the Garden State Parkway, Ward called home.

Althy, sounding like a crow, cawed into the telephone.

"Ward, damn you! Where are you? Why haven't you come home for supper? That poor man has medicine to take."

"Look, Althy," Ward said. "He wants to ride around. Okay? He's sick and he wants to go for a ride, so I'm taking him. Anywhere he wants to go. You understand? I just called you to tell you, we're okay. We'll be out of touch for a few days, but we're all right."

"Ward—"

"Don't worry. We're all right. I'll call you in a couple of days," he finished and hung up on her.

The technique seemed to work fine. You said what you wanted to say and hung up. Telephones were a fine invention if you didn't let them get away from you. Don't answer the ring unless you've got nothing to do or are looking for trouble. Reverse the charges when you call long distance. Hang up after you finish saying what you want to, especially with Althy. It didn't seem right to tell her where they were headed. It was bound to make her mad, although he couldn't figure why. He'd call again once they got there, tell her, and then hang up before she could go through the song and dance about sick man, bed, and medicine to take. That was better. Saying anything in advance might lessen their chances of doing it. He was just superstitious enough to believe that.

About the time they crossed the slate-gray Hudson at Tarry-town, his father said, "You talk for a while. I'll just rest, and you talk."

"Talk? What do you want me to talk about?"

"I don't care. Talk about anything. Talk baseball. Tell me one of your stories."

He was holding that cream-puff hat in his lap again, holding it carefully so as not to disturb it as if it were a sleeping cat.

"Okay," said Ward. "I'll tell you a story that Mr. Coombs told me when I was little. He used to tell good stories. You remember him?"

"I sure do. He was a fine gentleman."

"Yes," agreed Ward. "He was some good batting practice pitcher. Well, he told me this story. I was probably ten at the time. Granpa was there, he seemed to know it. We were sitting in the front room at Dunnocks Head one summer evening, and Mr. Coombs turned to me and he said, 'Son, have I ever told you the story of the man who stole first base?' And he told me this story. You all right?"

"Fine. Go ahead with your story."

"Well, there was a player by the name of Germany Schaefer who was a clown, a journeyman ballplayer, but pretty good any-way. He played for Detroit in the early 1900s, about 1907, '08, around then. One day in a game against Cleveland the score was tied in the late innings. Schaefer was on first, and Davy Jones was on third base. Schaefer signaled for the double steal, which meant he was taking off for second on the next pitch. To draw the throw from the catcher. Then Jones was to take off for home with the lead run. Well, the pitcher wound up and Schaefer took off with a big whoop and holler for second base. But the Cleveland catcher,

ol' Nig Clark, he was too smart to throw down to second. He just
held on to the ball.

"Now the Tigers had runners on second and third, and on the
next pitch Schaefer hollered 'Let's try it again!' and let out another
whoop and took off for first base and dove in head first in a cloud
of dust. Clarke just sat there and stared, and so did everybody else
in the park. The damn fool had just stolen first base. Nobody had
ever run backwards on the bases before. There was no rule against
it. The umpires just stood there and scratched their heads like the
rest of the crowd. So there it was. First and third again. On the next
pitch be damned if Schaefer didn't let out another whoop and take
off for second again. By this time Clarke had had all he could
stand, and he let fly with the ball, and Jones started in from third,
and Schaefer beat the throw at second, and the throw back to
home was late, Jones scoring, and Detroit won the game by that
one run. And that's how Germany Schaefer stole first base."

"Ha, ha, ha," his father shouted. "That's a good story. I like it."

"That's the last time it ever happened," Ward explained. "Because right after that they made a rule that you had to keep
moving counterclockwise along the bases. They made it so you
couldn't go back."

"Well, how about that," his father said.

"So Germany Schaefer was the only man who ever stole first
base in the history of the game. That's what Mr. Coombs told me."

"Be damned," said Gordon Sullivan.

They rode along the lovely old sedate Merritt Parkway, a road
curving and climbing and dipping among neatly trimmed lawns
and nicely barbered trees. They crossed over the Housatonic and
picked up the Wilbur Cross Parkway. There were lots of toll
booths on the Wilbur Cross; you fed the Wilbur Cross quarters.

"Did you know this road is named after an English professor?"
his father asked. He had just made himself a martini with double
olives and handed Ward a can of Bud.

"No, I didn't know that," said Ward.

"Well, almost," his father said. "This fellow Wilbur Cross
taught English at Yale and wrote books. He was famous. He was
also governor of Connecticut in the thirties. That's probably why
they named the road after him, instead of for teaching English at
Yale, don't you think?"

The old man had taken on a funny bantering tone of voice, and Ward went along with it.

"Yes, probably. Governors have roads and hospitals named after them. English teachers don't."

"You're right," agreed his father. "It almost happened here though. It would have been refreshing. Cause even to consider this state the center of civilization."

They worked their way to Sturbridge where they stopped at the Yankee Drummer Inn for the night.

"Find a place to stop," his father had whispered and hunched in his blanket against the door.

Ward drove around to the first floor room and parked the car. His father was still asleep against the door.

"Dad."

"Uhh?"

"We're here. You need some help?"

"Son of God," his father moaned.

Ward went around to his side, opened his door, and practically lifted him out. He was unnaturally light and fragile feeling.

"Bring my hat. And the picnic box."

Ward settled the frail man on one of the four-poster maple twin beds. The room was furnished in bogus colonial fashion with a lively wallpaper pattern. His father didn't want to take his clothes off, just his shoes and socks, and he wanted to sleep wrapped in his Sears Roebuck summer light blanket. Ward put the hat on the nightstand where his father could get it if he wanted. No sooner was he settled awkwardly on the narrow bed than the sick man crashed into unconsciousness, his head thrown back on the pillow, his mouth open in an attitude of total exhaustion. Ward sat on the bed and smoked and strained to see the faint signs of his father's breathing. He looked horrible. Think baseball, Ward thought. Just keep thinking baseball.

In the morning Gordon Sullivan was yellow again and looked one hundred years old. It took Ward a while to wake him up. He let him sleep till it looked like they were going to run up against checkout time, 11 A.M., and then he shook his arm gently.

"Jesus, Mary, and Joseph," his father said opening his eyes a crack and blinking painfully against the brutal daylight.

"We have to get out of here," said Ward, "unless you want to

pay another day's rent. Maybe it wouldn't be a bad idea if we
stayed another day. You could rest up. We could go over to
Old Sturbridge Village in the afternoon if you want and look
around—"

"No," his father was up on one elbow now. "Let's keep moving.
Didn't one of your ballplayers say something like that? Didn't you
tell me that once?"

"Yes. It was Satchel Paige. Satch said, 'Keep moving and never
look back. Something might be gaining on you.' "

"That's right," his father smiled. "Let's keep moving."

"Fine. You hungry? Want any breakfast?"

"No. We still have some beer, don't we?"

"Yes, I bought some Narraganset just before we stopped last
night."

"Well, I'll have a can of beer. Help me with my socks. No, no,
boy. Get the can of beer first."

As the old man drank his beer, Ward rolled on his socks, zipped
up his canoe shoes, and finished by handing him his cattle baron's
hat. Ward left his father sitting in the Cadillac listening to the
news on one of the Boston stations, while he found the ice machine and freshened up the picnic chest.

They drove downtown. In a drugstore, Ward bought a leather
travel kit and stocked it with razor, blades, a can of shaving cream,
aftershave, a couple of black hardrubber combs, a little shaving
mirror, Ipana toothpaste, toothbrushes, one red and the
other green, and a little white plastic container of J & J tooth
string.

There was a men's haberdashery next door with a striped awn-
ing cranked out over the sidewalk. Ward went in there and bought
a couple of changes of underwear for both of them, some middle-
weight white athletic socks for himself and a couple pair of over-
the-calf black socks for his father Then he went a little crazy and
bought the old man a bottle-green short-sleeved sportshirt, another Manhattan white shirt, and a pair of khaki slacks. While he
was at it he got himself a pair of khakis and a navy blue T-shirt.
He paid for these items with one of his father's crisp hundred
dollar bills, got them to put everything in a cardboard box, and,
feeling more than ever like Clyde Barrow on the lam, went back
to the car.

His father was feeling poorly. They drove till they found a gas

station, and had the attendant fill it up and check the oil. Then
Ward parked the Cadillac over by the restrooms. His father lay
down across the front seat, while Ward peeled the old black socks
off and put on a pair of new ones.

"There now. Doesn't that feel better?"

"Sure it does," his father answered in a small, exhausted voice.

Ward retired to the restroom with the cardboard box and shaving kit. He changed his clothes and shaved. He felt a lot better after
that. He tried to get the old man to go in the restroom and shave,
but he just wasn't up to it. So Ward opened the door, propped him
up on the edge of the seat with his feet on the ground, and with
his light blanket around his shoulders like a barber's sheet, Ward
lathered him up and shaved him. The old man sat patiently
through this with his hat on his lap, his eyes closed, not speaking.
His face looked very yellow against the white lather.

They got on the Massachusetts Turnpike and headed for Boston. It was a nice day, high hard blue sky, cool New England
weather.

"Goddamn," his father said, apparently revived by the flawless
sky, the hard edges of the trees and houses. "This is a nice ride,
isn't it?"

It was moving on toward noon. He was trying to eat half a ham
and cheese sandwich but having better luck with his vodka martini.

About one o'clock, still west of Boston, he asked Ward to pull
over. He'd gone a gray-green; his eyes were glassy and bulged out
of his head. Ward stopped the Cadillac on the shoulder of the
road, and the old man dragged his pillow and blanket over the
guard rail and collapsed right there. Ward sat on the guard rail,
smoking and drinking beer and watching the traffic pass by. Once
or twice the Staties passed, and he hid the beer under his new
T-shirt, the can almost unbearably cold against his belly. A little later,
his father woke and didn't seem to know where he was.

"Boy?" he whispered. "What the hell's going on? Where am I,
anyway? What am I doing out of bed?" He was cold and clammy,
covered with a fine sweat, his eyes bulged out of his head and his
tongue seemed to stick to the roof of his mouth.

Ward took him by the hand, helped him up, and got him to sit
down on the guard rail.

"We're just out for a ride, Dad. Right? We're just going for a ride. How you feeling now?"

His father shut his eyes and nodded his head: all right. A wave of hot air, like a shock wave from an explosion, struck them from a car that streaked by with a tearing sound. They sat together on the guard rail, Ward watching his father whose eyes were still shut, neither of them saying anything or finding any need to.

"Help me," his father said after a while. "I don't think I can get back in the car."

Ward helped him get back in, and they started out again.

"Talk," said his father. "Tell me some more baseball."

Ward shook out a couple of cigarettes and lighted them both up. "The Red Sox," he said handing him a cigarette. "Still playing tough. Yazstremski is having a wonderful year."

"Yazstremski," said his father. "The man who made them forget Williams."

"No, there'll never be another Williams."

"Pull over," his father said.

Ward pulled the Cadillac to the shoulder of the road. His father threw open the door and had a case of the dry heaves for about fifteen minutes. Ward smoked and tried not to watch him or to listen. When they were back on the road, Gordon Sullivan cracked a couple of cans of beer. They rode along in the air-conditioning, the rushing green world outside, the streaking cars signaling in the bright high sunlight, reeling in the long, monotonous stretches of macadam punctuated by the morse code of the broken white line.

When they crossed the New Hampshire line, Ward stopped at a market and bought a cold case of Narraganset and some more ice and stocked up the picnic chest again. They were out of the ham and cheese sandwiches, but neither of them was hungry anyway.

About four in the afternoon they reached the toll bridge at Portsmouth and crossed over into Kittery.

"Here we are," said Ward.

"The Piscataqua is not a river," said the old man. "And Kittery is not a town. Show me a real river. Show me a real town."

"What town? What river?"

"Take me down to the Kennebec. That's a real river."

They went up the Maine Turnpike, which pierced straight arrow through the pinewoods and the granite ridges. It was a lovely afternoon. They turned off the air-conditioning and rolled down the windows.

"Smell that air," his father said. "It's actually *fragrant*. It's so clean it smells good."

Ward exited at Falmouth and they ran along down Route 1.

He looked over at his father who was taking everything in quietly

"How do you like it?"

"I like it fine. It's beautiful country. Must have been crazy to move away from here. How do you like it?"

"It's good. It's a great trip."

In Brunswick, Ward stopped at Mike's Hot Dog Stand to get a couple with everything. Granpa and he used to make this a regular stop on Saturdays if they were up this way. Ward was hungry, having had nothing all day except for the Narraganset. Now he was feeling headachy from the sun and the beer and definitely ready for a little food.

"You want something, Dad? How about a hot dog?"

"No thanks. I'm not hungry."

Gordon Sullivan sat with the blanket around his shoulders like a shawl. He looked very small and thin and very sick.

Ward got out and started toward the store, but his father signaled him back to the car. He was sitting there wrapped in the blanket, looking at Ward with a faint smile on his gaunt yellow face.

"What is it, Dad?"

"You got a cigarette?" he asked.

"Yes, sure. Here."

Ward shook one out. The old man took it in his thin yellow fingers but made no move to light it.

"Here," Ward said. "You want a light?"

"No," his father smiled. "Not just yet. Thanks, son."

"Okay," said Ward. "I'll be out in a minute."

"Right," his father said.

Inside the shop, pungent with the smell of hot dogs and onions, it was dark and it took a second for Ward's eyes to adjust after the bright daylight.

"Mawnin'" said the fellow behind the counter.

"I don't suppose you have any limeade on the premises?" Ward asked him.

"No, all's we got in that line is Orange Crush."

"No, it's sublimeade I'm after."

"Pahd'n?"

"Never mind. Just give me a bottle of Moxie."

Ward was hungry as all get out. He bought two hot dogs with everything. He hadn't had a bottle of Moxie since the last time he was in Maine, twelve years ago. When he got back to Dunnocks Head, the first thing he'd always do was to walk up to Nicholson's Variety Store and get a bottle of Moxie. Sipping that cool bitter drink was all the evidence he needed to know that he was home for sure. Now he took a swig of the bitter drink and started out the door with his two hot dogs.

As he walked back to the Cadillac, he saw that his father had pulled his hat at a jaunty angle down over his eyes. He seemed to have fallen asleep in the corner made by the angle of the leather seat and the door. But when Ward opened his door, he knew it was more than sleep this time. His father was too still. Below the dude ranch hat, the sweat pasted his fine hair to his forehead. The blanket had fallen away, exposing the wrinkled two-day old white shirt; he was motionless as a photograph.

"Dad."

Ward shook his father gently by the arm. But it was no good. He was really dead. Ward got out of the car and dumped the hot dogs into the trash bin outside of Mike's. He swigged his Moxie and looked across the street at the empty bandshell on the commons. Brunswick was a nice little town. Williams was a better hitter than Musial. He was probably a better hitter than Ruth, maybe even better than Cobb. He looked back at the Cadillac, and the dude asleep against the window.

Ward got back in the car and drove down past Bowdoin College and Ernie's Drive-In, down the back road past the Navy Air Station to Bath. He drove downtown, past the sepia brick buildings circa 1890, the staunch old Federalist post office, originally the Customs House, past Shaw's Bookstore and the concrete town hall with its sun-struck golden cupola, right down to the Public Landing. There was the navy-blue Kennebec and, down river, the steel bridge, painted green, with the elevated center section that glided up and down to let the ships pass through. It was a fine sight.

"There's the Kennebec," Ward whispered to the dude ranch hat. "There's that damn river you wanted to see."

He drove the Cadillac up the hill to Washington Street where all the big, square white houses of the old ship captains were and he turned left and went on down across Center to High until he came to Ewell Saltonstall's Funeral Home. He hadn't seen Ewell Saltonstall for fifteen years, since they played town team baseball together. Ewell played third base and wasn't bad. He had an offer from the Browns, but he was a realist, sensing that his talent was estimable whereas death was limitless, and so he decided to go into the funeral parlor business with his uncle.

Ward lighted a cigarette and went up the walk to the big house, the best looking one, naturally, on the block. He rang the bell. Ewell himself opened the door. He was wearing glasses and a suit and had a belly on him. With that postman's bag fastened like a leech to his middle, he'd never in this life get down for another ground ball.

"Hello, Ewell."

"Well, for Pete's sake! Ward Sullivan," he cried. "Where did you come from? I haven't seen you in fifteen years!"

"Ewell?" The tone of Ward's voice put aside the social questions.

"What?" Ewell's face changed to dead serious.

"I need you to help me with my father."

"Your father?"

"Yes. That's him out there."

Ewell Saltonstall's eyes followed the line laid out by the jerk of Ward's head, to the big white Cadillac convertible at the curb. It looked like there was a cowboy asleep against the door.

NINETEEN

I'LL TAKE CARE of everything."

Good old Ewell.

Ward allowed his old teammate to lead him into the hall. He wobbled as he walked. His legs, he discovered, had turned to mush.

"You want me to drive the car around back?"

"No, no. I'll take care of it," said Ewell. "Give me the keys."

"What?"

"Do you have the keys to the car?"

"Yes. Right here." Ewell's twinkling blue eyes and robust dark hair, his air of friendly competency made Ward just want to turn everything over to him.

"I'll take care of everything," said Ewell. "You just wait here." His good-natured face was moderately flushed, purplish around the nose. The whites of his eyes were a little yellow. Otherwise he looked healthy. He was calm, had things well under control. A fellow could relax with Ewell around.

Ward stood in the hallway and watched his old buddy go down to the curb and, without looking one way or the other, matter-of-factly open the door and slide behind the wheel. Nothing out of the ordinary here, folks. Just a cowboy asleep against the door. The high-ceilinged hall was quiet and subdued, thickly carpeted, the wainscoting painted white. The dark old grandfather's clock ticked in a white-painted corner made by the turn in the stairway. The car moved, and the cowboy hat against the door slid out of view. In a minute Ewell came in from the back and handed him the keys to the car.

"The car's parked in the driveway," he said. "Now don't you worry about anything. I'll take care of your father. Where you staying?"

"I'll get a room at the New Meadows," Ward said. "Ewell, he just died. I went into Mike's to get a hot dog, and when I came out he was dead. Just like that."

How could a thing that had been coming on so long catch him unawares? He didn't know, but it had. Ward brushed his hand across his eyes, and when he brought it away it was wet.

"Christ," he said, "I must be crying."

"That's all right. People naturally cry at times like these."

"But I didn't even know it. That's what gets me."

He began to shake and suddenly he was racked with sobs that hurt his chest. Was that pathetic animal noise—not so much the sound of grief as it was of fear—coming out of him? He hid his face with his arm, leaning against the cool wall.

"Shit," he said after awhile, his forehead still against the wall.

"That's all right," said Ewell, putting a hand on his shoulder.

"I'm a fucking mess," said Ward.

"No, you're not. You're going to be all right. Come back here and sit down."

The funeral director took him by the arm and Ward, half blinded by mortifying tears, permitted himself to be led down the hall to the pine-paneled office in the back. There he found a rolltop desk with a green-speckled goose-necked lamp on it just like Granpa used to have. Sitting in the comfortable room they worked everything out for the obituary in *The Bath Times;* Ewell said he would send a copy to the *Sentinel* too.

"The money," Ward said.

"What?" said Ewell.

"He's got money in his pants pocket. About $1,600. We can't —"

"I'll get it," Ewell said.

He came back smiling and extended the crisp bills, folded in the middle. It was attached to the little silver money clip in the form of a dollar-bill sign that Ward had given the old man for his birthday about ten years ago.

"Is this it?" asked Ewell in his easy comfortable way.

Ward took the money and put it in the right front pocket of his khakis.

"Yes, that's it," he said.

They talked about a casket; Ward decided on a good one. Ward told Ewell he wanted his father buried in the family plot in Dunnocks Head. His father's own parents were buried somewhere on Swan Island, and there was no one else left in his family, except for some cousins in California. If anybody deserved repose in the old Webster cemetery, he supposed it was his father. It never occurred to him to ask Althy for permission. He just told Ewell to go ahead and do it.

The black hair stitched on the back of Ewell's hand glistened as he wrote on the pad. He looked up, his face ruddy with good health, his blue eyes quite empty of anything but the next question.

"What was your father's religion?"

"He didn't have any. He was baptized a Methodist, I guess. His mother was a Methodist, I think."

"I was thinking about a minister for the service."

Ward looked at him blankly. For some reason the word service brought up the idea of silverware, not a funeral.

"He doesn't need any," Ward said.

"How about a Unitarian?"

"A Unitarian what?"

"A minister. A Unitarian minister."

He remembered Althy had once said that Unitarians were just atheists with children. Not that he had anything against Unitarians. They were all the same to him.

"I know what he'd really like," Ward said.

"What's that?"

"Pachebel's Canon in D Major," said Ward. "He told me once that he'd just like to have that played at his funeral, and then for everybody to go home."

Yes, that was it. Years ago the old man seemed to enjoy classical music, having a small collection of records, mostly piano concertos by Mozart. But he'd said he liked Pachebel's Canon in D Major best of all. Sublime, he called it. Play that at my funeral and then send them all home, he had said. Of course at that time it seemed to Ward his father was only joking around to demonstrate his fondness for this particular musical composition. But now in recollection it didn't seem like any joke. It looked to be right on the money.

"It's a beautiful composition," conceded Ewell. "But most people want a minister to say a few words."

"That's all right," said Ward. "Let's do it his way."

He had left Saltonstall's Funeral Home at that point, leaving his friend feeling dubious about the propriety of music to the exclusion of the human voice in such matters. Ward drove directly to the New Meadows Inn and rented a room. The tourists were beginning to swarm over the coast at that time of the year, but they had not yet discovered the New Meadows since it was off the beaten track and not in the guidebooks. The rooms were small, pine-paneled, simple, and comfortable.

After settling in, he drove back to Bath and bought a blue suit, white shirt, tie, and shoes at Bennett's Men's Store—his funeral uniform, the stuff his father wore every day. How did he ever stand it? Ward hadn't worn a tie since his high school graduation, hated the things. You couldn't breathe with that thing choking you. Hated suits and white shirts too. He didn't own a suit, so he couldn't tell Gordie to bring it along for him. It was an awful waste of the old man's money. He was putting off the phone call home, but at last, all his shopping done, he put through the call and told Althy what had happened. Then he went back to the pine-paneled room with his cardboard boxful of clothes and lay down just to take a little nap before dinner. When he opened his eyes again, it was the next day. He had slept long and hard and dreamless. It was almost noon. After a nice breakfast in the dining room—pancakes, bacon, and two big glasses of milk which tasted so good after all the ham and cheese sandwiches—he drove down to Dunnocks Head.

The old house sat in the weeds next to the humpbacked buildings of the boatyard. It was not in bad repair by the looks of things. Cousin Duncan took care of it after a fashion, according to Althy. The paint was starting to go, but it wasn't really bad. A few of the scalloped shingles looked loose on the mansard roof. But the porch traveling across the front of the house turned the corner as firmly as ever.

The barn was beautiful with its diamond-shaped windows in the hayloft and its cupola which matched the one on top of the house. The one on the barn was without window glass and contained a weathervane, a black sheet-iron ship pointing by turn to the first letters of the four quarters of the wind which were set at right angles on the cupola. Ward walked through the tall grass behind the barn, past the corral built to contain Scott's pony when he was little, toward the cemetery at the edge of the dark green piney woods. The fog was still in the woods at this hour. The trunks of the trees were still blackly wet with the morning's rain. The cemetery, its spiked fence down in places, was on a little hummock. Standing in the middle of the cemetery, he could see down across a field full of little Christmas trees to the Kennebec. The fog hung above the river like a ghostly banner slowly roiling in the wind. The old stones around him were covered with lichens. The carved letters, sandpapered by the wind and rain, were smooth as old coins. Stones for all the old and accounted for Websters, whether their bones were here or not. A marker for the old Captain, for instance. Numberless children, dead in infancy, leaving nothing behind but a Christian name and a burial stone. Sailors and their wives who had weathered many winters—they were here too. Those killed by Indians, even. Even a stone for Scott Prothero and a small white marble stone for Sarah's stillborn child, Carol. No stillborn ever lived so long. Unknown but known anyway. The markers rode on the little fenced-in hill above the Kennebec, right at the edge of the dark green woods. Yes. It was a good place for his father. He would like both the view and the company. Ward walked rapidly back to the car through the tall wet grass, soaking his khakis to the knees. He sat in the car for a minute trying to figure out what he should do next. He decided to drive over to Bath and have a drink at the Boathouse and rest up for the next call home.

In the upstairs bar of the Boathouse, big windows looked out on the foggy river. The taste of the beer, his second, lingered zestily on his tongue and a nice sensation of unclinching was building above his eyes and in his throat. The bartender was a girl from Long Island with lank orange hair, almost the rusty orange and coarse texture of an orangutan's pelt. She had a ready smile, a friendly, eager, husky voice and pale blue eyes. They were round, like a pigeon's. He liked her. She minded her business, which seemed to be taken up with counting bottles and writing on napkins, except when he talked to her and then she was very attentive. His surroundings were fine. He relished them every bit as much as the beer.

Outside was the fog. In the fog lay the city of Bath, not far from Dunnocks Head. He could feel the country around him like a tonic, and he relished the peculiar sharpness of the salt air, the sensation of dancing reflected light, the slightly tense excitement of knowing the ocean lay close at hand on every side, putting another rachet in the pulse beat.

"You from around here?" asked the girl with a pleasant smile.

"Yes," Ward answered, and of course it was no lie. He'd been from around these parts all his life.

"Where do you live?" she wanted to know.

"Dunnocks Head. The old Webster place."

"It's a pretty little town," she conceded. "But I don't know the house."

"Well it's on the other side of town, on the way to Small Point. We haven't actually lived there for years. My grandmother and I just decided to move back."

"Oh that's nice," she said and went back to counting her bottles.

Just why she thought that was nice wasn't clear, but now that he'd made these declarations they took on the authority of fact. What he had said in no way seemed a lie. A prophecy maybe, but not a lie. Yes, he thought. I can't go back again. I'll have to stay here.

On the phone that night he talked about the arrangements with his brother.

"Terrill says I can't come to the funeral," said Gordie "He says it's too long a trip."

"That's all right," said Ward. "You take care of yourself. We can handle it up here."

"Goddamn it, I should be there."

"It's more important for you to take care of yourself. Dad would want that. You're the man now, kid. We're all relying on you. So you have to act responsibly."

"Will you explain to the people up there?"

"Sure. Don't worry about it. Just get well. Kid, I have something else I want to say."

"What's that?"

"I'm not coming back."

"Good. Thank God. At last you're going to do something."

"I don't know whether it's the right thing . . ."

"It doesn't matter," said Gordie.

". . . but I'm going to stay up here for a while. I can't go back to that job at the factory. I don't know what I'll do yet. But this seems like a good place to find out."

"Good," said Gordie. "Damn good."

"I'm going to ask Althy to come up here and stay with me."

"You are?"

"Yes. She loves it up here. I think she ought to be up here now that the good weather's back. You and Avis can handle things down there."

"Well, you talk to her about that," said Gordie. "It's all right with me. Anything you two work out. Avis went over and got her this afternoon. She's staying with us tonight. You want to talk to her now?"

"Okay. Put her on."

"Wait a minute. I think she's in the kitchen."

It really didn't take a whole lot of convincing.

"Althy," he said. "When you come up for the funeral, bring everything you have or at least everything you want that will fit into two suitcases. I'll drive down to Portland and pick you up if you let me know what flight."

"Bring everything? What do you mean?"

"Bring everything," he said. "We're going to stay up here, open up the old house again. What do you say?"

"What about your mother?"

"We'll take care of her. Everything in its own time. I'm staying up here, Althy. I'm not going back to Pennsylvania. There's nothing there for me. I'd like you up here with me."

"It's your mother I worry about," she said.

"Don't worry. We'll work something out, in time."

"How is the weather anyway?" she wanted to know.

"It's beautiful," he said.

Despite the fog and rain, it seemed to him that it was.

In the barn littered with the junk of several generations—giant dollhouses, wooden sleds so heavy as to be almost unmoveable— behind a dust-dingy, spider-black sleigh, Ward found the Captain's little catboat covered with an old piece of canvas. The same one found floating in Casco Bay by the Coast Guard, bereft of the ancient sailor with the sick leg and his black dog called Lucky. Cousin Waterhouse said the patrol boat towed the cat home and eventually it ended up here, stored in the barn along with everything else no one knew what to do with.

"There's one just like it in the museum at Mystic," said Duncan studying the graceful lines of the little boat between puffs on his pipe. "You wouldn't think a boat with that much beam could be so pretty."

"How wide is it?"

"It's almost eight feet. It's only sixteen feet long. It's got the dimensions of a giant bathtub. But look at her."

The canvas decking was painted orange and the smooth sided planking showed in faint gray lines through her white topside paint. The wood trim had all turned dull and gray.

"I guess it was a pretty boat once."

"It could be again," said Duncan.

"You think it could?"

"Sure. Why don't we fix it up?"

"Fix it up? Hell, you've already said you'd help me build a little place in the spring. When are we going to have any time?"

"We've got plenty of time," said Duncan. "We've got all fall and winter. That's more than enough time."

Ward looked at the boat again.

"I don't know how to sail," he said.

"Nothing to it," said Duncan. "We'll teach you. She'll need new lines. Probably the sail's no good. It's canvas, anyway. You'll probably want Dacron. It'll cost some money to fix her up. Not too much though. Most of it we can do ourselves. She'll need to be sanded, new bottom paint, everything. That coaming will be beautiful when it's cleaned up."

"How old is she?"

"That boat?" said Duncan. "Your great-grandfather probably had that built in 1920 or '21. Your mother and my father were just little tykes. My father often told me about what fun they all had sailing in it."

Well, they set about it. It turned out they did have time.

Ward found the work pleasant enough. Wearing a surgical mask, he sanded the wood trim till it had the clean smooth look of sandalwood. Duncan would stop in after work in the evenings usually bringing along his boys, Joe and Andy, to see how the work was coming and offer a few suggestions. On weekends, he helped with anything tricky. Andy, four years younger than Joe, told Ward, "You get it in the water next spring, and I'll show you how to sail it."

At ten years old this boy had his own little boat, a melon seed so-called, and had been a sailor for five years.

"Sounds good, Andy," said Ward. After all, a man who could not learn anything, had stubbornly resisted the simple facts of life for twelve years—what could he do but put himself into the hands of a child?

Altogether there was plenty to do that fall, the kind of jobs that took orderly thought beforehand, but once organized, could be done without a lot of difficult thinking.

Time. Strange to say there seemed to be plenty of it. He and Duncan went down and looked at that ten-acre plot Ward had bought with part of his bonus money so many years ago, land located right across the cove from the old Captain's cottage.

On part of this land, an old meadow opened to the water. Doubtless a farmer, having no poetic intentions in mind, had once cleared this land so his sheep could graze. In the process he had created a nice open vantage where a man, if he wanted to, could pause to relish a view of the bay onto which the cove opened. It made a scene pretty as a picture postcard, as Althy was heard to say. Ward and Duncan agreed that just at the edge of this meadow, yet still among the trees, would be the spot for Ward's little place.

The Captain's old cottage, green and scalloped shingled, needed paint and some windows, but was basically solid, they discovered. The porch which ran across the front was mostly rotten. However, the roof needed to be patched only in one place.

Of course, the cottage, empty for years, was full of rubbish— bottle caps, broken beer bottles, peeling wallpaper, and general dirt—which made the place thoroughly unattractive. Duncan said he knew a man and his boy who would clean out the trash for a reasonable price.

"There is plenty of furniture in the barn," said Duncan. "You get this cottage cleaned up and so on, you'll have a nice little income. It'll pay your grandmother's taxes."

That sounded good. A summer property only. Not right for what Ward had in mind, as it was gaunt and cavernous and three stories high, a typical overgrown Victorian cottage. What he wanted for himself was a house he could heat easily and use comfortably in the winter too. On this subject he said to Duncan, "I saw an old Franklin stove in the barn. I wonder if that would heat a little place in the winter."

"Probably not so good," said Duncan. "What you want is an airtight or maybe a combination like your grandmother has."

"An airtight?" Ward said.

He got a book out of the library in Bath and found out about it. He discovered an airtight stove was made from sheet iron and had tight joints and controlled drafts. You could build a fire in one of these and it might last all night. It was pretty damned efficient, except for the creosote in the chimney. You could heat an average-sized house forever if you had a ten-acre woodlot. It was unbelievable. You could harvest enough cordwood every year, about seven or eight cords, and if you knew what you were doing, that ten acres would provide you with fuel till the sun dimmed and went out. It was one of the most beautiful facts he'd ever run across.

In this way, between the boat in the barn and the plans for the spring, the time passed easily enough. He got a job in the Bath A & P as the vegetable clerk. It paid all right and kept the daylight hours from hanging heavy on his hands.

That winter Ward and his grandmother fixed up three rooms and closed the rest of the house. The center of this snug little fortress against the elements was the big old square kitchen with its combination electric and wood-burning stove. Here they took their meals, watched the television, did their talking. They dragged in a couple of overstuffed chairs and ottomans and a fossilized wrought-iron floor lamp from the parlor, and fixed up a little corner for themselves. Althy made over the dining room into her private domain. It opened right off the kitchen and she seemed quite satisfied with the arrangement.

Ward set up in the old study down the hall in the front of the house across from the parlor. He remembered it well from his childhood. In the big bay window were the table and chairs where Granpa and the Captain played their continuous game of cribbage. There too stood the powerful brass telescope on its tripod, which the Captain, his head screwed to the eyepiece, used to sweep the Reach as far down as Squirrel Point. Ward remembered him peering through the gleaming brass cylinder, the old man small and spry as a chimpanzee, dressed as always in his finicky, faintly yellowed white shirt, glossy with starch and hard as cardboard. Sleeve garters held the cuffs back from his beautiful hands which moved quickly and nervously across any surface they touched.

The side windows looked out on the gray superstructure of the boatyard buildings almost lost in chest-high grass. A memory almost hidden in a shifting sea of weeds. Moldering on the ways was the old half-finished but never launched five-master, the *Arzamas*—named but never born. In the summer it was always a popular camera subject; the tourists came to snap it, stepping on each other's feet, as they gawked at it as at a prehistoric beast.

Between the windows stood a Franklin stove, Ward's source of heat that winter, and around the walls of the high, tin-ceilinged room were the books of five generations. Everything conceivable was there. Ward began to read a little bit again. He'd given it up a long time ago, but now in the long winter nights he took it up again, gingerly at first, and then with more relish. One of the nice things was to go from book to book without finishing one and without feeling bad about it. It occurred to him he was under no obligation to finish anything he didn't want to, and it was a fine feeling. For a starter he tried some essays by Francis Bacon; these he found powerfully interesting and amusing. It was great sport to watch the whirring of that fine precision machinery Bacon had mounted inside his skull. He moved on to the tales of A. E. Coppard, someone he'd never heard of, but didn't stay with them for long. He found a book of South Sea stories by Somerset Maugham and read all of them. His mother's name was in that book. Then he started *The Anatomy of Melancholy*, which he remembered liking as a child because it had thin pages and such lovely fine print, but he couldn't read it. So he got into *Don Quixote* and he read all of that, taking the better part of January to do it. Then he read a bunch of Dumas, read it quickly—*The Count of Monte Cristo, The Man in the Iron Mask*, and *The Three Musketeers*—and he discovered he liked to read again, that it was a confirmed pleasure to sit under a good light in a warm place with books all around you and have a fine spirited voice talking in your head while the wind rattled at the window and the snow blew across the yard in riffling, misty sheets like ocean spray. In another book with his mother's name on the flyleaf, called *The Fountainhead*, he found a letter addressed to her dated February 16, 1941, from Scott Prothero:

Dearest Sarah,
   I never saw such a dull war. It makes one almost sorry to want to fight, all this sitting around in England. Ask Waterhouse if we didn't see more action by the dark of the moon in the old days when you and

the old Captain thought I was in one place but I was in another. Here they turn out the lights once in a while and the Luftwaffe sneaks in and knocks down a few old churches but for the most part we just sit and decode messages. . . .

I hope you and Gordon and the children are fine. I believe you know I really mean that. Gordon is a good man. The minute I set eyes on him that day in the news room in Portsmouth I knew he was a good man and that in his way he would be what I could never be for you, even if the circumstances were different. I never had the power of constancy. That's the beauty of a card game. It ends when the money runs out. I love you, of course you know that; it will always be a given. But I have no talent for settling down; so it is just as well that it isn't possible. This way I'll be able to do more for you and the children. You are after all my family because you will have to be—

He poked around some more and found a warped leather-covered journal book whose pages were so dry some came apart like moth wings when he touched them. In it, written in faded pokeberry juice, he found an account of the first Webster, that youngest son of the Cape Ann clan, who came north to make something of the family's tree plantation and settled on the banks of the Kennebec, started a sawmill, and cut trees for masts for the Royal Navy. He built a double lean-to, lived on one side and stabled his mule and horse on the other. That first winter, which lasted from October till the end of May, he nearly froze to death. His horse, which had already lost its tail when a bear jumped on its back, was finally finished off that winter. This Webster—Aaron by name— went out one morning and found the animal frozen stiff, still standing in his stall. Strangely, the mule survived. The horse became his winter provisions, sorely needed, since in the woods the snow was so deep it made hunting difficult and game was scarce anyway.

I damn near froze last winter. Next year I am going to get a dog or squaw to sleep with. I don't know which yet but some kind of creature to help keep warm. I lean to the squaw for with patience I might be able to teach it to cook carry water and chop wood although it would be more trouble other ways. A dog don't talk. Neither does a squaw much if you don't teach it English. I ain't made up my mind yet.

He would decide on the squaw, the one whose name he couldn't pronounce or remember and so settled on calling her Cora. The one

by which he'd have several children including at least a couple of
females, naming them all Cora, as the story had it, as if in that one
monumental effort he had exhausted his ability to conjure any
more female names. This squaw would be murdered, tomahawked, in the kitchen of the fine new house, that later would be
burned to the ground by the Indians. That first Webster was away,
so the story goes, down to Kittery on important business. He
would lead his neighbors in a reprisal raid against the camps of his
former in-laws. The Indians, in turn, would attack his house, kill
two or three of his numerous children. Next time, he would marry
a respectable white woman and rebuild the house. Right here,
Ward thought, where the present house was. Right here on this
ground where you might find fragments of charred bone if you
dug in the basement, or where, standing at the kitchen window
some night, you might, if given to fantasy, mistake a shadow
under the trees for a squaw, standing stock-still, and looking toward the house.

In gray buckram notebooks, he found the old Captain's journals
describing his days at sea:

> . . . about noon a heavy Sea borded the Ship flooded the Carpenter Shop Galley Stor
> Room and our Room that is on the after End of the forward House on the Starboard
> Side The Hens were in the Storeroom They were washed out on Deck and all but six
> went over the Rail the Steward was washed acrossed the Deck twice the cook was cared
> Blue being in the Galley at the time Tea kettle Tea Pots Pans and Brooms were Floating
> about the Deck I was obliged to take all of my things out of my chest . . .

The crabbed journal was full of weather, latitude, longitude, ob-
servations of sunsets, sunrises, sky, moon and sun.

Reading in the quiet of a February night about a routine passage
to San Francisco, Ward was galvanized by the entry:

> May 3 7AM Latt 2.20 Long 112.10 Fire in the Booby Hatch. Ship on fire and
> enveloped all over just time to launch Boats with a Few Provisions and stand off. All
> Hands Safe at Nine Mast went overbd Staid by the burning Ship all Day and Night
> the Ship burning very Brightly and hoping some ship would be attracted Fire and take
> us off—Latt 2.04 Long 112.00.

It was of course the famous fire in the Pacific, the time when the
old Captain, who was young then, led his crew and passengers

over four thousand miles of ocean in open boats, a voyage of
forty-three days with only ten days' provisions.

*Tuesday, June 5 First part of this Day pleasant with high roling Sea Night Fine Latter
part cloudy Sea still large Wind light dryer in the Boat than for many Days We are
getting very weak. Bread gone a little piece of Ham & a Gill of Water. A Conspiracy
formed to Murder me. Minds unquiet   God is over all Latt 16.46.*

In a tin box he found more letters to his mother from Scott:

. . . . I think they proved one thing conclusively. If a man of sufficient
complexity of mind proceeds in a sufficiently perverse and persistent
manner he can succeed at length in kicking himself in his own ass out
the door into the street. The whole family has a decided talent for that,
to wit the Captain and his issues of Goldman and Sachs which nobody
could tell him wasn't worth a shit. Still those perverse old men, you
could learn something from them. Their lives were an open book. I
mean over at the office at the boatyard there are those journals. About
their sea voyages and their business on land. It's all there, spread out
upon the page, the lives of the Captain and his father, that consum-
mate thief and patriot. Everything they wanted to record, lots about
the weather for they were sailors and little about the women and
children at home, for the same reason. You could learn, Sarah. There's
lots you could learn about yourself in those pages. . . .

*Thursday June 7 5 Weeks in the Boat Provisions all gone but 1 small can. A little
Water left Beautiful June Day running all Day hoping to reach Sandwich Islands
failing Fast. I remind them constantly that I alone capable of finding Land by Chart
and Quadrant I can barely hold the Pistol they think I am the very Devil Everybody
very weak A Day or two more and all will be over O God Mercy on us and forgive
us our sins Latt 16.36 L 136—*

You remember when I asked is the Captain still trying to marry you
off and you said, 'He's trying but nobody's buying'? And I told you
to tell him to never mind because I'd take care of that? Well now you
know what I meant, don't you?

*Friday June 15 Saw Indication of Land yes the Birds and other but dare not say it
for fear of disappointment I sit in the Bows but I could no longer fire the Pistol if it
came to that. If it comes to that I don't believe they could move either Mexican Standoff
At 10:30 AM made certain of Land Merciful God with Us for when we nearly reach
Shore and lowered Sail the reef appeared unfavorable Unable to hoist Sail too weak
and helplessly drifted toward Rocks but passed through an all but concealed passage*

in Reef to Safety Except for this narrow Way would certainly have perished. A famished set of Men. After being in the Boat over 4 3 days 8 hours. Not a man could walk. All taken out and carried up by the kind Kanakas who try to outvie each other in doing all they can to lessen our Misery. Now comes the trial whether or not we can be rebuilt after such a trial. No passage of bowels for 2 2 days.

Well, it was very fine to sit before a cheery fire and read the letters and journals and confirm all the things one knew, somehow by accident and instinct, about the family. It was amazing how little of what he read—material spanning something like 250 years of family history—was really new to him.

He and Althy were making it all right. When he came home at night, the kitchen would be warm, and there would be fresh biscuits, baked beans, a cabbage salad. Fresh donuts. A pumpkin pie and those crisp molasses cookies Althy made that tasted so good with a glass of milk. He would watch a little television with her before going down the cold hall to the study to start a fire in the Franklin stove. It didn't take long for that little stove to make everything snug. Althy had found a couple of Hudson Bay blankets and a big feather-filled pillow upstairs, and he often wrapped up in these on the couch near the good reading light with *The Bath Times* or *The Brunswick Record* or a book or one of the journals. Or sometimes he just sat there and watched the fire crackle and dance in the small black stove.

Often there was company. At least once a week Duncan and his wife Eunice and the boys stopped by to visit after supper.

Frequently Ward was in his room by this time and Duncan would come down the cold hall, knock deferentially on the door, and wonder if he couldn't see the *Times.* And having quietly read it, he would leave with no more ado.

There were letters to write and telephone calls to make, of course.

"Dear Sarah," he began. And then was stumped for some time. "How are you?" he wrote. And crossed it out as it seemed too metaphysical a question so early in the letter.

He was not in shape for letter writing and he found it hard work. He was discovering you had to get in condition to do every single thing, that nothing came easy to a man, that each separate thing required a different kind of preparation if you were going to do it with any grace and not hurt yourself in the process.

Of course he received letters and phone calls too, which helped him understand how to go about making his own in turn. For instance, there was a letter from the kid.

". . . . I have worked it out. She didn't want the money of course. But she couldn't do much about it, could she? I set it up in a revocable trust. Ward, you should see your son. He is beautiful, has those cat-like gray eyes the Websters have. Terry has named him Gordon. Like a goddamn fool when she told me I began to cry. . . ."

Through these letters and phone calls, Ward learned that the Carlisle property had been sold, and the horses auctioned off. The shoe factory apparently was a hell of an asset, according to the kid, without a penny of debt against it, so naturally Gordie mortgaged it to the hilt. He said he liked the prospects of the Portsmouth paper so much that he bought another paper in Nashua, New Hampshire, then one in Rocky Mount, North Carolina. He also bought six hundred acres of farmland outside of Carlisle which he said would turn to pure gold in ten years, and bought an apartment house in Orlando, Florida. He said he'd like to start a newspaper in Maine, about Maine, and he'd be up next summer to look into it. Was he painting? Yes, sometimes, when Avis would leave him alone. She seemed to think he was working too hard. Old man Coppersmith had had enough of the agency business so Gordie bought him out. "We need a corporate headquarters anyway," said Gordie.

"We do?" said Ward.

"Certainly," said Gordie. "You're in this too."

It was hard for Ward to see how he was in on this, but he supposed the kid meant he intended this empire to be operated for the family's benefit.

Sarah was improving somewhat, according to reports. It was decided that next summer Gordie and Avis would bring her north for a visit. Then on the way back, they would deliver her to take up residency at Rosemont, that sanitarium west of Boston which had been the institution originally selected by the old Captain. Rosemont had been the starting point of Sarah's psychiatric wanderings, the place where his father as a young man, too confident for his own good, had received and ignored the doctor's warning concerning Sarah's propensity for violence. Sarah had fond memories of Rosemont, and in fact claimed she had spent the happiest years of her adult life there.

According to the kid, it was Sarah's version of a convent, a quiet place out of the world where she could repeat the rosary of her memories without being distracted.

"It's the only place for her right now," said the kid. He seemed to know what he was talking about. Surely there was nothing Ward could do for Sarah. Under the circumstances, the kid's plan sounded okay.

One night, not long before this telephone conversation, he had looked up from his paper through the blue caul of smoke fulminating about his head and found Althy standing in the doorway in her print dress, her swollen legs, which had no more curve or variation than an elephant's, planted stubbornly.

"What are you going to do about your mother?" she asked quietly. There was almost a menacing doggedness about the old woman.

He kept on looking at the printed page of the newspaper as if he hadn't heard her, as if she weren't now standing in the doorway waiting for his answer, with her head raised, exposing the scraggly old throat, the eyes bright and watery not so much with age and weariness now as with the silent passion of her case. The room was quite cold which seemed to add to the seriousness of the old woman's question. It suggested that his answer would be tested against a severe, unbending code of behavior, as old as the Kennebec itself.

"I don't know," he answered, turning his head to see her.

"Are you going to leave her down in Pennsylvania, locked up like an animal?"

Pennsylvania, mentioned in this way, sounded like one of the tributaries of hell.

"I don't know. We'll have to see."

It was hard to tell his grandmother that he didn't want anything to do with Sarah. Althy could handle Sarah, could stand to have her around, but he never could. He was happy to get away from her and the effect she had on him, which either froze his will or else made him want to hit her and everybody else around. She made him crazy because she was so weak, and she had quit on life. Maybe she made him mad because he was afraid that he didn't have the iron to stay with life either. The whole thing scared him.

He needed time to think about it. Or maybe time *not* to think about it. He wanted to just stay in his room and read the journals and the papers. Drink sublimeade under the elms in the springtime. He had no real stomach for people anyway. Maybe with a little time by himself he would find a way to be decent to Sarah—although he doubted it. There were some things you just never learned to handle. Anyway, it seemed to him he must save himself for the new things—the boat and the work in the spring—and not get tangled up in Sarah's problems again, no matter how cold and heartless Althy or anybody else thought he was as a result.

When he finally figured he was in shape for it, he wrote the letter he'd spent all winter getting in condition to write.

"Duncan Waterhouse, my cousin, and I are going to build a little house for me down on the land I got for some of my bonus money. It's on a nice little cove, right across from my great-grandfather's cottage, which we are going to fix up too. We are going to fix up his boat too, and I expect to learn to sail with some help from Duncan's boys who are both sailors. Gordie and Avis and Mother are all coming up to visit next summer. The house will be finished by then. I would like you and the boy to come too. I would like to see the boy and I would like to see you too."

Then there were the long nights reading and the fire burning in the old Franklin stove, the Hudson Bay blankets, even the cold crisp air and the heavy snowfalls and the pleasure of finding the roads clear in the morning after ten inches had fallen in the night and not only cleared but cleared to the macadam. There was the pleasure of fish too. They bought fresh fish at the market and brushed it with a little butter and broiled it—all kinds of fish, haddock, cod, mackerel, blue. It was all fresh and delicious; he had never liked fish so much.

In the spring they began work on his house. First they bought a secondhand anchor and some good line and rigged up a mooring for the catboat. Duncan presented him with a small flat-bottom dingy that he'd built in his garage. It looked a little like a box people might use to mix cement in. Duncan told him it was his to keep, to use to get back and forth to the mooring.

There were a lot of boards Ward would have to buy, and nails and wire and glass—lots of things. But the posts and beams were standing all around him, in the form of trees.

They poured the footers, cut the trees, put up the posts and

beams. The next thing they did was build the roof; it was a simple
shed roof, the high side of the slope facing the southwest. Over
the beams they laid sub-beams. Then they laid down boards,
heartside down, running with the slope of the roof to add to the
strength.

They laid strips of aluminum foil shiny side up in shingle fashion, lengthwise, and nailed one-inch spacers through the foil and
ceiling boards into the sub-beams. They put down another layer
of aluminum foil, laid shiny side up with the slope, and nailed
down another row of spacers. Then they laid a layer of roof
boards, put down another layer of aluminum foil and finally
finished with double coverage roll roofing. And what they had,
said Duncan, was a very satisfactory roof.

The boys helped out too. Joe could hammer a nail better than
Ward any day and naturally he took pleasure in demonstrating his
superiority. Between bouts of work, Andy showed him how to sail
his boat.

"You'll catch on fast," said Duncan. "That boat is a forgiving
boat."

Forgiving. Certainly that was the kind of boat he needed.

Andy kept it simple and direct.

"Point the nose just off the direction of the wind," he said.
"Whichever way you pull the tiller she'll go just opposite. If you
get in trouble, just let go of her tiller and slack off the sheet. She'll
come right up into the wind."

Fine. A forgiving boat and simple instructions. They glided out
of the cove, hit the crosswind between the islands and the boat
jumped forward, heeled over, dumped its rail under the seething
water. Ward fought the tiller, bracing himself on the centerboard
trunk to keep from pitching overboard. The boat, sharply heeled
over, shuddered as if about to go over.

Good Christ, what have I done? he asked himself.

Andy rolled around the cockpit and lost his sailor hat overboard.
"Let go!" he cried.

Oh yes. Let go. Ward remembered now and let go the tiller and
slacked off the sheet; the boat pulled up, mild as milk.

"Can't you remember nothing?" the boy said angrily, taking the
tiller. He brought the boat about and went back for his hat, leaning
over the side and scooping it up with his free hand while his other
steadied the tiller.

True, the instructions had been simple enough, within anyone's grasp, but he had not expected an attack from the wind as soon as he reached the bay, being unfamiliar with such things. Then, also, he was worried about getting hit by the boom, which he soon found was impossible if he stayed in the cockpit where he belonged—or got out of it to do something only at the right times.

The second time out, he sailed her right across the bay. He had a good steady wind and made it in one tack. He brought her around poorly, but at least pointed her into the wind even if he wasn't very decisive and momentarily the boat fell into what was called "irons," and then he got her around, the sail stopped fluttering and filled, and the boom came across, and the boat surged again.

"Now you're getting it," said Andy.

"I am?"

"Sure you are."

Andy was very definite and happy about it. Ward believed the boy found it somewhat embarrassing to have dealings with an adult who knew so little about something so pathetically simple as sailing a boat.

Before long he was sailing the bay by himself. He had to laugh, thinking about it, as he slanted across the wind and sunshine. The boat silent and swift as a living thing. Here he was in the Captain's boat. Out here on the bay. Was he out here looking for God too? Picking up where the Captain left off and getting about the same results? Who knows? But no matter.

Since the house was of elementary post and beam construction, it came along quickly. After they put in the floor and squared it off they built layered walls from the inside out. They first nailed vertical boards leaving holes for the doors and windows and next tacked up a layer of aluminum foil, shiny side in, and overlapping from above like shingles. Then they marked up battens horizontally about two feet apart, then put another layer of foil shiny side out, and then carefully located and nailed a row of vertical battens to which the outside boards were nailed. When they were finished the place had a little porch on the front with one end screened in, a kitchen and living room, two bedrooms, and a sleeping loft. They did the wiring themselves, and they put in a Norwegian stove that had the capacity to heat hot water. They built the table, chairs, the bookcase, and even a double bed, and lugged down an old sofa and

easy chair and other things from that treasure house barn at Dunnocks Head. The only thing they allowed the experts to do was
to dig the well and put in the septic system.

It was about this time that Althy decided to sell the old house.

"There's no point in me staying here alone," she said. "I'll get
a smaller place, maybe up to Bath."

"Well," said Ward. "Let's see what Gordie says when he gets
here."

"I can't keep it. I wish I could," she broke out passionately. "I've
lived in this house all my life. But I can't, I can't keep it any more."

"Let's wait to see what the kid has to say," Ward said.

She proposed to sell the old house along with 25 acres of the
remaining 125-acre parcel to a dentist from Massachusetts who
had a large family of red-haired boys and girls. The dentist told
Althy he planned to fix it up and use it as a summer place.

"They seem like nice enough people," Althy said.

"Let's wait," he told her. And she agreed.

Still she found it necessary to sell off in a series of Sunday sales
the contents of the barn—spool beds painted eggshell blue, the old
wooden sleds, garden implements, plate collections, stuffed sea
fowl from the Pacific.

"You take anything you want," she insisted. He took as much
as he could, and she sold the rest.

As a result, his little house took on quite a civilized and carefully
furnished air.

One day Eunice stood in the middle of the living room with her
hands on her hips, a look of grim satisfaction on her big-beaked
face. It looked like Andy was going to inherit that nose, which
grew like a gnarled tree root out of the middle of her forehead.

"Now," she said. "All this house needs is a wife and a baby."

"Oh shut up, Eunice," Duncan told her.

Indeed the time grew on apace when the place would be full of
visitors from Carlisle. This was accompanied by a last minute
exchange of phone calls and letters, followed by that uncomfortable silence meaning your visitors are enroute, a time in which any
honest person will confess to a mild sense of dread. Ward expected
to be made twice happy by his company. Happy to see them when
they all arrived. And happy again to see them all go away. The part
he especially wanted to get over was seeing Terry after so long and
of course seeing the boy for the first time. Now the boy, as he

called him, he realized was just a little baby, and this little baby wouldn't know what was going on at all nor could he say how-do or do much of anything, Ward supposed. But anyhow, for no special reason, Ward liked to think of him as: the boy.

On the morning his visitors were to arrive Althy and Duncan and his family were all down at Ward's place, getting things ready for the clam bake. The women did most of the work, and after a while he and Duncan took a sail, but Ward was too restless to stay out very long and they came back quickly. As they walked up the path from the dingy, Duncan said, "I guess you've never seen this baby?"

"No, I never have."

"Well, don't worry about it. He'll look just like any other baby. They don't look like kids for about two years."

Eunice and Althy stood by the heap of seaweed in which lay buried the afternoon's clam bake. Eunice leaned against a rake and watched them move up the path, closer.

"This'll be some good, I'll tell you." she shouted.

"I suppose you're nervous." said Duncan. "I would be."

"Let's have a drink, Waterhouse," suggested Ward.

"Thought you would never ask," said Duncan.

"Where you two going?" Eunice wanted to know as they passed her.

"Going up to the house to have a drink."

"*Now?* At eleven o'clock in the *morning?*"

"Oh, bush-wah, woman."

It really worked out to be not bad. It was simplified by the fact that he opened the door on Avis' side, and she started the kissing business right off by leaping out of the Cadillac and giving him a smooch.

"Gimp, you goddamn jerk. How are you?" she said, but knowing the answer to that anyway she added, "Look, here's your mother."

He helped Sarah out of the back seat, she smiling shyly at him. She looked very thin, and she wanted to kiss him too.

"Thank God, you're all right," she said, a remark everybody took to be a bit touched, and which made them laugh nervously.

"Hello, dear!"

"Mother!"

Everything was turning out to be sufficiently confusing not to be awkward. The magnate charged around the side of the car with a big grin on his face.

"You son of a bitch!" he said and he too hugged and kissed Ward, and Ward began to feel like some tribal totem that everybody was supposed to pass around and kiss for good luck.

Duncan was there, with his pipe in his mouth, asking appropriately dumb questions such as: how long did it take you? You come down the turnpike, did you?

"Well, now," said Eunice, to no one in particular.

Then Terry emerged with the baby. Now this potentially was the most awkward moment.

"What a beautiful baby!" squawked Eunice.

Terry's eyes fixed on the child in her arms, wrapped in a light cotton blue blanket. A silence grew up, a kind of alert clearing formed around Ward as they all, helplessly—even if they had made secret resolutions to the contrary, as he suspected they had —waited to see what he would say at first sight of his son. Of course he had no idea what to say. He was stuck for words.

Finally—after what seemed like a long time but was probably just a few seconds—he said, "Is this the boy?"

Only then did Terry look at him.

"Yes," she said.

Gordie stepped forward out of the expectant circle. "Jesus," he said, "I feel like one of the Magi." Everybody laughed nervously.

"Here, give the kid to his uncle," and Gordie held out his hands.

"Step back," said Ward. "You can try him out any time."

Everyone laughed delightedly except Sarah who was puzzled. "What he say?" she wanted to know.

He took the baby, warm in his blanket and still sleepy, and looked at the face of this child, the skin silken and glossy as a tulip petal, the closed lids curved beautifully over the eyes. Yes, indeed. As Duncan had promised, this boy was just a baby, looked nothing boylike at all, but nevertheless, was the most beautiful, profoundly peaceful creature Ward had ever seen.

"Careful, don't drop him, you boob," said Gordie.

"Come in," Ward said. "See the house."

"Here, let me take him," suggested Avis. His arms, now empty, still felt the baby's sweet warmth. He glanced in Terry's direction but she was looking elsewhere, being kept busy by Eunice.

"Is this your house?" his mother asked wonderingly, looking up the path to the house, dappled in the shade of the surrounding pines.

"Yes. Duncan and I built it. Come and see it."

"Duncan always was clever," said Althy.

The afternoon had been planned to move things along so nobody would be made awkward by any long silences. Eunice and Althy had timed the clam bake to serve this purpose.

As Ward and Gordie made drinks for everyone, they all chatted easily on the screened-in porch. There was the baby to fuss over too. Duncan got the bassinet and the bags out of the car. Everybody was a good deal preoccupied by the child, except Sarah who sat in the living room by the window and looked out at the bay.

God, she looks thin and pale, thought Ward.

They ate on the porch at the long picnic table Ward and Duncan had built especially for the occasion just this week.

From Eunice's steaming pile of seaweed and rocks, everyone extracted a net bag containing clams, a lobster, a piece of chicken and an ear of corn. Althy had prepared some good fish chowder and there was plenty of bread and butter and beer. Everything tasted very good out in the fine air.

The boy had been put in his bassinet in a corner of the porch and had fallen asleep instantly despite the racket, doubtless a victim of the sleep-inducing effect of the salt air. Terry sat across from Ward and he was glad for so much conversation going on around the table and no time or silences which he would have to fill.

Ward looked out at the little catboat, moored fifty feet or so offshore. Dazzling as a gull on the water, it spanked its white bottom against the rippling green silk of the incoming tide.

"Have you ever been sailing?"

"No, I never have."

"Well, I would like to take you."

"Is it fun?"

"It's one of the most wonderful things you can do for yourself."

Joe and Andy finished fast and took their bat, ball, and gloves and went to the meadow. A couple of extra gloves had appeared, Ward noticed, and there had been some talk with their father before they left for the meadow about a game involving the adults later on. "Maybe," said Waterhouse. "No promises now. Go and play and let us finish eating."

Gordie engaged Duncan in a discussion of the merits of starting a weekly newspaper—not a paste-up of wire service stories or reprints—that exclusively dealt with Maine. Duncan lit his pipe and sat with his legs crossed, one hand supporting his weight on the picnic bench, blinking with a kind of canine deliberation against the fragrant smoke, and appeared to listen.

"What do you think?" asked Gordie.

Duncan said he didn't know. Gordie was prepared to discuss it further, endlessly it appeared.

Avis, sitting next to Gordie, said to Ward, "Look how pale and thin he is."

Indeed the kid did look thin and washed out.

"I try to get him to eat but he won't take time," she said.

"He looks pretty skinny," Ward agreed.

"He works too hard, Gimp. He works all hours of the day and night."

Gordie, pleased to overhear himself being discussed, turned from Duncan.

"I don't work too hard."

"Yes, you do," Avis told him. "You're trying to live three different lives at once."

"Well, you'll just have to take care of me."

"Tell him to slow down, Gimp. Before he kills himself."

"Slow down, Bro."

"Hell, what for?" Gordie smiled at large. "I'm having fun!"

"See what I mean?" asked Avis.

Nobody did.

"Come on, Duncan," said Gordie standing up. "Let's show those kids how to play ball. Come on, you guys."

And so Gordie and Avis and Ward, Duncan and Eunice trundled down the stairs of the porch intent on the meadow and the boys' bat and ball, leaving Althy and Sarah and Terry and the baby behind to serve as a gallery.

As it turned out, they elected Ward to be up first in a game of one-a-cat. Avis was the pitcher. She had appropriated Andy's ball cap and wore it with the bill sideways on her dark hair. The boy, feeling badly used, stood knee-high in what served for the outfield grass, skinny and bareheaded in the sunlight, far from what he took to be the original purposes of this game.

She threatened an elaborate windup, tried to cross him up with

a little pansy half-step toward third base and threw the ball into
the ground about ten feet in front of the imaginary batter's box.
Duncan, the catcher, had to go out and get it.

"Nice pitch, Avis."

"Hell, you ain't seen nothing yet."

The next pitch was slowmo, about eight feet high.

Out where first base was supposed to be, Joe dropped his glove,
twisting around in a complete circle, tortured beyond his limits by
these adult shenanigans.

"Come *on,*" he moaned, wanting a serious game. His mother
stood in left field with her arms folded, making it clear she was
there just for appearances' sake and didn't really count as a fielder.
Clearly the odds were against Joe.

"Hum, girl. Hum, girl," Duncan said to his pitcher as he threw
the ball back. Ward had to lean on his bat.

"Come on, you jerk," cried Avis. "Play ball."

"Hey, Terry," yelled Ward in the direction of the screened-in
porch where his audience sat, he knew, too dark behind the
screening to see.

"Yes?"

"Is the kid watching?"

It was Althy's voice that answered.

"He's watching all right," she said. "He's sitting right up here
with his eyes fixed on whatever it is you're doing out there."

"Well that's good," said Ward. "I wouldn't want him to miss
this hit."

Out on the mound, Avis snorted.

"You're going to hit shit. You never seen my fastball. My *real*
fastball. You'll be lucky if you even *see* this pitch."

"I'm ready," said Ward. "I don't know if Waterhouse is ready
though. I don't believe he's ever seen a fastball, have you, Waterhouse?"

"Fire when ready," said Duncan and crouched stiffly.

"You think this is a girl's pitch coming," Avis shouted to Duncan. "But this is no girl's pitch coming. You never saw a girl's pitch
like this before, Waterhouse."

"All right," he said calmly.

But she still wasn't finished.

"Take that pipe out of your mouth, Waterhouse, and get ready,"
she told him.

"I'm ready, for Chrissakes."

"Wait a second," Ward stepped out of the batter's box and cupped his hands.

"Gordie!"

"What?" came back his brother's voice, a mild faint bird cry in the deepening afternoon.

"Get back, kid! I'm going to hit this one a country mile!"

"Okay!"

The kid turned and bounded like a gazelle toward the dark trees at the edge of the clearing.

3737217

Made in the USA